Praise for Bentley Little

The Association

"With this haunting tale, Little proves he hasn't lost his terrifying touch. The novel's graphic and fantastic finale . . . will stick with readers for a long time. Little's deftly drawn characters inhabit a suspicious world laced with just enough sex, violence and Big Brother rhetoric to make this an incredibly credible tale."

—*Publishers Weekly*

The Walking

"Wonderful, fast-paced, rock-'em, jolt-'em, shock-'em contemporary terror fiction with believable characters and an unusually clever plot. Highly entertaining."

—Dean Koontz

"Bentley Little's *The Walking* is the horror event of the year. If you like spooky stories, you must read this book."

—Stephen King

"*The Walking* is a waking nightmare. A spellbinding tale of witchcraft and vengeance. Bentley Little conjures a dark landscape peopled by all-too-human characters on the brink of the abyss. Scary and intense."

—Michael Prescott, author of *Last Breath*

"The overwhelming sense of doom with which Bentley Little imbues his . . . novel is so palpable it seems to rise from the book like mist. Flowing seamlessly between time and place, the Bram Stoker Award–winning au-tho̶ ̶ ̶ ̶ ̶ ̶ ̶ ̶ ̶ ̶ ̶hi̶s̶ ̶a̶u̶d̶i̶e̶n̶c̶e̶ . . . is superb . . . ter̶ ̶ ̶ ̶ ̶ ̶ ̶ ̶ ̶ ̶ ̶ ̶ ̶ ̶ ̶ ̶ ̶ential to be a major sle̶ ̶ ̶ ̶ ̶ ̶ ̶ ̶ ̶ ̶ ̶ ̶ ̶ ̶ ̶ *kly* (starred review)

continued . . .

The Ignored

"This is Bentley Little's best book yet. Frightening, thought-provoking, and impossible to put down."
—Stephen King

"With his artfully plain prose and Quixote-like narrative, Little dissects the deep and disturbing fear of anonymity all Americans feel. . . . What Little has created is nothing less than a nightmarishly brilliant tour de force of modern life in America."
—*Publishers Weekly* (starred review)

"*The Ignored* is a singular achievement by a writer who makes the leap from the ranks of the merely talented to true distinction with this book. This one may become a classic."
—*Dark Echo*

"Inventive. Chilling."   —*Science Fiction Chronicle*

"A spooky novel with an original premise."   —SF Site

"Little is so wonderful that he can make the act of ordering a Coke at McDonald's take on a sinister dimension. This philosophical soul-searcher is provocative."
—*Fangoria*

"*The Ignored* is not average at all."   —*Locus*

The Revelation
Winner of the Bram Stoker Award

"Grabs the reader and yanks him along through an ever-worsening landscape of horrors. . . . It's a terrifying ride with a shattering conclusion."   —Gary Brandner

"*The Revelation* isn't just a thriller, it's a shocker . . . packed with frights and good, gory fun. . . . A must for those who like horror with a bite."   —Richard Laymon

"I guarantee, once you start reading this book, you'll be up until dawn with your eyes glued to the pages. A nail-biting, throat squeezing, nonstop plunge into darkness and evil."   —Rick Hautala

The Store

"*The Store* is . . . frightening."   —*Los Angeles Times*

"Must reading for Koontz fans. Bentley Little draws the reader into a ride filled with fear, danger, and horror."
          —Harriet Klausner, *Painted Rock Reviews*

The Mailman

"A thinking person's horror novel. *The Mailman* delivers."   —*Los Angeles Times*

University

"Bentley Little keeps the high-tension jolts coming. By the time I finished, my nerves were pretty well fried, and I have a pretty high shock level. *University* is unlike anything else in popular fiction."   —Stephen King

THE
RETURN

Bentley Little

A SIGNET BOOK

SIGNET
Published by New American Library, a division of
Penguin Putnam Inc., 375 Hudson Street,
New York, New York 10014, U.S.A.
Penguin Books Ltd, 80 Strand,
London WC2R 0RL, England
Penguin Books Australia Ltd, Ringwood,
Victoria, Australia
Penguin Books Canada Ltd, 10 Alcorn Avenue,
Toronto, Ontario, Canada M4V 3B2
Penguin Books (N.Z.) Ltd, 182–190 Wairau Road,
Auckland 10, New Zealand

Penguin Books Ltd, Registered Offices:
Harmondsworth, Middlesex, England

First published by Signet, an imprint of New American Library,
a division of Penguin Putnam Inc.

First Printing, September 2002
10 9 8 7 6 5 4 3 2 1

 REGISTERED TRADEMARK—MARCA REGISTRADA

Printed in the United States of America

PUBLISHER'S NOTE
This is a work of fiction. Names, characters, places, and incidents either
are the product of the author's imagination or are used fictitiously,
and any resemblance to actual persons, living or dead, business
establishments, events, or locales is entirely coincidental.

BOOKS ARE AVAILABLE AT QUANTITY DISCOUNTS WHEN USED TO PROMOTE
PRODUCTS OR SERVICES. FOR INFORMATION PLEASE WRITE TO PREMIUM
MARKETING DIVISION, PENGUIN PUTNAM INC., 375 HUDSON STREET, NEW
YORK, NEW YORK 10014.

For Judson and Krista Little,
who know a lot about the
weirdness in Arizona

Prologue

Zane Grey awoke with a twisted neck and a knotted back. Grunting, he pushed himself out of bed and made his way over to the window. He looked through the trees, past the sloping meadow in which his horses were corralled, to the tan wall of rock that was the base of the Tonto Rim.

He'd had a difficult time sleeping again. There'd been noises near the cabin: branch snappings and stone rattlings that could not be attributed to animals or to the wind. They seemed especially loud in the darkness of the moonless night. He'd also heard unearthly howling from somewhere up on the Rim; a low, strange wail that sounded like neither man nor beast. It was the howling that had really set his nerves on edge.

He was not a timid man. He'd hunted bear in Colorado without the benefit of a guide. He'd fished alone in a rowboat in a gale off the coast of Oregon. He'd lived half his life out of doors with nothing but a saddle blanket and a knife between himself and the wild. But the sound of that creature or demon or whatever it was up there on the Rim made him want to pack up his bags and hightail it back to civilization.

Demon?

He was not superstitious. But neither was he so closed minded that he refused to deny the possibility that there were things in this world he did not understand. Hell, the Bible talked of demons. And who was he to contradict the Good Book?

He stood for a moment at the window, leaning on the sill so as not to put pressure on his back. In the meadow, one of the horses whinnied and moved skittishly against the fence.

Word back in town was that even Indians avoided the top of the Rim, though they usually chose to make their homes atop plateaus for protection against marauding enemies, utilizing the natural fortresslike qualities of the geological formations. That was something to think about. He had no love for the red man, but he had to admit that they knew about the land, knew how and where and why to build their villages, knew what they needed to do in order to survive in this harsh country.

He straightened, grunting with pain as his back cracked. Part of him was still wary of going outside, even though the sun was up and the darkness gone. But he refused to let himself be frightened like some old lady. Rubbing his aching neck, he walked out to the outhouse to do his business, then brought in some water from the well, and set the kettle on the stove. The embers were still warm from last night, and he placed another log and a patch of kindling in there, using the bellows to resurrect the fire.

As he always did here at the cabin, he began the day with eggs and a slab of bacon, washing them down with hot black coffee. After breakfast, he walked back outside and looked in the dirt for any footprints, hoofprints, or claw marks. He circled the cabin three times but, as before, he found nothing to indicate that anyone or anything had been there save himself.

Already the Arizona sun was warm on his scalp, with sweat beginning to bead beneath his hairline. It was going to be a hot day—was there any other kind here in the summer?—and he strode out to the meadow before the temperature rose too high and the horses were put off their feed. Dead beetles, dried pine needles, and crushed sandstone crunched beneath his boots as he walked down the narrow weed-lined pathway. He'd been warned not to buy this land by more than one person in town, but the only advice he had ever listened to was his own, and he wasn't about to take the word of those local bumpkins on matters such as real estate.

He opened the pasture gate and started toward the barn, where he kept the oats and barley. The dark feelings of the night were already fading, as they did each morning. Daylight seemed to dispel any lingering dread and render ridiculous his nocturnal fears. Still, a vestigial anxiety remained. Last night had been the worst by far, and it was not quite as easy as usual to shake off the conviction that something evil and unnatural lurked in this section of the Tonto.

The horses came up to him, looking for food, and he patted their flanks, first Virgil's, then Tenny's. He pointed them toward the salt lick and sent them on their way. "Chow's coming," he said, then chuckled. "Just hold your horses." He made his way through the pasture, keeping an eye out for snakes.

It was in the barn that he saw the colt.

There should not have been a colt in there. He had only two horses, both stallions. There were no people on the property other than himself, and there should not have been any other animals.

But that was not what caused him to stop in his tracks. That was not what filled him with the urge to flee.

It was the animal's face. The bloody flared nostrils, the crazily bulging eyes, the wildly tangled mane, the too-wide mouth with its teeth bared in an impossibly savage grin.

Horses were not supposed to smile, and the presence of that human attribute on the face of a dumb beast was not only inappropriate but horribly wrong.

He did not even stop to think, his reaction was so instinctive. Reaching for the loaded rifle he kept on the wall, he whipped it off its hook and shot the colt in the head. The animal collapsed. Yet even in death that disturbing wildness remained, every single element of the colt's appearance abnormal.

And there was an air of . . . something *else* in the barn. He could not explain it, could not describe it, but it lingered nonetheless.

Still carrying the rifle, he hurried back outside, to the safety of sunlight. He wanted to get away from that dark clapboard structure with its dead crazy colt.

Perhaps the rumors were true. Perhaps Indians *had* always avoided this area, thinking it evil or cursed. But it did not seem to him that this was something old reasserting itself. No, this evil was something new, something emerging, something being born. He did not know how he knew this, but he felt it to be true.

He took a deep breath and looked back toward the barn, hefting the rifle in his hands. He needed to dispose of the horse's body. He didn't want to see it again and definitely didn't want to touch it, but the thought of the dead colt lying next to the stalls all night with that wild look on its face while he heard noises outside his window and howling up on the Rim . . . well, the prospect of that seemed much, much worse.

Virgil and Tenny wandered over, nuzzling his side, thinking he'd brought out their feed. The horses' presence bolstered his flagging courage, and he was grateful for their company. "Come on, boys," he said, slapping their flanks. "Let's see if we can't get you something to eat." He led the animals to the open barn door. He half thought that all would be normal upon his return, that he would discover he had imagined it all or, at the very least, that some of the craziness would have eroded from the colt's face. But the animal looked as bizarre as ever, and when both Virgil and Tenny balked at moving past the threshold, Zane decided that he, too, would be better off staying out of the barn. At least for the time being.

"I guess you'll have to make do with hay this morning," he told them.

The pasture was full of grass and he'd dumped two half-bales of hay by the far fence, so the stallions weren't about to starve. He led them over to the hay, made sure they started eating, then headed back to the cabin. Maybe later, after he drank a little courage and the sun rose higher in the sky, putting some more distance between himself and the night, he'd come back and figure out what to do with the colt's body. But until then he was going to stay as far away from that hideous abomination as possible.

He walked up the cabin steps and, once inside, closed and bolted the door. He was behaving like a woman and was ashamed of his foolishness, but no one else was around and he had to admit that he felt safer inside, behind locked doors.

On the table was the unfinished manuscript for his new

book, "Under the Tonto Rim," and he riffled through the pages, looking down at the words with disdain. It was romanticized hogwash, a portrayal of the West that existed only in his mind. He thought of the noises last night, thought of the colt in the barn. He should write a book about what life was *really* like under the Tonto Rim.

But no reader would believe that, he knew.

Not even in a work of fiction.

One

1

His first memory was of Delaware Punch.

The memory was pure and undiluted: a tactile sensation of cold and a taste of sweetness. He recalled a shack out in the middle of nowhere on a dusty road where his mother bought him the bottled drink. He hadn't known back then what his father did for a living, had not found out until years later, but his mother had a paper route, and with no one to baby-sit, she'd take him along each day, bouncing along the washboard roads with him in the backseat while she drove the old Rambler barefoot, folded papers in the front next to her. In his mind, the shack, a general store, was at the exact middle of his mother's route, and every afternoon they drove out into the desert, tossing out papers at the heads of ranch driveways, before turning around at the store, stopping for drinks, and delivering the remaining papers to other ranches on their way back to town.

Only he wasn't sure how much of his memory he could trust, because he saw the store as having a bareboard porch with a raggedy overhang and one of those metal soft drink iceboxes next to the door—an image he recalled seeing in a recent commercial. Did he remember what he'd seen or just what he wanted to have seen? It was impossible to tell where his memory was true and where imagination or cross-referenced images filled in gaps and blanks.

He could still remember the taste of the Delaware

Punch, though. That part was for real, and it was for that reason that he chose to believe the rest of it as well.

2

When he thought about it objectively, Glen realized that he must be going through some sort of midlife crisis. But it did not feel that way to him, and he was not at all sure if his behavior could be so conveniently categorized.

He left work on Friday fully intending to make a quick trip out to Arizona, put the land up for sale, and be back in time to participate in the conference call with programmers from the San Francisco office on Sunday afternoon. He shut off his computer, locked his desk drawer, said good-bye to Gillian, Quong, and Bill, and headed home to pack. His plan was to bring along the deed and all of his mother's papers, find some local real estate agent in Kingman to handle the sale, and return to Southern California immediately.

But even before he pulled into his driveway, he knew that was not going to happen. He had decided on the spur of the moment, while sitting at a stoplight and watching a blonde in a red Mustang pull into the 76 station on the opposite corner, that he was never going back to his job at Automated Interface again and, as he clicked the garage door opener and drove into the garage, he was filled with an almost euphoric sense of freedom.

He could do anything he wanted. Nothing was keeping him here; there was no reason for him to continue with this deadening, unfulfilling existence. He had no wife, no family, no girlfriend, and with his mother gone, there were no more appearances to keep up, no one to whom he had to justify his lifestyle. He'd read somewhere that the death of the last parent enabled one to finally become an adult, freeing a person from the role of child and allowing him to do what he wanted to do without any outside constraints. That was how he felt. He was devastated by his mother's passing, of course, and this week he had shed more tears than in the previous twenty years put together. But he had to admit that he also felt an underlying sense of liberation, as though he were finally free to start living after years of remaining in a holding pattern.

He had no specific dreams, no concrete plans—only a vague desire to travel, to see things, to go places. He was acutely aware of the fact that he had only one life and it was already half over. It seemed like only yesterday that he had graduated from high school, and yet here he was, thirty-five, his twenty-year reunion already on the horizon. And what had he done with his life, where had he gone?

Nothing.

Nowhere.

His mother's death had brought home to him the fact that time was passing quickly. He intended to make up for wasted opportunities by doing what he wanted to do rather than what he should do. He was going to indulge in all those things he had avoided out of fear or a misguided sense of responsibility.

He left everything behind. His job. His home. His friends. His entire life. He packed some clothes and toiletries, locked up the condo, dropped by AAA to pick up maps and tour books for every state, and hit the road.

He'd been born and raised in Phoenix, but he hadn't been back to Arizona in over five years—since his father died. His mother had sold the house and moved out to California to be closer to him, and while she'd talked about going back and seeing her friends, trying to get him to commit to a trip before his each and every vacation, somehow he'd avoided it. He'd been selfish. He hadn't wanted to spend his limited time off chauffering her around old haunts, and he regretted it now. It would have been easy to accede to her wishes, and it would have made her happy.

He spent the night in Vegas. Because of a Friday night traffic jam of fleeing Southern Californians on Interstate 15, he didn't get there until after eleven, but the city was still wide awake, sidewalks crowded, streets ablaze with multicolored lights and signs.

Amazingly enough, he had never been to Las Vegas before, and he found the city to be a big disappointment. The lavish hotels and resorts that looked so spectacular and enticing on television turned out to be cheap and tacky and crammed right up next to each other. He ended up staying on the fifteenth floor of a high-rise hotel in a room that smelled of stale cigarette smoke, and though he dropped twenty dollars at the hotel casino before retiring, he didn't enjoy it.

He drove to Kingman in the morning and spent nearly an hour driving unnamed dirt roads outside the city, looking for his parents' property. He wanted to see the lot first before talking with anyone, so that he could take some measure of the land, but his father's map was hopelessly out of date. Finally he broke down and went to a real estate agency. The overly solicitous realtor manning the otherwise empty office was busy, waiting for a couple with whom he was closing what appeared to be a pretty big deal. He gave Glen a map of the city's outlying areas, traced a route to the property in red ink, and told him that he'd have another agent meet him there in an hour.

He drove north out of town down a wide dirt lane that he was pretty sure he'd taken earlier, then turned onto a poorly graded road running over a flat, ugly section of desert. A bleached and weathered sign announced the name of the would-be development: SUNSHINE ESTATES. His parents had bought the property here after his father had retired, long after he was out of the house. As far as Glen knew, it was for investment, and he doubted that either of his parents had set foot on this land since they'd been suckered into buying it. A lot of people fell for such scams, but he was surprised that his father had been taken. Naturally suspicious and cynical, the old man had railed about the stupidity of people who bought items sight unseen through catalogues or television offers, and had constantly warned him about the duplicity and untrustworthiness of salespeople.

Yet he'd come out here and bought this worthless desert land.

Not a single home had been built on any of the properties in the intervening years. The parcels were well marked, though, and Glen had no trouble finding his parents' lot.

Their property was bigger than he would have thought. The barbed-wire fence paralleling the road ran nearly the length of a city block, from the small numbered sign that marked the parcel's eastern boundary to the dented cattleguard that granted access to the land at its western edge. He pulled onto the lot and stopped, getting out of the car. He didn't know what he thought he'd learn by coming out here on his own or what he thought he'd do. Pace off square footage? Run the soil through his fingers? Catalogue the plants? He ended up briefly looking around at the flat, barren land, then sitting in his car with the tape player on, waiting for the real estate agent.

A white Blazer drove up twenty minutes later. He saw the dust before he saw the vehicle, a moving cloud that followed the path of the road until it reached the cattleguard. The real estate agent who emerged from the SUV was a woman carrying an overstuffed clipboard. Tall, thin, blond, she had big eyes behind small fashionable sunglasses. "You must be Glen!" She approached him with an outstretched arm and a wide pretty smile. He was reminded of Sandi, though he hadn't thought of her in years and hadn't seen her since they were both seniors in high school.

"Yes." He shook her hand, conscious of his slick sweaty palm against her cool dry skin, and slightly embarrassed by it.

"Hello," the woman said. "My name's Sandi."

It couldn't be.

He looked closely at her while trying not to be obvious. She was about the right age, and there were definite similarities in appearance . . . so it was possible. Even the voice was a maybe. But she hadn't said anything to indicate that she knew him, and she'd shown not a flicker of recognition when she laid eyes on him for the first time. The realtor he'd talked to at the office had obviously given her his name, and if it was his Sandi, she would have at least asked him if he used to live on Trask Avenue in Phoenix.

He could ask *her*.

But he didn't.

He wasn't quite sure why. He was curious, but he

supposed at bottom he didn't really want to know. It was true that he hadn't thought of Sandi for a long time. Now that he had, though, he wished a better life for her than second-string real estate agent in Kingman, Arizona.

The woman sorted through the papers on her clipboard and started giving him a rundown on recent sales in this area and the desirability of those lots vis-à-vis his parents' property, but he only pretended to listen. Instead he thought about Sandi. He'd had a crush on her for nearly a decade, although he had told no one about it, least of all her. He even remembered the first time he'd started thinking of her in that way. They were at the Lions' Fair, a tacky, overpriced carnival put on by the meanest old men in town for the ostensible purpose of raising money to help crippled children. Their families went together each year, the kids and grown-ups pairing off once they reached the park where the fair was held. He and Sandi wandered around, bought some candy, played a few games. Then she announced that she had to go to the bathroom. They made their way over to the line of portable toilets set up on the periphery of the microscopic midway, and she told him to stand guard outside because the doors had no locks and she didn't want anyone busting in on her. From his guard post he could hear the sound of her rattling belt buckle, and he realized that behind that thin plastic door she had her pants down—and that he could open up the door and see her.

He didn't, of course, but from that point on he was acutely aware of the fact that he was a boy and she was a girl. It changed his behavior enough that they drifted apart and eventually stopped being friends, but he never stopped having a crush on her. In high school he had a falling-out with his best buddy, Allan, because Allan had started dating Sandi and, though he wouldn't admit it, Glen was jealous.

He looked at the realtor again as she rattled off the dimensions of the lot and what she thought he could get for it. No, he told himself. This wasn't his Sandi. His Sandi was living in Puget Sound working as a manager for a topflight software company. Or if she was still in

Arizona, she was a successful businesswoman married to an equally successful businessman and they lived in a six-bedroom house with a four-car garage in Scottsdale.

"Now," the agent said, "are you dead set on putting this property up for sale?"

"Well . . . yeah," he told her.

"The reason I ask is because you might want to hold on to it. I know people have a tendency to just clean house after a parent's death and liquidate all assets. And it's easier, sure. But sometimes parents' investments are worth maintaining. I think that's the case here. This area's growing, particularly with the expansion of communities along the Colorado River. And while there's no water, sewer, or electricity out here yet, it's only a matter of time. You're still young, and if you don't need the money, I'd suggest keeping the land. Your parents obviously saw the potential here, which was why they bought this lot in the first place. If you held on to the property until retirement, I'd be willing to bet that you could quadruple the amount that you'd get for it today." She smiled. "I know this probably sounds suspicious coming from a realtor, but remember, I'm cheating myself out of a perfectly good commission here. *I'd* be better off if you sold the place."

She wasn't cheating herself out of anything. What she was telling him in her veiled circuitous way was that it would be next to impossible to find suckers like his parents and that she doubted she'd be able to unload this land on anybody—and even if she could, it wouldn't be worth the trouble.

He hadn't thought he'd make a fortune off the property, but he had been counting on a little extra income from the sale. It didn't really make any difference, though. He didn't need the money. At least not yet. And if he was going to change his life, he ought to change it, and not count on residuals from the past.

"I don't like to gamble on investments," he said. "And since I don't have any sentimental attachment to this place . . ."

She was suddenly all business, her friendly, helpful manner replaced by a flat, no-nonsense terseness.

No, he told himself again. This wasn't his Sandi.

He told the woman to put the property up for sale. And started driving.

3

Springerville was a small town near the New Mexico border that was situated at the tail end of the Mogollon Rim, where the mighty plateau degenerated into a series of increasingly desertlike foothills. Coming down off the Rim, Glen could see a smattering of trees and a huge tan dome that looked ridiculously out of place among the flat homes and fast-food restaurant signs below.

It was lunchtime, and he was hungry. He'd spent last night in the town of Randall at a courtyard motel that promised a continental breakfast, but they served only one measly muffin and a miniature carton of watered-down orange juice.

He hadn't intended to stop in Randall at all, hadn't even known there was such a place. He'd driven aimlessly after leaving Kingman: eating lunch at Flagstaff, where he shopped at a huge used bookstore. Then he traveled the Lake Mary Road to Strawberry, Pine, and Payson because he liked the way it looked. At dusk, he'd found himself in Randall, so that was where he stopped for the evening.

And there was something cool about that, something gratifying about not making plans and simply holing up for the night at wherever he happened to be.

The motel hadn't been half bad—it had cable at least—and this morning, after grabbing his microscopic muffin and pathetic little orange juice, he'd looked through the rack of postcards in the lobby. Most featured corny retouched photographs. There was one of a half-jackrabbit, half-antelope creature called a "jack-alope," another of a fisherman hauling a whale-size trout out of a lake with a boat trailer. Two of them featured different doctored photographs of the same subject: a Bigfoot-like creature dubbed the "Mogollon Monster" that was supposed to roam the wooded plateau above town. He thought about getting one of the postcards to send to Gillian, Quong, and Bill back at the office, but then decided it might be better to make a clean break and just disappear. He'd changed his mind after checking out and bought a Mogollon Monster postcard, but it was still sitting on the seat next to him because he had no idea of what to say or how to say it.

Glen drove slowly down the two-lane highway that doubled as Springerville's main street. The dome turned out to be part of the high school, although he had no idea what the out-of-proportion structure could possibly be. Past the spate of gas stations and generic fast-food outlets was the downtown area, which consisted of a vintage single-screen movie theater showing a surprisingly recent film and a series of small shops housed in a block-long stretch of connected Western–style buildings. The town's lone mural, on the side of an old motel, depicted John Wayne as he appeared in *True Grit,* patch-eyed and grimacing.

There was something charming about Springerville. The sidewalks were empty, and the only other vehicles on the road were two dusty pickups and a battered Jeep, which somehow added to the rustic allure.

Sunday, he thought. Everything was closed up because it was Sunday and everyone was at church.

That seemed quaintly appealing, too. A town where people actually went to church, and Sunday was still different than other days in the week.

He stopped at Los Dos Molinos, a gaudily painted Mexican restaurant just outside of town that turned out to have the hottest food he'd ever eaten in his life. The place was crowded—he'd chosen it precisely because there were a lot of cars in the parking lot, figuring locals knew the best places to eat—and he sat down at a wobbly unoccupied table in the center of the room. The waitress handed him a menu before putting down a basket of tortilla chips, a tiny bowl of salsa, and a huge pitcher of water. Absently, he picked up a chip and scooped up some salsa, biting into it.

Immediately, his throat clenched up. He sucked in air, an instinctive reaction that resulted in an embarrassingly loud wheezing sound but offered absolutely no relief from the burning. He frantically searched for his glass through tearing eyes. He quickly gulped down both water and crushed ice before pouring himself another glass from the pitcher and downing that as well.

He had never tasted anything so hot, and it took several minutes of sucking on ice to dissipate the fire in his mouth.

He glanced around the restaurant. He seemed to be surrounded by families. At the table next to his was a mother with two young sons. One of the boys, having obviously burned his tongue on the salsa, was frantically breathing and fanning his mouth between gulps of water, while his brother laughed uproariously. Behind him, a man and woman about his age had a stroller parked next to their table, a little bonneted baby sleeping peacefully if awkwardly on the seat. In the rear of the restaurant, a man in a sheriff's uniform was talking earnestly to a bored teenage girl who could only be his daughter.

He supposed this abundance of families should have made him feel lonely, self-conscious about his own solitary state, but for some reason it did not. Instead, he felt hopeful and optimistic. The life before him was wide open, and suddenly anything seemed possible.

He remembered, as a child, watching a television program called *Then Came Bronson*. He had no idea how many seasons the show lasted, or whether it was a popular or critical success. All he knew was that it had had a major impact on him. It featured a young man on a motorcycle who roamed America, getting involved in people's lives before inevitably moving on, and it had seemed like the coolest thing possible.

That's who he felt like now: Bronson. He could go anywhere he wanted, stay as long as he chose, meet . . . whomever. And for the first time, he thought that his life was pretty damn good. He had no idea what the future would hold, but right now he was happy.

Midlife crisis.

There was that phrase again, and he supposed that was a possibility—which was why he had given no thought to selling off his condo and his possessions, why they were still waiting for him back in California—but for the moment he was content to move forward, to start anew, to behave as though he had left that old life permanently behind and was never going back.

The waitress returned with his meal. He was prepared for the spiciness this time and kept both his water and iced tea handy as he took a small exploratory bite. Either his taste buds had been numbed, or the dish wasn't as hot as the salsa, because he found that he was able to eat the food without gasping for breath.

Behind him, the couple with the baby were talking about some local Indian ruins that they'd recently toured. "What I liked was that they let you go down into the kiva," the man said. "At Montezuma Castle and most of these ruins, you can only look at them from the outside and walk around them. It was neat to go inside there."

"I thought it was creepy," the woman told him.

"When Brianna grows up, I'm going to teach her to be more adventurous, more like me."

"Over my dead body."

He didn't really want to listen in on their conversation, but with no companion of his own, he could not help hearing what was going on around him.

His ears tuned in to the low lecture the cop was giving his daughter, though he could only make out occasional words and phrases.

". . . expect . . . take responsibility . . . actions . . . that girl Janet . . . lucky I was the one . . ."

At another table, close to the kitchen, three guys who looked like cowboys were discussing the relative merits of Dodge, Ford, and Chevy pickups.

By the cash register, two old men who had just walked in were debating whether dogs behaved differently when the moon was full.

Glen finished off his enchilada, and took a bite of rice. He'd been planning to drive aimlessly across country, taking roads that looked interesting to him and seeing where they led. But he thought now that he might remain in Springerville. At least for a few days. He liked the town from what he'd seen of it, and eavesdropping on the conversations around him only made him more inclined to hang around a while.

He could see himself living in a place like this, getting some menial job, renting a rundown ranch house that he could fix up on the weekends. Maybe he'd meet a pretty local widow or a young single mom, and they'd get to know each other and eventually start dating.

He'd seen too many movies.

The waitress brought the check. He paid, left a tip, then walked outside. The air was hot and still, with a bracing absence of humidity that he remembered well from his childhood in Phoenix. His car was near the front of the small parking lot, but he didn't feel like driving right now and decided he'd rather walk off a few of the calories he'd just put on.

He started back toward the downtown, following a narrow footpath through the weedy lots that abutted the road. As he'd noticed on the way in, most of the shops were closed, this being Sunday, but he was able to look through the front windows into the businesses. There was a small consignment store that carried only baby clothes, an attorney's office, a used bookstore, a plumbing supply shop.

One unmarked storefront had an open door, and he peered in the window and saw photographs and a scale model of what looked like an Indian ruin. He remembered what the couple in the restaurant had said and, out of curiosity, walked inside.

A rattling swamp cooler attached to a blocked window at the back of the building attempted to alleviate the oppressive heat, but only succeeded in making the place more humid. Glen nodded to the bearded, short-haired young man standing behind a counter, then picked up a pamphlet from a table next to the door. *Huntington Mesa Ruins.* On the cover was a color photo, an aerial view of what had once been a sprawling pueblo community, but was now little more than a series of interconnected adobe walls and a handful of partially extant structures. Inside, next to a descriptive paragraph, were individual black-and-white pictures of the more impressive facets of the ruins. All the photos had also been blown up to poster size and mounted on the wall of the place.

Glen looked at the scale model, with its little loin-clothed figures, depicting what the Indian community had probably looked like in its prime. Then he walked over to a glass case housing arrowheads and pieces of pottery and artifacts that had been discovered in the ruins. He looked up at the man behind the counter. "Are there tours of the ruins?"

"Sure are. Five dollars for adults, three dollars for children. It's a fifteen-minute ride out to the site, and the guided tour takes about forty-five minutes. So figure an hour and fifteen, an hour and twenty all told. We provide the transportation, but you have to bring your own drinking water—and we seriously suggest that you do so. It's hot, it's summer, and there is very little shade at the site. It's easy to get dehydrated. A hat or bandanna wouldn't be a bad idea either. And sun block."

"I'm in," Glen said. "Where do I sign up?"

"Here. At the museum. But we only give two tours a day. At ten and two." The man looked up at a wall clock. "It's nearly one now. If you want to come back in an hour, we'll be ready for the afternoon excursion."

Glen nodded. "I'll do that. Thanks."

He walked back to the restaurant and his car, drove over to a Circle K, where he gassed up and bought a forty-four-ounce Coke, then cruised around the outlying area for a good half hour, taking an interesting dirt road that began next to a Mobil station and ended up at a chicken ranch in a box canyon.

By the time he returned to downtown Springerville, it was nearly two. He quickly pulled next to the curb in front of the museum, hoping he wasn't too late. He locked the car door and hurried inside. But when he passed through the doorway into the humid air of the building, he saw only the bearded young man behind the counter.

"Am I too late?" he asked.

"Not at all."

"Then where's the tour group?"

The young man smiled wryly. "I guess you're it. Do you still want to go? It's okay if you don't, but this is the most complete ruin of its type discovered in Arizona in the past twenty years. It's something to see. And it's not every day that you have the chance for a one-on-one personal tour." He nodded. "By the way, my name's Vince."

Glen wasn't sure how long he'd be in town or whether

he'd never pass this way again, so he said that he would
indeed like to take the tour. He paid his five bucks, and
Vince locked up the museum, then drove him in a Jeep
out to the top of a low mesa in the desert north of town.

The ruins were indeed impressive. They walked
through the first floor of a largely extant freestanding
adobe structure that was believed to have been some
sort of primitive apartment house. Then they passed
from one low crumbling wall to another as Vince described the series of half-wood, half-adobe dwellings that
had once stood on this spot. The guide was throwing all
sorts of facts and figures at him, and though Glen nodded politely, he wasn't really that interested. He liked
seeing the ruins, liked walking through the partially excavated archeological site, but historical minutae held no
allure for him.

In the center of a slightly raised circle ringed by
stones, a ladder protruded from a square hole. "This is
a kiva," Vince explained, motioning toward the opening.
"The kivas were—and are—ceremonial chambers hidden and kept secret from outsiders. This particular community had six kivas, although this is the only one we're
opening to the public." He pulled a small squarish flashlight from his back pocket. "If you'd like to go down
and check it out, be my guest. It's pretty small, so when
we have regular-sized tours, I only let in one guest at a
time while I stay up here and hold the ladder. But if
you'd like, I could go down with you."

"That's okay," Glen told him. "I'll feel better with
you up top. Just in case the ladder breaks or the place
collapses or something."

The guide laughed. "It's not likely. But I'll stay here
anyway and try to describe what you're seeing."

There wasn't much to see. A round room with smooth
walls and a sooty ceiling. He thought about the couple
in the restaurant. The man was right. Going down into
the kiva was fun. But the woman was right, too. There
was something spooky about it, and he came back up
the ladder pretty quickly.

Despite having grown up in Arizona, Glen had never
been to any Indian ruins before. There were some off
Washington or Van Buren or one of those presidents'

streets in Phoenix that he remembered passing as a child, but his parents had not been big on cultural or historic sites, and they'd never stopped.

Now, looking at these crumbling adobe structures, he realized for the first time how new America was, how recent the arrival of white people. According to Vince, this Indian settlement had already been abandoned for hundreds of years before the Pilgrims landed on Plymouth Rock. The knowledge made him feel small and insignificant somehow, and when Vince asked if he had any questions, he simply shook his head, and the two of them rode back to town in silence.

"Well, thanks," Glen said as the guide parked the Jeep in the alley behind the museum. "That was interesting."

"You're welcome. Hope you enjoyed it."

The two men climbed out of the vehicle.

Glen wiped the sweat from his forehead with his hand. He felt dehydrated. He'd brought his forty-four-ounce Coke with him, but most of that had been used up on the trip over, and he'd been too embarrassed to ask Vince for a sip from his canteen. The skin on his face felt tight, and he knew that he'd gotten burned. He should have listened to the guide and put on sun block.

His discomfort must have been obvious, because Vince said, "There's some cold water in the museum's fridge, if you'd like some."

Glen nodded. His car was parked on the street and he had to pass through the building anyway. "Thanks."

Vince unlocked the back door and turned to the left, where a small square refrigerator sat underneath a cupboard next to the bathroom. This close to the swamp cooler, the air actually felt good. Pulling a Styrofoam cup from a package inside the cupboard, Vince handed it to Glen, then took a plastic pitcher of water out of the refrigerator and poured. The water tasted cold, fresh, nice. Glen downed the cup, then had one more.

Vince put away the pitcher, closed the refrigerator. "Listen, are you by any chance looking for a job?"

Glen frowned as he crumpled the cup and tossed it into a wastepaper basket. Looking for a job? Did he appear in need of employment? He didn't think so. He was cleanshaven, and before he'd gone out on that Jeep ride, his hair had been neatly combed. Granted, he wasn't wearing his best clothes, but he had on his usual weekend outfit: jeans and a short-sleeve shirt. Typical leisure attire.

Although, come to think of it, he hadn't had much time for leisure the past few years. And when he examined his clothes more closely, he realized he had a slightly frayed collar on a style of shirt that had not been in fashion for the past half decade.

"See, my friend Al's overseeing a dig up near Bower. It's a pueblo site they discovered last year when the county was looking for a new landfill location. The job would only be a summer gig. Al teaches at ASU, and he spends his summers doing field research, conducting archeological excavations. Usually, he just recruits students, but I guess this year the pickings were pretty slim." Vince chuckled. "Why a young healthy coed wouldn't want to spend her three months of freedom earning minimum wage, living in a hovel, and digging in the desert is a mystery, huh?"

Glen smiled.

"So what do you say? You interested?"

Ordinarily, his response would have been an automatic no, but he'd been operating on a different, less logical level since leaving work Friday afternoon. Chance and intuition had been calling the shots on this trip, and he saw no reason to change that. He would just go with the flow and see where it led.

And it seemed to be leading him to say yes.

He'd always been an underachiever trapped in an achiever's body. He was not, by any stretch of the imagination an *over*achiever. He had not gone to Harvard and graduated at the top of his class and started up a multimillion-dollar Internet company. But he had gone to the perfectly respectable UC Brea and had gotten a good job with a major software firm. He had always felt like something of a fraud, though, and he had to admit that the idea of digging through dirt, looking for arrowheads and pieces of pottery for the summer, appealed to him.

He was still not used to his new—

midlife crisis
—lifestyle, was still stuck in his middle-class mode of thought, and he wanted to explain to Vince that he wasn't a bum, that he was only available for this work because he had voluntarily quit his well-paid corporate job to travel around the country. Like Bronson. But he realized that the other man would not care In this world, his past and pedigree weren't important.

"Yes," he said. "I'm interested."

"All right, then. I'll give Al a call, and we'll set you up."

Two

1

Cameron had been wanting to ask the question for three days, ever since they'd come to the Boy Scout ranch, but he hadn't wanted the other boys in his troop to think he was a wuss, so he'd held his tongue. He'd been nervous, though, worrying about it. Finally, this afternoon, after lunch, when he found himself alone with one of the scoutmasters, he asked.

"When are you going to tell us about the Mogollon Monster?"

It was what the ranch was famous for, what attracted most of the scouts to it, the high point of the entire week for a goodly portion of boys who came here each summer. But Cameron had never liked ghost stories or horror movies, and being out here in the wilderness was spooky enough without having to hear about real life, honest-to-goodness monsters that roamed the area.

The scoutmaster chuckled, mistaking his anxiety for anticipation. "Don't worry. We'll get to it. No troop has left here yet without hearing the story of the Mogollon Monster." He leaned forward, and Cameron thought there was something threatening in the man's eyes. "And no troop has ever heard the story and not been scared of Jim Slade's cabin."

Peach-fuzz hairs bristled on the back of Cameron's neck. He looked to the left, just outside the ranch gates, where the dilapidated cabin sat underneath the deep shade of the giant ponderosas, half buried beneath overgrown vines. Even in broad daylight the place was creepy. The doorless entryway and too-small windows held in an inky blackness that, shade or no shade, should not have been anywhere near that dark. There was a cracked and broken rocking chair on the ramshackle porch, and it was the rocking chair that freaked Cameron out the most. Dil Westerly, a scout from Tempe and one of his cabin mates, said that a boy from Cabin 10 had seen the chair rocking by itself, and ever since, Cameron had lain awake at night, listening for the creak of old boards. The thought of the monster was scary, yes, but somehow the ghosts in that haunted cabin seemed even scarier. Monsters roamed around, wandered through the forest, came and went. The ghosts and the cabin were *always* there, right next to the ranch, visible from almost any spot day or night. He looked into the shadowy doorway of the cabin and shivered. He would rather listen to the story of the Mogollon Monster every night than have that cabin so close by.

That changed at the evening campfire.

It was The Night, and they all knew it. One of the scoutmasters must have let the news slip, because word traveled fast. By the time the sun went down, they were all seated around the big fire. Everyone knew that tonight they were going to hear the story of the monster.

Scoutmaster Anderson was in charge of the evening's entertainment, and he started off in a roundabout way.

"Any of you ever hear of Zane Grey?"

In the front row, Toby McMasters raised his hand. "My dad belongs to his book club. He writes westerns."

"*Wrote* westerns," the scoutmaster corrected. "Zane Grey died in 1939. For a while he lived near here, in a cabin at the foot of the Rim. But something scared him off, and he left Arizona never to return." The fire crackled, snapped, then dimmed a little, making the surrounding forest creep a little closer. "It was the Mogollon Monster."

The boys grew hushed, wiggled in their seats, and settled in to hear the tale. Cameron felt cold and sweaty at the same time. He didn't want to be here, wanted to be home with his mom and TV and nice soft bed, but he was stuck. If it wouldn't have marked him for life as King Pussy, he would have plugged his ears. Instead, he focused his gaze on the campfire and tried not to pay attention to the words being spoken.

"Back then it was called the Tonto Rim, not the Mogollon Rim. 'Mogollon' was an Indian word, and no one used Indian words back then except Indians. But, still, everyone called the creature who lived up here the Mogollon Monster. And that was because it had been in these parts so long that only Indians knew what it really was. And it was so horrible, so terrifying, that there were no English words that could even describe it.

"Zane Grey wrote westerns, books about cowboys and gunfights, and maybe he'd read too many of his own stories because by the time he moved out here to Arizona, he thought he was a tough guy. That's why he lived in a cabin so far away from town. People tried to warn him, but he was a mean old cuss and wouldn't listen to anybody. Or maybe he did listen and just wanted to prove how unafraid he was. They told him that strange things happened on the Rim at night, that scouts and trappers had heard terrible inhuman screams, that animals had been found slaughtered and ripped apart limb from limb, that even trees had been torn out and uprooted. But he didn't care. He bought the cabin and went out there to live.

"Old Zane used to hunt in the daytime, and write at night by candlelight." The scoutmaster's voice took on a deeper, more ominous quality. "Until one night. The *last* night."

One of the other scoutmasters threw a branch on the fire and at once, as if on cue, all the boys screamed, startled by the sudden explosion of sparks. Nervous laughter followed immediately afterward. Scoutmaster Rogers, the one who'd put the wood on the fire, grinned, pleased to have gotten the reaction he'd obviously intended.

But Scoutmaster Anderson wasn't grinning. His face bore an intensely sober expression. He was clearly taking his assignment to scare the scouts very seriously, and he was *working* at it. This was not just an evening's entertainment for him; it was a mission. Something about that seemed wrong.

Cameron had been trying to concentrate on the fire

and on not listening to the story, but he had not been very successful. Against his will, he had heard almost every word. And he could not seem to look away from Scoutmaster Anderson's face, glowing eerily orange with the flickering light from the flames.

"No one knows exactly what happened that night. But there was a miner coming in from Colorado and hiking down the General Crook Trail, a miner who'd never been here and didn't know the area and didn't know he was supposed to stay away from the Rim at night. The miner said there were noises coming from that section of the forest that were unlike anything he'd ever heard. He'd been planning to make camp for the night, but he was scared and kept going instead, not stopping until he hit town at daybreak.

"After the people in town heard his story, they got together a posse and went out to Zane Grey's cabin. The door was wide open and inside, the tables and chairs were smashed, the bed and couch ripped open by something with huge claws. There was slime on the floor. And blood. Outside, the ground was hard—it was summer and hadn't rained for some time—but there were footprints in the dirt, the footprints of a creature huge and heavy, twelve-feet high at the least, and terribly deformed. The prints looked like a bear crossed with a person crossed with a spider. Some of the men wanted to leave, but they all stayed, scared as they were, and the posse followed the trail to the barn, rifles loaded and ready. The barn was empty, but it was even worse than the cabin. One whole wall had collapsed, and the hay bales were covered with black mold that was . . . *moving*. The three horses in the stalls were standing stock still and drooling, with wild looks on their faces. They'd gone completely insane.

"They shot the horses, then burned the barn. And then they got out of there before night fell.

"Zane Grey had just disappeared. There was no sign of him. Everyone thought he was dead, but he showed up in another state sometime later. He refused to talk about what happened in Arizona. The only thing people knew was that after that night, after he saw the monster, his hair had turned completely white."

There was a pause in the story as the scoutmaster drank from a glass of water. A warm breeze had sprung up, and it bent the campfire flames to the left, caused the branches of the pine trees to susurrate. The boys murmured among themselves. Darren Holstrom, next to Cameron, whispered that he thought he'd heard a scream from somewhere far atop the Rim the other night. He was pretty sure it was the Mogollon Monster.

"The monster went wild after that," Scoutmaster Anderson continued, and though his expression remained serious, there seemed to be a certain glee in his voice. "All of the ranches along the foot of the Rim were abandoned as it started attacking the people who lived there. Cattle were mutilated, turned into piles of bloody bones and scraps of flesh. Babies were stolen and eaten, only their skin left behind. Horses went mad and some even killed their owners.

"The Indians said that the monster sometimes went on rampages, angered by people trespassing on its territory, but even the oldest of them could not remember anything like this.

"And then it was over. The attacks stopped, and eventually hunters and trappers and fishermen started going back into the forest along the edge of the Rim and then even on top of it. Nothing happened to them. No one saw anything strange; no one was killed or hurt or chased away. After ten years or so, people even started moving back to the ranches.

"Everyone in town—not the Indians, but everyone else—thought the monster had either died or moved on. There was talk of Bigfoot in California by then, and some people thought that the monster had moved there.

"And then Jim Slade built his cabin."

Cameron couldn't help it. He glanced to the right, where the cabin sat in vegetative darkness beyond the boundary of the Boy Scout ranch, and he shivered. He didn't want to hear the rest of the tale.

"Jim Slade grew up in these parts. He knew the story of the monster just like everyone else. And just like everyone else, he thought it was over with, a thing of the past. Maybe he even thought it wasn't true, that it was just a made-up tale to scare little kids with on hot summer nights.

"It *was* true, though.

"There were hints. Shortly after he built the cabin, he found a dead bear on top of his woodpile—with its head missing. The pond where he watered his horses—where our pool is now—went dry overnight, and in the mud at the bottom were weird claw prints that looked like nothing Slade had ever seen. And strangest of all, there were no birds or bugs or mice or pests of any kind on his property. None of the usual forest critters would come near his place. It was as if Nature herself was afraid.

"The monster killed him on his wedding night."

Scoutmaster Anderson looked down at the ground, as if trying to decide whether or not to continue, and Cameron felt the urge to shout out to him, to tell him to stop, not to go on. But, of course, he kept silent.

"It was a girl from town, a girl he'd grown up with. Her name was Maria and she was the daughter of the Baptist minister. She didn't want to live so far from town, and she told him that she was afraid of the Mogollon Monster, but he said she was being stupid and backward. This was where he lived and this was where she would live, too. The Mogollon Monster was just an old superstition. Maria didn't believe him, but her love was stronger than her fear, and they got married in a big ceremony at the Baptist church with her father performing the rites. Half the town showed up for the wedding. After the reception, Maria and Jim rode back out to the cabin.

"A storm blew up that evening. A big old summer monsoon. But there was something weird about it. The thunder didn't always sound like thunder. Some of it did—but some of it sounded like a creature, a *big* creature, growling. It was their night and they tried to pretend that there was nothing wrong. They tried to be happy and content, but the storm was getting wilder, the noises were getting weirder. There was no electricity out here back then, only a generator Jim Slade set up in back of his cabin. All of a sudden the lights started flickering. They went off, then came back on. Went off and came back on. During one of those weird growling thunders, the lights went off for the last time, and the sound of a huge crash came from the back of the cabin.

" 'Don't go out!' Maria begged him. 'Stay here and wait until morning!'

"But Jim told her to sit there and wait, and he got out his long rifle and stormed out the back door of the cabin.

"He never came back. Maria waited and waited, growing more and more scared, and finally she couldn't help it and started screaming out his name. There was no response. The storm seemed to be tapering off, but she was afraid to leave the room to see what was going on outside. There was no phone, so she couldn't call for help, and the lights still had not come back on, so she waited in the darkness, unable to sleep, until morning.

"When the sun came up, she finally went outside." The scoutmaster's voice lowered. "The monster had gotten him. Torn his face clean off. She found it hanging from that dead tree by the side of the cabin, draped over a branch.

"That was seventy-five years ago . . . today."

The scoutmaster flipped on his powerful flashlight and pointed the strong beam across the camp to the abandoned cabin outside the ranch gates. The light played across the overgrown vines, the blackened openings that had once been a door and some windows, the rocking chair on the porch, the dead tree on the north side of the dilapidated structure.

The flashlight switched off, and Scoutmaster Anderson said in a low tone, "Sleep well, boys. Sweet dreams."

They switched on their own flashlights and walked back to the cabins in silent groups. Even the toughest among them had been quieted by the offhand horror and formless narrative of the story. Campfire yarns usually had some sort of big finish, and when the scoutmaster came to the end of his tale, Cameron had tensed up, waiting for someone dressed in a Bigfoot suit to jump out and scare the crap out of them.

But it hadn't happened. The story simply ended, and something about that was unnerving. It made everything seem a lot more real, a lot more serious.

The ranch seemed darker than usual, and Cameron

told Darren, who was walking with him, that the counselors and scoutmasters had probably left a few of the lights off or had somehow turned down the intensity in order to scare them.

"It's working," Darren admitted.

"Maybe they're going to throw a dummy out from behind one of the buildings, or maybe they rigged up some sort of fake corpse that they put in the path so we would see it." Cameron kept talking, trying to convince himself more than his friend, because deep down he thought that the adults *weren't* doing anything different or special, weren't trying to trick them, and that things were spooky and scary because it was all real.

At least, he consoled himself, their cabin was at the end of the row farthest away from Jim Slade's creepy little shack. Of course, it was also the cabin closest to the foot of the Rim. So if the monster came down the side of the cliff in the middle of the night . . .

No. He didn't want to start thinking about that.

They made it to their cabin safely, saw nothing weird on the way, and once they were safely inside, all was normal, all was right, and they had no problem forgetting about the Mogollon Monster.

Well, not forgetting about it.

Ignoring it.

But it was a different story after lights out. They all tossed and turned, anxious and ill at ease, but gradually the noises silenced as, one by one, the scouts in the cabin fell asleep: Jimmy, Art, Julio, Darren. Pretty soon Cameron was the only one awake. And he remained awake, listening, as the rest of the camp shut down. He heard two scoutmasters talking over by the chuck house, heard the clatter and rattle of equipment being put away in the barn, heard the adults say good night, and walk off to their respective cabins. There was a pause before the sounds of people gave way completely to the sounds of nocturnal nature, a brief interlude when all was quiet, and then the crickets started chirping, the frogs started croaking, the owls started hooting.

Everyone was asleep.

And still Cameron remained awake. Seconds passed, minutes, a half hour. He imagined the hands on a clock moving slowly, slowly, and found himself wondering what time it was. He tried to count sheep, tried to think of nothing but blackness, but none of it did any good. He simply couldn't fall asleep. He desperately had to take a leak, but there was no way he was going to leave the cabin. If he couldn't hold it the rest of the night, he'd just get out of bed and piss in the corner of the room and then try to blame it on someone else in the morning. He gritted his teeth, tried not to think of water.

And something changed.

He didn't know what at first, but he figured out almost instantly that the crickets and nighttime creatures had suddenly gone silent.

A shiver passed through him. His mouth was suddenly dry and he no longer had to pee. He wanted to reach over to the next bed and shake Darren awake, but he couldn't seem to make his muscles move. His arms remained stiffly at his sides underneath the sheet.

Gravel crunched outside, a slow heavy sound, as though something big were moving through the camp. A strange wind blew through the screen, a movement of air that felt oddly fluid, as though it had the density of water. Cameron breathed in quickly, a deep breath that he intended to hold until whatever this was—

The Mogollon Monster

—passed by, but the air he inhaled was thick with the stink of something rancid, and he gagged, coughing. He immediately clapped a hand over his mouth, praying that he hadn't been heard, that no green muscular talons would slice through the screen and slash his stomach open. He closed his eyes, shutting them tightly enough to cause tears, and waited for the blow that would end his life. Yet it did not come and did not come and did not come, and he fell asleep in that position—hand over his mouth, eyes squeezed shut—though he had no idea how long it took or when it occurred.

He was awakened by shouting.

"OhmyGod! OhmyGod! JesusChrist! HolyJesus!"

It was Scoutmaster Rogers' voice, and it was joined a moment later by the shouts of other scoutmasters and counselors, all of them shocked and horrified.

Cameron felt a sinking feeling in the pit of his stomach, but he quickly pulled on his pants like the rest of the boys and hurried out of the cabin. He knew where the startled voices were coming from even before stepping out the door, knew where the scouts would be running to, knew exactly where they would find whatever this horror turned out to be.

Jim Slade's cabin.

He was right. A crowd of men and boys had gathered around the rundown shack. The boys, who were talking excitedly on the way over, were all silenced the second they dashed out the ranch gates and reached the shack.

Cameron arrived just before Darren. His eyes went first to the rocker on the porch, but there was nothing unusual about it. He saw that the other boys and men were all turned toward the side of the cabin, and he followed their lead. They were pointing at something high up, something small and shapeless and disgustingly slimy.

He drew closer and felt suddenly sick as he realized what it was they were looking at.

Scoutmaster Anderson's face, hanging from a branch of the tree.

2

Bonnie Brown didn't like the Anasazi Room.

None of the female employees liked being alone in the museum at night. Most of them felt uneasy in the Colonization Room, with its metal conquistador uniforms and life-size mannequins depicting diorama scenes of Spain's seventeenth-century forays into the New World. A few of them didn't like the Natural History Room and the stuffed animals with their glowing glass eyes. But when she told them she felt uncomfortable in the Anasazi Room, they all laughed at her. It was in the new wing, for one thing. The lighting here was brighter than in the museum's original section, and the exhibits were all behind glass and spaced far apart. The Anasazi Room was particularly benign. They had no bones or mummies as in the Garfield Museum, not even any statues, figurines, or costumed dummies. There were only artifacts: spears and arrowheads, jewelry and beads, jars and vases, baskets and metates.

But she still didn't like it.

Bonnie looked up at the clock. The museum closed at nine on Fridays, but by the time the stragglers left, it was usually closer to nine-thirty. Then she had to count up receipts, tally the guests and reconcile the number with that on the turnstile counter, back up the day's computer work on diskette, and set all the building alarms before she could finally leave.

She was halfway through the receipts when the phone rang. It was Richard. He was home and bored and waiting for her, and he wanted to talk dirty. "Phone sex," he called it. She'd never understood his desire to describe sexual acts to her over the phone, but she tolerated it. Right now, though, she wanted to get out of here as quickly as possible, and she told him that she didn't have time for this right now.

"Come on," he begged. "You know what I'll do to you when you get home, right?" He started describing something he *knew* she didn't like, and she firmly told him good-bye and said she'd be home within an hour.

She hung up the phone.

And heard a noise from the Anasazi Room.

She looked left, into the new wing. All of the patrons were gone, the doors to the building were locked, and she was the last employee left. No one was in the museum except her. The lights were still bright, she had not yet turned them to half-power, but that didn't make up for the emptiness or the knowledge that she was here all alone.

The noise came again.

It was a rattling. No, not exactly a rattling—more like a clicking, a clattering, a chattering made by the rapid tapping of stone against stone.

She stood, grabbed her key ring, walked slowly down the wide empty corridor toward the Anasazi Room.

Again she heard the sound.

It wasn't stone against stone, she told herself. It was the rattling of the air-conditioning unit, some sort of perfectly explainable mechanical problem that seemed spooky only because it was night and she was all by herself with an overactive imagination in this big empty building.

The noise did not stop this time. It continued, competing with the clicking of her heels on the hard polished floor. She stopped outside the wide entryway to the Anasazi Room, listening to the rhythmic tapping, aware that it was in time with the over-rapid beating of her heart.

Without going in there, she knew what was causing the sound.

The metate.

A whisper of cold passed over her skin, leaving goose bumps in its wake.

She'd had a nightmare about the grinding stone the first night after the object had been installed in its case. It was a fairly recent acquisition, and a seemingly innocuous one. Aside from pottery shards and arrowheads, metates and their manos, or pestles, were just about the most common Native American artifacts found in the Southwest. Every museum in the Four Corners states had a storeroom full of extras, and every trading post, tourist trap, and gas station had one or two for sale to unsuspecting customers at outrageously inflated prices.

But she'd dreamed about it anyway, and in her dream the object had been carved not out of basalt but out of bone, the petrified bone of a dinosaur or some other prehistoric monster. It was oddly shaped, and, viewed from a certain angle, its irregular chips and shadowed bumps gave the impression of a scowling, malevolent face.

Bonnie thought of that now and steeled herself. She should not have come down this way. She should have stayed at the desk, finished her work quickly, and fled the premises.

She peered into the room. It was far darker than it should have been. The overhead lights were out, though she had not turned them off, and the lights in the display cases were off as well.

All except for one.

A lone spot shone on the metate, on the curved basalt grinding stone and its worn, vaguely phallic mano.

She had to fight the instinctive urge to flee. She still had no idea what it was about that particular object, out of all the hundreds of artifacts in the museum, that had given her the heebie-jeebies, but she knew now that her feelings had been right on the money. The thing might look like an innocent piece of carved rock, but it was haunted or cursed, and now its true nature had been made manifest.

It was after her.

No, she told herself. She just happened to be in the wrong place at the wrong time. This was impersonal, entirely unrelated to her. It could have happened to anyone. Wilton or Robert or Patrice or Jorge.

But it hadn't.

Slowly, the mano began to move, at first turning like a compass, then rocking back and forth before finally flipping up and down lengthwise in a manner that was not only unnatural but obscene, the staccato chattering of its repeated impact on the grinding stone impossibly loud in the stillness.

Bonnie ran.

She didn't know she was going to do it until she did it. She'd intended to wait and see what happened next, perhaps to try to turn on the lights before calling someone to take a look. But the obscenely animate mano atop that stolid heavy metate seemed directed specifically at her. Before she had time to make a logical decision, her body was obeying a more primal impulse, and she was racing away from the Anasazi Room, trying desperately to keep herself from screaming.

She ran back down the wide corridor, key ring jingling in her hand, until she reached the front desk. She threw the receipts in the drawer, locked it, then got the hell out of the building as fast as her feet would carry her, quickly locking the front doors, but not taking the time to set the alarms. Her hands were shaking as she fumbled in her purse for the keys to the car, and even as she sped out of the parking lot and bounced onto the street, the Jetta's radio cranked, she could hear in her mind that horrid clattering of stone on stone.

If she'd had a cell phone in her car, she would have called Stephen, her supervisor, or maybe even the police, and told them exactly what had happened. But she didn't, and by the time she pulled into her driveway, the desire to save face and avoid embarrassment had reasserted itself. She did call Stephen from the hall phone, but told him only that she'd heard a suspicious noise in the Anasazi Room. When she'd gone to investigate, all the lights had been out, so she'd locked up the untallied receipts, locked the front doors, and left.

"You should have called me from the museum," Stephen said. "You should have dialed 911. You know a patrol car would have been there in five minutes."

"I know," she said. "But I thought I might be in danger. There weren't even any custodians left. I was alone in the building, and I thought the best thing to do was get out."

Stephen sighed. "Well, it can't be helped. I'll call the police and meet them down there myself. If they find anyone, I'll give you a call. Otherwise, I'll see you in the morning. I want to go over this with you."

She was sure he did. Stephen was not one to let protocol lapses pass without extensive lectures and disciplinary action.

Richard was already in bed waiting for her, waiting for sex, and she decided not to tell him anything. She took off her clothes, climbed onto the mattress, and they made love—first in her favorite position, then in his. Afterward, she took a quick shower, and they fell asleep next to each other, cuddling.

She was awakened after midnight by a noise downstairs.

A thump.

It was her imagination, she told herself, a sound left over from a dream. But when the thump came again, she quickly reached over and shook Richard awake. "I heard something downstairs," she whispered.

He was instantly alert, scrambling out from under the covers and grabbing his bathrobe from the back of the chair. Neither of them believed in owning guns, but Richard slept with a baseball bat under his side of the bed, just in case. He scooped it up, hefting it over his shoulder as he treaded carefully across the hardwood floor toward the door, careful not to step on any of the creaky boards.

"Be careful!" Bonnie whispered.

He held a finger to his lips, shushing her.

The sound came again.

Thump.

He stepped out of the bedroom into the hall, quietly closing the door behind him, and she suddenly wanted to call him back. She didn't—he needed the element of surprise, and yelling would only alert the intruder—but at that moment she was filled with a frantic desire to get him back into the bedroom, to lock the door, and call the police, let them handle it.

And she knew exactly why.

From somewhere near the stairwell came a short sharp cry. And a loud crash.

Then silence.

And a thump.

Thump.

She tried to tell herself it was a home-invasion robber, a rapist, a murderer.

A person.

But she knew that wasn't the case. She knew what was making that noise. She'd known from the beginning.

The metate.

The thumping sounded closer, and with it came a familiar chattering, the unmistakable clattering of stone against stone.

It was outside the bedroom door.

She screamed. A loud piercing cry with no end, a shriek that required no breathing, no intake of air, and continued endlessly, issuing from her open mouth without any conscious effort.

She was still screaming when the door was bumped open and the grinding stone lurched across the threshold into the bedroom, its mano chattering crazily.

And she had not stopped by the time it reached the bed.

Three

1

Glen sat on a plastic booth bench in the Bower Jack in the Box, nursing his coffee and staring out the window at the chaparral-covered hills west of town. Vince had called his friend Al, the ASU professor, who had agreed to meet Glen here at eleven this morning and then drive him out to the site.

He was excited at first, meeting the archeologist friend of a guy he'd run into at the small town where he'd stopped for lunch. Sort of cinematic, something that would lead to a series of adventures for the ultra-cool hero.

Something Bronson would do.

But a night in an un-air-conditioned hotel room, a four-hour drive through some of the most godforsaken territory known to man, and forty-five minutes in this fast-food joint had given him time to think.

What was he doing here?

Maybe his mother's death had triggered this irrational behavior. Maybe he was suffering some sort of delayed reaction, some post-traumatic stress disorder that was manifesting itself in the form of a second adolescence. Maybe—

He was saved from any more self-analysis by the arrival of Al Wittinghill. The archeology professor looked just the way an archeology professor was supposed to look. Dusty clothes, khaki vest, tan skin, bald head, graying beard. Glen was the only customer in the place, so the other man recognized him right away, and he walked over, hand extended.

"Mr. Ridgeway?"

Glen stood. "Dr. Wittinghill, I presume?"

"Call me Al."

They shook.

"I must say, this is the oddest recruitment I've ever had. I just casually mentioned to Vince that we were shorthanded up at the site this summer, and all of a sudden he's calling me up and telling me he's found someone willing to dig." The professor smiled. "Not that I'm complaining. Recruiting on my own this year brought in a total of five people. I can use all the help I can get."

"I'm not . . ." Glen cleared his throat. "I don't know what Vince told you, but I'm not any kind of archeologist. I just stumbled into this. I was taking a tour of the Indian ruins in Springerville, and he asked me if I would be interested in working at an archeological site. I've never done anything remotely like this before. I'm . . . I'm a computer programmer, for Christ's sake."

"That doesn't make any difference. Even my students aren't all archeology or anthropology majors. One of them's getting his degree in business administration. He's here because he thinks it will be good life experience. So don't worry. You don't have to be an expert. You just have to be willing to take direction."

"I guess I can do that."

"Good, good. Let's head out to the site, then. I'll give you the ten-cent tour, introduce you to our intrepid band, then we'll get you settled in a cabin. I don't know what Vince told you about payment—"

"Nothing."

Al chuckled. "Well, there's a reason for that. We do provide free lodging. The university rented some cabins that used to be part of an old motor court on the south side of town. The only one still available has no air conditioning, but you can bunk up with Ron or Buck in one of the refurbished cabins if you want. As for wages, you get a small stipend of a hundred dollars a week. That barely pays for meals—if you stretch it—so you're not going to be making any money on this deal. I'd pay you more, but that's all my budget will allow, and I'm on the same scale as everyone else. We're not in it for the money. If you were thinking you were going to make a killing, now's the time to tell me and bow out gracefully."

"No," Glen said. "That's fine."

"Thank God!" Al grinned, clapped him on the back. "We need you. We really are shorthanded." He started toward the exit. "My Jeep's out front. You can follow me if you have a four-wheel-drive vehicle. Otherwise, we'll leave your car here and come back for it."

Glen nodded out the window. "That's my Saturn. The white one there."

"The Jeep it is, then." They walked out of the Jack in the Box into the dry eastern Arizona heat. "The site's not that far, but they never got around to making a real road to it. There's just a sort of half-assed trail, and you need high clearance to get through. Hop in and buckle up."

Glen followed him out to a battered, open-topped Jeep with no discernible color, and they drove through the center of town, turning left on a narrow half-paved road next to the Circle K. They passed a block of small, slummy single-story homes. Then the road wound around an irregularly shaped trailer park before heading between two low hills. To Glen's surprise, the road stopped just on the other side, abruptly ending at the foot of a scrawny juniper tree.

The professor did not hesitate. He swerved right before the tree, and then they were cutting through high dead weeds, bouncing over unseen bumps and troughs. If there was a trail here, Glen certainly couldn't see it, but Al steered the Jeep to the left and to the right confidently. A few moments later, Glen was able to discern the twin ruts created by the passage of tires, and then they were around another hill and bouncing down into a relatively flat, arid valley. Ahead, sunlight glinted off several parked vehicles, beyond which was an open excavation bordered by a mound of tilled soil.

"Did Vince tell you how this site was discovered? They were scouting locations for a new landfill. This is all county property, and they chose this spot because of its relatively close proximity to the highway. But when they ran the first backhoe through here, they unearthed a bunch of pottery and arrowheads—most of which they shattered and destroyed with their machine. As these people usually do, they stopped digging, looked at what they'd found, then went back to work. But when they ran into a section of adobe wall, they knew they had something here. The supervisor didn't want to make any decisions on his own, so he stopped all work, called someone in county administration. The news went up the chain of command and then they called in the university.

"It was kind of a last-minute thing. I was actually going to take my team to an old excavation near Rio Verde that has not been fully examined, but when this site was discovered, we altered our plans and came here." He glanced over at Glen. "*This* is a find."

They came to a stop next to a mud-spattered van with oversize tires and a back window covered with faded environmental stickers.

"Hop out. We'll have a quick look around; then I'll take you back to your cabin—"

"There's no reason to take me back. I'm ready to go right to work. It's just a waste of time to make an extra trip."

"I don't know if the good folks at our local Jack in the Box are going to be thrilled with your car sitting there all day."

"Parking's reserved for customers, right? I bought a cup of coffee."

Al laughed. "I'll back you on that. Push comes to shove and they have your car towed, we'll take them to court."

"Deal."

"All right, then. I'll introduce you, show you around, and get you started."

They got out of the Jeep, walking up the mound of dirt and ducking under a waist-high rope strung between metal stakes that marked the perimeter of the site. On the other side of the mound, all grass and vegetation had been cleared. A succession of low trenches connected a series of increasingly large man-made depressions. Here and there, sections of extant adobe walls protruded from the hardpacked ground. In the center stood a freestanding canopy underneath which were tables, chairs, and several large ice chests.

"This is our excavation. Like I said, we're a small crew this year. Just me, Melanie, Judi, Ron, Randy, and Buck. That's less than a third of the size I usually have. And we have to get as much done this summer as we can because there's no guarantee the site will be here next year. The university is petitioning to have this declared a state historic site, but this is county land, and they're under no legal requirement to preserve or protect it. All they have to do is grant us access for these three months, and allow us to cart away what valuables we can find. Unless we can prove that this is a unique archeological discovery or that it's extensive enough to warrant further study or has the potential to attract tourists, it's conceivable that by next summer this will all be a dump, or paved over and used to store maintenance equipment."

"So, what kind of Indian ruin is this?"

"It's an Anasazi pueblo, probably built between 900 to 1000 A.D., judging by the construction techniques and artifacts we're finding."

"Anasazi?"

Al chuckled. "You really are coming into this cold, aren't you?"

"I—" Glen began, embarrassed.

"Don't worry. It's fine. We'll teach you everything you need to know. Right now we're just looking for warm bodies and a willingness to work."

With an ease born of long practice, he slipped into professorial mode. "The Anasazis were the North American equivalent of the Mayas, Incas, and Aztecs, a highly evolved, highly civilized people who created a sophisticated culture. They lived in great cities. Mesa Verde, in Colorado, for example, was home to some seven thousand people.

"The word 'Anasazi' means 'the ancient ones' in Navajo. It's a reference to the fact that they were a people whose existence had passed into the realm of myth. The dominant culture in what is now the Four Corners states, the Anasazi disappeared sometime in the thirteenth century, abandoning their big cities much like their South American counterparts. Fiction writers have tried to portray this disappearance in a mysterious light, as though it occurred overnight, as though one morning everyone suddenly vanished. But most archeologists believe that a prolonged drought led to a gradual migration of the people, who scattered throughout the Southwest, reconvening in smaller, more easily sustainable communities, primarily the pueblos of northern New Mexico." His eyes twinkled. "But I'm not at all sure that the fiction writers aren't right."

They reached the first of the workers, a shirtless and seriously tanned young man using a fold-out foot shovel to dig a small round hole in the center of a larger square hole. He was sweating profusely, and when Al introduced him as Buck Hill, the young man stopped digging for a second, used the back of his hand to wipe the perspiration from his forehead, nodded a curt greeting, then went immediately back to work.

Several feet away, two other students—a pudgy young black woman and a rail-thin white guy with red hair and a sunburn to match—were shaking a large open-ended box with wire mesh on the bottom. Dirt and gravel were falling through the mesh onto a soft-looking pile of soil below. Next to them was a folding table on which were situated various artifacts.

"Judi Rhodes and Randy Tolleson," Al announced. The two looked over. "This is Glen Ridgeway. He's signed on with us for the rest of the trip."

"Glad to meet you," Judi said, smiling broadly. "It's about time we had another person to share our joy."

"Our misery," Randy corrected.

They both laughed.

Judi offered her hand. "Nice to meet you."

"Thank you," Glen said, shaking. "Nice to meet you, too."

Randy held out his hand. "Likewise."

"So what are you doing?"

"Sifting for the small stuff: teeth, beads, necklace fragments, what have you. Buck and Melanie have already gone through this pile, so there's probably nothing left. We're just double-checking."

Glen nodded.

"They're good kids," Al said as the two of them walked away. "They're both grad students, and they've been with me for the past three summers. Most thorough workers I've got. Ron, on the other hand . . ."

On the opposite side of the biggest section of exposed adobe wall, a bald and heavily tattooed young man was photographing the site with the largest and oddest-looking camera Glen had ever seen. He wore a Walk-man headset and didn't hear Al when the professor shouted out his name. But he must have seen the older man waving in his peripheral vision because he looked up at them and pulled down his earphones. "Yo."

"Ron Sedaris, our resident photographer-slash-pottery reconstructor. This is Glen Ridgeway."

Glen feigned a smile, nodded.

The bald kid nodded back.

An awkward pause followed, and then Al cleared his throat and started walking toward the southwest corner of the excavation. "Weird guy," the professor admitted after Ron had put his headphones back on and they were out of range. "But he knows his stuff."

They stepped into a narrow shallow trench and followed it to a larger sunken square.

"Finally, Melanie Black."

A pretty woman with a dirty-blond ponytail, clearly several years older than the other students, was at the far end of the indented section of ground, kneeling on a green pad and cleaning off a piece of pottery with a small brush. She was frowning, and she stood, turning the artifact over in her hands, examining it. She looked up at them briefly, said hello, then went back to the pottery shard in her hand, the expression on her face one of confusion and consternation.

Despite the professor's reassurances, Glen had been feeling hopelessly out of his depth. What was he doing? He knew nothing about archeology, had never even seen an Indian ruin until yesterday and was only here because of his idiotic resolve to act more spontaneously. With each worker he met, that feeling intensified. He'd been wondering whether to tell Al directly that he'd changed his mind and wasn't interested, or simply slink off in the middle of the night and disappear. He'd been leaning toward the latter.

But seeing Melanie caused him to reevaluate that plan. Maybe it was the fact that she was his age, or because she looked like a normal person, someone he could relate to, but he suddenly felt that coming here wasn't such a dumb decision.

Melanie dusted off the piece of pottery, her frown deepening. "This is strange."

"Did you find something?" Glen could hear the excitement in the professor's voice.

The woman nodded.

"What is it?"

"It's a shard from what looks to be a pitcher, judging by the pieces surrounding it."

"What's so strange about that?"

"There's a picture on it, a singular image rather than a continuous design."

"Yes?"

She held up the object, turned it toward him. "It's a picture of me."

2

Within two days, Glen had decided he definitely liked Melanie.

She seemed to enjoy his company, too. Like Judi and Randy, they worked as a team on specific projects, Al having designated her as Glen's archeological mentor. Unlike the others, she was not one of Al's students but a schoolteacher from Bower, who spent her summers engaged in activities that both corresponded to her interests and dovetailed with her classroom curriculum. She taught Arizona history at Bower Junior High, and last summer she'd signed on at Wupatki to shepherd youth groups through the national monument. The year before that, she'd been down at Tubac, acting as a docent at the state park, giving tours of the fort. Her degree was in cultural anthropology, and over the years she'd made a lot of contacts, so when she applied for summertime positions at these various historic locations, she was inevitably hired. The discovery of this new pueblo, right in her own backyard, was apparently a dream come true.

While Glen liked spending his days with Melanie, even enjoyed the work itself, nighttime accommodations were another matter.

His motor court cabin was a green stucco building in the shape of a teepee that housed a small round room with a single bed and a kitchenette, as well as a microscopic bathroom that would have felt right at home in a Winnebago. Although Al had provided him with a portable electric fan, it was hot as hell in there, and he had a difficult time falling asleep at night. But he couldn't see himself bunking with either Ron or Buck. Buck was a smug, irritating narcissist, and Ron was . . . Ron was just too weird. Judi and Randy were an item, so they stayed in the same cabin. Al had a cabin all to himself and would not be a bad roommate, but he showed a distinct disinclination to share.

Melanie went home at night to her own house.

Glen wouldn't mind sharing a room with Melanie.

In addition to working as a twosome, they had taken to carpooling together. She picked him up in the morning at the motor court, and they drove in her pickup over to the excavation. Judi and Randy carpooled as well in their van.

On Friday, after they'd finished at the site, after they'd pulled tarps over their week's work and weighted down the corners with excavated rocks on the off chance that a storm might hit during the night, she offered to take him on a tour of the town, show him some local points of interest. He accepted gratefully, and this time, instead of dropping him off in front of his teepee cabin and then heading home, she parked the truck and got out with him.

He had not made his bed that morning, last night's burger bag was still sitting atop the TV, his dirty razor was laying in the bathroom sink, and he was trying to think of a polite way to keep her out when she tapped his shoulder and motioned toward the sidewalk. "Let's take a walk."

She smiled at him, and he realized that she'd understood his dilemma. He felt embarrassed all of a sudden. "If you—"

"Come on," she told him, laughing. "I saw that look on your face. You didn't expect company. You're a guy. Need I say more?"

He smiled sheepishly. "It's a pigsty," he admitted.

"I don't care about seeing your little motel room anyway. Let me show you around town."

From the beginning, they'd had an easy working comeraderie, both at the excavation and on their carpooling trips, but he expected an awkwardness to creep in now that they were on a purely social footing. It didn't happen. They talked comfortably as they walked past the used-car lot, past the Dairy Queen, into the center of town.

Glen wiped the sweat from his forehead. They'd gone a little over a block, but he was already drenched. "I'm still not used to these temperatures."

"It's a hot summer," she agreed.

"I'm having fun, though. I mean, I have nothing to compare it to. I've seen archeology types sorting through the mud and tar by the La Brea Tar Pits on my way to the L.A. County Art Museum, but that's as close as I ever came to any kind of archeological experience. I like this, though. I think it's interesting."

"Yeah," Melanie said. She gave him a quick, obligatory smile, but it faded quickly.

"You don't think so?"

"I didn't say that."

"You didn't have to."

They kept walking.

"What's the matter?" he prodded.

She shook her head. "Nothing."

"What is it?"

"I told you. Nothing."

"Is it that pottery shard you found with your picture?"

She didn't reply.

"It is, isn't it?"

"It's not . . . *just* that," she said.

"What then?"

She took a deep breath. "There's something weird about that pueblo."

Glen felt a tiny surge of adrenaline, a slight increase in his pulse. He understood from her tone of voice what she meant. He had not felt anything himself, and he didn't really believe in the supernatural or the paranormal. But the drawing on the pottery, though crude, did look an awful lot like Melanie. "What makes you say that?" he asked.

"We've found other things, other artifacts that don't belong or that simply aren't . . . right."

"Like what?"

"Buck found a figurine two weeks ago, a stone carving. It wasn't a totemic figure, it wasn't a god or a demon or any kind of spirit, as most of these are. It was of a woman, an ordinary, average Anasazi woman, dressed in everyday clothes—only her face was contorted into an expression I can't even describe. It was the most horrifying carving I've ever seen." She pointed to her bare arms. "I have goose bumps just thinking about it.

"But that wasn't all. It was wrapped in rotted feathers bound together with strings of intricately beaded leather, as though it had been used as part of some shamanistic ritual. Attached to the bottom of the figurine, also by leather cord, was the mummified hand of an infant."

"Jesus," Glen breathed.

"Yeah."

"And there's been more?"

She nodded. "Judi and Randy found the jawbone of a horse so horribly deformed that we didn't even know what it was at first. It was in a garbage pile, a pit filled with castoff food and broken household items. A horse's jaw should not have been in that spot in the first place, and this thing . . . it looked like the jawbone of a monster. They also found—I know this doesn't make sense, but it's true—a leather pouch containing Greek money and, next to it, what Al has identified as a Saxon children's toy. They're both from roughly the same time period as the pueblo, and while it's possible that someone came by later and placed them there, it's not too probable. From the positioning of the items and the obviously undisturbed ground where they were found, it looks like they were in the pueblo when it was abandoned. Only as far as anyone knows, the Anasazi never had any contact with or knowledge of either the Greeks or the Saxons.''

Melanie licked her lips. "And then there's . . . my picture. It's creepy enough to find strange things buried in the ground for hundreds of years that don't make sense or can't be explained. But when one of them involves you personally, it . . . it . . ." She shook her head helplessly. "I don't know how to describe it. It's just worse is all. You start feeling like you're the target of something. You wonder if it's just a coincidence or if it's like one of those old mummy movies and you're the reincarnation of some princess that the monster's going to come after.''

"What does Al say about all this?"

She shrugged. "He seems excited, but I think it's more because these are rare finds and will help him protect the site. I don't think he believes there's anything out of the ordinary. Who knows? Maybe he's right.''

"But you don't think so."

She shook her head.

"He said something to me when he first brought me out on Monday, something about archeologists thinking Anasazis had devolved into other tribes, but fiction writers thinking that something mysterious had happened. He seemed to side with the fiction writers. Maybe he's working out some sort of new theory about their disappearance, and he doesn't want to let on or say anything about it until he can publish it.''

"That's not so far-fetched," she admitted.

"Maybe all this stuff supports his theory. Maybe that's why he's so excited.''

"I hope so. It makes it a little less eerie somehow."

"So you're not going to quit?"

Melanie frowned. "Quit?"

"I thought you were scared that—"

"It'll take more than that to scare me away. It's spooky, I admit, but once I start a job I finish it. Besides, I want to find out what happens.''

Glen smiled. "Good," he said.

She started to say something, then stopped and smiled herself.

They walked in silence for a moment, but it was a comfortable silence. They'd reached the downtown area by this time, the original Main Street, not the newer one with the gas stations and fast-food outlets, and she pointed out the old Bower Hotel, now home to medical offices, dental offices, and a few failing boutiques. She showed him the former sheriff's office, now an antique store, where rumor had it that Doc Holliday spent an involuntary evening on his way to Tombstone. They stopped in at Yellis' Soda Fountain, unchanged since the early 1900s and still owned by the same family. Melanie was obviously a frequent customer, and she bought a box of lemon drops, the type Glen had not seen since childhood.

They turned off Main and walked down a tree-lined residential street with beautiful old homes that seemed completely out of place in this dumpy little town.

Melanie popped a lemon drop in her mouth, then offered him one. "So tell me about yourself," she said. "I assume you're not married. Otherwise, you wouldn't be out here digging in the dirt all summer. Divorced?"

Glen shook his head. "No. And no significant other either."

"I'm sorry. Did you have a bad breakup?"

"From who?" He smiled wryly. "To be completely and totally honest, I haven't even had a girlfriend since college."

She raised an eyebrow.

He held up a hand. "I know how that sounds, and I know I should probably lie and pretend that my social awkwardness stems from the fact that I was involved in a long-term relationship and have been out of commission for a while. But the truth is, I never found anyone. And what's even more embarrassing is that I didn't really make an effort to look. I graduated, went to work, and suddenly I looked up and years had passed and my life was exactly the same as it was a decade ago. I'm not a workaholic or anything. It's not that I didn't have time for a relationship. It's just . . . well, I guess I sort of got into a rut and didn't know how to get out."

"You're out now."

He smiled. "Yes, I am."

"You know," she said thoughtfully, "you're the wave of the future, that type of new modern American I've been reading about: cut off from regular human contact, interacting only with coworkers and people on the Internet. You're probably one of those millionaires next-door, living in a modest little condo, eating frugally, never buying new clothes or new cars, and after you're dead, your neighbors will find out you had all this money that you had stashed away and could have done something with."

He felt embarrassed because she was a lot closer to the truth than he wanted to admit. Not about the money. But about the lifestyle.

He changed the subject. "What about you? Are you seeing anyone?"

Melanie was silent for a moment, then pointed down at the sidewalk. "See that?"

"What?"

"Those words."

He bent down to look at a name imprinted into the corner of the sidewalk square. " 'F. J. Black,' " he read. " 'Cement Contractor.' "

"That's my great-grandfather."

Glen was not sure exactly what this had to do with the topic at hand, so he said politely, "Oh. Your family's in construction?"

"He was a murderer. There are people's body parts buried in these sidewalks."

He looked at her, not sure if she was joking.

She wasn't.

"He was the most notorious serial killer in Bower history. The *only* serial killer in Bower history. He murdered sixteen transients between 1910 and 1935. This was a mining town back then, and a lot of workers drifted in and out of here, especially during the Depression. Every couple of years, he'd pick out some young man without a family, have a few drinks with him, take him out behind the lumberyard, and kill him. He'd chop the body into little tiny pieces and then mix the pieces in with the cement of whatever he was working on at the time. The town sidewalks were his biggest and longest project, and they got most of the bodies. Of course, no one found out about any of this until after he was dead, when my great-uncle Horace found his most recent victim out in the lumberyard, part of the body mixed in with some mortar, the rest in the dirt. They only found out about the others because my great-grandfather kept track of them in his ledger, along with his list of materials and expenses. He didn't write down names, but he wrote down descriptions and specified where he'd disposed of their body parts." She stared down at the sidewalk as she spoke, unwilling to meet his eyes. Her voice was low, unusually subdued.

"Everyone in town knows that. And they know that I'm his great-grandaughter. People are nice to me, I have friends, I'm a part of the community . . . but I'm not exactly prime dating material. The men of Bower aren't beating a path to my door. In the back of their minds is the thought that there's a mass murderer in my family, and that maybe his genes have been passed down to me." She smiled ruefully. "Not exactly the kind of thing men like to think about on a date.

"So, to answer your question, no, I'm not seeing anyone."

"Wow." Glen did not know what to say. What was the appropriate response to that? He shook his head, stunned. "Wow," he said again.

"Kind of see me in a whole new light now, don't you?"

He looked at her in surprise. "No," he said. And it was true. Her revelation was shocking, but it did not alter his opinion of her, did not reflect on her in any way, at least not in his mind. The past was past, and what happened had occurred decades before she'd even been born. Hell, he knew next to nothing about his own ancestors. For all he knew, they could have tortured people during the Inquisition, come over to America to slaughter Indians, and then worked their way up to lynching black men.

"I wasn't planning on telling you that," she said softly. "At least not for a while. I haven't told any of the others, not even Al."

"My lips are sealed."

"I guess I just thought you should know."

He wasn't sure what she meant by that.

"You know, the past doesn't die. It's with us all the time. The sins of the father and all that." She looked down at the ground, at the imprint in the cement. "I've thought sometimes that maybe that's why I teach history, why I spend my summers doing these amateur archeological things. Maybe I'm just trying to understand why we're such slaves to what went before."

Glen shook his head. "Maybe that's true in a small town, but not in the big bad city. I know people who've reinvented themselves three or four times over. They don't even have to answer for their own previous actions, let alone the actions of others."

"I wish I could do that, start over someplace where no one knows me."

"Why can't you?"

"I live here."

"So?"

"My job's here, my parents are here . . . I just . . . I can't."

Glen thought about his own mother, his own life. "Well, you leave almost every summer—"

She laughed. "And a liberating experience it is, let me tell you."

"Why not make it permanent? You know, I was trapped in a life I didn't want until my mother died—"

"That's the thing: your mother died. You wouldn't have left otherwise. You wouldn't have quit your job. You wouldn't be here."

"No," he admitted. "But I should have done it a long time ago. And you should, too. You don't have to go far. Springerville, say. Or Randall. You could work for a school there, live your own life where people know nothing about your family background, define for yourself who you are, yet be close enough that you could still come back and visit your parents on the weekend if you wanted to."

"That does sound tempting."

"There's nothing stopping you."

"I'll think about it." She smiled at him, and there was

gratitude in that smile. If he'd been more confident, if he'd known her longer, if he were a different type of person than he was, he would have hugged her. The moment seemed to cry out for it. But instead he smiled back at her, and they resumed their slow stroll down the street.

He found himself trying to imagine what she had been like as a child, as a teenager. She was his age at least, and he wondered if they would have gotten along if they'd met back then; if they would have been high school sweethearts, going to school dances, going out on dates, marrying young and having kids. Would that life have been better than the one he had now?

They continued walking. There was a long pause in their conversation, this one awkward. He glanced through the large front window of a well-kept house. Inside, the living room lights were on, though dusk had not yet arrived. A boy and a girl were sitting on the couch watching television. Their mother was seated on a nearby lounge chair, reading a magazine. He turned back toward Melanie. "So," he ventured, "would you like to go out on a date sometime?"

"Isn't this a date?"

He cleared his throat nervously. "I don't know," he said. "Is it?"

She took his hand, and he felt the softness of her fingers against his, the smoothness of her cool palm. She smiled at him, squeezed. "It is now."

3

Melanie awoke feeling good.

It had been a long time since she'd awakened on a day off feeling anything but restless and out of sorts. She peeled and grated potatoes and made herself hash browns for breakfast, which she ate on the back porch while watching a hyperactive group of sparrows dart between her two lemon trees. The sky was clear, but the temperature was not too hot, and it looked like it was going to be a very pleasant day.

She'd dreamed about Glen, and it was a sexual dream,

the first she'd had in a long, long time. She was not a person who ordinarily remembered her dreams, and on those few instances when she did, they were usually nightmares. But this time was different. She and Glen were making love on soft meadow grass near a mountain stream; she was on top, the warm sun shining on her bare back, and everything was perfect.

That euphoric feeling was still there when she woke up, was still there after breakfast, was still there after she'd changed the sheets and made the bed and vacuumed the house.

She would be meeting Glen after lunch. They'd planned to go out this afternoon with Randy and Judi. Ron and Buck would have come along in an instant—all of the ASU students were going stir crazy here on their days off and were grateful for anything that would help kill time—but the four of them had made a concerted effort to keep their plans quiet.

Her morning was free, though, and she felt so good that she decided to drop by and see her parents. Ordinarily, she made her obligatory weekly visit on Sunday evening, arriving just before dinner and leaving almost immediately after, but today she thought she'd actually spend some time with them, and she drove across town to her old home.

She pulled up in front of the house. Neighborhood kids she didn't know, but who would doubtlessly be in her class a few years from now, were playing kickball on her parents' lawn, using the willow tree and the corner of the garage and the flower box as bases. They stared at her suspiciously as she parked her car and got out, walking up to the front door. She felt like the intruder here, and while she smiled at the children, she felt relieved once she was inside, the door closed behind her.

"Mom!" she called out, walking into the family room. "Daddy!"

Her mother stood up from the couch. "What a surprise! We didn't expect you until tomorrow, dear. What's the occasion?" A frown passed over her face. "There's not any problem, is there?"

Melanie laughed. "No. I just thought I'd stop by and pay you guys a visit."

"Well, we're grateful."

Her father shifted in his easy chair. "You're here just in time. Your mother's trying to drag me into her drama league."

"We're doing *Death of a Salesman* this season, and I think he'd make a perfect Willie Loman. Look at how beaten down he is."

"I've been telling her that maybe someone who's *interested* or someone with some *acting talent* might be better."

"You can't spend the rest of your life just sitting in that chair watching sports and court TV shows. You're retired now; you can do anything you want."

"And I don't want to hang out with a bunch of queers and old ladies redoing some play that's been done better a million times before."

" 'Queers and old ladies,' huh? Yeah, you'd better watch out. There might be some *nee*groes there, too."

Melanie stepped in. "Mom? Obviously he doesn't want to do it. Daddy? Racism, sexism, and homophobia are nowhere near as charming as you seem to think they are. Now, why don't we all just forget about the drama league for a little while and try to have a nice normal conversation, like a regular family?"

Ordinarily, her parents would have chuckled and they all would have settled down to talk in a happy, everyday way. But, instead, they both lit into her for having "teacher-itis" and treating them as though they were seventh-grade children, her mother saying Melanie thought she was better than they were because she'd gone to college, her father telling her that she was an ungrateful know-it-all not half as smart as she thought she was. There was real animosity in it, and Melanie was taken aback. What had brought this on? She and her parents had always had a great relationship, a loving, sitcom-family relationship, and to her this came completely out of the blue. She was more hurt than she let on, and she excused herself, going into the kitchen ostensibly for a drink of water, but really to settle her nerves.

Strangely enough, things were calmer when she returned. Everything was back to normal. It was as if the vehement argument had never happened, and after a minute or so of awkwardness, Melanie told them about her week. She loosened up as she spoke, and she talked about Glen, saying how nice it was to have someone her own age at the excavation.

Her mother read between the lines instantly. "Why didn't you tell us about him before? Have you two gone out yet?"

"He just started this last week, and we haven't been on an official date yet, but we sort of went out last night. We took a walk. I showed him around town, and then we grabbed some food at La Casa. I think you'd like him. Both of you."

"It's about time," her father said.

"George!"

"She's no spring chicken." He turned toward Melanie. "You were already six years old by the time your mother was your age."

"Thanks, Daddy."

"Well . . ."

"Speaking of the excavation, your father found some Indian pottery."

He snapped his fingers. "That's right! I forgot to tell you." He struggled out of his chair. "I was digging a hole for those new sprinklers I'm putting in, and I came across this piece of pottery. Strangest damn thing. You and your friends dug holes to China in that yard when you were little and never found so much as an arrowhead, but now that they discovered that Indian ruin you're digging at, stuff seems to be coming up everywhere." He shambled down the hallway. "Wait a minute. I saved it for you."

She started to follow him back to his den, but stopped in the hall to look at the framed photos of herself that her mother had used to decorate the walls. A new baby picture had been added since last week, replacing a much cuter one that had hung there for twenty years. An outline of the older, larger frame was visible around the new one, and she wondered why the photos had been switched after all this time. "What do you mean, 'stuff seems to be coming up everywhere'?" she called out.

"George Kelvin said he found an Indian necklace while he was planting roses. And Helen's grandkids dug up a mess of arrowheads." He emerged from the den holding a triangular pottery shard that was black on one side, brown on the other. Between his fingers, she could see the white lines of a decorative pattern. "Come on, let's go back into the family room. The light's better. You can see the picture."

The picture.

Her pulse accelerated. She thought of that other piece of pottery, with its eerily accurate rendering of her face, and suddenly she was not sure she wanted to see what her father had found.

But she followed him back out to the family room, where he held up the shard so it was illuminated by the sunlight streaming through the sliding glass door.

The picture was crude, primitive, in the style of the early Anasazi, although it looked more like the simple renderings of cave art than the more elaborate designs usually associated with pottery.

It was her parents' house.

She took the object from him, feeling cold. She glanced from her father to her mother, but both of her parents' faces were blandly calm. Obviously, neither of them had recognized the image for what it was, and for a brief second she thought it was *her*. She was reading into the picture an interpretation that wasn't there. Maybe she had imagined the depiction of her own face on the pitcher shard as well. But, no. That wasn't the case. She had witnesses. The others had seen her likeness in the artwork. All of them had noticed the strange resemblance.

She examined the pottery fragment. The specificity of the image unnerved her. The building depicted was a single-story ranch house with a covered side stoop and a centered chimney. Such structures did not exist, had not even been conceived of, during the time of the Anasazi. Once again, the most logical explanation was that this was fake, that someone had painted this recently and planted it. But Al's examination of her previous find had revealed it to be legitimate, and she knew enough about Anasazi art to know that this, too, was real.

Oddest of all was the fact that she could see a figure peeking out of the front window, a small, simple face that bore no resemblance to anyone in her family. The crazily off-center visage looked like a cross between a clown and a crash-test dummy.

She was suddenly glad that her parents had not noticed the similarity between the pottery art and their house. It was childish and superstitious, but she felt better for the fact that they were out of the loop, as though not knowing would protect them.

Protect them from what?

She had no idea. It was not even a concrete thought, more a vague feeling, but almost immediately it solidified into certainty.

"You think it's an important piece?" her father asked.

"Oh, George," her mother said. "Give it up."

"*She* seems pretty impressed," he insisted.

"It's rare," Melanie admitted. She spoke carefully. "Most pottery from this period, from this area, had either no ornamentation or had just a repeating geometric pattern that circled the entire pot. The fact that this is a stand-alone image is different."

"See?" he said triumphantly.

"I'll take this to Al and see what he thinks."

"Go ahead. But I want it back. I found it on our property and it's mine."

She tried to smile. "Especially if it's rare and worth money, huh?"

"Especially."

"Okay," she lied.

She left soon after, explaining that she was going to meet some friends. Her father said good-bye and settled back into his easy chair, flipping on a football game, while her mother walked her to the door. "You'll be here tomorrow for supper?"

"Of course."

Melanie opened the screen and stepped outside.

"So when do we get to meet this guy?" her mother asked.

Melanie looked back. Through the mesh, she could see her mom smiling.

She smiled herself. "I don't want to scare him away."

Her mother laughed. "I'm happy for you. You deserve it."

Melanie turned away, embarrassed. "Thanks. I'll see you tomorrow." She waved good-bye and walked down the porch steps. The kids were gone, having taken their kickball game to the end of the block, but old Mr. Babbitt was out next door, watering his lawn, and he waved at her. "How are you, Melanie?"

She waved back. "Fine, Mr. Babbitt. How are you?"

"Fine, fine."

She'd known Mr. Babbitt her entire life, and she used to stop by the house every time she visited her parents, but ever since Mrs. Babbitt died two years ago, she'd stopped. She felt guilty about it, but the truth was that she felt uncomfortable around the old man.

Still waving, she hurried over to her car and hopped in.

She spent the next two hours before the date reading the newspapers and magazines that had been piling up, eating a light lunch, taking a *thorough* shower (just in case), and choosing clothes. Shortly after noon, she picked up Glen at his teepee cabin, and they met Randy and Judi at Denny's. They'd made no specific plans, and over milkshakes and iced teas, they tried to figure out something to do. Bower's lone theater was showing a mid-level action movie that none of them wanted to see; they'd all been to the park and its adjacent "historical museum" more times than they cared to; and window-shopping in the town's small business district had long since lost its appeal.

"I don't understand why we *have* weekends off," Glen said. "It seems to me that if there's this big rush to get as much done as possible during the summer and there's a shortage of volunteers, Al would want us to keep working."

"School policy," Randy told him. "Funding is always contingent on following bizarre and irrelevant rules to the letter, and apparently this time, Al's obligated to work only five days a week."

"He doesn't mind," Judi said. "He gets to work on his findings, flesh out his report, and every other week he speeds back to Tempe and the university. For the rest of us, though . . ." She shook her head. "No offense, Melanie, but Bower is not exactly a hub of activity."

She laughed. "Tell me about it."

The waitress who brought their drinks was not the one who had taken their order, and she smiled shyly as she placed the glasses on the table. "Hi, Miss Black."

Melanie recognized the waitress as a girl who'd been in her class several years back, though she could not remember her name. She smiled back. "Hello. How are you?"

"I got married last year. To Dwayne Bunker. Remember him?"

She didn't, but Melanie nodded. "I'm happy for you."

That was one of the unfortunate aspects of small-town life: constantly running into old students. When she went to the grocery store, the clerks and boxboys were ex-students. When she went to the movies, the kids in the ticket booth and at the concession stand were ex-students. When she called someone out to trim her trees, they were ex-students.

That wasn't such a problem for most of the other teachers. Bower Junior High (or "B.J. High" as the more discontented students snickeringly referred to it) had an extremely high turnover rate—Bower was not exactly the garden capital of the world—and it seemed to be primarily a stopover for new teachers on their way to jobs in the cities and districts they really wanted. But she was born here, grew up here, lived here, would probably die here, and even when her students grew up, there was still that distance. She was always "Miss Black" to them, and while they were nice to her and unfailingly respectful, it was impossible for her to develop the sort of easy cameraderie other people had with them. She was only thirty-four, had only been teaching for a decade, but sometimes she felt like an old spinster school-teacher who was destined to end up alone in an overcluttered house with a townful of acquaintances and no family.

It was why she spent her summers on projects with people from outside of Bower. If she ever hoped to meet someone, to have a life beyond the narrow boundaries within which she'd been living, she would have to look elsewhere.

She glanced over at Glen.

Now she had met someone, and the ironic thing was that it was right here in her own backyard.

Her own backyard.

She looked down at her purse on the booth seat next to her, spread open the twin flaps and saw on top of her makeup and sunglasses the pottery shard her father had found. But . . . something was wrong.

She squinted, bent over to look closer.

The face in the window was gone.

The house was the same, but that wild visage was no longer there. That was impossible, and as she thought about those crudely drawn features, she shivered involuntarily, a short spastic shudder that passed through her whole body.

"Anything wrong?" Glen asked, looking at her.

She thought of telling him, but at the last second shook her head, pulling together the sides of her purse. "No," she said. "No, everything's fine."

Four

1

"So how did that make you feel?"

Cameron looked away from the psychiatrist's steady gaze and shifted uncomfortably in the oversize chair. "I don't know."

"Were you frightened?"

Of course, dipshit, he wanted to say, but he simply shrugged. He was only here because he had to be. All of the scouts who'd been at the ranch were required to see a counselor to make sure that what they'd seen hadn't screwed them up. Part of him wanted to confide in the man and tell him the truth, describe what he was really feeling; but another, more logical, part reminded him that there would only be this one meeting, that the psychiatrist didn't know him from Adam, didn't care about him, and would never see him again.

So he answered the overly personal questions in as impersonal a manner as he could, wanting only to finish the session and get the hell out of this office so he wouldn't have to sit here and dwell on—

Scoutmaster Anderson's face

—what he'd seen.

Finally, after what seemed like an eternity longer than math class, the psychiatrist stood, smiled at him, and said they were through. The old man shook his hand in a way that Cameron assumed was supposed to make him feel like an adult, but instead made him want to laugh.

He handed Cameron a business card. "Here is my number. Feel free to call me anytime if you would like to talk. I can tell you right now that you will continue to have nightmares about this incident for quite some time. You may even start to feel anxious during the daytime, perhaps find yourself fearful of places and people that did not bother you before. Scottsdale is not the Rim Country, so there won't be as many physical reminders as there could have been, but just be aware that your reactions and feelings may not be what you expect and may not be something that you can control. So if you need to, you can call me and we can talk about it."

Cameron nodded. But who would pay for that? he wondered. Psychiatrists weren't free. Probably, Dr. Jeifetz would send a bill to his parents for anything beyond this first visit.

It didn't matter. He didn't need any extra help. He could handle this. He wasn't a *complete* wussboy.

His parents were in the waiting room, and his mom smiled at him and walked him outside to the hallway and the elevator, while his dad stayed behind and talked to the doctor. He wondered what the psychiatrist was saying, what his opinion *really* was, but Cameron tried not to let it bother him. He needed to get on with his life and pretend that everything was normal.

Afterward, they drove home.

There'd been changes in the neighborhood since he'd been away at camp. The biggest and best was that Devon and his gang of bullies had been broken up. He didn't know what had happened to the other boy and his pals, but their parents were still here and they were gone. The rumor was that they'd been arrested for beating up some kid whose dad was a lawyer and were now in juvy. But no one knew any more than that or even knew if that was true. The adults had to know, but they weren't talking. Both his parents and Jay's, however, were letting them play on the block unsupervised, so obviously wherever Devon and his gang had gone, they weren't coming back anytime soon.

The other change was that the Dunfords had moved out. They'd only been here for six months, so their leaving was no great loss, but it fueled speculation about their house. No one had been able to stay there more than a year since the Abramsons left, and the kids on

the block had long cherished the belief that the place
was haunted.

Cameron didn't want to think about that. Not after
what he'd seen.

They pulled into the driveway, and before they'd even
gotten out of the van, Jay had ridden up and was jumping off his bike, having obviously been waiting for them
to come home. Across the street was another flurry of
activity as Stu and his little sister Melinda ran out of the
house and came over.

He was glad to be back, was happy to be in the city,
surrounded by buildings and people, instead of being out
in the wilderness surrounded by . . . God knew what.

The Mogollon Monster.

He was a big hero now. Everyone wanted to hear the
story of his adventure at the scout ranch. Even kids he
didn't know or didn't like, kids from way over on Third
Street, begged him to tell them about seeing the torn
face hanging off the tree. The last thing he wanted to
do, though, was keep reliving that terrible morning, and
in a way he wished he had told Dr. Jeifetz about his
dilemma.

"So what'd the shrink say?" Jay asked after Cameron's parents went in the house.

Cameron shrugged. "Not much." He swiveled slowly
on his heels. "Except that I'm . . . *insane!*" He screamed
and leaped toward Melinda, hands extended, and the girl
ran crying back across the street toward home.

"Good one," Stu said shakily.

Jay laughed. "Thank God, you're back. It's been a
long week having to hang out with these weenies."

"I'm not a weenie!" Stu said.

"You're a weenie," Jay told him.

"I'm glad to *be* back," Cameron admitted. He realized
his mistake the second the words left his mouth.

Stu saw the opportunity and pounced on it. "So where
were his eyeballs?" he asked. "Were they with his face
or were they still in his head?"

Cameron sighed. "Could we talk about something
else? Do I always have to entertain you clowns and do
all the talking?"

"Yeah," Jay said, hitting Stu in the back.

"Hey!"

"Hay is for horses, mostly for cows." Jay kicked Stu's heel, sending the smaller boy sprawling.

Stu quickly got back on his feet. "I'm telling my mom!" He followed the path of his sister across the street.

Cameron nodded. "Thanks."

"No problem." Jay looked around to make sure no one was eavesdropping and no one else was coming. "So where *were* his eyeballs?"

There was an afternoon thunderstorm, a monsoon from the north, and Cameron was glad. The kids playing street soccer all scattered to their respective houses, and he, too, went home, ostensibly to get out of the rain. He must have retold his story twenty times since getting back from the shrink's, but instead of desensitizing him to the events, the repetition only cemented the horror in his mind and made it harder for him to think of anything else.

Luckily, his parents left him alone, didn't bug him about it, and he hid in his room, closing the door and pretending to be playing with his Game Boy. In reality, he sat staring out the window into the backyard, wondering, as he had so many times since that terrible morning at the scout ranch, where the monster had gone and what it was doing. He was acutely aware of the fact that it could have been him rather than Scoutmaster Anderson. He recalled the crunch of gravel outside the cabin, the sickening smell of rotted food. The creature had been close, had passed within a few feet of him, and if it had seen him, if it had known he was awake, it might have gotten him instead. He recalled also how a *change* had come over the world just before the monster had passed by, how everything had gone silent, how he'd wanted to cry out but couldn't, how there'd been that strange heavy wind. The memory was tactile, specific, not merely a one-dimensional remembrance but a sense-surrounding re-creation of the event that he knew he would be able to recollect at any time.

And suddenly—

it happened again.

The world outside grew instantly darker, as though a filter had fallen over the window, and the air became thick, liquid. He wanted to run out of the bedroom, but could not move, wanted to call out to his parents, but could not scream. Outside, he thought he saw a shadow in the rain, a hulking figure that should have shambled, but was instead lightning quick.

The Mogollon Monster.

Cameron looked away, concentrating on the shelf above the desk that held his rock collection and scouting awards, trying to ground himself in reality and make sure that he'd seen what he thought he'd seen, that he hadn't just imagined it. His mouth felt dry, and he swallowed hard before again looking out the window. The backyard was empty. There was only the lemon tree, the fence, the old swing set, and his dad's barbecue soft-focused by a heavy curtain of rain. There was no monster, no—

He saw it again.

It was standing between the tree and the fence, and this time it didn't look so big. It was the size of a teenager maybe or a short man, certainly not the Bigfoot-like beast whose shadow he'd witnessed a moment before. The rain and the angle and his own mind had conspired to make it appear so large. But its existence was not just a trick of his imagination. The thing was actually there, and somehow the fact that he could see it, even if it was smaller than he'd originally thought, was more frightening than any vague glimpse or ephemeral shadow could ever be.

He could make out no specifics through the rain-blurred glass, could only see a hairy, silhouetted shape, but he knew that the monster was staring at him, and he was filled with a coldness that seeped all the way down to his toes.

He blinked, and it was gone. The air was once again normal, light. He could move, he could make noise, and the dark filter that had settled over the world disappeared.

Cameron fell back on his bed, trying to catch his breath. The monster had followed him here to Scottsdale all the way from the scout ranch. He didn't know how, didn't know why, but he knew it was true, and he wondered if his face would be hanging from the lemon tree in the morning.

What could he do, though? Tell his parents? Jay? Stu? Melinda? What if that put them in danger? What if it came after them next?

The shrink.

Yeah! Dr. Jeifetz. He had the psychiatrist's number. And the monster certainly couldn't track telephone calls (and even if it could, a small part of him said, at least the shrink wasn't a friend or family member).

But his parents would overhear his conversation with the doctor—there was no way around that, the phone was in the kitchen—and then his dad would go out to try to find the monster. And then . . . ?

His head was pounding. There seemed no way out.

At the very least, Cameron thought, he needed to document what he'd seen, to get it down on paper . . . just in case.

He rolled off the bed and walked over to his desk, where he opened the top drawer and took out a sheet of unlined paper. Taking a pen from the pencil holder, he tried to draw a picture of what he'd seen out the window, but he couldn't quite remember what the figure looked like. That was weird. The image should have been burned permanently in his mind. Instead, he found the memory fading, the shape of the creature blurring and blending with those of other monsters: Bigfoot, Frankenstein, Dracula.

Still, he drew what seemed to him to be a close approximation, and it looked even better once he filled in the tree and the fence and other objects from the backyard. Something was still missing, though. Something wasn't quite right. He stared at his drawing and tried to figure out what was wrong.

It might have had wings, he thought. Maybe that was—

No. The hair.

Cameron quickly scribbled in a chaotic rat's nest. Yes. That was it.

He shivered. It was as though he'd triggered the key that ended a hypnotic trance. His fading memory re-

versed itself, and he suddenly knew *exactly* what he'd
seen. He looked at his drawing, looked out at the rainy
backyard, then ran out of his bedroom toward the living
room, where he hoped to God that his parents were safe
and sound and waiting to give him comfort.

2

It was only an arrowhead.

So why did it make him feel so weird? So guilty and
creeped out? It was as though he had a mummy in the
house, like he'd unearthed the remains of some ancient
Indian shaman, illegally stolen it from a protected burial
ground and stashed the dried body in the closet. The
feeling was the same. Especially in the middle of the
night when he got up to take a whiz. The arrowhead
was lying atop the bureau in the living room, and each
time he left the bedroom and crossed the hall, he sped
by the darkened archway that separated the back of the
house from the front and hurried to the safety of the
bathroom.

Lately, he'd taken to leaving the living room light on.

And the hall light.

And the bathroom light.

And the kitchen light.

All because of that arrowhead.

Eric Jackson looked from the television to the bureau,
and though he couldn't see the flattened artifact from
this angle, he felt a tingle of cold spread down his back.
He'd actually had a dream about an Indian sitting on
the foot of his bed, an ultra-realistic dream in which he
thought he'd awakened to see an intimidating figure sitting ramrod straight on top of the covers, facing away
from him, facing the open door.

The only thing was, he wasn't sure it *was* an Indian.
He assumed so, because of the context and because of
the arrowhead, but there was something strange about
the shadowy form, something odd and unfamiliar he
could not quite place. He woke up with goose bumps

and lay there for the rest of the night with the lamp on, resting only fitfully.

He'd found the arrowhead in his side yard, while digging a hole in which to dump his used oil and filter. It had been at the top of an overturned shovelful of earth, a chipped, brown triangle that stood out in sharp relief against the dark blackish soil. He thought that was strange. In all the years he'd lived here, all the holes he'd dug for various reasons, he'd never come across even an interesting rock, let alone an Indian artifact. Still, he picked it up and pocketed it and finished digging. He'd forgotten about it until that evening when he emptied his pockets before taking off his clothes and climbing into bed. He'd put it on the nightstand with his keys, wallet, and change, and the next morning he'd washed it off and placed it on the bureau in the living room next to the railroad spike he'd found while camping, among his collection of geodes.

Eric looked at the clock on the VCR.

Nine.

Tomorrow was a workday, and he usually went to sleep about this time, but he decided to stay awake awhile longer. Even with the lights and the television on, he still didn't feel entirely safe in the house, and he was reluctant to go to bed while that thing lay out there in the open.

As ridiculous as it sounded, even to himself, he was filled with the certainty that the arrowhead posed a threat to him. This was not something he'd been willing to acknowledge before, but now that he'd finally admitted it, he felt better, free, as though he'd been relieved of a huge burden and was able to act the way he wanted to instead of putting up a false front.

Eric stood. He'd never live this down if anyone found out about it, and he was ashamed of himself for being such a pussy, but he knew what he had to do if he was ever going to get another decent night's sleep in this house. He walked into the kitchen and emerged a moment later carrying a sandwich-size Baggie. Taking the arrowhead from the bureau, he quickly dumped it into the plastic bag. Part of him did not even want to touch it, and for a fleeting second he thought he should don work gloves and use them to place the artifact between the pages of a Bible, but there was a limit to how obsessive he was willing to get.

Outside, the street was empty and lights were off in over half of the houses. The moon was full but hidden behind a stray cloud, giving the world below an odd and eerie cast. He tossed the Baggie with the arrowhead into the rear of his pickup, then went back into the house to get his keys and lock up.

He drove to Bower's Lake.

It wasn't really a lake—more like a pond, a glorified mud puddle, even—but because it bore the name of the town's founder, its status had long ago been upgraded. It lay five miles outside of town, beside a control road halfway between the highway and the Willet Draw ranger station. Eric came in from the west end and pulled to a stop next to the gnarly scrub oak that was the only tree near the water. The moon had emerged from behind the cloud and the landscape was bathed in bluish light. There was plenty of illumination to see by, and for that he was grateful.

He got out of the truck and walked around back to retrieve the plastic bag. The arrowhead inside was black and its edges looked razor sharp, its point perfect, despite the hundreds of years it had been in the ground. He didn't really want to touch the object again, but he knew the bag would probably float, so he took a deep breath, stuck his hand in the bag and pulled out the arrowhead. Cocking back his arm, he threw it as hard as he could, watching it soar over the meadowgrass, and fall into the center of the pond, where it hit with a satisfying plop.

A wave of relief washed over him, and Eric looked quickly around to make sure there was no one else around, that no one else had seen him, before hopping back in his truck and hauling ass for home.

3

"Jerod! Come here!" Ricky looked up from the hole he'd been digging and motioned his friend over.

Jerod, busy trying to extract nails from the four-by-four they'd confiscated from the dump and were planning to use for one of the new room's posts, took his time about responding. Ricky was his friend, but the boy had the attention span of a flea. He was always overreacting to small shit, getting hyped up over things that didn't even matter, and Jerod had learned a long time ago to ignore him for the first few calls. If it was unimportant, his friend would give up trying to get his attention and move on to something else. If it turned out to be real, then the boy would come over and get him.

"Jerod!"

They were adding on to the clubhouse again. The club had already expanded from the original single room to a sprawling structure that took up almost the entire side yard. Over Easter vacation they'd even added a lookout tower, making a trapdoor in the roof and constructing a four-sided fence up top. Now they were going to make a basement, a sunken hideout, and Ricky was digging a hole while Jerod was figuring out a way to shore up the sides so it wouldn't cave in on them. They'd gotten the idea from an old rerun of *Hogan's Heroes* on Nick at Nite, and to Jerod's mind this was going to be the coolest thing ever.

Which was why he didn't want to waste his time on one of Ricky's little half-baked worries.

He glanced over, saw his friend excitedly jumping up and down on the lip of the hole, which was about five-foot square and three feet deep.

"This is big, dude! This is major!"

His interest piqued, Jerod wiped the sweat from his forehead and carried his hammer over to where Ricky was eagerly motioning him over. "What is it?" he asked.

Ricky jumped into the hole and crouched at the bottom, pointing to a black open space in the corner where his shovel had broken through. "There's like a cave down there or something!"

Jerod followed his friend in. He leaned over and

peeked into the ragged aperture. Sure enough, he could tell from the way the sunlight stopped several feet down that whatever was down there was deep.

"Should I tell my mom?" Ricky asked.

Jerod looked at him. "No way! She'll have this whole place roped off and won't let us back here until your dad's buried everything and cemented it over. We need to explore this on our own first."

Ricky grinned.

They started digging furiously, Jerod using his hammer like a pickax to expand the opening, Ricky scooping out dirt with his shovel. There was indeed some sort of chamber down there, but it didn't look like a cave. It looked man-made. The sides appeared to be intentionally constructed, made out of mud or cement or adobe. As sections of ground began to fall through and the breach broadened, it became clear that the space beneath them stretched under the rest of the clubhouse and even under Ricky's home.

Finally, the opening was big enough for them to fit through, and they stopped working, wiping the sweat off their faces and pausing to catch their breath.

"Should I go and get a flashlight?" Ricky asked.

Jerod shook his head. "Too suspicious. It's the middle of the day. Your mom'll want to know what you need it for." He poked his head through the opening. "I think there's enough light."

"Who's—?"

"I'll go in first."

Jerod turned around and lowered himself through the opening, sliding backward on his stomach. Luckily, the wall of this underground chamber was irregular. Individual bricks protruded here and there, as if intentionally providing footholds for those attempting to climb up or down. He jumped the last few feet, and stepped forward to look around. Behind him, Ricky hit the dirt floor with a grunt.

The chamber was huge, easily the size of the auditorium at school, and while the area immediately surrounding them was clear, Jerod could tell that most of the room was crowded with a jumble of oddly shaped objects.

Buried treasure?

Visions of pirate loot and ancient Indian gold caused the blood to race in his veins. They might be rich!

The light died out just past the opening through which they'd come, and he was not able to make out exactly what was accumulated on the floor. They stood in place for a moment, waiting for their eyes to adjust. Gradually, the contents of the room came into focus.

"What do you think they—?" Ricky began.

And stopped.

Skeletons. The cylindrical room was filled with skeletons. Skulls, rib cages, leg bones, arms. The fleshless remains of literally hundreds of bodies had been dumped or left or buried down here, some whole, others broken and in pieces.

"Holy shit!" Ricky breathed.

Jerod was petrified—he had never seen anything like this, not even in his nightmares—but he refused to show fear. Especially not in front of Ricky.

He took a hesitant step forward, acutely aware of the fact that generations of dead bodies lay before him. This was like a community tomb or something, a burial room, someplace where an entire village sealed up their dead. Probably Indians.

He hadn't been aware of it until now, but he'd been holding his breath. He let out a large exhalation and breathed in hard. All of the bodies had rotted down here, lying in this sealed chamber for years, for centuries, until the corpses became bone. Jerod half expected to smell the fetid stink of decay, but his nostrils and lungs filled only with dry and slightly musty air that was not at all unpleasant. To his left and right, whole skeletons lay stretched out in the dirt, like the posed figures from one of his pirate models. In front of him, a mass of bones sloped gradually upward, a wall of ancient remains. He tried to tell himself that the spirits or souls of these people were not here. They had gone to heaven or hell, but he could not help thinking that this was a haunted spot, that the ghosts of at least some of the dead still lingered in this underground lair.

He would have expected Ricky to be nervously chattering away, asking a thousand questions, and the fact that his friend was silent made everything seem even more ominous.

Jerod took another step forward, his eyes adjusting further to the dark, and he squinted into the dimness in a vain effort to make out the far end of the chamber.

From off to the right came the dry musical sound of bones rattling.

He turned, and saw in the gloom a skeletal arm . . . beckoning.

They ran like hell, Ricky in the lead, scrambling to get up the wall and out. They were screaming as though banshees were chasing them, and once they were on top, in the yard, they ran screaming into the house, shutting and locking the door behind them and yelling for Ricky's mom to call the police.

Five

1

"God *damn,* this is exciting!"

Al was grinning like a five-year-old with a box of candy. He'd just come back from examining a burial chamber found by two kids in a backyard, and he could hardly contain his enthusiasm.

Glen looked up from the folding table where he was brushing off a piece of pottery. "Is it really as big as they said?"

"Bigger. This is the single biggest burial chamber I've ever seen, and I'd venture to say that it may be the biggest yet discovered in North America, at least in terms of the number of entombed bodies. We're sitting on an amazing piece of history here. I just . . ." He took off his hat and scratched his bald head, grinning. "I can't describe it. This is so damn . . . I don't know. It's fantastic."

"Will this make it easier to get your protected status?"

"No doubt about it. No doubt at all. We could end up with a national monument designation if all goes well."

Melanie put down her sifting box and pushed a stray strand of hair from her face. "You really think this site is that important?"

"This site is important because of its location, the number of artifacts, and the quality of the ruins, as I've maintained all along. But that's only part of it. This could quite possibly be the most significant North American archeological find of our lifetimes. What I propose to you is that the entire town of Bower and this surrounding area is built upon the site of a massive Anasazi settlement, a city two to three times bigger than that at Mesa Verde. Mesa Verde was home to seven thousand people at its peak. We could very well be talking ten thousand here. We haven't found our Cliff Palace or Pueblo Bonito yet, but even without a single dominating structure, the sheer scope and size of this makes it easily the largest Anasazi community yet discovered." He grinned uncontrollably. "There were *hundreds* of skeletons in that burial chamber. Hundreds of them! I've never seen anything like it."

The others had stopped working and gathered around, drawn by Al's passion for the subject, and Glen had to admit that the professor's enthusiasm was contagious. There was the sense that they were part of something momentous, that they were present at the making of history. Crouching down, Ron took a photo of Al to record the moment for posterity.

"I'm going to gather up a few things, then call Smith over at Interior and McCormack at ASU, tell them about these new developments. I suggest that you all finish up what you're doing and knock off work early. I'll meet you in town at Patrick's Bar. Drinks are on me!"

Glen awoke with the dawn and stared out the triangular window of his teepee cabin at a truly majestic sky. Billowing pink-orange clouds of sunrise expanded outward from the eastern horizon, and the sun itself, hidden behind the hills, exuded broad, perfectly defined rays that looked like something out of Creation or a cereal commercial.

He slipped into his jeans and walked outside barefoot and shirtless. The slight tang in the air, a hint of cold, made him think of autumn, though summer had not yet passed its midpoint. He looked around him. Even the dried brown weeds at the end of the parking lot were infused with the dawn's magic, the slanting light granting them a transcendence they should not have had.

The orange in the sky brightened as the sun rose, preparing for a final burst of color before fading into the duller colors of the day.

He used to be stirred by such sights, and he could not

for the life of him remember when that had stopped. As Glen stared up at the clouds, he could appreciate what he was looking at in an intellectual way, but it did not move him. Time was when he had mapped out whole futures based on moments like this, imagining whom he would marry and where they would live and what they would do after seeing a particularly impressive array of wildflowers in a meadow or a rainbow against a backdrop of hills.

But no more.

He stood there for a moment longer, then walked back into his room, shaved and showered.

He thought about Melanie. Was he serious about her, or was this some sort of temporary infatuation, a situational romance, like those people who became instantly close during natural disasters, but discovered they had nothing in common after life returned to normal? He had finally sent that postcard off to Gillian, Quong, and Bill, and the fact that he had chosen to remain in touch with them, that he hadn't completely severed ties with his old life, made him think that this was just a temporary respite, and that he would eventually return to the real world, to jobs and computers and freeway commutes.

Besides, the dig only lasted until the end of August. What was he going to do after that? Al and his students would return to ASU. Melanie would go back to work at Bower Junior High. What was he supposed to do? Get a job at Jack in the Box?

At the pueblo, the mood was upbeat. Everyone was exhilarated by the possibility that their work here was not merely interesting but important, and Al had to caution them to focus on the small stuff, on the here and now. Archeology was in the details, and oftentimes the less showy work yielded the most significant results.

For Glen, the excitement of yesterday had worn off a little. Yes, he was glad to be present at such a significant place and time, but he felt slightly detached from it all. Maybe if he'd been here from the beginning, he'd feel more a part of it, but as it was, he was happier for his coworkers than he was for himself.

After work, Melanie dropped him off at the motor

court. She had to attend a summer session school board meeting in order to find out her schedule for the next school year, so he was on his own tonight. Judi, Randy, and Buck were going out for Mexican food and invited him to join them, but he begged off and instead walked down the highway to the grocery store, where he bought cheese and bread and luncheon meat for sandwiches.

He stepped up to the checkout counter.

"How do you expect to pay for this?"

Glen frowned. Was it his imagination or was the clerk at the register being deliberately rude? The man was frowning at him as though he were a habitual shoplifter. Glen was reminded of an incident the day before yesterday, when a teller at the bank had given him a dirty look as he'd cashed his paycheck, acting like he was trying to rob the place. Was it because he was an outsider? Or because he was digging at the pueblo? He'd told Melanie about it, and she said that she, too, had noticed a change in people's behavior, that ever since individuals had started discovering Indian artifacts in their yards, they'd seemed suspicious of the university team.

There's something weird about that pueblo.

Melanie's words had never been very far from his mind, and while nothing unusual had been unearthed during his time at the site, save that shard with Melanie's picture on his first day, the possibility had always been there. Maybe that was why he hadn't been as gung-ho as everyone else about all these new discoveries popping up around town. He had turned down Al when the professor had invited him to see the burial chamber, and he realized that the reason he had done so was because he was afraid.

There *was* something weird about that pueblo.

Glen handed the disapproving clerk a twenty, took his change, and left the store. Was the old woman walking through the doorway glaring at him? Was the young man pushing his infant son in a shopping cart eyeing him suspiciously? Maybe he was just being paranoid, but he felt as though he was the center of attention, the recipient of hostile glances from everyone he met, and as he walked back down the highway, he looked down at the gravel shoulder before him, not wanting to see the faces of people in the passing vehicles.

The police arrived at the motor court shortly before midnight. Glen was awakened by shouting and doors slamming and the flashing of red and blue lights that easily penetrated the sheer fabric of his drapes. He watched for a while out the window, but there were too many people, too many lights, too many shadows. His sleep-addled mind could not seem to make sense of the chaos, and he finally lay back down in the bed, covers over his head, facing away from the window.

In the morning, he discovered that Ron had been arrested for taking obscene photos of underage girls and posting them on his web page. A high school girl from Bower had filed a complaint with the police.

After being drugged and tricked into taking toilet shots, *she* said.

After he wouldn't give in to her demands and pay more money than they'd originally agreed upon, *he* said.

The word was that he'd made all of his "models" sign release forms and that the folder containing those release forms was one of the things the police had confiscated. Al had been to the police station and was pretty sure that Ron would be released quickly, but he was still worried about the university's liability in this, as well as the public relations damage. Like Glen, he had noticed that the residents of Bower were not exactly enamored of them or their project, and the professor was concerned that this incident would hinder the prospects of getting the site the protection it deserved.

"I always thought there was something weird about that guy," Judi admitted.

Randy grinned. "Want to check out his website?"

She punched his shoulder.

"You're not on there, are you?"

She punched him again, harder.

Al was gone for most of the afternoon, and the rest of them worked alone and unsupervised. They were subdued. Even Randy and Judi's comfortable banter took on a forced, brittle quality before subsiding into silence. Glen was glad that he and Melanie were working apart today. He didn't feel much like talking to anyone. The professor returned sometime after three, making a short general statement to them all that echoed his cautious optimism of the morning, then settling down at his customary chair and table under the central canopy.

Glen returned to his work. He was digging and scraping the hardpacked ground in the northwest quadrant, having already unearthed a cache of small shells and a scrap of a yucca fiber pouch. Then he came across an object much larger than any of the other artifacts he'd found today, an incongruous expanse of rounded bone. He picked at the hardened soil, chiseling out the shape.

Frowning, he brushed dust off the object. It was a skull, he could see now, but he couldn't quite place it. It wasn't wolf or bear, wasn't horse or deer or mountain lion. In fact, it looked . . . vaguely human.

But not quite.

He was no expert. What little he knew about nature came almost entirely from the Discovery Channel. Once he'd completely freed the skull from the surrounding dirt, he called Al over to look at his find. As he waited for the professor to make his way to this section of the pueblo, he recalled what Melanie had said about the other things that they'd found here, the unexplainable things, and a chill passed through him as he looked at the yellowed skull.

"Where is it?" Al asked, stepping over the low adobe wall.

Glen motioned toward the ground at his feet.

He knew instantly from the change of expression on the professor's face, the quick shift from professional obligation to unqualified excitement, that this was big, this was significant.

"What is it?" he asked.

Al shook his head, knelt down, and examined the object, his fingers running over the smooth curved bone, touching the small slanted eye sockets, the snoutlike nasal cavity, the sharp and overlarge teeth. Whatever it was, the thing had had a big head, and Glen thought of a phrase he'd heard somewhere or read: *There were giants in those days.* What was that from? The Bible?

Al stood, took off his hat, and gazed down in wonder. "What a day," he said. "First Ron, now this. I guess everything does even out."

"Is it . . . human?" Glen asked.

"That's the question, isn't it?"

"You mean, you don't know?"

"I can guess, I can speculate, but do I know for sure? No. I can tell you this much: I've never seen anything like it, never even heard of anything like it, and if I'm right, if it is what I think it is," he said, a note of triumph in his voice, "it confirms a theory that I've long held to be true, but that has pretty much been the laughingstock of academia for the past decade. I'll be honest with you. This"—he pointed at the skull—"is why I'm here. It's what I've been hoping to find every summer since I started these excavations. Not this specifically, not this skull, but some indication that we are on the right track, proof that our theories were not just idle speculation." He looked around. "Damn, I wish Ron was here to take a picture. Do you know where his cameras are? Are they back in his room?"

Glen shrugged. "I guess so. I don't know."

"I need to tell the others about this. We need to talk about it." Al held up a hand. "Listen up!" he announced, speaking loud enough for everyone to hear. "I want you all to come here! I have something to show you!"

Melanie and the students put down their tools and instruments, stopped what they were doing and made their way through the maze of pueblo half-walls to the room in which Glen had been working.

"What the hell's that?" Buck asked, pointing at the skull.

A smile spread across Al's face. "*That* is what I want to talk with you about."

"Is it from a caveman?"

Al's smile, if possible, grew even wider. "I'd be willing to bet that its age is concurrent with that of the Anasazi bones in that burial chamber—although there's no way we can prove it right now." He crouched down and carefully picked up the skull, turning it over in his hands. It was nearly twice the size of the professor's head. "Glen is the one who discovered this. It's a skull, obviously, but it's not from any animal I've ever seen, and despite some surface similarities, I don't believe that it is human."

Glen shifted uneasily on his feet.

"Then what is it?" Melanie asked. He thought he heard in her voice what he was feeling.

"The Anasazi ruled this realm for nearly a thousand years. In the latter half of the thirteenth century, a severe drought lasting several decades hit the Southwest. Virtually no rain fell, rivers ran dry, and the Anasazi disappeared, their major settlements left deserted.

"They devolved into cannibalism at the height of the drought. At least, that's the most recent theory. Anasazi coprolites with proteins that would only be present if the defecator had ingested human flesh were found several years ago at Ute Mountain in Colorado, confirming what had been merely a widely disputed hypothesis." He paused dramatically. "But maybe it wasn't the drought. Maybe something *else* made them turn to cannibalism.

"I know this sounds unbelievable, but bear with me. There is a pattern of civilization abandonment, for want of a better term, throughout the Americas. The Mayans, in fact, disappeared at almost the same time, in nearly the same way, as did the Anasazi. The assumption has always been that wars and environmental factors fragmented these civilizations, that the people scattered and the smaller tribes which came afterward were all descended from these great cultures. But the thing is, none of these tribes exhibited the same mastery of art, science, and mathematics as did their supposed forebears. There were similarities, sure, but more the copycat attempts of a less talented people than the legitimate inheritance of true descendants."

"So where did they go?" Melanie asked.

"It is my contention that, in the case of the Anasazi, an outside force is at the root of this disintegration, behind the cannibalism and the abandonment of cities. This could mean some sort of invisible force like radiation." He paused. "Or it could be a specific being, a monster if you will, that somehow influenced or corrupted or even coerced the Anasazi into modes of behavior that were not native to them and that eventually destroyed their civilization."

Glen looked down skeptically at the skull. "And that's what you think this is?"

"I don't know. Physical anthropology is not my area of expertise. But Pace Henry, a friend of mine from NMU who's over at Chaco Canyon, *is* an expert in that field. We've been working together on this theory for the past ten years without any evidence to support us, relying solely on reading between the lines of existing facts. This is the first concrete confirmation that the accepted conventional interpretation of events does not tell the whole story, that perhaps our ideas have some validity.

"That's what Pace has been hoping to unearth at Chaco Canyon. Again, you students already know this, and Melanie probably does, too, but for the benefit of Glen, Chaco Canyon is one of the great unsolved mysteries of the Southwest. A Southwest Stonehenge, if you will. It was supposedly a place of great power, and there were massive edifices constructed at various points of the compass, aligned with celestial phenomena. Like other Anasazi settlements, it was abandoned abruptly, but unlike other cities, the doorways to the buildings were sealed up before the people left. No one knows why, but Pace and I believe that they discovered something at that location that caused them to rethink their entire worldview, that . . . well, scared the hell out of them.

"So they left. But before they did, they took the time to meticulously close up every entrance to every building, using rocks and mortar to block all doors, all windows, every way in or out of their structures.

"Why? To protect whatever was inside from some sort of outside invader? To lock something in that they didn't want to get out? I suggest to you that it was the latter, although if they did manage to capture this creature, it escaped, as no trace of any such thing was found at the site. In fact, no trace of any such thing has ever been found anywhere." He paused. "Until now."

Judi squinted at the skull, moved around to examine it. "This creature certainly wasn't trapped or sealed in any sort of prison or tomb."

"No," Al admitted.

"So you think that in the middle of its wholesale slaughtering of pueblo dwellers it just . . . had a heart attack and died?"

"I don't know. I don't even know if this is it, if it's one of a series of such creatures, or if this is something entirely unconnected." He chuckled. "And for the record, I don't think it slaughtered the Anasazi. I think it made them disappear."

Looks and glances were exchanged, but no one said a thing.

"I'm aware of how all this sounds," the professor assured them. "Don't think I'm not. I expect my credibility in your eyes is hovering somewhere around the Grover Krantz level. But, as I've said, ours is only a theory, and if the facts take us elsewhere, we are prepared to follow their lead. But at the moment, our interpretation appears to be as valid as any other, and it also explains some of the discrepancies that plague the conventional wisdom."

There was silence for a moment. No one spoke.

Randy cleared his throat. "There's no skeleton," he said. "The head was obviously separated from the body."

Al smiled. "Yes."

"That suggests some sort of ritualistic killing," Randy mused. "It indicates that our pueblo dwellers ascribed importance to this death. They either wanted to ensure that this guy remained dead and could not be resurrected, or else he was used as part of some standardized rite or ceremony."

"Exactly."

"Perhaps it was a figure of worship," Judi said, warming to the subject. Glen heard the intrigued tone of her voice. "A dark diety. In that case, this beheading might have served to ward off evil repercussions."

"You think this was a god?" Buck asked.

"Maybe *they* thought it was a god. Maybe it was some sort of . . . freak, and they ascribed magic powers to it." She shrugged. "Or maybe Al's right. Maybe it *was* responsible for the disappearance of the Anasazi."

Buck looked unconvinced.

"I'm going to call Pace right now," Al said, "and see if he can come out. I doubt it, and if that's the case, what I want to do is send you, Melanie and Glen, over to Chaco Canyon tomorrow with the skull. I'd go myself, but I have Ron's incarceration to deal with. I'm expecting word from the university about our liability and responsibilities at any time—and . . . well, to be honest, I want to do some excavating of my own and see if I can find . . . who knows?" He grinned happily. "I have no idea what to expect, and I can tell you I'm pretty damn excited."

"Couldn't you just take some pictures, scan them, and e-mail them to your buddy?" Buck asked.

Al shook his head firmly. "Pace needs to see the real thing. He'll probably want to do some tests as well. Besides, he'll have a place to put it and much better security. I couldn't leave it out here with the rest of our artifacts, and the idea of keeping it in my motel room . . ." He trailed off. "No. It'll be much safer with Pace. This piece is far too valuable to be treated so casually. We can't afford to lose it."

The professor looked at his watch. "It's getting late. I want to get some photos of the site as is before we proceed any further. So I need a backup cameraman. Any of you know where Ron keeps his equipment? Anyone know how to use it?"

They broke up soon after. Al assigned them new duties, and everyone remained at the excavation until the summer sun was nearly down.

Glen dreamed that night of the skull. In his dream, it was screaming at him from the inside of a glass museum case and its voice was that of his mother.

2

They set off shortly after dawn, with the sun still low behind the eastern hills and the sky to the west not entirely divested of night color. Melanie brought coffee and donuts, and after an initial round of obligatory conversation, the two of them settled into a sleepy early morning silence. The only sounds in the car as they headed north toward the interstate were the chewing of maple bars, the slurping of hot java, and the quiet drone of Bower's rapidly fading radio station.

The skull was packed tightly in a sealed box and locked in the trunk, but Glen still felt ill at ease. He didn't want the thing in his car at all. It seemed even creepier now, on the second day, the unnaturalness of its size and animalistic-yet-human shape serving to remind him of Al's speculations as to its origins. Plus, that voice from the dream was still echoing in his head.

The radio station finally disappeared completely as they approached the junction of I-40, and Glen motioned toward the box of cassettes on the floor near Melanie's feet. "You can check through there, see if there's anything you want to listen to."

She sorted through the box and picked out a Pat Metheny compilation, which he took as a good sign. It was one of his favorites.

He stared out the window at the flat, nearly featureless landscape, then looked over at her. "Why did Al pick us?" he asked. "And why did he want both of us to go? Shouldn't one of us have stayed? I mean, with Ron gone, he's really shorthanded. One of us could have taken that thing. It's not like it weighs a ton."

She wrinkled her nose mischievously. "Maybe he's playing matchmaker." Glen looked over at her again, and she shrugged. "Actually," she admitted, "Al told me why he sent us. Because we're not students. We're not affiliated with the university, so we're less likely to try to capitalize on this or use it as a stepping-stone for our own careers. Besides, he's pretty confident that the site will be here next summer. This is a significant find, and with practically everyone in town digging up artifacts, he's fairly sure that protected status is a given."

"Even with the Ron situation?"

"They can't hold that against Al. Besides, that's just a sideshow. And it's not something Al knew about or had any control over."

"But why both of us? Why not just you? Or me?"

"I don't know," she said. "Because it's a long drive?"

They reached the New Mexico border by midmorning, gassed up at Gallup, then continued on. Chaco

Canyon was a national historical park, but it was not easily accessible and not located near any town or city. According to both Al's written directions and Glen's AAA map, the quickest and most direct route was fifty miles down a state highway and then another forty miles or so over a dirt road that led to the Indian ruins. But the state road was closed, not merely blocked off with cones, but obstructed by a berm of gravel, and when Glen looked at his map, he saw that the only other way to reach their destination would be to continue on to Albuquerque, then head north through mountains and a series of small towns until they reached another thirty-mile dirt road that would bring them in from the east. It was a long and roundabout route, adding several extra hours to their trip. But there was no way to avoid it.

"We'd better get moving," he said. "We have a lot of miles to cover."

They ate lunch in Albuquerque, stopping off for burgers and a bathroom break at a roadside McDonald's before once again heading out. The gas tank was still half full so he did not fill up, a stupid decision he regretted when they found themselves passing through towns that could more correctly be called hamlets—small communities that did not appear to have electricity, let alone modern gas stations.

New Mexico seemed poorer than Arizona, and another world entirely from California. The towns they drove through could just as easily have been in *old* Mexico. There were no fast-food joints, no supermarkets, no shops, or banks, only old adobe buildings of indeterminate function and small wooden homes adjacent to open fields. He saw outhouses in back of the homes, saw dark-skinned men actually riding horses along the side of the road.

One of the villages—a nameless community situated among the green trees of a narrow, river-carved valley—did have an independent service station, a hand-painted sign on top of the faded shake roof announcing simply: GAS.

Glen pulled into the station, running over a length of black cable that caused a loud bell to ding somewhere inside the rundown building. They both got out of the car and stretched. The lone gas dispenser was the old-fashioned kind. There was no place to swipe a card, no automatic bill taker, only a locked pump with a skinny nozzle. When it became obvious that no one was going to come out and meet them, Glen walked into the open office. "Hello?" he called. "Anyone here?"

No one was behind the counter or the cluttered metal desk, and he poked his head into the dark garage. "Hello?"

The place appeared to be abandoned. He walked out of the office and around the side of the building. No one stood near the air and water hoses. There were only metal racks filled with bald tires out back. He returned to the car, puzzled. "I can't find anyone."

"Maybe the attendant went out to get some lunch or something," Melanie suggested. "This is a small town. People don't lock their doors." She looked around. "Why don't we try over there?" She pointed to an adobe house that had been turned into a Mexican restaurant.

"Okay."

She grabbed her purse out of the car, and they trekked across the sun-baked asphalt, not only feeling the heat but seeing it in the thick wavy air that emanated from the road. Above, the sky was a deep perfect blue, although an army of puffy white clouds was advancing from the north.

The utter silence seemed odd. He heard cicadas and the scuttling of lizards in the dry grass, but no human voices disturbed the still air, no music or machinery marred the quiet. The town seemed empty, abandoned, and Glen suddenly had a bad feeling about this place.

The door to the restaurant was open, although the interior of the building was dark. Two white plastic tables on the porch were unoccupied, new place settings atop one, dirty plates and glasses on the other. Glen and Melanie exchanged a look but said nothing. They walked up the porch steps and into the restaurant. Here again, they saw a mixture of used and unused tables, and here again there was no sign of life. Glen stepped behind the cash register, peered into the kitchen. "No one," he reported.

"What do you think's going on?" Melanie asked.

"I don't know," Glen said, but he was thinking about the skull.

"Don't you think it's kind of weird? I mean, here we are on this mission, and we run into a situation that seems to parallel our pueblo dwellers? What are the chances of that?"

He wanted to simply go back to the gas station, get in the car and drive on. Of course, he'd noticed the parallel, but he'd hoped that she hadn't. Now he was afraid that she would want to stay and explore, look for other people, try to find out what happened.

Sure enough, he felt her hand on his arm. "I know we should get out of here," she said. "I'm sure you want to get as far away from this place as possible. Which is probably a very sensible idea. But don't you think we ought to at least look around a bit and make sure there's no one . . . hurt?"

"What I think we should do," Glen said, trying to sound logical, "is call the state police from the next town up and let them figure it out. Who knows? Maybe this really is a little ghost town with only one or two guys living here. We're assuming that everyone disappeared, but that might not be the case. Maybe the gas station has been abandoned for years and that's why no one's there—"

"This restaurant was obviously not abandoned years ago. Those dirty dishes look pretty new."

She was right.

"Why don't we give ourselves ten minutes?" she suggested. "If we haven't found anyone by that time, we'll leave."

"All right. Ten minutes. Starting now."

They walked out of the restaurant and down the porch steps. "Which way?" he asked.

Melanie looked around, then pointed up the alley-sized dirt road to the left of the restaurant. Twin rows of shacklike houses headed away from the highway. "There," she said.

"We can't just walk into people's homes."

"No, but we can knock on doors."

Knock they did, on several of the more likely looking candidates—houses with cars or trucks parked in front of them—but no one answered, and they heard no noise from inside any of them. They walked past a small orchard of cherry trees. At the end of the road was a small adobe church. There seemed to be a lot of such churches in New Mexico, Glen thought. It was obvious even to him that they predated nearly every building he'd ever laid eyes on. Melanie explained that many of them had been built before the United States was even a country, some of them before the Pilgrims had landed at Plymouth Rock.

"History is written by the victors," she said as they walked up the dusty street. "That's why we're always told American history through a British-centric lens. It always starts in the East and moves west. But the truth is that America was settled here first. There was a governor's mansion and a sitting Spanish governor in the civilized city of Santa Fe when the Pilgrims sat down to their primitive first Thanksgiving. But that doesn't fit into the myth. We're supposed to think the brave colonists tamed a savage land occupied only by a handful of nomadic natives and that after they fought for their independence and set up a stable democracy, they moved inland and settled the Wild West. We're not supposed to realize that there was already a cultured European civilization here."

Glen laughed. "Sounds like your classes are probably pretty interesting."

"I get complaints from parents," she admitted.

Theirs were the only voices on this silent street, and the sound of their footfalls echoed off the flat fronts of empty houses.

As they drew closer, Glen realized that the church was of very primitive construction with a narrow windowless design. This was a Christian house of worship, but there seemed something pagan about it, as though the needs and requirements of an older religion had been incorporated. He recalled reading somewhere that Christmas and Easter were appropriated holidays, that no one really knew when Christ was born or died and the way the early church had recruited believers was to piggyback their sacred days on earlier, earthier celebrations. There was something of that here, and it seemed an uneasy mix. Glen felt a faint chill as he walked toward the building, and he had the sudden desire to turn around and leave. He did not want to see what was inside.

They walked up the short wooden steps.

Opened the heavy double doors.

The interior of the church was dark, but sometime in the last century electric lights had been added, and Glen found a panel of switches in the vestibule. He flipped them on. The chapel was suddenly illuminated by two wrought-iron chandeliers that hung on thick chains from the arched ceiling, with frosted bulbs made to resemble candle flames. The nave was empty, as was the chancel at the head of the church, and Glen looked up the aisle between the pews toward the altar. The front of the chapel seemed strange and it took him a moment to realize why. The steps. They were flat and wide, made from rock rather than adobe or cement, and they seemed far older than the surrounding floor. Large inter-laced stones of various hues formed vaguely geometric patterns on the way up to the altar. They looked just like a series of steps they'd uncovered at the pueblo, steps leading into what Al said had been a ceremonial chamber. Spanish builders must have constructed their house of worship on the remains of a much older site.

Glen and Melanie walked forward, cowed into silence by the sacred atmosphere of this place. They passed the heavy pews and a wrought-iron stand of unlit votive candles.

The church was small and narrow, and the transept consisted of two shallow alcoves. Tall dark wood panels of considerable age formed triptychs on the indented walls, their painted pictures faded by time but still clearly visible. The scenes depicted were not of Jesus and the crucifixion, or Adam and Eve in the Garden, or any other traditional subjects. Instead, they were strange, almost surrealistic paintings featuring at least one figure who was very familiar.

"My God," he breathed. "That's me."

He turned toward Melanie, but she seemed to be in shock, the expression on her face mirroring the way he felt.

Glen stared at the left transept wall. The panels

seemed to tell a story, and while he wasn't that familiar with the Bible, he had the feeling that the tale told here was not a parable from the Good Book. In the first scene, he was standing beneath a canopy, surrounded by low, tan half-walls. A bright sun shone in the sky. At his feet was a pile of bones. The panel depicted the excavation at Bower, and Glen stared at it, his head reeling. It had been a leap for him to acknowledge that there was something odd about the pueblo and its artifacts, but this was a quantum leap beyond that. He had quit his job, tooled east with no destination in mind, and through a series of flukes had ended up working at an archeological dig. Yet a couple of hundred years ago, some artist or monk or priest way out here in the wilds of New Mexico had painted a picture of him at that site. He must have had some sort of *vision* about it.

It all involved such a complicated and convoluted series of coincidences that it boggled the mind. Had all of this been somehow preordained? Was he *supposed* to be here at this time? Was he *meant* to find these paintings? Glen didn't know, but he felt manipulated, a pawn in the grip of some omniscient force able to bend reality to its will and orchestrate seemingly random events into a grand design.

He was a hairsbreadth away from hopelessness, ready to concede his utter lack of free will, when he suddenly realized that he was looking at this all wrong. There were always multiple explanations for everything, endless possibilities even for seemingly connected events and facts and conclusions that appeared to be set in stone. Sure, his being here to see these paintings could be the culmination of some elaborate plan, but it could also be entirely accidental. Or there could be some explanation that he was just too stupid or myopic to see. Hell, maybe the figure wasn't even him. Maybe it was some historical character that just happened to resemble him.

No. He knew that wasn't true.

His eyes moved on to the second painting in the triptych. In this one, he was again at the ruins of the pueblo, only he was facing a bright white light, a radiating circle that almost looked like a star. Into this light, twin rows of men and women in both ancient and modern dress were walking.

In the final panel, he was not depicted at all. Instead, the clothes he'd been wearing, some sort of brown suit, lay atop a monstrous pile of bones ten times the size of the one in the initial painting. The white light was to the left of the bones, and against its backdrop a strange-looking figure was silhouetted: a thick, powerfully built man with a mane of wild orange hair.

Glen walked immediately across the church, past the front pews, to the right side of the transept. Here, the paintings were, if anything, even more bizarre. In the first one, Glen was back, this time with a young boy. Both of them were walking, passing a group of kneeling Indians and a pack of twisted, deformed dogs. In the sky above, the wild-maned man stood on the sun.

The second panel showed dead trees and fallow fields next to a deserted city with square, nearly identical buildings. The only figure in the scene was the man on the sun, still in silhouette.

In the final picture, the orange-haired man was in a cave or a darkened room, facing Glen and the boy, who both held what appeared to be lengths of rope with jagged bolts of lightning shooting out the ends. The wild man was screaming, either in terror or pain. On the wall behind him was a stone wheel covered with carved symbols.

"What does this mean?" Melanie asked. Her voice was hushed, reverent.

"I keep a disposable camera in the car," Glen said. "In case I get in an accident. I'm going to go get it and try to take pictures of this. We can show it to Al or his friend. Maybe they can figure out something from it." He started back toward the entrance.

"Wait!" Melanie said. "I'm not staying here alone!"

He grabbed her hand, and they stepped out into the sunlight, blinking at the brightness as they walked down the steps, waiting for their eyes to adjust.

"You want to come with me?" Glen asked. "Or—?"

Melanie took a few more steps away from the church. "I'll wait here. Hurry."

He ran down the dirt road toward the highway. The

hot sun made him sweat, but it didn't penetrate the bone-deep cold that had taken root within him while inside the chapel. He reached the car, grabbed his camera from the glove compartment, and hurried back up the street.

He was breathing heavily. "I need to exercise more," he said, wiping his forehead.

She smiled perfunctorily.

"Just let me catch my breath."

"I'll take the pictures," she offered.

"You wait here," he told her, pulling himself together. He started toward the church.

"I'll come with you."

"No. I'll be back out in a minute." He walked up the steps and inside. The lighting was dim and he didn't have a flash, so he took two close-up photos of each panel and three of each triptych. The camera only had twelve shots. He wished it had twenty-four—he would have taken the whole roll—but it probably wouldn't make much difference. Either there was enough light in here or there wasn't.

When he emerged from the church, Melanie seemed troubled.

He frowned. "What is it?"

She looked at him strangely. "I . . . I've been keeping this from you," she said. "I don't know why. It . . ." She reached into her purse, pulled out a shard of pottery. "My father found this in his yard. Back in Bower."

He took the object from her, examined it. On the clay surface was a crude drawing of a house, a contemporary house. "Is this—" he began.

"Like the picture of me, it's authentic. At least I'm pretty sure it is. It's Anasazi pottery, and that's Anasazi artwork." She licked her lips. "The thing is," she said, "it changes. The picture. Sometimes there's a . . . a face peeking out of that window. Sometimes the face is smiling. And sometimes it's not. I don't know which is worse."

"I don't see a face now."

"No. It's asleep maybe, or . . . I don't know. That's my parents' house there, the one I grew up in. I've kind of been thinking of this thing like a crystal ball. Not one that tells the future, but one like in *The Wizard of Oz,* where the witch lets Dorothy see what's happening back on the farm. That's why I think of that little face being either awake or asleep."

"You think this thing's living in your parents' house?"

"No, it's not that. It's . . . oh, I don't know."

"What's it look like?"

Melanie took a deep breath. "It's weird looking, and it kind of reminds me of a clown in a way. But it also reminds me of that silhouette in those panels back there." She nodded toward the church. "That thing with the hair."

The cold within Glen erupted on his skin in goose bumps.

"Leave it," he said. "Here."

"What?"

There's no reason to keep it, is there? Dump it, get rid of it. That thing creeps me out. The skull in the trunk's bad enough, but that's just . . ." He shook his head. "Let's just toss it, get the hell out of here and move on."

"I don't know. It's part of the pueblo. We might need it to piece together a more accurate history. It wouldn't be right to just abandon it here."

"You didn't show it to Al, did you?"

"No," she admitted.

"And you probably weren't going to. Look, it won't be missed. There's plenty of pottery there. And bones. And more ruins. It's not needed." He looked into her eyes. "I don't want that thing traveling with us. I don't like it."

"I don't like it, either."

"But?"

"But . . . I don't know. Maybe I'm afraid to let it go, afraid something might happen."

Glen was silent. That was a possibility. He didn't know anything about this stuff. They were equally in the dark here. He handed her back the piece of pottery.

Melanie's hand closed around the shard. Then she suddenly cocked back her arm and threw it. The object landed in a clump of dried weeds to the right of the church steps.

"Fuck it," she said. "Let's make a clean break."

Glen didn't know why, but it made him feel better. They might not know what was going on, might be caught up in something far bigger than themselves, but they were still free to make their own decisions. That had to count for something.

"Let's go," he said.

They started toward the car.

"So should we tell someone about this place?" Melanie asked. "*Should* we call the state police?"

"I don't know," he admitted.

"It doesn't look like any crime's been committed, but . . ." She gestured around. "This town's abandoned. Everyone's disappeared."

He felt as though he were in one of those 1970s TV movies, where the intrepid hero and his girl find themselves in an empty city only to discover that the population of the entire world has suddenly disappeared. It was stupid, he knew, but he experienced a mild case of panic, a sudden need to drive to another town, make sure there *were* people left in the world. What if, he thought, the next town was abandoned? And the next? And the next? What if they drove back to Albuquerque and the entire city was deserted, riderless cars left on the freeway, unattended burgers sizzling on the grills of fast-food joints, hoses still running on empty lawns?

A plane buzzed high overhead.

Glen felt an irrational sense of relief—and a need to get away from this village as fast as humanly possible. They increased their pace and reached the highway just as a pickup truck rattled past. The driver honked and waved.

They walked past the Mexican restaurant and across the highway to the gas station. Out here, back on an artery connecting them with civilization, the dread engendered by the church paintings and Melanie's changing piece of pottery seemed less pervasive, less immediate. The gloom and sense of hopelessness that had stolen over him at the end of that dirt road now seemed once removed, and he was filled with an almost irrational exuberance, a feeling that he could do anything, that there was no way any unseen force or power could impose its will on him.

"We're not going to get to Chaco Canyon by dark," Melanie said as they reached the car, "and if your map's right, there aren't any towns or any place for us to stay on the way. I sure as hell don't want to spend the night in the car parked outside some closed visitor's center. Why don't we head back to Albuquerque for the night, give Al a call and head over in the morning?"

"He's not going to be happy. You know how anxious he was to get the ball rolling on this."

"We have no choice."

"All right," Glen said. "But forget Albuquerque. How about Santa Fe? I want to see your famous governor's mansion."

Melanie grinned. "Santa Fe sounds great!" She stood on her tiptoes and gave him a quick kiss.

"Then Santa Fe it is."

The sun was going down by the time Glen pulled into the hotel parking lot. They'd called from the road and made reservations, picking a place randomly out of the AAA book. It turned out to be a pretty good choice, a two-story inn with faux Indian architecture, only three streets down from the historic plaza. He sat there for a moment, then looked over at Melanie, clearing his throat. "Uh, where are we—?"

"Same room, same bed," she said.

He smiled. "I was hoping you'd say that."

It was the best night of his entire life. They bought Subway sandwiches and ate them in their room, lay next to each other on the bed watching reruns of *Seinfield,* and took a long slow bath together before making love. Despite everything that had happened, the evening was perfect. It was as though they were suspended in a bubble protecting them from the real world, and he found that he could forget about the day, pretend that they hadn't come across a deserted town where a three hundred-year-old church had murals of himself, and where they'd left Melanie's haunted pottery shard.

She'd brought a book with her, a Phillip Emmons

novel, and while she read he thumbed through the complimentary copy of *Santa Fe Style* that had been left on their nightstand. They were cozy, comfortable, and he was filled with an uncharacteristic sense of well-being. This was what he'd been searching for when he set off from Automated Interface that day.

He put down his magazine and watched her for a while, admiring the still way she sat, the graceful way she turned a page, her smooth pretty face that managed to look both kind and intelligent, even in repose.

"You look kind of like a baby-sitter I had," Glen told her.

Melanie laughed, glancing over at him. "What?"

"I had a crush on her. I was about ten or eleven, maybe. Usually, this old lady from across the street, Mrs. Garson, was my baby-sitter when my parents went out. But sometimes she was busy baby-sitting other kids, and my parents had to find someone else. High school girls mostly, although I don't know where they found them—a service maybe, or word of mouth from one of my friends' moms. Anyway, there was this one girl, very pretty, very nice, and I remember she let me stay up past my bedtime and taught me how to make chocolate milkshakes. She had long blond hair parted in the middle and John Lennon glasses and she wore one of those hippie peasant skirts—you know, down to her ankles and pink with little flowers on it.

"She only watched me once, but I never forgot her. She was the best baby-sitter I ever had." He smiled. "And she looked a little like you."

Melanie sat up and kissed him. "Glen Ridgeway, I think I have a crush on *you*." She switched off the lamp on the nightstand, and seconds later she was on top of him.

Six

1

"Dude!"

Standing next to Jay and Stu, Cameron stared at the cat. It sat in Stu's backyard, in the middle of the lawn, looking up at them, and on its face was the freakiest expression he had ever seen. It sent cold shivers through his body, made his balls tighten.

"You weren't lying," Jay said, awe in his voice.

"No," Stu said, but there was no satisfaction in the acknowledgment.

Cameron didn't know what was going on. All he knew was that Stu's pet was making him feel the same way he had at the scout camp—

The Mogollon Monster

—and at this moment he wanted to be anywhere but here. He thought of the figure he'd seen in the rain, and he had no doubt that this was connected. The truth was that nothing had seemed right since that afternoon. Everything since had had a malevolent tinge, like he was seeing the skull beneath the skin, the dark truth beneath the happy world that everyone else experienced. He'd tried explaining it to Dr. Jeifetz, but he could tell that the shrink didn't believe him, was putting it all down to stress from seeing what had happened to Scoutmaster Anderson.

The cat twisted its head around, then snapped it back, simultaneously jumping into the air, legs flailing.

As one, the three boys turned and fled, running

around the side of the house and not stopping until they reached the street.

"Holy shit!" Jay said, stopping to catch his breath. "What was that?"

"I told you!" Stu said. "I told you!"

Cameron looked back toward the house, half expecting to see the freakish cat leaping through the side yard after them, but there was no sign of the animal. His heart was thumping crazily, and if anyone had tapped his shoulder at that moment, he probably would have jumped a mile. He wanted to tell his friends about the figure he'd seen in the rain, but he didn't know how to describe it and had no idea how to explain its relation to the cat. Hell, he didn't even know himself. Not really. All he knew was that all of this weird stuff was somehow tied together.

"So he's been like that since this morning?" Jay asked.

"I don't know. Usually Trix comes in for Friskies at breakfast, but there was no sign of him. I found him in the backyard about ten minutes ago, and I came to get you guys."

"What'd your parents say about it?" Jay asked.

"My old man isn't home. He went to Home Depot, and . . ." He shuffled his feet, looked down. "I didn't tell my mom."

"Why not?"

"I don't know. I just . . . I don't know. Scared to, I guess."

Cameron knew exactly how his friend felt, that unfamiliar jumble of fear and confusion, and it further cemented his belief that everything was connected.

Jay looked over at him. "What do *you* think it is?"

Here was his chance. He could say what he thought, explain what he'd seen. But instead he found himself shaking his head. "I don't know," he mumbled.

"I don't think it's rabid. It's more like it's . . . possessed." Jay looked around for confirmation.

"Yeah," Cameron said, able to get out that much. Stu just looked scared and unhappy.

From down at the end of the block came a strange wail, a hackle-raising cry that sounded like a cross be-

tween a baby's scream and a lion's growl. The gooseflesh
that had been starting to recede on Cameron's arms returned again in full force. An animal was walking down
the sidewalk toward them. Well, not exactly *walking*. It
was more of a limping, lurching skip, a freakishly unsettling movement that made them freeze in their tracks.
Cameron wasn't sure what it was at first. It was unlike
any animal he had ever seen, more like something out
of a nightmare, but as it drew closer, he saw that, like
Stu's cat, it was a twisted version of a normal pet. Only
this one was a dog.

"Oh, my God," Jay said. "That's Bear!"

He was right. Cameron recognized Jay's dog even before his friend finished speaking. For a brief wild second
he thought that maybe all of the pets on earth had un-
dergone this metamorphosis simultaneously, that this
was the beginning of some global role reversal like
Planet of the Apes, where other animals would take over
for humans. But then reason reasserted itself and he
thought that it was probably some disease or something
that had been passed from one animal to another in the
neighborhood.

No, that wasn't true. That's not what he thought.

The Mogollon Monster.

Whatever it was might be very well confined to this
neighborhood, but it was not a disease, and it had nothing to do with germs or bacteria or science. It had to do
with the figure he had seen in the rain and the way that
he had been frozen and the air had been heavy and
reality had *shifted.*

"Fuck," Stu breathed. "It happened to your dog, too."

Bear stopped.

Then lurched-hopped-skipped forward.

Then stopped.

Then yowled and lurched before stopping again.

Behind them, Stu's dad's pickup pulled into the driveway, having driven in from the opposite direction. Cameron felt a welcome rush of relief. An adult! Someone
who could take over and handle the situation.

Stu's dad got out of the cab and slammed the door,
walking back to open the tailgate. "How's it going,
boys?" When none of them responded, he frowned and

came over. "What is it? Anything wrong?" He followed their eyes and pointing fingers, and a funny look crossed his face when he saw Bear. The dog was now one house away and walking in circles, its head cocked at an almost impossible angle. Its teeth were bared, its lips turned up in what could only be called a smile.

"What the . . . ?" Stu's dad took a step toward the animal, then turned back toward them. "That's your dog, isn't it, Jay? That's Bear."

Jay nodded.

"You boys better step back. Why don't you get behind the truck there?" He started forward.

"Dad?" Stu called out.

"What?"

"Shouldn't you have, like, a weapon or something, just in case?"

"Hey!" Jay said, but his protest was halfhearted. This wasn't his dog anymore and he knew it.

"I'm just going to take a look. I'm not going to do anything."

"Mr. Haynes?" Jay cleared his throat. "Maybe you should stay back, too. Or call someone. Like the police or something. Bear's . . . he's not right. There's something wrong with him."

"Just like Trix!" Stu called out. "Trix is the same way! The same thing happened to him!"

Other people were coming out of their houses now: Mr. Green, Mrs. Dilbay, Mr. Finch. They'd obviously seen the dog's bizarre antics through their windows and were coming out to investigate. Cameron hoped that somebody *was* calling the police or someone *did* have a weapon. Stu's dad, even all the dads in the neighborhood, couldn't fight something like this. The brief sense of relief that he'd felt dissipated as he realized that no adult, no matter how strong, no matter how much authority he had, would be able to go up against something that could do this to Bear.

Mr. Haynes approached the dog cautiously. "Hey, buddy," he said softly, keeping up a stream of calm, comforting chatter. "Hey, Bear. How are you, sport? How's a boy?"

Without any warning, the dog leaped in the air the

way Stu's cat had, legs flailing. Only he didn't fall back down. He shot forward, through the space above the sidewalk, flying, hitting Mr. Haynes full in the chest, knocking him over. Before anyone could react, before anyone even knew what was going on, the animal's smiling, twisted mouth was snapping crazily and biting through skin, through flesh, through rib, burrowing into Stu's dad's chest. The three boys started screaming, along with all the other men and women on the street, but Mr. Haynes didn't have a chance to scream. He was dead before his brain even had time to tell his mouth to cry out. Bear grunted and snuffled through the bloody viscera, twitching periodically in a jerky, unnatural manner and letting out that eerie wail.

Gary, the Spenglers' oldest son who was in the army and back home on leave for a few days, heard all the yelling and came running out of their house. When he saw Mr. Haynes on the ground and Bear tearing into him, Gary automatically grabbed two bricks from the low wall bordering his mom's flower garden and came running across the lawn.

He threw the first brick, which hit Bear in the head, tearing off a chunk of flesh. Even in his altered state, the dog knew enough to back off. Then Gary was upon the animal, and he drew back his arm and brought the second brick down with all of his might, again and again. The brick hit Bear at an angle, a corner imploding the dog's eyeball, sinking into fur and tissue, cracking skull. Cameron was relieved to learn that Bear could be killed, thrilled to see the animal crumple on the spot, slumping onto the cement sidewalk in a pool of still-spilling blood.

Maybe there was hope.

Stu ran up the driveway and into his house in tears, screaming for his mom. The adults gathered around the fallen bodies. And as the sirens started up at the fire station down the street, Cameron pulled Jay behind the pickup and tried to describe what he'd seen on that rainy day, starting from the beginning.

2

Arthur Wessington saw it for himself, then quickly grabbed the nearest wall phone and ordered Kuhn to close the museum. Then he placed another call to Clarke. The security guards began smoothly and efficiently herding patrons out of the building, informing them that there was a gas leak and that the museum would be closed for the remainder of the day while the problem was fixed.

Only there was no gas leak.

A fetish in the Anasazi exhibit, a nasty little thing with an enormous phallus and a scowling face made out of bear bone, had somehow come to life.

Arthur watched the hideous figure lurch across the enclosed display case, its oversize organ tipping over another smaller figurine and tapping loudly against the clear Plexiglas. The expression on its face had not changed, could not change, but it looked angrier somehow, as though frustrated by its inability to escape imprisonment.

Sergio, Tress, and Patrick were huddled together, watching, standing close but not too close. Tress was the one who had called him, and at first he'd thought it was a practical joke. But the joke went on too long, and he could tell from her tone of voice that she was deadly serious. When he came downstairs, he had seen that it was true.

He was not as shocked as he would have been a few months back. He'd heard through the grapevine that similar episodes had taken place in museums throughout the Southwest: Tucson, Santa Fe, Denver, Salt Lake City. Artifacts were supposed to have moved on their own.

He hadn't believed any of these stories, but he believed them now. The first thing he was going to do after they got this situation under control was call some of his colleagues at those institutions and get hard reports, find out exactly what had happened and where. The fact that this was not an isolated event, was part of something much larger, made it much more frightening.

He was not even sure whether he *would* be able to get the situation under control.

"This is probably on the security video already," Patrick said, "but maybe we should film this so we have some proof, so it's not just our word." He cleared his throat. "You know, after the fact."

Of course. Arthur mentally kicked himself. "Get the camera from my office," he told Patrick. "Not the one we use for inventory, but my personal one. It's in the bag behind my desk."

The assistant curator hurried off.

Arthur turned his attention back to the fetish. It seemed even angrier now. It wasn't the face—or wasn't *entirely* the face, for the expression carved into the bear bone was indeed fierce—it was more the movement, the harsh, purposeful jerks that propelled the figure across its display case, kept it knocking hard against the sides.

The Plexiglas was shatterproof, so he shouldn't have been worried that the fetish could break out . . . but he was. In his mind, he saw it smashing through the display case, tumbling onto the floor, righting itself, and lurching toward him. It was small, its legs were stationary, and it couldn't move fast—he could easily outdistance it—but he saw himself running away, getting in his car, and frantically driving home while the thing slowly and inexorably came after him, not stopping, no matter what obstacles were in its way, no matter how long it took.

Someone shouted from somewhere toward the back of the museum, and almost simultaneously the phone started to ring. Arthur looked over at Tress and Sergio, and after a split-second of hesitation, he ran out of the permanent exhibits gallery and down the wide corridor toward the source of the panicky shouting, which appeared to be the cataloging room. His heart was pounding like a kettle drum in his chest. Already he could see the security guards clustered around the open door, sense the terror in their postures.

Clarke saw him first, and the guard's face showed visible relief as he waved Arthur over. "Thank God, you're here!"

"What is it?" Arthur asked.

"Here." Two of the security guards moved aside to let him pass, and Clarke and Kuhn walked into the cataloging room with him.

Artifacts were moving across the floor. Hundreds of them. They were off tables, off shelves, out of boxes—masks, tomahawks, axes, arrowheads, pottery, carvings, toys, tools, sandals—and they inched along the smooth shiny floor in a uniform direction, toward the door, as if all were imbued with the same purpose. Kel and Mai, two of the museum's researchers, along with a volunteer grad student Arthur didn't know, were huddled behind the big oak desk on the right side of the room. The tide of creeping artifacts had not yet reached the desk, but once it did, the three young people would be cut off, unable to get to the door.

"What should we do?" Mai asked. She was in shock, her face without expression, her voice robotically matter-of-fact.

"Get out!" Arthur ordered. "Get out now!"

It was as if the three had been frozen, encased in ice, and suddenly the ice had shattered. Mai's blank immobility disappeared. She started screaming, and in seconds she and Kel and the grad student were scrambling around the desk, practically pushing each other over in their desperation to get across the stretch of open floor to where Arthur and the guards stood.

Arthur herded them all through the doorway, out into the central corridor. Everyone kept looking over their shoulders as they passed by him, half expecting a pack of arrowheads to come whizzing through the air. But nothing like that occurred. The tools and toys and relics were moving forward slowly at an unchanged speed. If the workers could all just get out of this room, they'd be safe. None of the objects could open a door; none could even reach the knob. There was no way the artifacts could escape.

Clarke was the last one out, following close on Arthur's heels, and he slammed the door shut behind him. Keys jingled nervously as he locked it.

They stood there for a moment, looking at each other. No one said anything.

But the corridor was not silent.

Underneath their heavy breathing, from the far end of the partially lit hallway came a steady repetitive sound, a *click-tap, click-tap,* and Arthur turned to see the Anasazi fetish lurching implacably toward them. It had broken out of its case, and was angrily making its way down the corridor, its stiff bone feet clicking on the polished cement, oversize organ sticking straight out in front as if to ward off all comers.

Tress and Sergio had followed him, apparently not wanting to be alone with the fetish, and were standing with the security guards, but Patrick was still gone, upstairs in his office getting the camcorder, and Arthur found that worrying. He wanted everyone here, in the corridor, where he could see them. He didn't like the idea of any of his people being alone in far-off parts of the building.

"What the hell's that?" Kel asked.

Arthur was about to answer when a muffled bell dinged and Patrick emerged from the service elevator next to the men's room. The bone figure swung around on unbending legs to face the assistant curator. Though the carved object was small, a trick of the light threw an enormously exaggerated shadow before it, dominating the hallway.

Patrick had started for the gallery, but he saw everyone standing at the end of the corridor, and he stopped in his tracks. He stared at the oncoming fetish. He had plenty of room to pass by on either side of the little figure—*all* of them had plenty of room to pass by—but everyone remained rooted in place.

"Get out!" Arthur shouted at him. "Call the police!"

Patrick was already videotaping.

Good boy, Arthur thought.

"What are you going to do?" Patrick called, still taping.

"There's a whole roomful of them!" Mai yelled, terror in her voice. "They're coming after us!"

"We're going out through the conference room and the custodial office!" Arthur said. "Finish taping and get the hell out of here! Call the police! We'll meet you outside!"

Patrick took a step forward, crouched down, then

stood again, the arm with the camcorder dropping to his side. "Got it!" he called. "See you there!"

Arthur caught Clarke's eye. "Let's get out of here," he said. "Move."

The guard started ushering people toward the side hallway. Murmurs, hard breathing, various sounds of human movement all served to cover up the horrible *click-tap, click-tap* of the bone figure, but Arthur remained constantly aware of its exact location.

Behind them was a loud thump and then another as the first of the artifacts hit the closed door of the cataloging room.

They hurried down the hall, through the conference room and the custodian's office to the exit. Arthur was the last one out, and just before he stepped through the door, he heard an impossibly high-pitched whine, a grating, screeching noise that sounded like a bird being dragged to its death by the braking metal wheel of a train. The terrible sound spoke to him on some level, and he had the horrible feeling that it was the fetish, calling out to him, trying to entice him back. He quickly slammed the door and followed the others outside, away from the building, toward the safety of the street.

Seven

1

They were on the road by seven the next morning, eating breakfast burritos in the car, having purposely chosen a route that would not take them through that empty unnamed town. They had called Al to tell him about the delay, but only got his answering machine. They'd also left a message for Pace Henry.

Melanie glanced over at Glen as he drove. She'd expected their lovemaking to make a difference today. And it had, in the hotel, in the bed, before they'd gotten up, when they were still holding each other. But now, in the car, in daylight, it was as if the sex had never happened.

No, that was not true. It had happened; they both knew it, and it would probably happen again tonight. But he was one of those men who compartmentalized their lives, and she knew that he was not capable of fully integrating their new status into their working relationship. At least not yet. He saw her looking at him, gave her a quick uncomfortable smile, then took a sip of his coffee and focused his attention back on the road.

The car skirted the southern edge of a low mountain range. The road before them stretched across an open sloping plain, landscape shifting from the high desert of the Santa Fe area to a much starker terrain. They'd gone through a lot together yesterday, and the experience had drawn them closer. That was good. She did not know what sort of future this relationship had—if any—but at least she knew that the attraction was not merely physical or the result of circumstances.

She spotted a dead carcass by the side of the road. Not a coyote or a squirrel or a skunk as she'd seen throughout this trip, but a cow. Two vultures suddenly flew up out of its open rotted rib cage, feathers flapping.

Melanie followed the carcass with her eyes, watching it through the window as they passed. As her head turned to the rear, she caught sight of the car's trunk. She quickly faced forward, trying not to think about the skull. She suppressed a shiver. They hadn't talked about the skull on this trip, had talked of everything else, yet she knew that both she and Glen felt the same way about the object.

They drove on for a while in silence. Finally Glen said, "Why was I in those pictures at the church?"

"I don't know," she said.

"Why was your parents' house on that pottery?"

"I don't know."

They were heading into an area of low buttes and sculpted rock. They passed a pair of twin sandstone hoodoos that looked like elephants' feet.

"The camera's still in the glove compartment, right?"

She checked. "Yeah."

"Good. I want to get those pictures developed and show them to someone. I . . ." He shook his head, at a loss for words.

Melanie put her hand on his arm. "I know."

It started to snow an hour later, while they were traveling through a series of low eroded hills with the earth-tone striations of a Georgia O'Keeffe landscape. It was hot outside. They'd been using the air conditioner since they got into the car this morning, and the small flat clouds stretching endlessly across the sky were white without a hint of gray.

Yet snow was falling, light swirling flurries at first, then an ashy-looking curtain of white that cut down visibility to a matter of feet. Glen slowed down. "Where the hell did this come from?" He turned on the head-lights, but if anything they made visibility even more difficult, highlighting the falling snowflakes to the exclusion of all else.

They crept forward slowly, the speedometer oscillating

between fifteen miles per hour and an even slower speed that the needle registered as zero. The snow was starting to stay on the ground, rocks and sand and an occasionally visible thistle disappearing under a blanket of white. Luckily, the road remained clear, the asphalt retaining enough warmth to melt whatever fell upon it.

And then suddenly the snow was gone. They were back in the blazing sun of the desert, white clouds in the blue sky above, and the car was being buffeted by winds so strong that Glen's hands tightened on the wheel at ten and two. His knuckles whitened as the vehicle was pushed from the shoulder to the centerline and back again. "Jesus!" he said.

His voice showed his annoyance, but something else as well: surprise with an edge of fearfulness. Melanie knew because she felt it, too.

Theirs was the only car on the highway, and the wind harassed them all the way to the turnoff for the dirt road that led to Chaco Canyon.

Where it died completely.

As they crossed from pavement to dirt, the powerful gusts disappeared, not lessening, not slowly abating, but stopping instantly, as though the off switch to a monstrous fan had been thrown. They had only thirty miles to go, and when the car started bumping along the washboard road, free from the rocking pressure of the outside winds, they thought their weather problems were over.

But then it started to rain. Again, they could see no rain clouds in the sky, only the benign blue and billowing whiteness that had been with them since Santa Fe. Yet in a matter of seconds, they were caught in a torrential downpour that made it difficult to see and threatened to turn the road into mud.

"What if we get stuck out here?" Melanie asked. "You don't have four-wheel drive in this thing, do you?"

"No."

"So what if we get stuck in the mud? What are we going to do?"

As if to illustrate her point, the rear end of the car fishtailed.

Glen once again gripped the steering wheel grimly. "We'll make it."

Then the hail started.

There was something . . . biblical about this weather, Glen said. Or at least she thought he said. It was hard to hear above the clattering of the hail on the roof. Such abruptly changing and clearly delineated meteorological phenomena seemed deliberate, as if something was conjuring up obstacles to keep them from reaching Chaco Canyon.

The skull.

That abomination in the trunk was the sole reason they had come, but she wished they could stop the car, toss that damn thing onto the side of the road, and speed on. She had the crazy feeling that if they did so, all of this would stop, this weather weirdness and whatever came next would be over.

Whatever came next.

Yes, she realized. She expected more.

There were a surprising number of cars by the Chaco Canyon visitor's center, more hardy souls than she would have thought having braved the weather and the bad road to get here. Or had they? Glen's white Saturn was spattered with mud and looked as though it had been in some sort of off-road endurance race. The other vehicles in the parking lot merely looked dusty. Had all of these cars and trucks been here overnight and avoided the snow and rain?

She thought not.

Maybe they'd come from the opposite direction.

No, that road was closed.

Only they had experienced the storms.

Glen and Melanie left the skull in the trunk and walked into the visitor's center. An old couple was chatting with the uniformed ranger behind the counter, while a girl, who appeared to be their granddaughter, spun a rack of postcards. Several other couples and a family with two smirky teenage boys were looking at exhibits in the center's museum, and two women were reading through souvenir books in the adjoining gift shop.

Glen walked up to the counter and waited until the ranger finished talking to the old couple.

The ranger—STEVE M. according to his name tag—bid

good-bye to the man and woman, then turned toward Glen, smiling. "Welcome to Chaco Canyon."

"Hello," Glen said as Melanie sidled in next to him. "Could you tell us if Pace Henry's here?"

"Pace? I think he's off right now. Let me check." The ranger went through the doorway behind him, into an office, and spoke quietly to an older man at a desk.

"We're from Dr. Wittinghill!" Glen called out. "Dr. Al Wittinghill! We're expected!"

Steve returned a moment later. "He's out at site three, our active excavation. I could page him for you if you want."

"That'd be great," Glen said.

Melanie wandered into the gift shop while they waited. The other customers were looking through post-cards and Native American knickknacks, but she headed over to the wall opposite the window, which was lined with dozens of thin, photo-heavy books about Chaco Canyon and other national parks and monuments throughout the Southwest. She picked up the Chaco Canyon book with the best cover shot and started flipping through it.

When Glen joined her, Melanie asked, "What do you think that was? With the weather?"

"I don't know."

"But you don't think it's normal?"

Glen looked up from the book. "No," he admitted. "You?"

"No."

They went back to flipping through the pages, not wanting to talk about it anymore.

Pace Henry arrived much sooner than they expected, coming in through the door that led out to the ruins trails. The fact that he was out of breath when he entered the visitor's center showed how anxious he was to see what they'd brought. Ranger Steve motioned toward them, and Pace walked over. "You're Glen?" he said. "And Melanie? I'm Pace. Al's colleague."

He looked different than she thought he would. He was much younger than Al, for one thing. He looked more like a college student than a professor, albeit a college student from the seventies. There was something familiar about him, and in a blink Melanie figured out what it was. He looked like Jeff Bridges in that godawful remake of *King Kong*; long hair, full beard, and all.

Pace frowned. "Did you bring it? I thought Al said—"

"It's still in the car," Glen told him. "I'll go get it."

Pace wanted more details, or at least a different perspective than the one provided him by Al, and he asked Melanie to tell him her version of how the skull was discovered.

"Glen's the one who actually found it," she explained. She described to him what happened and what Al had said and how excited he'd been. She told him about the wacky weather on the way over, not specifically stating that she thought it was connected to the skull, but letting him draw his own conclusions, and she was about to go into their adventures yesterday when Glen returned, lugging the heavy wood box. Pace immediately rushed over to help, both of them holding on to the box and sidestepping across the open floor.

"My workroom's around back," Pace said, nodding at Melanie. "Could you get the door?"

She moved in front of them, opened the door, and Pace led them around the side of the building and through a separate entrance into a large room with cinder-block walls, numerous shelves and glass cases, a pair of deep metal sinks with a green garden hose in between, and long wooden tables on which were sorted various bones and artifacts.

"Let's set it down here," Pace said. They placed the box on a cleared section of the table closest to the wall, and he picked up a screwdriver and started prying open the sealed top.

"Did you get ahold of Al?" Glen asked.

Pace shook his head. "Tried a couple times last night and once this morning, but no response. I left messages on his machine."

"Us, too."

"A lot must be going on if he hasn't called back," Melanie said. In her mind, she saw Al unearthing a burial chamber in which something dark and tall and slimy was buried but not dead.

She pushed the thought away.

"Maybe we should try again," Glen suggested.

"Go ahead. The phone's on the shelf next to the sink." Pace motioned behind him.

Melanie and Glen walked over, and Glen took the number out of his wallet and dialed. She could tell from the long wait that there was no answer on the other end. Once again, he left a short message, telling him that they were at Chaco Canyon.

Across the workroom, Pace had carefully unpacked the box, withdrawn the skull, and placed it on the table. He was expertly using an X-Acto knife to slice open Al's tightly wound bubble wrap.

The skull had lost none of its ability to unnerve. Melanie looked at the oversize teeth, the slanted eye sockets, the snout. Whatever it was, the thing had been hideous, more monster than man, and she could think of no animal or living creature to which the skull corresponded.

Pace was momentarily at a loss for words. He stood there, examining the skull, tracing its contours with one wary finger.

"Wow," he said finally. He looked up at them. "Hey, were you able to get in touch with Al?"

Glen shook his head. "No answer."

"Too bad."

They all stared for a moment at the oversize skull.

Pace started quizzing Glen about his unearthing of the object, wanting his side of the story. As he spoke, Pace examined the skull more thoroughly, turning it over, using a magnifying glass and a thin hooked instrument to study the sharp, disproportionately large teeth.

"So neither of you saw the burial chamber Al described to me, is that correct?"

"I . . . didn't want to see it," Glen admitted.

"I didn't go either," Melanie said. "But Al was very excited, and I have to admit it sounded impressive. I know photos were taken."

"Photos? Damn! He should have sent them to me."

"We'll make sure he does when we get back," Glen said.

"He told me there were hundreds of interred bodies, and that they looked . . . dumped, as though this were a mass grave and there'd been no time to go through the usual ceremonial procedures, as though a lot of people died at once, and they'd simply needed to get the bodies in the ground quickly."

"And you think this thing caused it?"

Pace didn't answer, but turned the skull back over. It seemed to be frowning at them, Melanie thought. Had it changed expression? No, that wasn't possible. She had simply not noticed before. Or was now ascribing to the shape of its bone structure an emotional component that wasn't there. But it seemed to her that its facial cast looked different than it had before, angry and more unpleasant.

"What do you think it is?" Glen asked, staring at the skull. His voice was low. Awed or frightened or both. "Al told us his theory—*your* theory—that there was some sort of catalyst, a creature maybe, that led to the disappearance of those Indian tribes. Do you think this is it?"

"If you want my professional opinion, as an anthropoligist, I have to say that I have nowhere near enough data to make that determination, and that in all likelihood I won't be able to conclusively answer that question, no matter how many tests I run." He paused, and ran a hand through his hair. "But if you're asking my gut reaction, my *feeling* . . . Yeah. I think this is it."

Pace thought for a moment, then covered the skull with a blue tarp. "Let me show you something," he said.

They left the workroom. Pace carefully locked the door behind them, then returned to the visitor's center to tell Ranger Steve not to let anyone in until he returned. He led them behind the building, down a rock-lined path cordoned off from the public with a length of rusted chain and a cheap aluminum sign that read: EMPLOYEES ONLY. The path passed over a small rise, then wound around a pair of open pits that were unmanned at the moment but obviously excavations in progress. Ahead, at the edge of a low, heavily eroded mesa, Melanie could see a smallish ruin with an open roof.

It was hot, and she wiped the sweat from her face with a finger. She was struck by how divorced she felt from the vanished world around her, how alien it all seemed. This was the history of the United States, yet she felt apart from it, a third party with no connection to these ruins, these people, and she was reminded of how Wallace Stegner had once called this nation's past "other people's archeology." It was true. In Africa, in Scandinavia, in Asia, people could dig down into the earth and find the bones and artifacts of their ancestors. And their ancestors before that. And their ancestors before that. All the way back to the beginning of time. But the Americas were not like that. Even before the British, this had been a continent of serial conquerors, and digging into the earth brought up only the remnants of defeated cultures and dead civilizations.

They reached the site, a nondescript rock structure that appeared to be a single-family dwelling. That was odd. As far as she knew, the Anasazi had lived in pueblos, the equivalent of apartment houses, great interconnected structures where an entire village would reside. She had never seen a small house, set apart like this, with no adjacent structures.

She wanted to ask Pace about it, but he was already walking through a small, almost completely square doorway, ducking under the tree-branch lintel and entering the roofless room beyond. She and Glen followed.

Inside, the walls were smooth adobe, well preserved after all this time by the aridity of the desert. On them were painted arrows and spears, sharply angled birds and simplistic, rectangular people. There was color—white and brown and black—but only the smaller figures had been painted in. The larger birds and people were sketchlike, line drawings with only the heads and feet in color.

"As near as we can figure, this was a storehouse of some kind. Although, why it was located so far away from the other structures of the community is not clear. It is also quite small for a storehouse, and the murals suggest some sort of ceremonial usage." He smiled sheepishly. "The truth is, we don't really know *what* this building was. We're guessing."

Pace moved forward, gesturing at the paintings on the

walls. "I want you to look at this artwork so you can compare it to something I'm going to show you in a minute."

"What are we supposed to be looking for?" Glen asked.

"Nothing in particular. I just want you to note the style and technique, the primitive characteristics of the painting."

"Okay," Glen said.

Melanie stepped up to the wall on the right, looked at the pictures, committed them to memory, and nodded. "All right."

"This way." Pace led them through another small door into a long narrow room where the mid-morning sun shone at a slanted angle, illuminating an elaborate mural on the facing wall. "We don't show this to the public," he said. "For obvious reasons."

Indeed, the mural portrayed the most graphically depicted sex acts Melanie had ever seen. These were not the simple featureless figures with engorged, overemphasized pudenda or gigantic, crudely rendered phalluses that were so common among primitive fertility-based cultures. Instead, exquisitely detailed and remarkably colorful scenes of debauchery were painted on the smooth adobe, with individual focal points bordered in black as though the viewer was supposed to be looking through a window. In one, an older man was standing atop a tree stump holding his penis, and either ejaculating or urinating into the willing mouths of a trio of young women spread-eagled on the ground before him. In another, an overweight woman was on her hands and knees while another thinner woman sat behind her, the second woman's face buried in the buttocks of the first. Two women licked the opposite sides of a prone man's erection. A man was copulating with a female bear. At least a dozen other figures were engaged in various types of unnatural sex acts.

"It's Sodom and Gomorrah," Melanie said.

"Remarkably similar," Pace admitted. "Even more so when combined with the narrative provided by the accompanying pictographs." He pointed toward the narrow side wall. "According to that, the community depicted here was prophesied to end cataclysmically due to its decadent ways, its destruction brought about by an unspecified supernatural being. Less than fifty years after these paintings were made, Chaco Canyon was abandoned, its windows and doors sealed."

Melanie was still staring at the explicit painting before her. Not only did the mural look as though it had not been created by the same artist as the artwork in the previous room, it did not look like it came from the same culture. There seemed something more modern about the graphic detail here, an individuality in the presentation that had not been seen even in European art until half a millennium later.

Glen must have been thinking the same thing. "Were these—" he began.

"They were done at the same time as the others," Pace said.

Melanie felt chilled, though she was sweating and the sun felt hot against her head.

"Now let me show you what's on the *other* side of this wall." Pace ducked under an arched entryway to the center room of the ruin.

Though there was no ceiling here, either, the chamber seemed darker, and was measurably cooler than the rest of the structure. She also noticed a strange smell—not the sour, musty deadness found in most ruins, the scent of sand and rock and long-departed life, but a fresher, harsher odor, subtle yet tangible, that bizarrely struck her as gasoline mixed with rotted vegetables.

Pace was facing the wall next to the entryway, and Melanie and Glen both turned to look in that direction.

At the painting.

This one was done in a more traditionally primitive style. It resembled the artwork back in the first room— or perhaps its sister mural on the other side of the wall, only drained of life and individuality. It depicted a solidly built, squarish creature with wild bushy hair. The creature was humanoid—that is, it had two arms and two legs—but it was not human. Even this crude representation imparted the feeling of something profoundly alien. Not "alien" in the sense of outer space, but "alien" as in utterly unknowable. It was the same creature they'd seen in the tryptich of the abandoned church, and that connection made it seem much more ominous.

They stared at the figure.

"It is a god," Pace said softly. "Or a devil."

Melanie felt uncomfortable looking at the painting. Her brain suddenly made the association. "Why did you take us out here?" she asked Pace.

"Because I think you have the skull of this being, a supernatural entity predicted to destroy the Anasazi society, the entity that *did* destroy that society."

Melanie could believe it. The bushy-haired figure was, hands down, the most evil-looking creature she had ever seen. It cast a shadow over the entire room, a pall that encompassed the walls, the floor, even the narrow strip of sky above. The air itself here seemed wrong, affected by the unnatural creature depicted on the wall. She found it hard to breathe, her throat and lungs filled with a parched harshness.

Glen was asking Pace a question, but even though she was only a foot away, she couldn't seem to hear their words. The sound was muffled, indistinguishable. She squinted at them, trying to read their lips, then turned back to the painting on the wall.

Her heart skipped.

Had it changed positions?

She suddenly wanted to—*had* to—get out of this room, this building. No, the figure hadn't moved, but there was definitely something different about it, and the fact that its appearance could change terrified her. She thought of the shard of pottery she'd left back at the empty church yesterday, with its disappearing face in her parents' window. Reality, she understood now, was not solid and dependable, as most people thought, as she'd always thought. It was ever fluid, shifting.

Gasping, panting, trying desperately to catch her breath, she fled the chamber, fled the ruin, and waited outside in the hot unfiltered sun until Glen and Pace emerged. They'd obviously come out to check on her, concerned, wondering why she'd bolted. She expected questions, expected them to ask her what was wrong, but neither of them said a word.

They felt it, too, she thought.

They returned to the visitor's center in silence, walking slowly back over the dusty path until they reached the cement sidewalk and the workroom.

The skull was gone.

It was impossible but true. They searched the room, and Pace questioned the staff, but no one knew anything about it. No one had gone back there, and while ordinarily such a locked-room mystery would have thrown suspicion on everyone within shouting distance, all three of them instantly believed the denials. This was not a normal theft.

Melanie asked Ranger Steve if there had been any calls for her in their absence. When he said there'd been none, she tried to call Al again, but the land line seemed to be down and the cell phone didn't work out here.

"Kind of convenient," Glen said.

She didn't respond, but she'd been thinking the same thing.

The three of them stood in the middle of the visitor's center, between the museum and the gift shop, while around them tourists walked in and out of the building. Melanie glanced over at the museum, her attention drawn by the skull of a sloth encased in glass. "Where do you think it is?" she asked Pace.

He shook his head helplessly. "Haven't a clue. Any ideas?"

Melanie had plenty, but she didn't want to speak them aloud. She wouldn't be surprised to see the skull suddenly appear in one of the museum's exhibits, or back in the trunk of Glen's car, ready to return to Bower. She could even imagine it back *in* Bower, returning on its own in some mysterious, unspeakable way, positioned once again in the hole Glen had dug.

But her gut told her something different. She really thought it was in the ruin they'd just visited, that spooky little building out there on its own, with its open roof and unholy murals, and in her mind's eye, she saw it on the ground before that bushy-haired figure in that dark cold chamber.

Pace led them once more on an obligatory search of

the workroom and the park service's storehouse, even on an inspection of the picnic grounds adjacent to the visitor's center, but they found nothing.

"Where are you two planning to spend the night?" he asked as they walked past the public restrooms.

Melanie looked at Glen.

"We didn't really have any plans," Glen admitted. "We thought maybe we'd find a motel in Gallup or something."

"It's getting late. Gallup's far, and we have an empty cabin you can use. Why don't you stay here? We can talk some more over dinner. I haven't had an opportunity to speak with Al, so I'd like to sound out the both of you about some of my thoughts here, what I think we might do and what we should concentrate on. Since we can't get ahold of him, you can be my messengers and tell him what we've discussed."

"Well . . ." Glen said hesitantly.

Pace ran a hand through his thick hair. "As Al probably told you, we've pretty much kept this under wraps. And we'd like to keep it that way until we publish." He gestured back toward the visitor's center. "So I can't tell them in there, can't talk about this with any of my friends or coworkers. But you two *know*. Hell, you were there, you found it." He took a deep breath. "And I think I want to talk about it tonight."

Glen was nodding, and Melanie, too, understood. "All right," she said, catching Glen's eye. "We'll stay."

"Great." Pace smiled. "That's great."

2

They left early, before dawn, and arrived in Bower just after noon.

They'd been gone only two-and-a-half days, but it seemed like a month. The roads, the buildings, the cars on the street, everything had the slightly distanced unfamiliarity that came with an extended break in the routine intimacies of daily life. Before heading out to the site, they stopped first at Melanie's house to go to the bathroom, and while she went first, he quickly unloaded their suitcases from the car. On the long trip back, Glen had agreed to give up his primitive lodgings in the motor court and move in with her. The invitation was open-ended, and while he knew he'd be there until the end of summer and the end of the dig, what was going to happen beyond that neither of them knew.

While he went to the bathroom, Melanie phoned her parents. She'd tried to call from the road several times, but the line was always busy. When he emerged, she was just hanging up, and he could tell from the relieved expression on her face that her parents were all right.

After grabbing two bottles of Snapple from the fridge, they headed out to the excavation in Melanie's truck. Glen sped off the highway and down the dirt road, filled with an unfamiliar sense of urgency. He pulled next to Al's Jeep in the crowded makeshift parking lot and they quickly got out and hurried up the mound of dirt, not speaking, not needing to. They ducked under the rope.

The site was abandoned.

Glen stood staring, his eyes searching the various pits, trenches, and half-excavated walls for any sign of movement. It was the town all over again. He didn't know how he knew, but he did. What's more, he'd been expecting it. He glanced over at Melanie, and she, too, seemed unsurprised. After what they'd seen in that church and what had happened at Chaco Canyon, nothing was shocking anymore.

They stood for a beat longer, then walked slowly through the partially unearthed ruins, looking for . . . what? Charred bones? Piles of ashes? Empty clothes?

There was nothing, only the sun, only the wind, and they made their way over to the canopy in the center of the excavation, where an extra-large Jack in the Box cup filled with water sat atop the table, having remained there so long that there was not even any condensation on the outside of the cup.

When did this happen?

Glen looked out over the empty excavation. He saw Al's Panama hat on the ice chest next to Buck's Walkman, saw Judi's purse lying next to a pick and pail. They were gone. All of them. They'd disappeared, and he had no illusions that they were just missing and would eventually return. Whatever happened to them, they were never coming back.

He picked up a spiral notebook filled with Al's small cramped writing, looked down at a sift box filled with pieces of pottery. What if he had been here at the time? What if he were one of the missing? He could not muster much emotion over the prospect, and it occurred to him that it was because he knew he would not really be missed. He had no family left, no close friends. There was no one to care. Oh, Melanie might feel bad for a while, but then she'd get on with her life and it would be as though he had never existed.

Life was so transitory and ephemeral, an individual's existence so small and ultimately pointless.

He thought of his mother. He had avoided thinking about her as much as possible these past several weeks, and he understood now that he'd been afraid to let himself dwell on her passing, afraid that if he did so, he would succumb to despair. He'd done the same thing after his father's death—although he hadn't been aware of it until this moment. He'd thrown himself into his work, had purposely not thought about either his dad's death or life, had carefully partitioned off those thoughts and memories. With his mother, he'd cried, he'd grieved, and he thought he'd gotten it out of his system. But then he'd given up his job and his former life for a taste of freedom and the open road, and he realized now that one of the reasons he'd run away was because he didn't want to deal with the loss, didn't want to face those feelings.

He stared down at the sift box, then up at the blue, blue sky.

Why was he thinking of all this shit now?

Melanie found his hand, squeezed it, not looking at him, but glancing around the excavation as if expecting a monster to pop out at any second. "What do you think happened?" She seemed more shaken than he did. Or rather shaken in the right way. She had not been surprised by what they'd found, but she was horrified, and obviously frightened. "Did they just disappear in a flash? Did creatures come and take them, physically carry them away? Did they put up a fight? What the hell happened here?"

Glen didn't know and he was glad he didn't know. It was cleaner this way, easier to take. If he were aware of the messy details, if he started imagining the specifics of what they'd gone through, what they'd felt, he might not be able to continue.

"It's like the town," Melanie said softly. "Like the church."

"Yeah."

"Do you think we should . . . look?"

She didn't have to explain; he knew exactly what she was talking about. Glen turned toward the northwest quadrant. His heart was hammering in his chest. He didn't really expect to see anything other than an empty hole, but a part of him was afraid to look, afraid that something *might* be there.

Something?

The skull. He was afraid the missing artifact would be nestled snugly in the ground exactly where he'd found it.

"I'll check," he told Melanie.

Glen made his way through the half-excavated pueblo to the room where he'd discovered the skull. To his great relief, he found only a ragged open cavity in the hardpacked ground. It had been expanded since he'd left—obviously Al had been looking for additional bones—and a chisel and trowel lay on the dirt nearby, but there was nothing weird or strange or out of the ordinary, and for that he was grateful.

Melanie followed him. She looked down at Al's abandoned tools. "Who's going to notify their families?" she wondered.

"I don't think anyone even knows this has happened yet. We're the only ones."

"We have to tell the police, then. File a missing-person's report."

She was right, of course, but Glen was embarrassed that such an idea had not even occurred to him. He looked at Melanie. He was her age, a little older actually, but she seemed more mature, able to operate more easily in the real world.

"Maybe we should go now," she said, glancing around nervously. "It could happen again."

Glen nodded. He thought it was over—whatever had

happened here, they'd missed it—but he understood her worry, and the last thing he wanted to do was hang around this place.

They started back toward the front of the pueblo, but when they reached the canopy, Melanie stopped. "Look." She pointed.

Two boys on bikes were pedalling furiously toward them over the rolling countryside, jumping small indentations in the ground, speedily circumventing boulders and the occasional trees. He hadn't seen anyone on their way out here, so he figured the kids must have ridden across the grasslands from town rather than taking the roads. The boys drew closer, sliding to a stop as they reached the rope that cordoned off the excavation, and Glen was able to make out the expressions on their faces. They were terrified of something, and he automatically looked at the rolling plain behind them to make sure they weren't being chased. Melanie's grip on his hand tightened.

The boys ran through the pueblo, jumping over shorter ruin walls, over to where he and Melanie stood.

"Is Dr. Wittinghill here?" the shorter one asked breathlessly.

Glen shook his head. *No,* he was about to say, but before he could even get the word out, the other boy was shouting.

"Where is he?"

Glen fixed the boy with a flat stare. "Who are you?"

"Jerod. And that's Ricky. Where's Dr. Wittinghill?"

"He's gone. We don't know where he is."

"Then *you* gotta come with us."

"Who are you?" Glen repeated.

Ricky spoke up. "We're the ones who found the . . . the . . ."

"Burial chamber," Jerod finished for him. "And—"

"It's all different now. They changed it all."

Jerod turned on his friend. "Just shut up and let me tell it, will you?"

"I—"

"Shut up!" Jerod yelled.

"Calm down," Melanie said. "Just tell us what happened."

"They moved," Jerod said.

"What moved?"

"The bones. We saw them move before, like they were alive or something. But now they made themselves into things. Like a fence. With a gate. And a table and chairs. And a . . . I don't know what. Like a sculpture."

"It's scary," Ricky said, nodding his head.

"It is," Jerod admitted.

"And it's right below my house."

"And we don't know what to do."

"Did you tell your parents?" Glen asked.

They looked at each other.

"What?" Glen said.

Ricky started crying. "I don't know where they are."

Jerod nodded, swallowing hard. "His mom's supposed to be home, but she's not, and when we went down to his dad's store, no one knew where he was." Jerod licked his lips. "My parents are in Tucson. I'm staying with my grandma. But I don't want to tell her. I can't tell her."

"I think they might be down there," Ricky sobbed.

A shudder passed through Glen, quick and sharp like a piss-shiver.

I think they might be down there.

He hadn't wanted to see the burial chamber, even with Al to guide him, had been afraid of it even then. Now just the idea of that dark death cave caused him to suck in his breath.

"We'll come with you," Melanie told the boys.

What? Glen blinked, looked at her face, saw that she meant it, and he realized that she had not had the same reaction to this as he had. He could still see the goose-flesh on his arms—pinprick points of raised skin that corresponded to individual hairs—but the skin of her arms was smooth and unaffected, the reassuring smile she directed at the boys honest and heartfelt.

Ricky wiped his eyes. "I told you."

Jerod looked skeptical. Relieved but skeptical. "What about Dr. Wittinghill?"

"We'll let him know about it when we see him again. Right now, let's go. Toss your bikes in the trunk. We'll drive you."

The boys shared a glance.

"We can't—" Ricky started to say.

"We're not supposed to ride with strangers."

"We'll follow you," Melanie suggested. "You take your bikes, lead the way."

Jerod nodded. "Okay."

Ricky lived in a tract house in the newer part of town. Bower was not exactly a hotbed of growth, so the "newer part of town" consisted of a ten-year-old subdivision adjacent to flat, cleared ground overgrown with weeds where a second subdivision had been planned but never built. They walked through the house, Ricky calling out, "Mom! Dad!" just in case, but neither of his parents was home. They passed through a sliding glass doorway into a large backyard. On their right, near the side of the house, were several waist-high mounds of dirt.

"It's over there," Jerod said, pointing.

Glen and Melanie walked over the grass to the mounds, which he could now see continued into the side yard, where a tall sprawling clubhouse cobbled together from disparate boards and doors and discarded signs stood at the far end. Just before the clubhouse was a large pit about six feet in diameter.

"Down that hole," Jerod said.

Ricky was crying again.

"Don't worry, hon," Melanie said. She put an arm around him. "We'll check down there, and if we don't find your parents—and I'm sure we won't—we'll go to the police and tell them, okay?"

"The police?" Ricky repeated, panicked. "You think they're dead?"

"No, no. They're probably just out shopping or something. Don't worry. The police do this kind of stuff all the time. They're not always out there catching bank robbers. Usually, they just help clear up misunderstandings. Like this."

Glen wasn't sure she should be soft-pedaling what would probably turn out to be an unsolvable tragedy, but he knew enough to keep his mouth shut. He passed between the hills of dirt, stopping at the foot of the hole.

A makeshift wooden stairway, more ladder than steps, descended into the darkness.

He did *not* want to go down there.

Nevertheless, he turned back around. "Do you have a flashlight I could use?"

"There's one in the club," Jerod said. He ran up one of the mounds and leaped from top to top before sliding down the last one and kicking open a small hidden door in the clubhouse. He crawled inside, then emerged with a battery-powered torchlight. "Here. We use this for our camp outs."

"Thanks." Glen took the light, flicked it on, and pointed it at the hole. The rickety, ladderish steps were illuminated all the way to the bottom, as were the sides of the sloping hole, but the burial chamber itself remained in darkness. Only a stray skull at the foot of the makeshift staircase was visible, black eye sockets and perpetual grin daring him to come down.

Glen fought the urge to turn away and flee.

"Stay here," he ordered. Gripping the torchlight tightly, he started slowly down the steps. It grew colder as he descended into the ground. His nostrils filled with the unique musty scent of old death.

He stopped at the bottom and shone his light around. The burial chamber was much larger than he'd imagined. The adobe-walled room extended farther than his hand-held illumination could reach, and he understood Al's excitement. The professor must have been overjoyed at the sight of so many undiscovered Anasazi skeletons.

But the boys were right. Things had changed. From Al's description, this had looked like a mass gravesite, whole skeletons lying next to each other on the dirt floor, placed into niches in the walls, a mountainous accumulation of bones stacked along the far end of the crypt. But now it looked like . . . nothing he had ever seen. There was not a complete skeleton to be found. All the bones and skulls had been separated and rearranged into a king-size table and half a dozen chairs and, like the boys said, a low fence that ringed the chamber and appeared to have a working gate. There were piles of smaller bones, bastard complements of the dirt mounds up above, as well as shelves, a trunk, a chest of drawers, a bed, and several freestanding lamps, all made from the fleshless remains of long-dead people. He did not know what was holding the bones together, and he did not want to know. It was like a room in Hell, and dominating everything was what the boys had called the "sculpture," a horrible travesty of art that stood fifteen feet high and consisted of stacked and fitted skulls. It resembled nothing so much as a Cubist-constructed demon, a twisted distorted figure with a square disproportionate head. What lay beyond that, in the darkness, he could not tell.

"You want me to come down?" Melanie shouted from the top of the stairs.

"No! Stay up there!"

"I'm coming! Shine your light on the steps!"

He heard her footfalls on the wood above him and swiveled his light so she could see where to walk. She descended slowly, holding on to the rickety wooden rail with one hand, the other balanced against the adobe wall. When she reached the bottom, he moved the light so she could see the chamber, and he heard her sharp intake of air.

"Yeah," he said.

She was silent as she took it all in. "Do you see anyone down here?" she asked finally.

He shook his head.

"Hello!" Melanie called, and he wanted to put his hand over her mouth, afraid that she might be alerting something to their presence.

"Anybody here?" she yelled out.

"Mom!" Ricky called from above. "Dad!"

"Stay up there!" Glen said sharply. "Don't come down here!"

"We're not!" Jerod shouted.

Glen breathed deeply. He was jumpy. He had believed the boys even before coming down here, but now that he'd seen it for himself, he was much more frightened.

And Ricky and Jerod were right about the bones.

They *were* moving.

He saw nothing overt, nothing that he could prove,

but he heard noises, sounds, the dry scrape of bone on bone, the click of hard calcium striking its counterpart. Each time he swiveled his light to look, everything was still, but when he turned back again, he always noticed some slight difference. When he saw the expression on Melanie's face, he knew that she was aware of it, too.

He took a step forward, felt Melanie's restraining hand on his arm.

"Let's file that missing-person's report," she said.

Glen nodded. He wanted out of here, and he was grateful to Melanie for insisting that they leave. He didn't know what was causing all this, or what it meant, but like that room in Chaco Canyon with the wild-haired figure, this chamber felt evil.

Evil.

If he'd been anywhere else, the thought would have made him laugh. That word was not even part of his ordinary vocabulary. It seemed like something from the past, an archaic term for an outmoded concept.

But he knew now that there *was* evil. It was real, and it was here.

They piled the boys back into the truck and headed to the police station, following Melanie's direction. They were nearly there when she suddenly sat up sharply in her seat. "Ron!" she exclaimed excitedly, turning toward him.

Ron! Of course! They'd forgotten all about Ron and his midnight bust.

"Maybe he can help us!" Melanie said.

"If he's still in jail."

He was. And after explaining to the desk sergeant what the boys had told them and what they'd seen at Ricky's house, after each of them filled out and signed a report about it, after they gratefully pawned off the kids to a detective who promised to track down Jerod's parents and then find Ricky's, after they filled out their *own* missing-person's reports for Al, Judi, Randy, and Buck, he and Melanie met with Ron in a locked, bare visitation room.

The young man was angry.

"Where's Al, goddammit? He said he was going to

get me a lawyer and arrange bail, but I've been sitting in here for the past three days and haven't heard word one!"

"Three days?" Melanie asked.

He sensed something in her voice because the anger was instantly replaced by wariness. "Yeah," he said. "Since Tuesday morning." He looked from Melanie to Glen. "What's happened? Why are you here?"

They told him.

"Fuck howdy," Ron breathed, sinking back in his chair.

Glen leaned forward. "We thought you might be able to tell us something—"

"Are you kidding? I don't know what the hell's happened. I'm more in the dark than you are."

That was true.

"They're gone? Really? All of them?"

Glen nodded.

Ron shook his head, stunned. "Fuck." He looked up. "So where does that leave me?"

"I don't know." Glen looked over at Melanie, who shrugged helplessly. "Did Al get you a lawyer or anything? Have you met with—"

"I haven't met with shit. I've just been . . . waiting." Ron took a deep breath, trying to calm himself. "I guess that explains why Al's been MIA."

"I don't know how these things work," Glen admitted. "What I know about jail and lawyers I learned from television."

"Me, too," Melanie said.

"You think I'm some expert? I know about as much as you do." Ron stood, clearly exasperated. "You can't let me rot in here. Somebody has to get me out." He seemed almost ready to cry. Despite the shaved head and all of the tattoos, he looked like a lost little boy. "I didn't even know she was underage. And she agreed! I have her release form!"

"Are they mistreating you?" Melanie asked.

"No. There's no one else even in the jail except me right now, and the cops . . . they treat me all right, I guess." He shook his handcuffs. "But I've never been in jail before. I have to get out."

"Did you call your parents?"

"No, I can't. They wouldn't understand. And I don't want them to know."

"We'll call ASU," Glen told him. "Maybe Al already got the ball rolling. They have to have some kind of legal aid. You're a student, right?"

"Yeah."

"Well, there's probably some sort of student services that could help you. I'll call. Find out."

"Couldn't you . . . ?" Ron cleared his throat. "Don't you have some money? I'll pay you back, I promise."

"How much is your bail?"

"I don't know. I'm not sure it's been set yet. If it has, no one's told me."

Glen looked over at Melanie, sighed. "I'll see what I can do."

"We'll be back," she promised. "With help."

Walking up the cinder-block hallway to the lobby of the police station, Glen shook his head. "We came here to file missing-person's reports because everyone at the site vanished after we found the skull of an unknown monster that may be responsible for wiping out an entire race of people a thousand years ago. So how did we end up trying to find legal aid for a pornographer?"

Melanie smiled, and took his hand. "The Lord works in mysterious ways, my son. The Lord works in mysterious ways."

Eight

1

"Get back, everyone! Please! Get back!" Lieutenant Armstrong stood at the barricade with a bullhorn as other officers walked the line, making sure no one tried to get into the ruins.

And a lot of them wanted to.

That was the weird part, Cameron thought. They could see what was going on, but they still needed to feel it, touch it, experience it for themselves.

God damn, adults were stupid sometimes.

Maybe not, he thought. Maybe it wasn't their fault. Maybe they were being drawn in there, pulled, like metal to a magnet.

He shivered.

He and Jay were standing across the street from Pima House Ruins, had been there for the past two hours. The ruins were just down the street from their neighborhood, off Camelback Road near downtown Scottsdale, and though it was a state park and a famous place and within walking distance, the only time he'd actually been there was on a field trip in third grade.

But they'd heard this morning from Fat Josie, who lived over on Arbor and who'd ridden over on her bike specifically to tell them the news, that cops were roping off the ruins and keeping people out because there was, like, a Bermuda Triangle in there. A man had walked into the ruins and just disappeared. And then another man had gone after him and then *he'd* disappeared. And then a *police dog* had vanished. Now they were roping off the whole place.

So he'd told his parents he was going to Jay's, Jay told his parents he was going to Cameron's, and the two of them immediately sped over, watching from across the busy street as the crowd swelled, as more police arrived, remaining on this side of Camelback because they were afraid to move any closer. Noises were rising from within the ruins, horrible hackle-raising sounds that were not screams, not growls, not thunder, but somehow incorporated all three.

Cameron also saw movement in there, a furtive rushing from adobe wall to adobe wall by someone or something that could not be clearly seen, even in broad daylight. It was this that kept them waiting, watching, rooted in place.

Just then an old man tried to sneak under the sawhorses and yellow ribbon that blocked of the ruins. Cameron was glad they hadn't decided to cross Camelback and stand on the sidewalk with the rest of the onlookers. These attempts to pass through the barricade and see what was going on definitely seemed like the result of some strange draw or force rather than simply stupid curiosity, and he was thankful they were far enough away that they were not affected by it.

Overhead, a helicopter with the Fox logo was circling in the air just above a police helicopter.

"News chopper," Jay said, pointing.

It was starting to feel like a block party. In addition to the locals and the police, news vans from the TV stations were arriving, and a snack truck had stopped and was selling drinks and doughnuts and candy.

Jay kicked a rock off the sidewalk into the gutter. "Too bad Devon and Chase and Kirk aren't here. We could push them in."

"Whatever happened to them?" Cameron asked. "Did anybody ever find out?"

"I heard they got sent away for a long, long time. I think they stole a car and then used it in a robbery and beat up some guy."

"No shit?"

"That's what I heard. Mike told me, and he overheard his parents talking about it. His dad's a cop, you know."

Cameron hoped it was true. Not the part about the guy getting beat up, but Devon and his buddies going away for a long time. The neighborhood was so much nicer with those assholes gone, and it was a relief not having to listen for the noise of Devon's motorcycle, to be able to play outside without tensing up at the sound of every starting engine.

Last year Devon and his pals had caught Cameron after school, picking him out of a crowd and shoving his face into a pile of dogshit on the small strip of grass next to the sidewalk. Cameron had puked, and then they'd shoved his face in the puke, while everyone stood around laughing at him. They'd let him go after that, but they'd *looked* for him each day after school, wanting to do it again, wanting to make him into a show. One weekend Devon had caught him on the sidewalk in front of Stu's house and had punched him in the stomach and then spit on him when he was down. "If you narc on me your ass is grass," he said, and walked away, laughing.

So if Devon and his friends really were in juvy or jail, that was great news.

Suddenly a woman across the street sprang forward, out of the crowd, ducked under the police ribbon, and made a mad dash for the closest ruin: a crumbling L-shaped adobe wall. Two policemen immediately scrambled after her, but she had a head start. She was yelling in triumph, arms in the air like a football player who had just made a touchdown, as she ran up the sloping sidewalk, jumping the low rail that blocked off the path from the ruins.

And disappeared.

Cameron saw it happen. It was quick, but he saw it. The second she left the path, there was a *shimmering* in the air, like a wall of mercury that had been disturbed, and then the woman was gone, blinked out of existence. At the last second, her shout of triumph sounded like a cry of agony, and it seemed to echo long after she had vanished, its shrillness swallowed up by the low growl/thunder/scream that continued to emanate from the ruins.

Something unseen ran from behind the wall to a partially reconstructed hogan.

The onlookers were stunned. Even Lieutenant Armstrong's bullhorn had temporarily gone mute. Cameron's first reaction was to turn tail and haul ass for home. But then the spell was broken. The lieutenant started barking orders again, the guy running the snack truck kept selling chips, people began talking.

"Holy shit." Jay turned to him. "What do you think it is?"

"You know."

"I know?"

Cameron met his eyes.

"You think *this* is the Mogollon Monster, too?"

"There's a connection, yeah." He cocked his head, as if listening. "Don't you feel that?"

"What?"

"That . . . heaviness. Like the air is thicker. Here, step back." Cameron retreated from the road onto the lawn of the house behind them, bringing Jay with them. Then he walked forward, stepping off the curb, into the gutter. The air engulfed him, liquid, oppressive.

"Fuck!" Jay said, his eyes widening. "I do feel it. You're right."

"That's what I felt both at the camp and in my room that day when I saw it in the backyard."

"But why is it here? And how can it do this?"

"I don't know."

"It's not just after you, then."

"Doesn't look like it."

"Back!" the lieutenant ordered the crowd through his bullhorn. "Stay back!"

"That's even scarier," Jay said.

Cameron nodded, forcing himself to swallow. "Yeah."

Policemen, at the lieutenant's behest, were fanning out, pushing the barrier forward, forcing people off the sidewalk and into the street.

The crowd was getting ugly. Something in the mood of the assemblage had changed, and it seemed only a matter of time before one or more of them broke through the barricade and followed the woman who had disappeared. They were no longer just onlookers; they wanted in. Even after what they'd seen, *especially* after what they'd seen, they appeared eager to experience for themselves that awful power.

Why?

The air pressed in on Cameron, dense and viscous, and he knew why.

"Let's get out of here," Cameron said. "Let's go home."

Jay nodded, the bravado of the early morning gone. They were witness to something here much bigger than both of them. As far as Cameron was concerned, they even *lived* too close to this place, and if he thought he could convince them to do so, he'd tell his parents right now to sell the house, pack their bags, and head to Vermont or Hawaii or someplace far, far away.

They started down the sidewalk and were about to turn left onto their own street when Jay stopped, pointed. "Oh, my God," he said. "Look."

Dozens of animals were coming up Camelback Road, all making their way toward the ruins. They weren't in a pack, although a coyote, two cats, and a squirrel were walking down the center of the asphalt nearly side by side. They were arriving independently, having been summoned or drawn here. Like Stu's cat, like Bear, they were hopping, lurching, moving strangely, their bodies contorted into humped unnatural positions, their faces frozen in crazed wild-eyed grins.

Traffic was backed up behind the animals, horns honking. Cars driving in the opposite direction were forced into the far single lane.

"You think the police are gonna stop 'em?" Jay asked.

"I don't know. Let's just get out of here."

"I want to see if—"

"Watch it on TV," Cameron told him.

Jay looked at the freakish animals, then again at the crowd surging in front of the barricaded ruins, and nodded reluctantly. "Yeah. All right."

They turned their backs on Camelback Road, heading up their own street. The air became lighter and easier to breathe as they moved away from the ruins, but the coldness Cameron felt did not lessen. Behind them, they heard a dog's bark that sounded uncomfortably like human laughter.

2

The crew finished the trail's midsection shortly before noon, and Shumway said they could break. Devon immediately walked uptrail, away from the others, who were already taking out their sack lunches and settling on the stumps and boulders surrounding the work area. Pete Holt, who'd been following him around like a puppy dog all morning for some goddamn reason, grabbed his lunch and hurried after.

Devon found a boulder out of sight of the others, facing a canyon wall, and sat down.

Pete leaned against a cottonwood on the opposite side of the trail, took a squished sandwich out of his bag. "Hey, didn't you bring anything to eat?"

Devon shook his head.

"You want part of my sandwich? It's peanut butter and jelly."

"No."

"I have an apple."

"No."

Pete nodded. "That's cool." He took a bite, chewed quickly. "Like I was saying, the great thing about the YCC is that we get to go into places that the public never gets to see."

Devon shrugged, lit a cigarette. He didn't give a shit. Most of the nerds-in-training who'd signed up for this gig were all gung-ho about the environment and the Indians and fuck knew what all. But he'd been sent here on court order, as part of his "community service," and while he was glad that he'd been sentenced only for the car, that they hadn't found out about the *other* thing, he sure as hell wasn't going to go all tree hugger just because he was serving his time in a national park.

And if that dickheaded judge thought that these clowns were going to change him, that peer pressure was going to somehow make him into a happy, smiley dogooder and accomplish what his parents and the school couldn't . . . well, that fuckwad had another think coming.

"See, there's these new ruins that they just discovered. The archeologists haven't even gotten to them yet, and it's going to be another decade or so before everything's looked over and catalogued and trails are made and the public's allowed in." Pete grinned. "But we can check it out now."

"Groovy," Devon said derisively.

Pete cleared his throat. "I was thinking of going over there after we get off this afternoon. There's not a whole lot to do around here, and instead of just hanging out with those doofuses"—he nodded down the trail—"I thought maybe me and you could go over to the ruins, explore, whatever."

Devon wanted to smile, but it wouldn't have been cool. The idea that this little twerp considered himself his pal, his equal, was pretty damn funny. If anything, Pete was even more of a dexter than most of the other corps workers.

Still, Pete was right. There *wasn't* a whole lot to do around here except sit around and play cards, attend nature talks, or do whatever chores the rangers wanted to pawn off on them.

And at least if he was out there on his own, he'd be able to smoke.

Devon nodded. "Yeah," he said. "Sounds all right. Just tell me how to get there."

He brought his motorcycle.

It was against the rules and probably against his sentencing agreement. He'd ridden to the park on it, but it was supposed to remain in storage until he left. From what Pete said, though, these ruins were way the hell out in God's country, and there was no way on earth he was going to hike that far.

He pulled up to the end of the service road behind the tourist cabins, their agreed-upon meeting place. Pete was waiting, and his eyes widened as he saw Devon's bike.

"You can't . . ." He shook his head, at a loss for words.

"Can't what?"

"There's no off-roading here," Pete said. "This is a *wilderness* area. It's *protected.*"

Devon smiled, feeling strangely satisfied. "Yeah? Who's going to stop me?"

"You're supposed to *walk.* You'll ruin the trail."

"I'm riding the bike. If you're gonna be a pussy, just tell me directions and I'll meet you there. If you want to pretend to be a man, hop on and we'll haul ass."

Pete hesitated only a second. "All right."

He climbed on the back of the motorcycle.

The ride was rough, the trail almost nonexistent. Even with Pete shouting in his ear, he made wrong turns and had to backtrack twice. They went through gullies and over hills, finally ending up on a low escarpment that overlooked a series of interconnected canyons.

Devon shut off the engine, got off the bike.

"There." Pete pointed.

He could see the ruins from the top of the bluff, and he had to admit that they did look pretty cool. Although he wasn't going to give this nimrod the satisfaction of letting him know that. Nestled against a cliff in the nearest canyon, highlighted by the slanted light from the late afternoon sun, the ruins consisted of a two-story adobe structure that appeared to be built into the rock wall, two, low, windowless dwellings that jutted out from the sides of the taller building, and a stone circle that abutted both. Trees and bushes grew wild in the canyon, hiding the ruins until recently. They were now only visible because a crew had cleared the brush.

"There's a narrow trail down the side," Pete said, "but I don't think you want to take your motorcycle there because it might get wrecked. Once we get through this first section, though, there's a rope ladder that goes down into the canyon. The workers left it. We'll be down there in five minutes, ten tops."

The boy was right. Ten minutes later they were standing in the stone circle, looking up at the buildings. The ruins looked a lot bigger from this vantage point, and Devon felt the same sort of thrill that all the other YCC-ers probably felt when they saw someplace like this.

Maybe he *was* being affected by working here this summer.

He pushed that thought out of his mind.

He turned to face Pete. "You've been here before, right?"

The other boy nodded enthusiastically. "It's bitchin'."

"You know what all these buildings and shit are?"

"Some. Come on, I'll take you on a tour. There's something you *gotta* see."

They went into the main structure, walked through a big room with a fire pit in the middle, and several smaller rooms with doorways built for dwarves. Pete had brought a flashlight, which was a good thing because even though the sun was shining directly on the ruins, the few windows in this structure were small and let in little light.

They walked all the way to the back of the adobe building. The light dimmed further, and only Pete's flashlight playing across the solid wall made him realize that this entire structure had been built out of a natural cave, with the adobe facade giving it the appearance of being completely man-made.

Pete grinned. "This is why we came."

"What?"

The flashlight beam landed on a square chiseled doorway in the far right corner. Like all of the others, it was short, but unlike the others there was no adobe frame or wooden crossbeam. There was only a sooty smudge above the opening.

"What's in there?"

"You'll see." Pete moved forward, ducked low, and walked crouching through the doorway.

Devon followed.

The chamber was small and dark, smelling of dust, dirt, and something faintly unpleasant. The air inside felt warm and stale, and he thought that whatever Pete wanted to show him had better be pretty damn spectacular because he was about to turn around and walk out of here. Or *crouch* out of here.

Pete's flashlight played across a freestanding boulder in the center of the room that was covered with symbolic etchings. Around the foot of the boulder were several jars of clay and some broken pots. As the flashlight moved down, Devon saw that broken pottery shards littered the stone floor of the chamber.

Pete squatted down. "Check *this* out." He sorted through a small pile of pottery, picked up a piece and handed it to him.

Devon gave it a cursory glance, tossed it back on the floor. "Yeah."

"No. *Look* at it." Pete picked the shard up again and pressed it into Devon's palm, shining his light on the item.

Devon looked down at the irregularly shaped object. There was some sort of painting on the dusty clay, and he squinted, finally grabbing Pete's flashlight and training it on the shard for a better look.

It was him and Pete.

Devon felt chilled, cold despite the warm stuffy air.

The figures on the ancient pottery were crude silhouettes, but there was no mistaking whom they represented. The figure on the right had spiky hair like he did and appeared to be wearing a bulky motorcycle jacket. The other shape was smaller and skinnier with bozo hair that flared out on the sides like Pete's. His first thought was that this was some sort of joke, that Pete himself had come out here earlier, painted pictures of the two of them on the pottery and had lured him to the site to show him. Which was just about the faggiest thing he'd ever heard.

But he knew even before he saw the other boy's face that Pete had nothing to do with what was in this room.

Devon had the sudden urge to bolt.

Pete took the flashlight back. "Weird, huh? And there's new things every time. I came here twice before, and the first time I found what looked like my dog on a jar. I couldn't find it again the next time. But I found a broken piece with, like, a picture of my mom. I left it against that wall. I wanted to see if it would still be here or if it would have something different on it." He walked over to the right side of the room, shining his flashlight around.

"Gone!" he announced.

Devon's chill intensified. He was no pansy, but this place was damn creepy. He didn't like the fact that they were all alone, that there were no rangers or workers or anyone else anywhere near these ruins. No one could hear them out here. No one could save them.

He tried to make his voice sound bored. "Hey," he said, "let's hit the road."

"Not yet."

Devon watched the flashlight beam play across the broken pottery in front of him as Pete returned. This wasn't just weird lights or spooky noises or shit like that, stuff off in the distance that would happen whether they were around to experience it or not. This was *personal*. It was aimed specifically at them, and that's what scared him the most. Whatever was doing this had known they were coming.

He picked up what looked like part of an old water jug. Etched on the side was a picture barely visible in the diffused illumination of the oncoming flashlight: his parents. He dropped the jug, and was gratified to hear the pottery break.

"Hey!" Pete called out, and this time there was anger in his voice. "What are you doing? You can't break these pieces. They're priceless."

"Fuck 'em," Devon said.

He was hoping Pete would suggest that they leave now, not wanting him to destroy any more precious artifacts, but the boy had not finished showing him everything he'd discovered.

"Now for the *real* treasure," Pete said. "If you thought that other stuff was cool, this is going to blow you away." He shined his flashlight into the far corner.

Onto a skeleton.

Devon nearly shit his pants. He backed up a step, involuntarily. He wanted out of here. He wasn't a nature boy. He was a city kid. This wasn't his turf, and not only did he feel lost, out of his element, but for the first time since he was small, he felt scared, really and truly scared. Not the way he had when he'd been arrested, not the way he had when those two skinheads had cornered him on the playground, but the kind of scared you got when you were six and you knew that the monster was going to jump out of your closet and kill you.

He stared at the figure slumped against the wall. It

wasn't the skeleton of anything he'd ever seen. It wasn't animal and it didn't look quite human, but it did have two arms and two legs, although the bones were short, oddly segmented and uncommonly wide. The freaky thing was that the skull still had hair, a wild mane like a 'fro. The huge hair seemed to give expression to the noseless face, an angry expression that lent a cruel malevolence to the slightly upturned toothless mouth.

"Cool, huh?"

Devon grabbed the flashlight.

"Hey!" Pete said.

"Just shut the fuck up for once."

Devon focused the beam away from the skeleton, on the ground, trying to ignore the goose bumps surfing down his arms and legs.

"What *is* it?" he asked, and his voice came out more hushed than intended.

Pete did not respond.

"Hey, I'm talking to you."

There was no answer, no sound.

Devon shone the beam around, but it lit only the boulder in the center of the room. And the broken pottery surrounding it.

Pete could not have left. Devon was near the doorway and would have felt or at least heard him pass by. There was no other entrance or exit, so it was impossible for him to have departed through another opening.

So . . . what?

He'd just disappeared?

Devon avoided shining the light on the skeleton until he checked everywhere else in the chamber that Pete could be. Quickly, reluctantly, he pointed the beam at the corner. No Pete. There were only the malformed bones, the wild hair.

He ran outside. He ducked to get through the door and sped through the other rooms on instinct more than memory, but finally he emerged from the ruins. The sun had sunk lower and had grown a little more orange, but there was still plenty of light. Dusk was at least an hour or so away.

He stopped crouching, stood at full height. "Pete!" he yelled at the top of his lungs.

The cry echoed down the canyon, bouncing back at him from the ancient adobe facades, but there was no call in response, no answer.

"Pete!" he yelled again.

He looked back at the small door through which he'd exited. The undersize rectangle was now completely black, the rooms inside bathed in the darkness of the coming night.

He got out of there fast. He hauled ass up the rope ladder, ran up the small section of trail, hopped on his bike, and sped back toward the visitor's center and the YCC cabins. Briefly—very briefly—he considered telling someone, reporting what had happened to Shumway or one of the rangers or someone in the visitor's center, but he knew that was out of the question. Besides, he was determined not to spend one more minute in this godforsaken wilderness. Court order or no court order, there was no way in hell he was going to stay here, not after that.

He went to his cabin, gathered up his belongings and took off.

He headed home.

The thought occurred to him that he might be blamed for Pete's disappearance. Someone may have seen them leave together, or Pete might have told a friend about his plans. He knew that the truth would sound ludicrous, and he began trying to think up a more plausible scenario should someone try to question him. He'd worked out a pretty good explanation by the time he pulled into his parents' driveway. He'd even come up with a legitimate-sounding excuse for his parents, to explain why he'd broken his sentencing agreement and bailed on the YCC.

The lights in the house were off, and though he didn't have a watch, Devon knew it had to be after midnight. The national park was a good six hours from home even cruising at top speed—which he hadn't been doing because he hadn't wanted to be pulled over by any cops.

He was glad his parents were in bed. If all went well and he was able to sneak into the house unseen and unheard, he'd at least get a good night's sleep before having to confront them in the morning.

Although he wasn't really sure how good a night's sleep he'd get.

He thought of the ruins, the chamber.

Shivering, he hurried up the walk, found the key under the mat, and quickly opened the door, anxious to get inside.

He locked the door behind him, acutely conscious of the sound the lock made as it clicked into place. The house was silent; even his parents' television was off, and he was careful to make no noise as he tiptoed down the hall to his bedroom. He slipped off his boots and crawled into bed fully dressed, falling asleep seconds after closing his eyes.

He awoke once and found that he'd twisted and tossed in his sleep. His blanket was tangled up by his feet and he was lying on his side, facing the window. Outside, backlit by a streetlight, he thought he saw a shadow on the slatted blinds.

A short squat creature with a wild mane like a 'fro.

No, he thought, he was imagining it. Or he was dreaming. Whatever it was, it wasn't real, it wasn't happening.

He quickly straightened the covers and pulled them over his head, making sure his feet and hands were tucked in, the way he had as a child, and he closed his eyes and forced himself to fall asleep.

He awoke in the chamber.

The smell woke him up, the odor of dust and dirt and that other thing, that unpleasant thing. The smell was stronger than it had been before, and he opened his eyes to see a piece of broken pottery next to his face, a jagged shard depicting a kid who looked a hell of a lot like Pete being impaled on an oversize stake.

There was hard ground beneath him, and he sat up instantly, head and heart pounding. His mouth tasted like dirt.

Pete's flashlight lay on the floor to his left, its dying yellow beam spread out and illuminating the right half of the room, the boulder, and the broken pots. Devon didn't know where the flashlight had come from, but he was pretty sure he'd taken it with him when he fled. In fact, he knew he had. It had been in his hand when he'd climbed up the rope ladder to the motorcycle.

That didn't matter, though. It was here now and so was he, and he reached for the object and trained its weak beam on the far corner.

The skeleton was gone.

A quick sweep around the chamber showed him that it was not anywhere within these four walls. He hoped to Christ that it was not waiting for him in one of the other rooms as he ducked through the small doorway and ran out of the adobe building as fast as he could.

He was barefoot, and the dirt beneath his feet felt cold and rough. The air was cold, too, but he was sweating, filled with terror.

He ran through the last doorway into the open and kept running. There was no moon, and his eyes were not able to adjust to the lightless dark that enveloped the canyon. The flashlight was useless, and he dropped it in frustration, thinking only after he heard it hit the ground that he should have saved it. He could have used it as a weapon.

Against what?

He ran faster.

He had no idea where the rope ladder was, and he was thinking that he should stop and try to get his bearings when he ran into a tree. Hard. He hit his head and fell backward onto the ground, landing flat on his ass.

He thought he was there for only a second, thought he'd simply closed his eyes and shook his head to clear it.

But he was back in the chamber, Pete's dying flashlight on the littered floor next to him.

This time he was not alone. His parents were standing on the left side of the boulder, staring unblinkingly at the opposite wall. Both were holding broken jars of clay on which were depicted scenes he did not want to see.

Were his mom and dad dead? He didn't know, but despite the wrenching in his gut he was afraid to check, afraid to find out.

He grabbed the flashlight, swung it around. The far corner was empty, but there were bones piled in the doorway, oddly shaped bones that looked neither human nor animal.

It came to him then. He finally recognized the smell,

that *other* smell, the horrible smell. It was the odor of fresh blood. He recalled how the trunk of the stolen car had smelled like this after they'd killed the retarded kid's dog, after Kirk had cut the animal in front of the boy and they'd stuffed its body in the trunk.

That was the smell.

Blood.

He didn't know why he hadn't recognized it before.

There was a percussive clattering as the bones in the doorway shifted, moved of their own accord.

Elsewhere in the room the sound was echoed as shards of pottery stirred, slipping against each other.

He looked wildly about, trying to figure out a way to escape. There was only the one door, but even in the dying light he could tell that more bones were in the entryway than there had been before. There was no way he'd be able to make it through.

He was going to die in here, he realized.

Why was this happening? Had he and that dweeb Pete disturbed what was supposed to remain untouched and were they being punished for it? Or was he being punished for his part in harassing the retarded kid and killing his dog? He'd never been religious, never been a believer, but maybe there *was* a God, some sort of cosmic judge who had decided to mete out divine retribution.

No, he thought. Even if God existed, He wasn't working out of the back room of an old Indian ruin.

This was something else. Something he did not—*could* not—understand.

The bones in the doorway shifted again, rearranging themselves into a shape he recognized, but did not want to acknowledge. He thought he heard a sigh, a word, whispered.

His name.

Instinctively, he ran to the center of the room where his parents stood next to the boulder.

"Mom!" he cried. "Dad!"

He reached for his father, who fell over backward, shattering on the ground as though he were made out of clay. The pieces of his body landed indistinguishably among the other shards on the floor.

Devon grabbed his mother's hand, but felt only a strange dry coolness, like leather that had just been taken out of a refrigerator. He was sobbing, and he whirled around, screaming to the room and anything in it: "I'm sorry!" He didn't know what he was apologizing for, but he *was* sorry, sorry for everything he'd ever done, ever said, ever thought, even though he knew that made no difference here, had nothing to do with this.

The weak yellow beam of the flashlight flickered once, then started fading.

"Help!" he screamed at the top of his lungs. "Help!"

He looked wildly around the chamber, and the last thing he saw before the flashlight died completely was that his mom had a 'fro.

Nine

1

Glen awoke before Melanie, and he rolled carefully onto his side to watch her while she slept. She dozed soundly, none of the chaos and horror of the past few days visible in the smooth lines of her face. Her brow remained unfurrowed, her eyes gently closed, her full lips parted as she snored lightly. The sun had not yet risen, but it was growing light outside, and he could clearly see the details of her soft attractive features, features that he had come to know intimately over the past few days.

Amidst all the things that were happening, he thought, one of the oddest was this. Them. This island of calm in the storm. Their budding relationship.

Budding relationship.

It sounded so corny, He'd never been one to think of life in Hallmark terms, and he felt embarrassed now to be so overly focused on and enthusiastic about his first real relationship in . . . what? Ten years? Fifteen?

He thought of Kim Mangram, his girlfriend in college, and he remembered the first time they'd had sex in his dorm room rather than in the car. She'd peed in the shower in front of him, and afterward they'd performed sixty-nine, using their mouths on each other, tasting each other's juices. "There are people who've been married for fifty years who aren't as close as we are," she'd said. It was a naïve and embarrassing overstatement, a cliché no doubt repeated and believed by every lover on the planet, and though he'd bought it at the time, he'd figured out over the years that such self-important declarations were generic and typical, the type of pronouncements ordinary people used to make them feel unique and special.

But he felt that way again with Melanie. The sexual acts they'd performed were no different than those performed by every other couple, the confidences they'd shared no more intimate or revealing, but it *felt* like they were. The two of them seemed closer than any other couple on earth at this moment, and it was a glorious feeling to have, an endorphin rush that made him feel awake, alive, and irrationally happy.

Melanie opened her eyes, surprised to find him watching her, but not made uncomfortable by it. She smiled sleepily and moved her head up to kiss him. They both had bad breath—"morning breath" the commercials called it—but neither of them cared or felt self-conscious, and again he wondered at the magic that had brought them together.

Magic?

Jesus, he *was* a walking Hallmark card.

Melanie stretched, sat up. "Busy day," she said.

Glen nodded. Ron would be out today, according to Zack Een, the lawyer they'd found to represent him. Glen thought "Zack Een" sounded like the moniker of a Martian, and the man himself seemed to fit his name perfectly, but Melanie had asked around and according to the teachers at her school who'd had previous need of legal assistance, Een was the best in town. Ron was paying the lawyer with credit cards, although Glen had had to pay the bail bondsman.

The police were looking into the disappearance of Ricky's parents (Jerod's had shown up and were fine) as well as the disappearance of Al and Buck and Randy and Judi. The cops were treating them like ordinary missing persons, going through the traditional investigational steps. But Glen had the feeling that they suspected something, that though they refused to admit it and were unwilling to act on it, they knew these were not run-of-the-mill cases with ultimately human explanations. It was a vibe he got from them, his reading of the covert glances the cops shared, the odd silences with which they greeted certain inquiries.

And it was not just the police. Everyone in town seemed weird and secretive, tuned into a hidden agenda that seemed to involve him and Melanie, but about which they were being purposefully kept in the dark. The hostility he'd felt before, which had been simmering beneath the surface, was now out in the open. In their absence, something had hardened the town's attitude against the excavation and everyone associated with it. When he'd gotten gas yesterday at the Circle K, an old woman on the opposite side of the pump had frowned at him. "Why don't you go back where you came from?" she said. Inside the convenience store, the clerk, a middle-aged man wearing a too-hip hat, had practically thrown his change at him, scowling. Later, at the drugstore, dropping off their film for developing, a group of young toughs had followed them up and down the aisles, pointing and laughing and making rude comments. When they walked back outside, they discovered that someone had thrown eggs at the windshield of his car.

Glen pushed away the covers and rolled out of bed, picking his underwear off the floor. "I'm going to take a shower," he said. "Want to join me?"

Melanie had showered last night, and she shook her head, sitting up in bed. "I'll make breakfast. Is French toast okay?"

"Fine," he said. He had only asked out of obligation and was actually relieved they wouldn't be showering together. He wasn't in a sexy mood and was glad he wouldn't have to pretend.

Ah, middle age.

He padded off to the bathroom.

By the time he finished showering, shaving, combing his hair, and dressing, Melanie had coffee and French toast ready, and they ate together at a table on her back porch, looking out at her well-tended yard. Several small brownish birds flitted from tree to tree, occasionally dipping into the birdbath on the lawn and shaking their wings in the water.

"Robins?" he asked.

Melanie smiled. "Sparrows."

"Oh," he said, embarrassed.

She laughed.

"I'm a city boy," he said in his own defense.

"I noticed."

The two of them sat in the sunlight, enjoying their breakfast, pretending for a brief while that all was right with the world.

The truth was that he didn't know what came next. Melanie had left a message with the office of the anthropology department at ASU, explaining about the dig, the disappearances, and Ron, but no one had yet called back. The two of them certainly weren't going to continue with the excavation alone, and he was not sure what Ron planned to do once released. Everything was on hold for the moment, and that was frustrating.

"I think we should call Pace," Glen said. "Let him know what's happening."

"You're right." Melanie nodded. "Why don't you do it?"

After breakfast, he did try to call Pace, but a female ranger who identified herself as Matea said that Pace had taken a four-day leave of absence and would not be back for three more days. He hadn't left a forwarding number and she had no idea how to get ahold of him. "He's probably out in the field somewhere," she suggested. "That's what he usually does when he takes time off."

"What do you think he's doing?" Melanie asked when Glen told her. "Looking for the skull?"

"I don't know," he said, but the image in his mind was of the bearded professor sitting alone in that adobe ruin, in the narrow dark room with the painting of that horrible creature, performing some type of ancient rite, while outside the weather shifted from rain to sun to wind to hail.

"I don't like it," Melanie said.

He looked at her. "I don't either."

He thought again of the painting of that creature. God or devil, Pace had said. Whatever it was, it had been nearly identical to the figure in those church paintings. He recalled the final panel in the second triptych, where he and a boy had been holding lengths of rope, facing the hairy-maned figure, while on the wall behind the creature was a stone wheel covered with carved symbols.

The figure was obviously at the center of all that was happening. But what was his connection to it? Was it because he had found the skull? And was that even an accident? Was it random chance . . . or had he been meant to dig it up? Had the whole thing been preordained?

The paintings in the church would indicate so.

Melanie walked back to the bedroom. "I want to stop by my parents' before we go to the police station," she called out.

"No problem," Glen said. He followed her down the hall, stood awkwardly in the doorway while she made the bed.

"Just a quick stop by. My father says everything's okay, but I want to see them, make sure nothing's wrong. Just in case."

According to Een, Ron was scheduled to be released at ten, and they pulled into the driveway of Melanie's parents' house by nine-thirty. "Just a quick visit," she promised. "Then we're out of here."

"It's okay. Don't worry about it."

"It's for my sake, not yours," she told him.

He'd only met Melanie's parents once, but that was just last week, and they both seemed to have aged a decade in that time. Her mother, Margaret, a small, chipper, rather outgoing woman, now looked dour and bedraggled.

"Come in, come in," Margaret insisted when she answered the door and saw who it was.

"We just stopped by to say hi," Melanie said. "We were in the neighborhood, so . . ."

"Well, you'd better come in and see your father."

"Why? He's okay, isn't he? There's nothing wrong?"

"What are you talking about?" Her mother frowned. "Are *you* okay?"

Melanie stole a glance at Glen. "I'm fine. I'm fine."

George was seated on a recliner in the living room, watching a basketball game. He nodded at them as they walked into the room, but offered no greeting. A careworn man to begin with, he seemed downright haggard.

Melanie sat down on the couch. "We're going to the police station after this."

Her father scowled. "To get that pornographer out?"

"Yes. To get that pornographer out." She sighed heavily. "Look, Daddy, we don't really have anything to do with that. We're just doing what Al would do if he were here. Mostly we're going because we want to find out if the police have discovered anything. They were supposed to go through Al's room over at the TeePee. Maybe they found something in his effects . . ." She trailed off, not bothering to finish.

"Someone else is missing," Margaret said, her voice small. "Besides your people and that boy's parents."

"Who?"

"Jack Connor. He went fishing out to the lake." She licked her lips. "He never came back. His truck's still there, and his fishing stuff, but he just disappeared." She cleared her throat. "People are starting to talk."

"Starting to talk?"

Her father stood, pointed. "About you."

Melanie looked incredulous. "Me?"

"You all with your excavation! You caused it!"

"What?"

"The past should remain buried! You don't dig it up!"

What the hell was that supposed to mean? Glen looked at Melanie. She seemed to be just as surprised and confused as he was.

The past should remain buried.

He thought about Melanie's great-grandfather. The murderer.

The old man seemed genuinely angry, and he remained standing, practically shaking, glaring at them. "This all started when you dug up those ruins, started taking things out of the ground that should've been left there forever. What do you expect?"

Glen stepped in. "I don't expect people to start disappearing because some bones and pottery were excavated by archeology students."

Margaret pulled her husband toward the kitchen. "Excuse us," she said in a sugary voice tinged with steel.

"Do you think they know what's behind all this?" Glen asked when they left the room. "It sure seems like your dad's afraid of something being found out, something he knows about but we don't."

Melanie shook her head, obviously at a loss. She looked baffled. "I don't know. I've never . . . This doesn't make any sense to me. You're right. It's like some bad secret-in-a-small-town movie. I can understand some superstitious yokels acting this way. But my father?"

"We're not superstitious yokels," Glen pointed out. "And we've been thinking along the same lines."

"I guess so," she admitted. "It's just . . . it's my *daddy*."

Melanie's parents returned, a strained smile on the face of her mother, a blank, noncommittal expression on her father's.

"Sorry," George said gruffly. "I guess we're all on edge here."

Glen hoped Melanie was going to quiz him, confront him, but it was her call, her family, and he'd follow her lead.

"What should've been left in the ground forever?" she asked, and he was proud of her for standing up to her father, impressed by her bravery.

George stared at her, not answering.

"You said—"

"I know what I said."

"Daddy, our friends are missing, that boy Ricky's parents are missing, and now I guess Jack Connor's missing, too. If you know anything or can help find them, you need to speak up. Tell us, tell the police, tell somebody."

"I don't know anything. I just know that certain things ought to be left well enough alone."

"I think what Melanie's asking," Glen said, "is how you know *which* things ought to be left well enough alone." He turned toward Margaret. "You said 'people are starting to talk.' Talk about what? Is there something we should know?"

Melanie's mother stood there with a plastic Nancy Reagan smile on her face. Her father pointed. "I don't know you, and I don't want to talk to you," he said. "Stay out of my affairs."

"Then talk to me, Daddy."

"There's nothing to talk about."

"Obviously there is."

"It's just obvious that your friends were digging up that Indian ruin and disappeared. The paper said that this boy's parents, that it was their yard that had that tomb. Jack Connor was probably involved in digging stuff up, too."

"What about that pottery shard you found?"

"I don't want to talk about it."

"Did you notice that it had a picture of our house on it? This house?"

"I don't want to talk about it!"

He had noticed, Glen thought.

"Something's going on here."

"That's what I said!"

Margaret was still wearing that plastic smile. She put a hand on her daughter's shoulder. "Maybe you'd better go," she told Melanie. "You know how your father gets—"

"How do I get?"

Margaret pretended he wasn't there. "Wait until he cools off. Try again later."

"We have to go anyway," Glen said. "We're due at the police station at ten."

Melanie was shaking her head. "I want to—"

"I'm not talking!" George said.

"Come on," Glen prodded. "We can come back afterward."

"I have nothing to say to *you*!"

"Who, Daddy? Me?"

"No. Him. He's the one who got you into this in the first place, who got us all into this."

Melanie was about to argue, and a part of Glen wanted to argue, too, but he pulled her toward the door, and she allowed herself to be led.

"What was that all about?" Glen asked when they were in the car and rolling.

"I have no idea." Melanie looked in the side mirror back at her parents' street. "But I don't like it."

Zack Een was waiting for them at the police station. Tall and geeky, wearing black pants and white shirt, no tie, he sat on a bench in the lobby, not reading, not talking on the phone, not writing, simply staring into space with a preternatural stillness that Glen found unnerving. All of the paperwork was completed, and all that was needed was Glen's signature on two forms, since he was the man who had fronted the money for the bond.

Glen signed where he was told. Een accompanied a uniformed officer through the security door toward the cells, and several minutes later, Ron emerged, still removing his keys and change from a sealed plastic bag.

"Thanks," he told Glen, walking over. "I owe you one."

Glen nodded, gave him a semi-smile, not sure how to respond.

"So where am I going to live?" Ron asked. "Can I go back to my motel room?"

"I guess so," Melanie said. "The university rented those rooms for the summer."

"Your computer equipment has been confiscated," Een reminded him. "For your sake, don't buy, borrow, or try to replace any of it. If we win, and I think we will since you do have signed releases, you'll get it all back. But for now, for appearance's sake, just stay away from computers for a while."

"What about my photo equipment? Has that been taken, too?"

"Yes, and any undeveloped film in your cameras is being developed."

"But I need that to document the site."

"Again, stay away from it for now."

"There's nothing to document at the moment," Melanie told him.

A strange look came over his face. "Oh, yeah."

"I'm through here," Een said. He addressed Ron. "Be in my office by ten tomorrow morning. We have a lot to get through before trial. Judge Okerlund's impressed by volume of documentation, so we'd better start generating some. Our case is good, and if we can just tailor our presentation to the judge's idiosyncrasies, I think you'll be free and clear."

"What about our countersuit?"

"We'll discuss that in my office," Een said quickly. "Ten o'clock. Tomorrow."

Ron waved as the lawyer started for the door. "See you then. Thanks."

"Countersuit?" Glen said.

"I'm not allowed to talk about it."

Glen looked at the bald and heavily tattooed student, and he wanted to say *I paid your bail, asshole. You're allowed to tell me anything I want to know.* But instead, he let it slide and walked up to the sergeant at the desk to ask about the status of the disappearances.

The detective in charge of the case was named Dyer. Short and stocky, with a thin mustache and perpetual air of busyness, he was in his office, sorting through a fat pile of very thin folders when the sergeant knocked on his doorframe. "Visitors, Chuck."

"Thanks."

The three of them entered the office.

Dyer frowned at Ron, then turned his attention to Glen and Melanie. "What can I do for you folks?"

"We're here about the disappearances at the—"

"Oh, yeah! I recognize you now. Did you remember something else?"

"No," Melanie said. "We were wondering if *you* had any information for *us*."

"Well, we've gone through Dr. Wittinghill's vehicle and hotel room, sorted through his belongings, and have found some interesting items, though not like the stuff we found in *his* room," he said, nodding toward Ron.

Ron snorted.

Melanie shot him a look of warning.

"There are no real leads, nothing that indicates what happened to Dr. Wittinghill or your other colleagues, but we did find a fax you might be interested in seeing. It arrived day before yesterday from a Professor McCormack at ASU, although there's no indication that Dr. Wittinghill ever saw it—which is why we're tentatively assuming that Wednesday was the day of the disappearances." Detective Dyer sorted through the files on his desk and finally pulled out a single sheet of paper from the bottom. "We contacted the professor and interviewed him over the phone. While he wasn't able to shed any light on the disappearances, he did reiterate what he says in here, that he'd like someone from your team to look at some new discovery at an Indian ruin in Phoenix. He wouldn't go into detail, but he sounded pretty excited about it. Maybe you should give him a call."

Glen read the fax, handed it to Melanie. "Do you have his number?"

"It's on there. Oh, wait a minute, that's his fax number." Dyer quickly rummaged through a messy stack of notepads and scraps of paper next to the file folders. He found what he was looking for, wrote down the number, and handed it to Glen. "Here."

"Thanks."

McCormack had left a message on Melanie's answering machine when they returned home, saying essentially the same thing that he'd told the detective and said in his fax to Al. He'd left two numbers—his office and his pager—and when Melanie called the office number, he was in.

Glen walked out to the kitchen to get himself some ice water, and when he came back into the living room, Melanie was just hanging up the phone, a strange look on her face.

Already his pulse was accelerating. "What is it?"

She shook her head. "He wouldn't say. Said there was something new they'd found at Pima House Ruins in Scottsdale and he wanted Al to look at it. But that since Al was gone, he wanted us to see it." She looked up at him. "He said it was urgent."

"Urgent?"

Melanie nodded.

"What the hell does that mean?"

"I don't know. But he sounded scared."

2

He wasn't prepared for this.

For the second night in a row, Vince slept in the museum, unrolling his sleeping bag on the floor next to the desk and leaving the office light on. The Springerville police had promised that a patrol car would circle the block every two hours or so, but even if that were true—and he had his doubts—such a cursory cruise would not necessarily deter or frighten away a person intent on doing damage.

Two nights ago, someone had broken in and stolen some of their most valuable pieces: an intact urn, two clay pitchers, a beaded necklace. The weird thing was that no windows had been broken, no locks had been jimmied. Whoever did this had somehow opened the bolted door, then shut it and locked it again.

Which was impossible.

If the archeological society had more money, they could install security cameras or hire a night watchman. But they didn't, and so Vince was volunteering to stake the place out and guard the museum.

He wasn't a big man, wasn't much of a fighter, and didn't believe in guns. He was here more as a deterrent than anything else, and if an armed robber came in, he wouldn't be able to do much with his little pocket knife other than make empty threats.

But it wasn't armed intruders he was worried about, was it?

No.

He'd learned *that* last night, when he was awakened shortly after two by an eerie clicking that seemed to come from one of the exhibits near the east wall. He could see from the dim shapes in the semidarkness that there was no one else in the museum besides himself, and he tried to think of an insect or rodent or mechanical object that could be making such a noise, but could not. The image in his mind, for some reason, was of the diorama, and he thought of those painted plaster figures moving about inside the glass case, gathering minuscule objects from the mock-up landscape and taking them into the pueblo model.

The idea frightened him. It was absurd. Still, he squinted into the gloom, trying to make out details within the diorama case, needing to know, but childishly afraid to leave the safety of his sleeping bag.

Click-Clickclick-Clickclickclick-Click.

What was making that noise?

He did not know, but he was afraid to find out. He spent the rest of the night ignoring the sound, trying in vain to sleep, hoping that he wouldn't hear the tinkle of breaking glass and the clatter of tiny plaster feet running across the tiled floor.

He'd found nothing out of place in the morning, everything undisturbed, and he'd tried all day to figure out what could have caused that noise, even going so far as to move the two cases that were flush against the wall.

He'd half convinced himself that he'd imagined it, but when it was time to hit the hay again, he'd left the light on in the office and moved his sleeping bag from the open area by the west wall to the space next to the desk, next to the phone.

Now the light was off.

And the clicking noise was back.

He had no idea when or how it had happened. All he knew was that he had fallen asleep with the light on and now there was only darkness.

Clickclick-Clickclickclick.

He wasn't prepared for this.

Quietly, Vince unzipped the side of his sleeping bag. He crawled out and stood up. The clicking noise was all around the room now, not just by the east wall. Last night's image of animated plaster figures was replaced by one of huge oversize bugs, science fiction beetles with pincers and impossible-to-penetrate shells. He looked around fearfully, his gaze moving slowly about the room in a clockwise direction, focusing on each object in order to make sure it belonged here.

The clicking stopped.

He turned around, thinking he'd heard a muffled thump behind him.

And saw it.

A shadow was moving on the wall above the cash register, an oddly shaped shadow with a human form and unruly hair and the herky-jerky movements of an old silent film. It seemed to have no source, no real object to which it corresponded. Only a combination of the streetlight across the highway and an overbright full moon allowed him to discern its presence at all.

The shadow paused, and though he could not make out any visible features on the flat black head, he had the distinct impression that it had stopped to watch him, that it was staring at him.

Then it was moving again in that old-time-movie manner, across the wall, over the map of Arizona, over an exhibit case, around the corner, over the front window. The shadow bled through the glass of the door—was inside, and then, a second later, was outside. It hovered for a moment in the air, backlit by the streetlight . . . then faded into nothing.

All around him exploded a sudden riot of movement as the doors to exhibit cases flew open, as glass shattered, as books fell from shelves. Vince scrambled behind the desk and reached for the light switch. He expected the lights to remain off, assumed the power was cut, and was already planning to grab the flashlight he'd stashed in his backpack, but the overhead fluorescents flickered on, bathing the room in harsh white light.

The artifacts were going crazy. Bowls and pots were rocking back and forth on their own accord. Arrowheads were spinning wildly on shelves. Necklaces were inching across tabletops like earthworms. Metates and their manos were chattering insanely on the floor. He'd assumed that the disappearance of that strange shadow had caused some sort of psychic power surge, setting everything in motion, but these things continued to move on their own, imbued with life, with purpose, not merely shaken by an outside force.

He'd heard rumors of this phenomenon the past few weeks, accounts of ambulatory artifacts—moving masks, walking dolls, pottery shards that rearranged themselves when no one was looking—so he was not the only one to experience this. An epidemic of animate relics was spreading throughout the Southwest.

But that didn't make it any less frightening.

All at once, he saw a broken spear flying at his head and he ducked. It clattered harmlessly against the wall behind him.

Amidst all the commotion, Vince saw two large carvings making a beeline for the door: totemic figures from the late Anasazi period. Unlike the other artifacts, which seemed content to move about the small museum, these two seemed bent on escape. It occurred to him that all of the accompanying sound and fury was meant to be a distraction, to keep his attention off the stone idols.

Glass shattered loudly as first one, then the other smashed through the front door and moved onto the sidewalk outside. He did not know what form of locomotion propelled the figures. They were each carved from a single piece of basalt and had no real legs, only the suggestion of legs on a tapered bottom of chiseled stone. Yet they sped quickly forward, not wobbling or lurching, but advancing smoothly, as if on wheels or rollers.

Behind them, a straw basket rolled over the lip of the door, followed by a waddling metate and a host of pottery shards.

He thought of calling the police, of calling Dana Peters, president of the archaeological society, but those artifacts were *moving*. Instead, Vince quickly grabbed the digital camcorder he'd placed in the side pocket of his backpack for easy access and hurried outside, stepping over flapping sandals and chittering strings of carved shells through the hole in the door, careful not to cut himself on the jagged glass.

It was a different world on the street. He'd lived in Springerville for the past nine months, since landing this internship, and something had changed tonight; there was an undefineable sense that things were not as they should be. The town seemed empty, abandoned, and as the contents of the museum moved onto the street, a horde of antiquities crossing the highway, they encountered no one else. Someone was *always* on the road, heading to or from New Mexico, and this absence of human activity was eerie.

Vince stayed a safe distance behind, taping. He hazarded a glance between the commercial buildings to the houses beyond, glad to see porch lights and the flickering of televisions, but hoping for a glimpse of an honest-to-God person. He knew he was being paranoid, but he wanted to know that everyone in town had not vanished into thin air.

Paranoid? Who was he kidding? He was chasing Anasazi relics down a highway in the middle of the night after they'd broken out of a museum. It was a *very* short leap to the mass disappearance of a townful of people.

From behind the chain-link fence of the junkyard, he saw the glowing eyes of Cliff Rogan's black Labrador staring at him, oddly luminescent in the moonlight. Ordinarily, the guard dog went into a jumping, barking frenzy if so much as a breeze disturbed the air. But now the animal was silent, unmoving.

Vince increased his speed, moving a little closer to the artifacts in order to get away from the dog.

Still no movement, still no sound.

The basalt figures veered left, off the highway, down a small dirt road. As the rest of the relics followed, he suddenly knew where they were going.

The ruins.

Or *back* to the ruins. For they had been excavated from Huntington Mesa, had been there for most of the past millennium. Now, apparently, they wanted to go home.

The road ended abruptly, but the artifacts continued onward, into the desert, toward the mesa. They obviously had no intention of taking the roundabout Jeep trail up to the pueblo. They were heading straight to the site.

They had *intention*?

Everything about this was horribly, crazily wrong.

Vince walked several paces past the end of the road, still taping, then stopped, shutting off his camera. There was no way he was going up to the ruins. Those kivas were creepy at the best of times, and the thought of being there alone at night, while those two statues and their followers moved through the ancient rooms, chilled him to the bone. He'd done enough, he'd done more than enough, and in the morning he would download what he'd filmed and turn it in to the archeological society, the police, the sheriff's office, and whoever else wanted to see it.

There was movement off to his right, and he jumped, heart lurching in his chest. An old Indian man was sitting on a rock, watching the scene. Like a living racist stereotype, he was wrapped in a Navajo blanket and held in one hand a bottle of whiskey. He did not seem scared, did not seem surprised, but was simply watching calmly as though this sort of thing happened every day.

Vince was about to ask the old man *why* he wasn't

shocked by the animation of these objects when the Indian pointed toward the top of the low mesa. "They come."

A chill passed through him. There were indeed figures on the mesa, strangely shaped forms with horns and hair and lumpy bodies illuminated by moonlight. They were walking, not on the edge, but on what Vince knew was a footpath, heading west, away from the ruins.

"But who are they?" he asked, and for some reason he was whispering.

"The Others."

The Others. He didn't like that. It occurred to him that this old man was a ghost, an apparition sent to explain all this to him and tell him what he was supposed to do. But the smell of the whiskey was real—and strong—and the same intermittent night wind that ruffled his own hair sent stray strands of the old man's salt-and-pepper mane flying.

"Who are 'The Others'?" Vince asked.

The old man took a swig. "Don't know. Not exactly. Only know they ain't us."

"But you've seen something like this before? You know what's happening here?"

"Nope."

"What about—"

But the Indian was already wandering off, not toward the mesa, not back toward the road, but through the boulder-strewn ground toward the light of a far-off ranch house, moving with the exaggeratedly careful steps of the inebriated.

"I just—" Vince called after him.

The old man held up his hand for silence, and kept walking.

Vince turned back toward the mesa. The figures on top were gone, and the artifacts had disappeared into the darkness of the night. A gust of wind blew cold against his face. He looked down at the digital camera in his hand, took a deep breath to steady himself, then started toward town.

In the morning, he drove up the trail to the top of the mesa, not knowing what he would find, just wanting to see if there was anything unusual after last night's . . . incident.

He wasn't prepared for the sight that greeted him.

Men and women, dozens of them, were crouched down, digging in the dirt with hands or trowels or kitchen spoons, looking for . . . he didn't know what. But it was something specific, because they were setting aside rocks and broken glass and even some decent-looking shards of pottery. They were dressed in their Sunday best, and that inappropriate attire made him wary. He got out of the car and began walking, but they were ignoring him, pretending as though he wasn't there.

He headed toward the pueblo, staring at the dirt as he did so. He saw no evidence of any of the missing relics, but the hardpacked earth was scarred. At first he assumed the cause was the totemic figures, the metates and arrowheads and other relics, but he realized that none of those objects was heavy enough to create such scoring on solid ground. When he looked closer, he saw what looked like claw marks and giant footprints.

Could it have been The Others?

He didn't think so. Admittedly, he'd only seen them briefly and from very far away, but they'd been normal size. In the moonlight, his first impression was that they were monsters of some kind. But since then, he'd had time to analyze what he'd seen, and he'd come to the conclusion that they were not monsters but people: people outfitted in ragged primitive costumes. He had no idea if they were dressed that way to frighten onlookers or as part of some bizarre ritual, but there was no doubt in his mind that they were human. Stupidly, he hadn't filmed them, a fact he hadn't even realized until he'd walked home. It would be a long time before that sight was erased from his mind, though.

Two juniper trees on the west side of the pueblo were shredded, their trunks cracked lengthwise and bent away from each other as though pushed by giant hands. The ruins themselves appeared the same as they had yesterday morning, the last time he'd taken a tour through here.

The men and women were still focusing intently on their digging activities. No one was talking, not even whistling or humming. They scooped out spoonfuls and shovelfuls and handfuls of dirt, oblivious to everything else around them.

These weren't the people from last night. These were people from town. He didn't recognize any of them, wasn't even sure how he knew this was true, but he did.

He considered making his circuitous way around the ruins, examining the partially walled rooms of the eastern house and the largely extant building that made up the western complex, but he knew where he needed to go. If anything was to be found here, it would be in the pueblo's ceremonial chambers, the secret rooms where the original dwellers had conducted their rites of worship.

The kivas.

He'd been aware since he first started giving tours of the site that many visitors found the single kiva that was open to the public unsettling. Quite a few refused to go in, and oftentimes those who did came out subdued and shaken. He himself had always been a little creeped out by it, but he'd assumed that was because he knew the specifics of some of the rituals that had been performed there.

Now, though, he was acutely aware of not only the underground rooms' sordid past, but the *aura* and the *feeling* he got from them.

Vince walked past an elderly woman, in a pearl necklace and flower-print dress, kneeling down and scratching the ground with a kitchen spoon and steak knife. He reached the public kiva, stepped up to the raised circle and grasped the top of the ladder, peering down into the opening. The walls of the kiva were slick, wet, slimy, completely coated with some sort of shiny black substance. At the bottom lay a skeleton, a headless skeleton that looked bigger than that of a man and oddly misshapen, too big to fit through the top opening, but nowhere near big enough to have rent the juniper trees or made those huge clawed footprints in the earth.

Where had it come from? The excavation at Huntington Mesa was ongoing. The archeological society coordinated efforts between several community colleges from various parts of the state, and surely he would have heard if anyone had uncovered a skeleton. Particularly one like this.

And where was the skull?

He crouched down, poked his head through the opening, wanting to get a closer look but afraid to descend the ladder.

The positioning of the decapitated skeleton in the precise center of the ceremonial room seemed ritualistic. Around the bones, the artifacts from the museum, both the ones he'd seen last night and the missing pieces from two nights before, were arranged in deliberate order, forming a rough geometric shape. This is where they'd been going . . . the faithful worshipping their god.

That was exactly what it was like, particularly with the two carved figures perched to the left and right of where the skull should be.

He withdrew his head from the opening, standing quickly. To his surprise, the other men and women had abandoned their single-minded digging. They had dropped their tools and were making their way toward him.

Or toward the kiva.

He moved aside, off the raised circle of ground, backing toward one of the rent junipers. The people did not alter their course. He realized for the first time that there were no vehicles up here other than his own. Everyone else had walked the several miles from town.

In their dress clothes.

The first man passed him, silent, purposeful, and Vince watched as he firmly grasped the top of the ladder and walked down into the chamber. A young woman in a tight red skirt followed.

The people began lining up, the queue winding around a freestanding adobe wall and around an excavated fire pit. The first man emerged from the kiva with a metate, followed up the ladder by the young woman carrying a basket.

Two old women went down, one after the other.

They climbed up a moment later, bearing broken pieces of pottery.

Two other people went down.

Vince stood there until each of the men and women had obtained an artifact from the kiva and had started off down the dirt road, on the long trip back to town. He could have stopped any of them at any time—what they were taking was museum property—but he hadn't wanted to—

he'd been afraid to

—and he'd let them go, waiting to see what would happen. After the last man left, a tall skinny guy who Vince was pretty sure worked at McDonald's, he gathered up his courage, stepped onto the raised circle and looked down into the kiva. As he suspected, there was nothing remaining. The number of artifacts had corresponded exactly to the number of people. Only the headless skeleton remained: large, thick boned and looking decidedly threatening in the darkness of the chamber. The smooth black walls gleamed wetly.

He practically jumped off the raised section of ground, almost tripping over a rock as he did so.

Reaching his Jeep, he watched the last man retreat down the road. He could not shake the feeling that the artifacts had come to the kiva to be blessed—or cursed— by the unnatural skeleton. Now it was the job of the men and women to disseminate the relics throughout the land, to spread the gospel as it were, and as the man's body disappeared and then his head on the downward sloping road, Vince let out a deep and long-held breath.

3

Henry Abel stood at the edge of the plateau, above the fire-scarred finger canyon, looking south. The view was beautiful. The Four Corners power plants must be off-line, he thought. The sky was blue, the desert air clear, and for once not even a trace of haze obscured his view of Shiprock. He'd been working as a ranger here at Mesa Verde for twenty years, damn near half his life, and though he'd been offered a transfer several times, he had always turned them down. This place spoke to him—the land, the pueblos—and if he could live out the rest of his days in southern Colorado, he would die a happy man.

He finished his salami sandwich, folded up the wax

paper, and put it in his pocket. This was his favorite lunch spot, although he occasionally ate at other overlooks and even in the cafeteria during particularly wet weather. But he felt most at home here, standing atop the mesa that had once housed the Anasazi's biggest city, looking out over the flat high deserts of northern New Mexico and Arizona.

It was hot today, and the chaparral brush, the piñon pines, and juniper—or what were left of them after the fires—were alive with the festive sound of cicadas. Hordes of the little critters were chirruping for all they were worth, the staggered sounds of individual insects like an endless musical round. Why in God's name, he wondered, would people choose to live in the concrete canyons of New York or the tamed green suburbia of the East? He'd been born in Ware, Massachusetts, raised in Hartford, Connecticut, but he'd never felt truly alive until coming west, moving to Tucson after receiving a track scholarship to the University of Arizona. He'd been sleepwalking before that, existing rather than living, and after his first semester in the desert, after spending fall and summer exposed to the rough raw glory that was the Southwest, he knew he never wanted to leave.

He pulled a Snickers bar out of his front shirt pocket. As he ate it, he stared out at Shiprock.

And it flickered.

What the hell was that? Henry blinked. He focused on the jagged volcano core, wondering if it was a trick of the distance or a sign that his eyesight was deteriorating. For a second there, the massive geological formation had disappeared and *wavered*, like a scene on a television with bad rabbit ears.

Henry continud to peer at the rugged peak, but whatever it was did not happen again. Probably nothing, he told himself.

He looked at Shiprock one last time.

Then he turned away, walking over the crunching bodies of dead cicadas to his Jeep.

That evening, Henry was leading a ranger talk when the cars came. The snaking line of headlights on the road from Cortez was clearly visible from the small outdoor

amphitheater where he was discussing the behavioral
habits of local squirrels and birds and deer.

Something was wrong. The park closed at sunset, and
only those who were already within its boundaries, those
who were camping or staying in the cabins or the lodge,
were allowed on the roads. Yet literally dozens of vehicles were making their way up the mesa.

"We haven't seen any squirrels at all," a soft doughy
man wearing hip-hop shorts announced. "No deer,
either."

"And not many birds," an old woman chimed in.

Henry tried to focus on his discussion. "Since the fires,
wildlife within the park has had to adapt to the changed
environment. Many existing habitats burned and the animals were forced to migrate . . ."

He kept talking, but his eyes remained on the line of
vehicles. He was getting increasingly nervous as he
watched the slow inexorable approach of headlights. The
last vestiges of day had disappeared from the west in
the past few minutes, blue fading into deep purple to
match the rest of the sky, and the string of lights seemed
brighter, more ominous.

Ending his ranger talk early, Henry tried to hurry everyone out of the amphitheater. He didn't know why,
but he wanted them safely in their cabins or lodge rooms
or tents before the cars and trucks arrived. He wanted
to protect them. The people weren't cooperating,
though. Too many were staying in their seats, talking
familiarly to each other, looking up at the stars. Others
were approaching him, wanting to ask questions. He
tried to usher them out, tried not to let his anxiety show,
but that was becoming harder and harder as the line of
vehicles drew closer.

The first pickup stopped in front of the amphitheater.
It didn't pull into the adjacent visitor's center parking
lot, but halted in the middle of the road.

Behind the pickup, in a chain reaction, the other cars
and trucks stopped.

The people got out.

They were carrying weapons. Not revolvers or assault
rifles, but older, more primitive weapons. Spears, axes,
bats, sharpened rocks. The vehicles were still running,

headlights on, and as much as anything else, that tightened the knot in Henry's stomach and made him want to flee.

They approached. Both men and women. Some of them were naked, others dressed in raggedy castoff clothes. Quite a few wore regular everyday duds, but these people, too, seemed peculiar and threatening.

Some of them had bloody hands.

Now his audience started leaving: Mothers shielding the eyes of children, husbands hurrying wives back to their lodgings and looking fearfully over their shoulders as they made their hasty exits down dimly lighted paths.

But they were already too late.

The townspeople attacked—for they *were* townspeople; Henry didn't know how he knew that but he did—and they attacked with fury, swinging handheld hatchets, leaping upon shoulders with upraised rocks, shoving spears through chests. They screamed unintelligibly, cries of rage that blended with cries of terror from the desperately retreating visitors. Within seconds, blood was streaming down the fitted rock steps into the pine-needle-covered dirt.

Henry ran away from the lights of the amphitheater, toward the shadows. But he didn't need to. The attackers ignored him, concentrating only on the tourists. Two naked men ran past him, beating a crying woman about the head with blunt blocks of wood. A woman pushed him aside to get to a little girl who had become separated from her family, gleefully stabbing her with a homemade knife.

He hadn't thought of it until now, but two days ago when he'd been in Cortez to buy some gas and groceries, he'd sensed indications that all was not right. Trouble was simmering beneath the normally placid surface of the town. The middle-aged man who worked behind the booth at the gas station, usually an impeccably dressed fellow, was wearing dirty cutoffs and a torn T-shirt. Dottie, the cashier at the supermarket, whom he'd known since the store was built ten years ago, didn't recognize him. Everyone seemed tense and out of sorts, and when he'd driven past the high school, he'd seen a large crowd gathered in the parking lot, watching a fistfight and cheering on the participants. He'd driven by too fast to get a good look, but the fighters seemed to be teachers or parents, not students.

Still, how had that turned into . . . this?

He had a walkie-talkie clipped to his belt, which was used to call for help and notify other rangers if there was a medical emergency or serious accident. He knew he should utilize it, but he was afraid to do so, afraid that if he alerted someone to what was happening here, his exemption from the violence would be revoked. He kept looking toward the road, toward the visitor's center, toward the lights of the cabins through the trees, hoping someone had seen the headlights on the road and was coming to investigate.

What if they did, though? What could any of his fellow rangers or park employees do against these lunatics? They could call the police, but he realized that maybe the police were already here.

The massacre was winding down. He had no idea if anyone had escaped, although judging by the limp, eviscerated bodies lying on the seats and steps and surrounding ground, he would be willing to bet that only one or two had made it out. The man in the hip-hop shorts was still alive, but he was screaming. An overweight woman in a dirty loincloth was sitting on his stomach and gleefully scalping him with a chunk of obsidian. Closer in, an old man was grunting like a pig as he rooted through the entrails of a little boy.

Henry remained in the shadows, willing it to end, waiting for them all to get back in their still-running vehicles and drive away. They didn't. Instead, they started running, as if on cue, down one of the paths away from the road, weapons held high, screaming. The path led to the new site, the one they'd discovered after the fires had burned off the brush. In seconds, they were all gone, the amphitheater suddenly silent with the soundlessness of the dead.

He had a chance to escape, to finally get out of here. He could run to the visitor's center, get the other rangers together, call for outside help.

He could.

But he didn't.

Where were they going? he wondered. And why? He stared down the path, saw only darkening gloom as it moved away from the lights. Were they aware of the new site? And what would they do there?

He had to know.

Henry walked across the amphitheater, trying to ignore the broken bleeding bodies, and started down the path. He could stay behind them, spy on them to find out what they were doing. They were loud up ahead, still screaming, but they sounded far away, as though they had continued to run, and he broke into a jog, praying that they hadn't left behind any sentries to guard their route.

He caught up to them at the house.

It was what they'd discovered after the fire had burned off surrounding trees and bushes. Built next to a low bluff, with the limestone cliff acting as a fourth wall, the structure was not intact, but it was in good enough shape that its purpose and origin were clear. There was no roof, of course, and the adobe walls were in various states of disrepair, but to a large degree the foliage had protected the building. The back room, constructed under an overhang, was almost completely preserved, and this was where the townspeople were headed. They had abandoned their weapons, most of them, and instead of screaming wildly, they were standing in line, silent and subdued, waiting to go in. The room was small, the size of a typical modern bedroom, and there was no way all of them could fit in at once, but those who were forced to wait their turn appeared surprisingly calm.

Henry thought of that guy from Chaco Canyon he'd talked to last week. What was his name? Picante? Race? Something weird.

Pace.

That was it. The guy had asked him if any unusual artifacts had been unearthed in the past month or so, if any unexplained occurrences had happened at Mesa Verde. Henry knew what he was talking about, he'd heard the rumors, too, but he assured the other man that nothing like that had been seen at Mesa Verde. He'd thought at the time about the house, however fleeting, but that discovery was several years old, and nothing unusual had ever happened there, so he hadn't mentioned it.

Henry was still in the shadows on the side of the path, still quite a ways away from the building and the line of raggedy people. But even from this angle and this vantage point, one thing was becoming increasingly clear. Men and women were going into the back room, but they weren't coming out.

Some of them were. But not most of them. While his original plan was to hang back and watch, he now wanted to see for himself what was happening in there.

They'd ignored him before, and he counted on his luck holding. He stepped bravely into the open and walked past the line of people, around a side wall on the opposite side of the house. No one stopped him, no one made a sound. Ten minutes before, everyone had been in a frenzy, slaughtering innocent tourists, and now they were as passive as sheep. He pushed his way past a nude young woman covered in mud and blood, past a long-haired man in a ripped mechanic's uniform. Before him, the adobe wall joined with the overhanging rock of the bluff. In the center, a black rectangle, slightly smaller than an ordinary door, was the entrance to the room beyond.

A tall, heavily tattooed man wearing dirty cutoffs walked up to the entrance, looked in, stood there for a moment, then turned away, and headed out of the house. Before the next person in line could step forward, Henry moved in front of him and peered through the doorway.

The back room had been transformed. Inside was a wonderland of bones, a beautiful fantastic world of white ribs and gleaming skulls and bleached pelvises, all glowing with some sort of inner light and arranged in a radiant display that for some reason reminded him of Christmas. The room had been empty before: bare adobe walls, bare dirt floor. Now, however, it was a spectacular showcase of . . . of what?

Skeletons, a part of his mind said.

That was true, but that was only part of it. For whatever had created this magnificent scene had turned those base ingredients into magic.

A hand touched his shoulder, and then the next man

in line was walking past him into the room. The man
ran his fingers along exposed ulnas and tibias and clavi-
cles, an expression of awe on his blood-spattered face.

And then he was gone.

It was quick, it was simple, a no-frills miracle, and
Henry was not only shocked but amazed and curiously
impressed.

No, not impressed. Attracted.

Yes.

He stared at the spot where the man had vanished
and felt the pull. The people here obviously knew what
would happen if they went into the room. Yet some still
walked in. *Most* walked in. He understood. He knew
why the last man had not turned away.

A rational part of his mind was telling him that he
should get back to the visitor's center, let everyone know
what was happening, warn them about this place.

But what was the point? Oblivion was so much nicer.
Just the thought of running all the way back, explaining
what he'd seen, trying to figure out what was happening,
helping to come up with some sort of plan, tired him out.

A woman in tattered rags tried to push past him, but
he stopped her with an outstretched hand.

"Wait," he said.

Smiling, he walked alone through the open doorway.

And ceased to be.

Ten

1

The trip to Tempe was tense. Returning from New Mexico, they'd been anxious, but they hadn't really known anything. Not for sure. And though they'd suspected that something had happened to Al, they could legitimately pretend that it hadn't, that everything was normal, everything was fine.

But this was different.

Melanie fidgeted with the notebook in her lap. Last night she and Glen had written down a chronology of events, and seeing it there in black and white, so matter-of-factly stated, had been a sobering experience for both of them, bringing home just how helpless and inconsequential they were in the face of all that was happening.

Outside, a single abandoned house sat behind a faded, once-gaudy sign announcing ARIZONA ACRES! NEW LUXURY HOMESITES!

Ron had wanted to come with them, but he'd been allowed out of jail only under the condition that he remain in town. The terms of his bail required him to stay within the jurisdiction of the Bower PD or face re-arrest. Een had made this very clear, but she and Glen reiterated it for him, and he said he understood, don't worry, he had no plans to jump bail.

"There goes my money," Glen joked when they left Ron at the motor court. But it wasn't really a joke. Melanie, too, had her doubts as to whether he'd still be in town when they returned.

Again, they took Glen's car. There was nothing in the

trunk this time, but it still felt like there was, as though the skull had left a residual trace, a psychic spoor, and their mood reflected this. They were testy with each other, and their sporadic attempts at conversation dwindled and then disappeared as rangeland gave way to forest and forest to desert.

They were a half hour out of Payson and nearly to Sunflower when Melanie asked, "Where are we going to stay?"

"Stay?" Glen said.

"In the Valley."

"I don't know. A hotel."

"You're unemployed and, believe it or not, I haven't saved a huge amount of money from my small-town teacher's job. I think we should ask this Professor McCormack if we're still drawing pay from the university. Maybe we can get them to foot the bill."

"I have money," Glen said.

"But how long will it last if you keep wasting it by bailing out ASU students and driving hundreds of miles at the behest of professors you don't even know?"

He shrugged, showing that such mundane economic concerns had not even crossed his mind. "Let's worry about that later."

Neither of them knew where at ASU the archeology department was located. Neither of them even knew where to find a non-stickered parking lot. So Glen parked in a nearby shopping center, in front of a Tower Records, and despite the intense summer heat, they hiked a block down to the campus and wandered around until they found a directory that led them to the right building.

Professor McCormack was in his office, a small cubicle piled floor to ceiling with books and bones, and built-in shelves housing a spectacular collection of Native American pottery. He was talking on the phone, and they heard him before they saw him, rough voice coming from the only open door, loud in the empty hallway: "Your mama was on her hands and knees, and I'm so big and buttfucked her so thoroughly that your daddy and two of his friends could go in there at once and not make an impression."

Glen rapped on the door frame, and the professor hung up the phone immediately, looking sheepish. "Sorry," he said.

"Who were you talking to?"

"White supremacist hotline. I call it periodically to harass them."

"Someone has to, I guess," Melanie said.

"That's the way I look at it."

"I'm Glen, and this is Melanie. We're from the Bower dig? Al's assistants?"

"Right, right. Come in, sit down. I've been waiting for you." McCormack stood. He was a big man, beefy and red faced, who looked more like a sanitation worker than a university professor. He shook both of their hands across the desk. "Sorry to make you come all this way, but . . ." His voice trailed off. He didn't seem like a man who was often at a loss for words, and to Melanie his reticence was worrying.

"But what?" she prodded.

"I wanted you to see it for yourself."

"See what?" Glen asked.

"There are two sets of ruins open to the public in the Phoenix metropolitan area: Pueblo Grande and Pima House. Nothing unusual has been reported at Pueblo Grande. But Pima House has been closed for the past three days because—" McCormack sighed. "I don't know how to say this in a way that doesn't sound insane, so I'll just spill it. People are vanishing in the ruins. Not getting lost but"—he snapped his fingers—"vanishing. Like that. And it's not just people. Animals, too. The police are on twenty-four-hour watch, guarding the place and making sure no one goes in. Five people are gone, though. Including one patrolman. And dozens of animals, who seem to be drawn to the site."

Melanie shivered. "Do people . . . know about this?"

"Oh, yes. It's been in the paper and on the news."

"Then why couldn't you tell us about it over the phone?"

He shrugged. "Paranoia. It's news here but it might not be news everywhere. And I wanted to make sure you'd come. Actually, I wanted Al to come, but since *he* seems to have disappeared, I thought it best to bring in some of his people." McCormack paused. "So where *is* Al?"

Melanie looked at Glen, letting him answer.

"We don't know. But he's not the only one."

"That's what the police said. But I'd like to hear your point of view."

Glen told him, starting with the items that had been unearthed before his arrival: the demonic figurine with the mummified infant hand attached, the pouch of Greek money, the Saxon children's toy. He went through everything, from their trip to New Mexico and the abandoned town and church to the bone sculptures beneath Ricky's house.

McCormack did not interrupt, but nodded all the way through. When Glen finished speaking, the expression on the professor's face was grim. "I don't know if you've heard, but there's been a rash of unexplained phenomena associated with Anasazi relics and ruins. Not just here but in Flagstaff, Santa Fe, Denver, throughout the Southwest. I didn't put any credence in those stories, not at first, but after what happened at Pima House, after what I saw for myself, I couldn't help but believe. And now, with what you've told me . . ." He shook his head. "That's why I wanted to talk to Al. He's something of an expert on unusual aspects of Native American culture, and his focus has always been on the Anasazi. To be honest, he's become something of a joke in the field, he and Pace. One of the worst-kept secrets in archeological academia is that they're working on some sort of unifying theory of Native American disappearances. I wanted to bring Al in because . . . well, because I thought he might have a unique perspective on what's happening." McCormack ran a hand through his greasy hair. "No, that's not true. I thought he might *know* what's happening. And what we should do."

"Have you tried contacting Pace?" Melanie asked.

"Six or seven times a day."

"Us, too," she admitted.

Glen nodded. "We think he's looking for the skull."

McCormack leaned over the desk. "Do you think he's disappeared? I mean, *disappeared*?"

"I don't know," Melanie said softly.

They talked awhile longer. The professor showed them photos he'd been e-mailed from other archeological institutions: a line of artifacts that appeared to be marching down a museum corridor; a human skull floating in the air above an excavated burial ground; before and after pictures of an Anasazi exhibit with well-lit museum cases first displaying baskets and tools and then empty and broken with shattered glass on the floor; and a series of photos featuring a shriveled, leather-wrapped mummy that changed its position in each shot.

"You said this was in the papers, on TV news," Melanie said. "Is it a big story?"

"There's a report from Pima House every day and it's usually the lead, even though there's been no change in the situation, so, yes, I'd say it was a big story."

"I mean, has it been picked up by the national news? Have they put together all of these individual events and connected them?"

McCormack smiled wryly. "The tabloids have." He opened his top desk drawer and pulled out a copy of *The Insider*. The banner headline read: ANCIENT INDIAN CURSE THREATENING U.S.

Glen took the tabloid from him, and shook his head. "You mean *Men in Black* was right?"

McCormack shrugged. "There's a kernel of truth to most comedy."

"But no one else?" Melanie asked. "CNN isn't broadcasting it? Or CBS? AP hasn't picked it up?"

"Not to my knowledge, no."

"How's that possible?"

He shrugged. "Illiterate yahoos are always talking about the media's liberal bias. There is no liberal bias. But there's an Eastern bias. And a metropolitan bias. Small towns in the West simply don't get covered, and as a result a lot of news goes unreported. Look at Bower. No TV station, no large city within a hundred miles, newspaper not affiliated with the wire services. If something happens there, who's going to know? Even the Phoenix and Albuquerque news outlets won't report it. How's Dan Rather back in New York going to find out about it?"

"But this is in the Phoenix area. It's on the Phoenix stations."

"Things happen all the time. People die or disappear, natural disasters occur. No one thinks anything of it. It's the price we pay for being alive on the planet Earth, part of doing business. This time, we just happened to be in the right place at the right time. We saw the connections. But I doubt if anyone else has—except the tabloids—and until they do, or unless we tell them, this isn't going to get much play."

Melanie wished the word was spreading like wildfire, that news organizations were informing the world, and that the government was recruiting from the best and the brightest, the top minds in a variety of interconnected fields, to find out what was happening here and how to stop it. It would be comforting to know that they could relax, that the big boys were on the case and the three of them didn't have to worry about the fate of . . . what? Some Indian ruins and excavation sites? The Southwest? The entire country?

More and more, she felt the weight of responsibility on her shoulders.

"Do you think we could see these Pima House ruins for ourselves?" Glen asked.

No, Melanie thought.

"That's why I asked you here. Let's go."

They saw the police cars and the helicopters from blocks away. Melanie felt a gnawing pain in the hollow pit of her stomach as they passed a crowd of excited onlookers standing before a barricade of temporary chain-link fence. McCormack drove his car up to a long sawhorse blocking the entrance to an adjacent parking lot, showed a policeman manning the entryway an ID card, and the sawhorse was moved aside so they could drive through.

There were a *lot* of onlookers, much more than there should have been for an incident that essentially had been stagnant for several days. They were animated, enthusiastic, as though they were attending some sort of revival meeting or entertainment event. She got out of her car, and heard the buzz of conversations from the assembled individuals. The mood of the crowd was what concerned her the most. They chose to be here, seemed to like being here, and there was something disturbing about their interest in such a deadly and horribly alien phenomenon.

Within the fenced boundary, the eroded remnants of the Anasazi buildings and the paths leading to them were cordoned off with yellow police ribbon. From somewhere inside came a low, intermittently thunderous growl, as though the earth itself were snarling at something. McCormack walked up to a uniformed officer standing next to the ribbon under a mesquite tree, consulting the top page of a sheaf of papers on the clipboard he carried.

"Rand," McCormack said in greeting.

The policeman nodded. "Professor."

"How goes it? Any change?"

"None."

"Have they finished mapping it yet?"

"If they have, no one's told me. Haven't even seen Sabian or Chang today."

"Some of our physicists and physical scientists are trying to determine the size, shape, and exact position of this vortex or whatever it is," McCormack explained. "If they can get a three-dimensional picture of it, computer-model it, they might be able to extrapolate from there and figure out some of its other properties. They started out with lasers and light beams, but there's no spectral anomaly; using those techniques, you can't even tell it exists. Light passes through unbent and untouched. So they went the low-tech route and threw a ball with an attached string. The string was cut off at the point of entry and Dr. Chang, who was holding the other end, got a shock—like a kick in the chest, he said—although string is nonconductive and there was no evidence of anything unusual on any of the string's fibers. They then threw ball and string, with the end tied to a stationary object, but for some reason, there was always a recoil and they could never precisely determine where the vanishing point was. Now they're tracking some sort of sensory projectile, an electronic mapping device ordinarily used underwater that feeds back data to a computer up until the second it disappears, and this seems to work, although the parameters of the vanishing point keep changing. They're not expanding or contracting . . . just moving. Shifting back and forth, Dr. Sabian says, and that's the theory they're working on now."

Melanie looked over the yellow ribbon, saw only paved paths winding between a benign-looking ruin. She shivered.

"How big do they estimate it is?" Glen asked.

"The size of a football field," McCormack said.

They were silent for a moment, looking at the site. Melanie glanced over at the crowd behind the fence. They wanted to get in, she thought. They wanted to experience it for themselves. They wanted to disappear.

And they were excited about it.

"Hey!" a policeman yelled behind them.

They all turned toward the parking lot, where a sleek orange cat ran across the asphalt from a neighboring yard, away from a pursuing policeman. The cat passed McCormack's car, darted between them, dashed under the police ribbon up the path—and vanished.

Rand snapped his pen and made a check on his clipboard. "Fifth one today," he said. "Fifth cat. Twelfth animal overall."

Melanie looked at the spot where the cat had disappeared, thought about Al and Judi and Randy and Buck. "Let's get out of here," she said, feeling sick to her stomach. "I've seen enough."

Glen nodded solemnly. "Me, too. Let's go."

Glen paced the terra-cotta floor of the McCormacks' ultra-large living room, trying to think, but his thoughts were muddled, his brain overloaded. He glanced out the tall twin windows at beautiful desert landscaping: saguaros and ocotillos surrounded by smaller bushier plants punctuated with the brightly colored flowers characteristic of drought-resistant vegetation. It was an exceptionally nice house, particularly for a college professor. McCormack's wife, he'd found out, worked for APS and was the real breadwinner of the family. The two of them were in one of the back rooms right now, no doubt arguing over McCormack's invitation for them to stay at his place.

"Sit down," Melanie suggested. "You're making me nervous."

He was making himself nervous. This should be the point where he and Melanie simply bowed out gracefully and let the authorities take it from here. He might have found the skull in Bower and the two of them might have run into some strange shit in New Mexico, but anthropology professors were looking into this now. And physics professors. And cops. All of them using their resources and considerable expertise to figure out what was happening and do something about it.

So why did he feel that he needed to stay involved?

Part of the reason was the triptychs in that church and those pieces of pottery with Melanie's face and house. The two of them *were* involved, whether they liked it or not. They had not asked to be drawn in, but strange events had been personalized to include them, and it was clear that they had been specifically chosen.

But part of it also was that he could not walk away, could not just cede his role to someone else. He'd been there at the beginning and he was going to see this through to the end.

Melanie, he knew, felt the same way.

Besides, one of those church paintings showed a line of people walking into a white light. What was that if not the vortex at Pima House? And subsequent panels depicted him battling that strange frizzy-haired demon, a boy at his side. If those prophesies were to be believed—and they'd been frighteningly on target so far—then he was going to be here all the way through.

Melanie was not in the pictures.

He pushed that thought out of his mind.

He turned toward her. "We didn't pick up our photos," he said. "The ones from New Mexico."

"Damn! You're right." She hit the arm of the couch with a fist. "We could've shown them to Dr. McCormack."

"After we get back," he said. "We'll send him copies."

But Glen realized that he didn't expect to go back. That was strange. What did he think they were going to do? Live in the McCormacks' guest room forever? Buy a house in Phoenix and settle down? Head back to California? It didn't make any sense. Of course, they were going back to Bower. Tomorrow, probably. Even if they did decide to go somewhere else, Melanie would have to return home for her clothes and belongings.

Unless she couldn't go back.

Unless she was dead.

She wasn't in the paintings.

He was going to make himself crazy thinking in circles like this.

McCormack and his wife emerged from the hallway, hand in hand. They *had* been fighting about the professor's impulsive invitation, he could tell, but they'd decided to put on a united front, and Mrs. McCormack—Alyssa—smiled at them. "I'm glad you'll be staying with us."

Melanie stood. "If you're sure it's not an inconvenience."

"I'm the one who's inconvenienced you," the professor said. "I made you come down here. The least I can do is offer you a place to stay."

"It's fine," Alyssa said, and her voice was sincere. "We're glad to have you."

McCormack beamed at his wife.

She let go of his hand, patted his arm. "I'm going to start dinner."

He looked surprised. "You don't want to—?"

"—discuss disappearing people for the thousandth time?" she finished for him. "No thanks." She nodded to Glen and Melanie. "Hope you like Mexican food."

"We do," Melanie said. "That'll be great. Thank you."

"Let's go into my study," McCormack said as his wife went into the kitchen. "I have photos Al compiled from previous summers' digs and a bunch of maps he gave me. I've been looking through them since the Bower police called me, but haven't been able to find anything in them that sheds any light on what we're dealing with. You two are new. Maybe you can come at this from a fresh perspective, pick up on something that eluded me."

They followed him through a hallway as wide as a room, into his study, a gigantic home office with a skylight, a wall of windows and the type of built-in bookshelves that Glen had seen only in movies. Maps and photo albums were piled on the oversize desk, and as McCormack started to explain where Al and last year's team had conducted their excavation, Glen's gaze landed on the nearest map and the word "Springerville."

"Vince," he said.

Melanie frowned. "Vince? Who's Vince?"

"He's the guy who got me into this to begin with. He's another friend of Al's, and he gives tours to these ruins near Springerville. What are they called?" He squinted at the map, trying to find the name.

"Which ones? Casa Malpais? Huntington Mesa?"

"Huntington Mesa! That's it. I took the tour and he recruited me for the Bower dig. He seemed to be pretty tight with Al, and I'd be willing to bet Al's shared some of his theories. He might be able to help us out."

McCormack frowned. "Vince . . ." he repeated. "Vince . . . I don't think I know any Vince."

"He's young. Probably an ex-student. What I was thinking was, I could call him, tell him what's going on, see if he knows anything about it or has any theories—"

"Use my phone," McCormack said, pushing it across the desk.

The professor only had phone books for the Phoenix metropolitan area, so Glen got the number for the Huntington Mesa museum by calling information. Vince wasn't there, but when Glen lied and said he was a friend and it was an emergency, the elderly woman who answered the phone gave him the number of Vince's apartment.

Vince picked up on the fourth ring. "Hello?"

"I don't know if you remember me. My name's Glen Ridgeway. I took a tour of your ruins last month, and you hooked me up with Al Wittinghill at the Bower excavation?"

"Oh, yeah. Hi." The young man's voice sounded different. Distracted, disassociated.

"I, uh, I've been working there since then, and, uh . . . something's happened," Glen admitted. "Actually, quite a bit's happened."

Suddenly Vince sounded interested. "Really?"

"Weird shit."

"Are you there now?"

"No. I'm in Scottsdale."

"Oh, weird shit? I know what you're talking about. The Pima House Ruins, right?"

"That's part of it—"

"My sister called and told me. Her family lives close by there, and she's worried it's going to spread. I don't know what she thinks I can do, but I have a few days coming to me, and I was going to come there tomorrow and see it for myself." There was a pause. "Actually, something happened here, too. Something like that."

"Al's missing," Glen blurted out. "It's happening everywhere."

"Al? Shit. What happened?"

For what seemed like the hundredth time, he went through the whole story from the beginning, starting with the weird artifacts found before his arrival in Bower, ending with this afternoon's trip to the Pima House Ruins.

Vince was silent when he finished, and for a second Glen thought he had hung up. "Hello?" he said. "Vince? You still there?"

"I'm here."

He didn't say anything else, and Glen looked at Melanie and McCormack with an I-don't-know-what's-going-on expression.

When Vince spoke again, it was in that distracted, disassociated monotone. "We had a break-in at the museum, or we thought we had a break-in, and I spent two nights sleeping there trying to catch the guy. I only heard noises the first night. But on the second night all hell broke loose. The artifacts were . . . alive. Some of them attacked me and some of them escaped. I followed the escapees outside and down the highway. They went right down the highway, two stone statues leading and a bunch of smaller stuff following. They eventually made their way through the desert outside of town and walked up to the top of Huntington Mesa, back to the ruins where we found them.

"I filmed all this on digital, and I e-mailed it to Al last night . . . although I guess he didn't get it since he's not there. I can e-mail it to you, too, let you see what happened. It's dark and some of it's unclear, but overall it's pretty good. It's not like those UFO films. You don't have to interpret what's happening. You can see."

"Do you have an e-mail address?" Glen asked McCormack. "He has some digital video he wants to send us of what happened in Springerville.

" 'DrMcCormack,' no period. The 'at' sign. Then 'Freelink.com.' I'm not sure my computer's equipped to handle video, but we can try it."

Glen repeated the address.

"Okay, I'll send it. But I'll bring a copy tomorrow just in case you can't access it." Vince paused. "Some other stuff happened, too. After I shut off the camera. I ran into this old—Navajo man, I think he was—and he was just sitting there on a boulder, watching and getting drunk. We saw people on top of the mesa all dressed up in feathers and masks and rags, like ancient tribal people, and the old man called them 'The Others.' He said he'd never seen them before and didn't know what The Others were, but he knew they were 'The Others,' and then he just sort of wandered away.

"Of course, I didn't go up there. I went back home. But the next morning, I drove to the ruins, and there were people up top, people from Springerville. They were all dressed up like they were going to church, and they were digging in the ground, looking for something. The trees around the ruins were all shredded and there were big claw prints on the ground, like some monster had stormed through there.

"I went to the front kiva, the one I showed you, and at the bottom were the artifacts from the museum. And a skeleton. You found a skull with no body in Bower? This was a body with no skull. I don't know if it's the same creature, or if there's any connection at all, but the people started going down into the kiva and picking up the artifacts. They climbed back up and took them home, and at the end the only thing left was that headless skeleton.

"I haven't been up there since. I've been afraid."

Glen felt cold just listening to the story. He remembered perfectly the Springerville museum and the Huntington Mesa ruins and could visualize everything Vince was describing. "I think we have a lot to talk about."

"I'll be in the Valley tomorrow afternoon. Why don't I give you a call when I get there? Do you have a number you'll be at?"

Glen gave him the number of Melanie's cell phone. The two of them said good-bye and hung up.

"He's coming to Scottsdale tomorrow. He'll give us a call when he gets here."

"You think he can help?" Melanie asked.

No, Glen thought, but he shrugged noncommittally. "I don't know. I hope so."

"All right," McCormack said. "We're on our way." He opened up a photo album. "Now, let's look at these pictures."

2

It was all coming to a head.

He didn't know how he knew it, but he did.

George Black stared at the collection of pottery shards he'd gathered from the yard the past few days, the ones with pictures of him, Melanie, the house, the Weird Man. He hadn't told his daughter about them, hadn't even told Margaret. He'd kept them there, hidden away in the locked bottom drawer of his desk, taking them out only when he was sure he was alone.

But that was nothing unusual, and he shouldn't feel guilty about it. There were a lot of things he'd never told his daughter, never told his wife. Everyone knew about his grandfather, of course. But he'd successfully erased that stigma, had forged a new identity for himself, based solely on his own qualities rather than the actions of previous generations. And one of the ways he'd done so was by service to his country. He'd been a hero in Korea, the most decorated infantryman Bower had produced.

That was one of his secrets, though, wasn't it?

He supposed everyone knew what those medals and commendations really meant. The decorations meant that he'd killed a lot of people. His government had trained him and provided him with equipment and transportation to another country, where he'd been ordered to murder people with dark skin and slanty eyes. But what the medals didn't tell was how much he'd *liked* killing those people. He'd murdered one North Korean sergeant with his bare hands and a rock, smashing his head repeatedly until it cracked open like a melon and all the blood and juices poured onto the dirt. Another he'd gut-shot from an inch away, feeling the hot gush of blood on his hand, hearing the wet sluicing sound of bullets rending flesh.

Why was he thinking about this now?

Because of the pottery.

He reached down to grasp the warm dusty clay, and the pictures responded to his touch. The Weird Man popped up in the house window, winked at him. Melanie stood mournfully in the open doorway. On another rounded fragment, a line of severed heads stretched along the top of the backyard fence. A small thumb-size piece of pottery showed a wild staring eyeball.

He'd been feeling strange lately. Not out of sorts but . . . different, as though he was changing, not quite the same person he had been. It was a stupid idea, but he couldn't seem to shake it, and it was all tied up with the pottery, with the pieces of broken, patterned clay he had found in his yard. It was almost like the pottery was radioactive and he was being contaminated by it.

Contaminated?

It was as good a word as any to describe the way he felt.

God damn those eggheads and their excavation. They'd brought all this upon him; they'd started it all.

And Melanie was one of them. That was the ironic part.

He looked down at the biggest shard of pottery. It *had* shown a full-length view of their house and yard, but now the house depicted was Brian Babbitt's, next door. He touched the other shards and saw Babbitt kneeling in front of a hole in the ground, saw him placing something indistinct on a table, saw him smiling broadly at a small hand without fingers.

What could it mean?

George glanced from one piece of pottery to another, trying to follow the painted images as though they were panels in a comic strip, but they didn't make any narrative sense. This was the first time he'd seen a picture of anyone outside of his family—except for the Weird Man, of course—and he didn't know what it meant.

"George!"

He quickly picked up the pottery shards and shoved them back in the drawer. What the hell was Margaret doing home so soon? The stupid bitch must have forgotten something and come back for it. She was supposed to be at the grocery store, and usually that meant he had at least a full hour to himself.

"George!"

He locked the drawer, pocketed the key, and hurried across the den, opening the door. "What is it?" he called down the hall.

Margaret poked her head around the corner. "That red light came on again. You forgot to fill up the gas tank and now we're almost out. I don't want to run out halfway across town and have to call you or walk."

He closed the den door. "Let me look at it."

"There's nothing to look at. The light's on and it stays on. I want you to go get some gas first before I drive anywhere."

"Give me the keys."

As he walked past Margaret, she handed him the keys, and he went out to the car, opened the driver's door, and got in. He inserted the key in the ignition, but did not turn on the engine. He tapped the clear plastic window covering the speedometer, pretending to be looking at something, then stepped out of the car. "You have two gallons left," he told her. "This baby gets twenty-eight miles per gallon. You could go fifty-six miles on what you have in there."

"But—"

"Stop at the gas station on your way if it makes you feel any better. But you could drive all around town twice, come home, and I'd still have enough to go out tomorrow."

Margaret looked relieved.

That was one thing that could be said for Melanie and women of her generation: they weren't dumb enough to fall for something as stupid as that.

Right now he was glad his wife was, however. He had decided that he needed to go next door and see Brian Babbitt, and he wanted her out of here. He didn't care if she ran out of gas at IGA and had to hoof it back. He wanted to make sure she would be gone for some time.

Why?

What was he planning to do?

He didn't know. But he wanted to be on the safe side. Just in case.

Margaret got in, started the car, and backed out of the driveway. She waved to him before putting the vehicle into drive and heading down the street. He waved back and stood in place until the car turned the corner.

Then he walked next door to Babbitt's.

He hadn't been over to his neighbor's house for a long time. He didn't know why, wasn't sure when the friendship had slipped back into acquaintanceship, but he realized when he saw the dead patchy lawn, the dusty, unwashed front windows, the trail of garbage on the driveway, that it had been quite a while since he'd been here or even looked over here. When Winnie had been alive, the four of them had socialized quite often, but recent contact had been limited primarily to greetings over the hedge as one or another of them came home or left.

The picture on the pottery had looked more like the *old* Babbitt place, the way it had been in Winnie's day, the way he thought of it in his mind, and for the first time he wondered if he was dreaming those pictures or imagining them. Maybe they were all in his mind and if he showed them to someone else, that person would see nothing unusual or out of the ordinary.

No.

The pictures were there.

And they kept changing.

George moved up the dirty driveway, then across a short cement walk to the stoop. He was about to ring the bell when the door suddenly opened and Brian Babbitt stood there in the darkness of the unlit foyer, wearing nothing but his glasses. The old man's nudity should have shocked him, but he had no reaction to the sight of that wrinkled sunken chest, those shriveled dangling genitals. When Babbitt motioned for him to enter, George walked inside.

If the outside of the house had changed, the inside was unrecognizable. In the living room, the furniture was gone, the carpet torn up. Where the furniture had been, on the bare cement floor, were beads and small stone carvings, hundreds of them, arranged in a round pattern that seemed familiar to him, but that he could not quite place. Babbitt hurried past him, sat down hard on the floor, and began to move several carvings, scooting one fat women catty-corner, sliding a deer atop a trio of turquoise beads. He looked like a kid playing with army men, and he picked up a nasty little figurine, a demon or monster of some sort, and held it to his ear, nodding periodically as though the stone object were whispering to him.

He put down the figurine, smiled at George. "That's how I knew you were coming," he said. "They told me."

It was the first thing either of them had said, but that didn't matter. They didn't really have to speak. They understood each other.

They suffered from the same obsession, George thought, and briefly it occurred to him that what they were doing was wrong.

Then he looked down at all the beads and carvings and felt a calmness settle over him. He was impressed with the sheer number of objects Babbitt had found, and he wondered if the old man had started searching in other places besides his own backyard.

George cleared his throat. "I've been finding pottery," he said. "That's how I knew you were in here."

Babbitt nodded and picked up a small carved horse, placing it on the outside of the circle. He stood, and George noticed without interest that he had an erection. "Come here," Babbitt said. "I want to show you what I found."

George followed him around the bar and counter into the kitchen. Some of the living room furniture was here: a lamp and end table smashed against the side door that led into the garage, a rickety bookshelf set on the counter next to the sink, touching the ceiling. Babbitt walked up to the refrigerator. The door was off its hinges and nowhere in sight, and the fridge was empty save for a strange black form that looked like a mummified animal.

"What is it?"

"I think it was a cat."

George stared at the dark wrinkled object with admiration and envy. *This* was a find. He had only unearthed pieces of pottery and a couple of arrowheads. Nothing like this.

"You can eat it. It tastes like beef jerky." Babbitt picked up a steak knife lying on the refrigerator shelf next to the cat and sliced off a thin piece from the mummified animal's back. He handed it to George, cut a piece for himself. "Try it. It's good."

George smelled the dried meat, then put it to his lips and nibbled on a minuscule portion. It wasn't bad. He put the whole thing into his mouth and chewed. Pretty good, really. Kind of tasted like beef jerky. Teriyaki beef jerky.

"To tell you the truth, I don't even know what made me think of trying it in the first place, but it seems like I've been craving lots of weird food lately. I don't know if my tastes are changing or what." Babbitt glanced around as if afraid of being overheard and leaned forward conspiratorially. "Every try child fingers?"

"Child fingers?"

"The fingers of children. They're surprisingly tasty."

"No, I can't say that I have."

"You should." Babbitt placed the steak knife back on the refrigerator shelf.

George looked out the kitchen window, saw only the indistinct form of his own house and poplar tree through the filthy translucent glass. He glanced back toward the living room and the army of carvings arranged in the round pattern.

"What's coming next?" he asked.

Babbitt stroked the head of the mummified cat and smiled. "I don't know," he said. "but whatever it is, it's big."

3

Eric Jackson no longer slept with the lights on.

He didn't know when he had stopped. But after he had thrown the arrowhead in the lake, he had found more. And more. And more. Every time he stubbed his toe, it seemed, he was uncovering another arrowhead. At first he'd left them where he found them. Then he tossed them into the garbage can in the garage. Somewhere along the way, however, they had ceased to frighten him. He had become intrigued with their differences and peculiarities, with the variances in size and shape and technique and materials. They had grown in number upon the bureau in the living room, taking the place of his geode collection, and in a transition so smooth he hadn't noticed it, he had stopped sleeping with the lights on.

Eric sat on the cold cement floor of the garage, fitting a chiseled obsidian tip into a bamboo spear of his own making. He'd stolen the bamboo from the Yamashitas' yard, and he planned to try it out this morning, see how well bamboo worked. He'd made over thirty spears, from different wood and branches, and he kept track of how well they flew, how accurate their aim, how strongly they hit, in a small green notebook he kept in his toolbox. Only three had been out-and-out failures, and those he'd destroyed, retaining the arrowheads for reuse. The rest lay stacked against the back wall of the garage, waiting.

Waiting for what?

He didn't know yet. But he would know when the time came.

He finished the bamboo spear and took it to the backyard, where he spent the next hour throwing it at a series of targets and meticulously recording the details of each throw. The bamboo was light and aerodynamically sound, and while the tapered end broke off twice and the spear did poorly on all of the strength tests, it *flew,* and Eric decided to get a larger length of bamboo and try again.

The Yamashitas' bamboo was all small. They'd

planted it only five years ago, when they'd moved to Bower. He'd already taken their biggest piece, and he tried to think of someplace else in town or in the county that might have bamboo.

The park.

He locked up the house and drove his pickup to the east end of town, parking in the lot next to the playground. Between the playground and the baseball diamond were the biking and running trails, the pond and stream, the area with the heaviest non-native foliage. If there was any bamboo to be found, it would be here.

Eric grabbed a pair of clippers from the toolbox in the bed of the pickup and walked past the swings, past the slide, past the jungle gym, onto the dirt path that led into the heart of the park. He kicked a potato chip wrapper into the water as he passed over the small bridge that spanned the stream. Luckily, the park was empty. No kids were playing on the equipment, the paths appeared to be empty and he heard no noise from the athletic fields. If he did find some bamboo, no one would see him steal it.

The brush grew thicker, and he slowed his pace, stopping to look behind a copse of cattails, peering between two tall camilia bushes at a batch of reeds at the edge of the pond. The path dipped, curved right. He didn't see anything that looked remotely like bamboo ahead of him and was about to turn back and try one of the forking side tails he'd passed, when he saw—

Feet.

There was a body in the bushes, short legs and small tennis shoes protruding from beneath a leafy, low-hanging branch. Eric stopped, stared, and waited to see if there was movement. When he saw no motion, heard no noise, he stepped carefully forward and lifted the branch.

A boy of about four or five had been killed and dropped off here in a sloppy attempt to hide the body. He was wearing cutoff jeans and a yellow Elmo tanktop. Eric could see marks of a rope around the child's neck, eyes bulging from a bloated strangled face. The kid's fingers were missing; they'd been chopped off.

What surprised Eric was not that the kid's body had been dumped here, but that it had not been stripped. Weren't the killers of young boys usually pervs?

Eric bent down to examine the body more carefully, though he didn't know what he expected to find. He was not horrified but strangely intrigued. There was no blood on the ground, despite the missing fingers, although a trickle of dried white spittle on a purplish puffy cheek led to a brackish puddle on an oversize leaf.

Eric suddenly realized he was hungry. His stomach was growling. Was someone barbecuing? Something smelled good—

The boy.

Eric frowned, then leaned closer, sniffed the skin of the child's arm. Yes, that was it. The kid smelled like . . . chicken.

Barbecued chicken sounded great right now. He'd been so absorbed in making and testing his bamboo spear that he'd forgotten to eat lunch. Now he was so hungry that he could barbecue the boy and eat him.

Barbecue the boy . . .

He pinched the kid's forearm, felt meat under the skin.

Why *not* barbecue him?

There was something wrong with that logic, Eric thought, but he could not remember what it was. Besides, such petty concerns were swept aside by what had grown into a monumental hunger. Damn! He was starving! He could not remember ever having been so famished, and he stood, looking up and down the path, listening for noises. The park still seemed to be empty.

Quickly, before he could change his mind, he squatted down and picked up the boy's body. It was heavier than he'd thought it would be, and he struggled to his feet. He didn't like cradling the kid in his arms, didn't like looking into those bulging eyes, and he shifted position, holding on to the legs and throwing the head and torso over his shoulder. He felt wetness through his shirt, but he didn't care, and he walked quickly back the way he'd come, smelling the sweet scent of fresh flesh.

At home, he stripped the body, washed it with the

backyard hose, and tenderized the meat, stabbing it with a fork and then dousing the boy with barbecue sauce.

The Weber wasn't big enough, but he had a barrel barbecue, a homemade contraption the previous owner of the house had left behind. He dragged it from beneath the jungle of interlaced spiderwebs on the fence side of the storage shed to the center of the backyard. He swept it out with a broom, filled it with charcoal and a few dried mesquite branches, splashed lighter fluid over everything, and set a match to it.

An hour later, the coals were ready. The boy had been marinating on the patio table, and Eric lifted him by one foot and one hand and placed him on the grill, gratified to hear sizzling. There was a slight flare of flames as the kid's hair burned off.

He stood next to the barbecue, watching.

Damn, the food smelled good.

Turning would have been tough, but he had an old pair of asbestos gloves in the garage, and he used them to lift the boy's body and awkwardly flip it over. By this time, the eyes had melted and blackened and no longer appeared to be staring. Dark grill marks slashed horizontally across what had been the face, making it look like an oddly shaped steak, and Eric mused that this could just as easily be a pig.

Long pig, he thought. And chuckled.

He used the asbestos gloves twice more, making sure nothing burned but everything was cooked. When it looked like it was done, he took a fork and peeled off a section of thigh, blowing for a second on the steaming meat and then placing it in his mouth and chewing it.

Juicy.

Good.

Still chewing, he walked into the kitchen, came back with a plate and a carving knife. He looked down at the cooked brown carcass and smiled.

Chow time.

4

Cameron woke up early, knowing something was wrong.

He didn't know how he knew but he did, and before he left his room, he got dressed, putting on his pants and shirt and shoes and socks rather than ambling out to the kitchen barefoot in his pajamas. He wanted to be ready to flee the house. Just in case.

He heard his parents talking in the kitchen, but when he went in, the room was empty. There were empty bowls and glasses on the placemats, Cheerios and milk and orange juice in the middle of the table, but his mom and dad were nowhere in sight. He walked out to the family room carefully, ready for anything. "Mom?" he said hesitantly. "Dad?" They weren't here either. Nor in the living room, their bedroom, either of the bathrooms, or the garage. He opened the sliding glass door and went outside, checking the backyard, the side yards, the front yard. Nothing. The cars were still here, but his parents weren't, and he stood on the front lawn, wondering what he should do. Check the neighbors' houses, call the police?

He walked across the street to Jay's.

Jay's parents would help him. He couldn't count on anyone else. Mr. Green, Mrs. Dilbay, Mr. Finch, all of the other people on the block seemed to have changed since Stu's dad had been killed. They were weird, hostile, as though blaming Jay for the actions of his dog and blaming Cameron for being his friend. But Jay's family was still normal, and he knew they'd help him find his parents.

He stepped up the curb, walked over the lawn, and slowed as he looked up at the house.

The front door was open.

Wide open.

That didn't mean anything. Bear was gone so they didn't have to worry about the dog running away. There was no reason they *had* to keep the door closed. Probably Jay's dad had carried groceries into the house and both of his hands had been full and he hadn't been able to close the door behind him. He'd probably be coming out any second to shut it.

Carrying in groceries? At seven o'clock in the morning?

Cameron stepped gingerly up to the front door, peering inside. The interior of the house was dark, silent.

He didn't want to go in, but he had to, and he stepped slowly over the threshold, holding his breath. There was no noise, not even the hum of a refrigerator or the sighing of toilet pipes, and when Cameron finally exhaled, his breath sounded as loud as a shout.

Common sense told him to call out Jay's name, then haul ass and bail if there was no answer, but he continued to creep slowly and silently forward. His shoes squeaked on the varnished wood floor of the entryway. The house grew progressively darker the farther he went in. The door behind him was open, but all of the drapes were closed and none of the lights were on as he passed into the gloomy living room.

Jay's mom was a fanatic housekeeper and, as usual, the room was immaculate. But when he looked toward the kitchen, he saw shadows within shadows, areas that, even with the curtains drawn, should not have been quite so dark. He turned away, not wanting to go in there.

Gathering his courage, he strode quickly across the murky living room to the hallway that led to the bedrooms and bathrooms. He'd speed through here quickly, and if he didn't find anyone, he'd go back to his own house and dial 911.

He poked his head into Jay's room, saw nothing, checked the first bathroom, then stepped into the doorway of Jay's parents' bedroom.

Where he stopped.

It was standing on the bed, hair frizzed out, arms bent at the elbows and stretched forward as though waiting to catch a ball. It was completely still, like a statue, but it was not a statue. While its eyes were deep-set and too dark to see within the shadowed face, Cameron knew it was staring at him.

It was the thing he'd seen in the backyard that day. *The Mogollon Monster.*

No. It wasn't the Mogollon Monster. He had the feeling that whatever this thing was, it was far more dangerous, far more evil than the simple Bigfoot clone described in that scout ranch story.

There was no indentation on the mattress where the figure stood, not a wrinkle on the carefully folded bedspread. The creature seemed to weigh nothing at all. Again, the air was heavy, liquid. Only this time it was as if he could *see* it. He was not incapacitated, though, he could move. He backed up slowly, then ran back down the hallway. Jay's parents had a Polaroid camera. He and Jay had used it once to take a picture of Stu swimming in his underwear, and he knew it was in the closet next to the front door. He dashed over there, praying that it had film, praying that the thing on the bed—

the monster

—hadn't left. He wanted to catch it on film so he could prove later that he wasn't lying or crazy.

If there *was* a later.

It was still standing on the bed when he returned. Cameron held up the camera and with shaking hands took a photo.

He tore out the Polaroid as he ran, the afterimage of the flash making it hard to see as he dashed down the unlit hallway. He sped out the front door, and in seconds was across the lawn and at the curb. He glanced down at the picture in his hand. It wasn't fully developed yet, but already he could see that frizzy-haired monster coming into focus atop the blurry bed.

He'd gotten it.

Cameron shoved the picture in his pocket and looked over his shoulder. As he'd hoped, he wasn't being followed. The creature remained in the house. Before him, the street was empty. Now that he looked, he saw that all of his neighbors' front doors were open.

This was a nightmare. This couldn't be real.

It was real, though, and he wondered if monsters were standing on the beds in all of those houses.

He had no idea what to do next, so he ran back home across the street. The front door, thank God, was not open but closed, the way he'd left it. At least he knew there were no monsters in his house. He'd dial 911, call the police, tell them what he'd seen, and they'd probably have someone over here in a couple minutes. They already had men stationed at the Indian ruins. All they had to do was send one of them up the street.

He knew he was not alone the second he stepped inside the house, but his first reaction was one of relief because he saw his parents sitting on the couch, watching TV.

Only the TV was turned off.

They were watching a blank screen.

Relief was replaced instantly by fear. He wanted to call out to his parents, wanted to run over to them, make sure they were okay. But he was afraid. They were not okay. Something was dreadfully, horribly wrong, and he couldn't even call the police because the phone was on the other side of the couch.

His mother nodded at the blank TV screen. His father laughed.

Maybe he could *run* to the police.

Cameron backed out of the house, closed the door behind him, then raced down the empty street, past the other homes with their open doors, toward Camelback Road and the ruins, toward police and people and the real world.

He was allowed to get two blocks down before his way was obstructed. He reached Clark, the second side street, and halted instantly at the edge of the curb. There were twin dust devils dancing on the asphalt. Impossibly tall, impossibly thin cyclones of sand that stretched into the air farther than he could see.

Dust *devils*.

They moved in tandem across the road from one side to the other, making sure he could not pass.

The dust devils had faces. His parents' faces. It wasn't like that old Tron game they had at the Retro Mall. The faces weren't stretched-out, flattened countenances wrapped around the bottom of the cyclonic dust cloud. They were more fluid than that, and at the same time more real, three-dimensional visages formed of swirling sand and leaves and trash.

Cameron stood there, breathing hard, sweating profusely. Collateral wind, hot and gritty, touched his cheeks, mussed his hair.

His mother's face nodded at him. His father's laughed,

the accompanying sound a sibilant hissing of grainy
wind. Those were the same reactions they'd had to the
blank TV screen at home, and Cameron sat down hard
on the curb. He wanted to cry, wanted to give up. The
dust devils pressed forward across the asphalt, moving
slowly, deliberately, and when he looked up again to see
the faces, they were both angry, mouths wide open as if
to yell at him or devour him.

Fear won out. Despair fled as quickly as it had arrived,
and he jumped to his feet and ran back the way he had
come, leg muscles straining, hurting as he pushed them
to their limit, desperate to escape the dust devils, this
neighborhood, everything. Doors slammed sequentially
on the houses as he passed them, but when he approached his own house, the door he'd closed opened
wide.

He slowed, stopped. It was pretty obvious that whatever was behind all this was bent on keeping him there.
It would throw any obstacle it could into his path in
order to direct him, like a lab rat in a maze, to the
destination it wanted for him.

Besides, where else did he have to go? Wasn't this
where he was heading anyway? His house was no longer
any of the things homes were supposed to be: it wasn't
safe, it wasn't reassuring, but it was what he knew, and
the impulse to return was instinctive.

He looked at the open doorway, heard the *click-clack*
maraca sound of front doors slamming up both sides of
the street. He thought of his parents and knew that he
had to go check on them, see what had become of them.

He entered the house warily, prepared for anything.
Nothing jumped him, nothing came at him, he heard no
strange sounds, but when he looked across the living
room, his parents were gone.

In their place, on the couch, were two brown carrots.

Dazed, numb, overloaded, he stepped heavily across
the room.

Maybe those weren't dust devils he'd seen. Maybe
they were giant carrots.

The connections here seemed to make sense on some
level he could not understand. He reached out to touch
the carrot on the left. It broke beneath his finger, crack-

ing like cheap porcelain before crumbling into dust. In the dust was a single white tooth. His mom's tooth. The one on the top in the front that was a little differently shaped than all the others.

He knew he was supposed to touch the other carrot, break it, see something of his dad's inside, but he did not, could not. He stared at the tooth, snow white against the brown dust, realizing for the first time that his mom was dead. He had assumed that already, but it had not hit him until now. Knowing that her tooth had been taken out, though, knowing that wherever her body was, it was missing a front tooth, made him understand in a very visceral way that his mother had been killed.

He looked at the other carrot.

His dad, too.

The doorbell rang.

What would it be now? His parents reincarnated as dwarves? Jay dead and still wanting to hang out? That frizzy-haired creature?

It didn't matter. He was beaten. He couldn't take any more. He wasn't going to run, wasn't going to fight. Whatever was going to happen would happen, and he would accept it.

The doorbell rang again.

He opened the door, bracing himself.

"Cameron?"

"Uncle Vince!" he said gratefully.

And he started to cry.

Eleven

1

As quickly as it had come, it was gone.

Except that Glen was not sure it really was gone. He had the feeling it had just moved.

He and Melanie stood in the Pima House parking lot while McCormack, several policemen, and a host of scientists carrying various types of electronic equipment walked up and down the ruins' trails. As always, a huge crowd stood behind the barricade, but this time they looked worried, disappointed. Television news copters hovered above.

No one knew when it had stopped. But early this morning, before dawn, one of the policemen charged with patrolling the perimeter had made a run for it himself. His fellow night-shifters went after him, wanting to grab him before he vanished.

But he didn't vanish.

He passed the spot where everyone else had disappeared, and kept going, over a small rise, around the side of the main house, before coming to a confused stop. His pursuers had halted long before, afraid of vanishing themselves, and they stared with undisguised shock.

An hour later, the state park was crawling with cops, scientists, investigators trying to determine whether the "vortex," as it was being called, had shrunk to a fraction of its former size or had disappeared entirely.

"What do you think it means?" Melanie asked in a hushed, awed voice.

"I don't know," he admitted.

"It seems ominous, the way it just stopped. Like maybe this was the preview, and now the main show's about to start."

She was exactly right. He hadn't known why this latest development was making him feel so uneasy—it was a *good* thing that the vortex was gone, wasn't it?—but she'd hit the nail on the head. The disappearances in Bower, the vortex here, all the bone sculptures and animate relics had been leading up to something, something bigger. Stage one was ending and stage two was about to start.

Melanie was about to say something else when her cell phone rang. She answered and immediately handed the phone to Glen. Vince was at his sister's house, he said, but things had come up and he wouldn't be able to make it today. He'd call them back tomorrow. What things? Glen asked, but Vince had already hung up.

"What is it?" Melanie asked, seeing his face.

Glen shook his head. "I don't know."

"Is he here in the Valley?"

"Yeah, but he said he can't make it today, that something came up, and he sounded . . ." Glen thought for a moment. "Scared."

Melanie sighed. "What now?" she said wearily, and that expressed his feelings exactly.

Glen looked out across the parking lot. One of the policemen—Captain Ortiz, if Glen remembered correctly—was talking to McCormack in a brisk officious manner. Immediately after the end of the short conversation, the professor hurried over. "An interesting development has happened on one of the streets off Camelback here. It sounds as though it's connected. A whole neighborhood has disappeared, everyone save one kid. I don't know any more than that. Some of our guys are going over to see what's what."

"I'll drive," Glen said.

McCormack was right: it *was* close. They could've walked. As they drove down the wide suburban street, following a police car, Glen didn't see anything out of the ordinary. These sorts of neighborhoods never appeared to have any people in them anyway, because the residents were always either at work or inside their homes. But halfway down the third block two patrol cars and one unmarked vehicle were parked at angles in front of a nondescript house.

Standing in front, talking to a team of detectives, was Vince.

The police car they'd been following parked next to the others, and Glen pulled into the adjacent driveway. The three of them quickly got out. While McCormack hurried over to talk to the officer in charge, he and Melanie made a beeline for Vince. The other man was obviously surprised to see him, but just as obviously grateful. Glen silently indicated that he and Melanie would wait around until he finished talking to the cops.

That proved to be sooner than expected. Looking exhausted, Vince walked over and suggested that they move farther away from the police so they could speak in private.

"What happened?" Glen asked.

Vince shook his head, not ready to talk yet, and Glen saw how young he was, how overwhelmed and out of his depth. The last time they'd met, Vince had seemed like a knowledgeable archeology professional and he himself had felt like an unemployed dimwit. Now he felt older and more experienced—and he realized with a start that he was not the same person he had been at the beginning of the summer, the person who had left Automated Interface to travel the country and find himself.

Vince cleared his throat. "I didn't tell them what happened back in Springerville. Maybe it was a mistake, but I don't think it's what they're looking for. I don't think they'll understand . . . and I don't think there's anything they can do about it." He paused. "I'm not sure what Cameron's saying."

"Cameron?"

A group of additional detectives had been interviewing a kid on the front porch of the house. They finished their questioning, and the boy quickly came over.

Glen sucked in his breath.

"This is my nephew, Cameron."

The boy.

Glen blinked, not quite believing what he was seeing. He felt an uncomfortable sense of déjà vu as he looked at Vince's nephew. Cameron looked uncannily like the boy in those paintings in the abandoned church. Same round face, same dark hair, same red shirt.

Glen didn't like this, didn't like it at all. Everything was coming to pass just as some unknown priest had imagined three or four centuries ago, and while he still held out hope that he had the capacity for free will, he was beginning to think that it was all predestined, that he was merely fulfilling some role that had been assigned to him long before he'd been born.

Glen watched the boy talking to his uncle. Maybe it wasn't true. Maybe he was seeing things that weren't there. He thought of the store that sold Delaware Punch on his mom's old paper route. Memories were faulty under the best of circumstances. Perhaps he was imagining similarities between Cameron and the boy in the paintings where there were none.

He wished they had the New Mexico photos so he could compare and make sure. Why the hell hadn't they picked up the developed pictures before coming down to the Valley?

"So what happened?" Melanie asked.

"According to Cameron, it started here before it started there," Vince said, motioning toward Camelback Road and the ruins beyond. "The pets on this street were affected over a week ago. One of them even killed a man."

"It started before that," the boy said in a quiet, hesitant voice. "It killed one of the scout masters at my boy scout ranch. Tore his face clean off. It followed me down here."

"It?" Melanie said gently.

Cameron nodded. "Whatever it is."

Vince told the rest of the story. He explained how his nephew had seen something outside the window of his bedroom after returning from the scout ranch and had drawn a picture of it; how one friend's cat turned strange and spooky; how another friend's dog had killed a neighbor; how people and animals had started disappearing into the ruins . . . and then what had happened today: missing people, the monster in the bedroom, dust devils with his own parents' faces, ceramic carrots that looked like the dust devils. Cameron chimed in periodically to clarify or correct, but for the most part kept silent.

"It's the scope of this I don't like," Melanie was saying. "Bower, Springerville, Chaco Canyon, Phoenix, almost every major site or museum throughout the Southwest. This isn't like a haunted house. It's big. Not that I believe in haunted houses, but that was the only analogy I could think of." She sighed. "Although, there's no reason for me *not* to believe in haunted houses. They're certainly no stranger than what we're talking about here."

Vince nodded. "I hear you."

"What really worries me is that in Bower the problem wasn't just the site or the bones or the Anasazi relics. The people in town were affected, too—and not in the way you'd think they would be. Even my father seemed weird. He was angry with us, with Al and the entire team."

"Hell," Glen said, "the whole town seemed pissed. It's like they blamed us, like they knew what was going on and thought we were the cause of it."

"Maybe they did know what was going on," Vince said softly.

"What do you mean by that?"

"Just a theory. But after I ran into that old Navajo man, while I was following those artifacts across the desert, it occurred to me that societies are unique entities not totally related to the people who make them up, and that they have memories, ways of retaining and passing on knowledge that individuals may not specifically know but, when confronted with, know to be true."

"A collective unconscious?" Melanie said.

"Maybe, maybe not. I don't know. But there are myths and stories indigenous to specific cultures at specific times. That old man knew enough to call those tribal people 'The Others,' but he said he didn't know anything about them: who they were, where they came from, anything. It was as though his knowledge was instinctive rather than rational, like a baby who's afraid of a black widow spider, but can't possibly know that the spider is poisonous or even understand the concept of 'poisonous.' It's just an automatic reaction. Knowledge that's hardwired in."

"Who do *you* think those people were?" asked Melanie.

Vince shrugged. "I have no idea. I've been thinking about it a lot, and I know they weren't from Springerville, but where they *were* from and why they were there . . ." He shook his head.

Glen tried not to look at the boy, tried not to think about him. "So how did the people in Springerville act? I mean, after you saw them up there in the ruins the next day?"

"Not all of them were there, just a couple dozen or so. But everyone in town seemed normal afterward. I didn't see any changes. No hostility. Nothing like what you're talking about."

"What about that . . . skeleton you said you saw?"

"The one in the kiva? The headless one?"

"Yeah. Is it still there, did you just leave it?"

"What else could I do? It's an archeological find, and I wasn't equipped to dig it out right then, and, well, to be honest, it was creepy. I didn't like being around it by myself. And now, after what you told me about that skull, I'm glad I didn't try to do anything more with it."

"You didn't happen to take a picture of it, did you?" Melanie asked.

Vince shook his head. "Do you have a photo of your skull?"

"Ron took some," Glen said, "but, no, we don't have them, and I don't know where they are."

"I'd bet they're from the same creature," Melanie said. "Bower and Springerville aren't *that* far apart, and since it appears that the creature was beheaded as part of some ritual, it makes sense that its body would be in a kiva. The scary thing is that the people who did this weren't content to just separate the head from the body and bury the two separately. They had to bury them a hundred miles apart at different pueblos."

Vince looked at his nephew, then up at Glen and Melanie. "Cameron got a picture of it," he said, speaking low. "The creature he saw. We didn't tell the police. I thought you should see it first. I don't know if it's the same one we're talking about or . . ." He nodded at Cameron.

Silently, the boy handed Glen the Polaroid.

It was one thing to see paintings, drawings, carvings. It was quite another to see a photo of the real thing. Glen stared at the picture, unable to look away, held captive by the sheer incongruity of the scene. There was a bed, a dresser, the nondescript furnishings of a suburban middle-class bedroom. But atop the bed, standing on the covers, was a creature with a dirty orangish afro. It was huge and out of proportion, but the face was what captured Glen's attention. Neither human nor entirely inhuman, with dark angry eyes and a cruel, slightly smiling mouth beneath a blank expanse of skin where a nose should have been, it was terrible, a ghastly visage unlike anything he had ever seen. God or devil, Pace had said of the painting in Chaco Canyon, and Glen was fully ready to believe the latter. There was something evil and unnatural and fundamentally wrong with the figure, and seeing it alive in a photograph brought this home in a way that nothing else could.

"Oh, my God," Melanie said, putting a hand to her mouth. "I've seen that before."

Glen nodded. "At Chaco Canyon."

"No."

"The church in—?"

"No."

"No?"

"No."

"Where, then?"

"It was a mummy in this tourist trap. I don't know why I didn't remember it before."

"A mummy?"

"Yeah. It was . . ." She shook her head. "I can't remember. It was either in southern Arizona, down past Tucson, or somewhere past Flagstaff on the way to Meteor Crater. One of those little roadside attractions. They had it in a Plexiglas box, and it was supposed to be an ancient Aztec king. I thought it was fake at first, and the friends I went with all laughed about it, but I remember the room it was in was un-air-conditioned and hot as hell and smelled. It was like something had died in there, and after that I couldn't be sure if the mummy was real or not. I mean, I didn't actually think it was an Aztec king, but I thought it might be the remains of a real dead man and not just a papier mâché mockup. One of my friends took photos of us next to the mummy case, which is what jogged my memory." She shivered, and her voice grew soft. "But that's what it looked like. I remember the hair."

Cameron swallowed hard. "Yeah. The hair."

Glen continued to stare at the Polaroid. Was this the same sort of creature whose skull he had found? The picture was dark, but there seemed to be definite similarities. This one was so much smaller, though. He thought of that unholy cave under Ricky's house, and he could easily see this creature sitting in the darkness, patiently piecing together various skulls and bones into fences and tables and sculptures.

Melanie touched his arm, and he jumped. Broad daylight, a completely appropriately touch, and he jumped. No one laughed, though.

"I think we should track that mummy down," she said.

"And do what?"

"Buy it, steal it, bring it back to study. Give it to Professor McCormack. Or Pace if we can find him. These creatures, these things, whatever they are, are at the heart of what's going on. We found a bodiless skull, Vince found a headless skeleton, the boy took a picture of one, we've seen cave drawings. This is our opportunity to examine one and . . . see what we can learn."

Glen nodded reluctantly. She was right.

"Can we keep the picture for a while?" Melanie asked Cameron. "I promise we'll take good care of it."

"You think I want that thing?" The boy gave her a disgusted look. "It's yours. I only took it so people would know I wasn't crazy."

"Maybe we should let the police see it," Glen suggested.

"You think they'd be able to do more with it than we can?" She shook her head. "We'll give it to them afterward if they want it."

Melanie's confidence gave him confidence. He looked at the Polaroid in his hand. What were they up against? What were these things?

McCormack walked up, confirming that policemen had gone into open houses and found half-eaten food and partially completed chores, but not a single person alive or dead. "They've vanished," he said. "And since they didn't go down to Pima House, I think there's a good possibility that our vortex has relocated somewhere very close by."

Cameron looked from his uncle to McCormack. "What do the Indians say is happening?"

Vince looked surprised. "What?"

"What do the Indians think is behind all this?"

The professor blinked, started to say something, then shut his mouth. Glen felt his own face redden with embarrassment. He glanced at Melanie. How ethnocentric could they be? All of the bizarre events that had occurred throughout the Southwest over the past few weeks had happened in or around Indian ruins and museums. Yet none of them had even thought to discuss what was going on with a single member of any tribe. Why had it taken a boy to figure out what should have been obvious to them from the beginning?

The police had failed, too, he realized. And all of the other scientists and experts with their metal detectors and laser scanners and Palm Pilots.

The past doesn't die. It's with us all the time. Melanie had said that when she'd told him about her great-grandfather the serial killer, and it was true. Attitudes and outlooks from previous centuries, politically incorrect positions denied and thought long discarded were still there in modes of thinking, systematic approaches. It had never occurred to any of them to consult someone who might have some cultural connection with what was happening. Even Vince, who had met and talked with an old Navajo man in the desert in the middle of the night, had not thought to seek out any other tribe member the day after he watched his fellow citizens loot the ruins.

"I don't think they know either," Melanie said. "But we need to ask them."

The detectives were returning, armed with more questions, no doubt, and Vince told them to go ahead and leave. This was going to take awhile. Implicit in his request was an admonition to get started on their unofficial investigation because the official one wasn't about to look in the places that it should. "We'll be staying at a motel tonight," he said. "I don't know where yet, but I'll call you."

Glen nodded.

Vince smiled wryly. "Bet you're glad you stopped off at Springerville for that tour, aren't you?"

"Don't think I haven't thought about that," Glen said.

He, Melanie, and McCormack headed back to the car. The crowd from the ruins seemed to have discovered that something equally interesting was going on here, for they were massing at the end of the block, which policemen were beginning to cordon off. News choppers were flying high above, circling both locations, waiting to see which turned out to be the bigger story.

McCormack wanted to return to Pima House, where his colleagues were still poking around with their high-tech instruments, but Glen said that priorities had changed. They had a possible lead and that he and Melanie needed to go back to the professor's home.

"Why? What is it? What happened?"

They filled him in on the details, the dust devils and ceramic carrots, explaining what Cameron had seen and how he had thought to take a Polaroid of the monster. Glen withdrew the Polaroid from his shirt pocket and let the professor see it.

"Did he tell the police?"

"He told us," Melanie said.

"We have to tell them. Let's go back to the ruins. We can give Captain Ortiz the photo and they can use it in their investigation."

"What are the police going to do with it?" she asked. "Put it in their file? Put it on a wanted poster?" She met his eyes. "If there was ever a time for out-of-the-box thinking," she said, "this is it. Police and law enforcement are trained to fight crime and find criminals. They aren't trained to deal with the supernatural. And whether you want to use the word or not, that's exactly what we have here."

The professor backed down. "So what's your plan?" he asked.

"Find the mummy. Buy it, steal it, do whatever we have to to get it back here so you, and Pace, if we can ever find him, can study it, examine it, and . . . figure out what we need to do," she finished lamely.

McCormack nodded.

They were woefully unprepared for this, Glen realized. How were they supposed to fight an enemy that was thousands of years old? That made people disappear? That had wiped out entire civilizations? They were completely out of their depth, but the awful truth was that they were the only ones who could fight . . . whatever this was.

Ten minutes later, he was pulling into McCormack's driveway.

Something was wrong.

He sensed it immediately. They all did. The air seemed too still, the world too quiet. Without a word, they got out of the car and hurried up to the front door.

The inside of the house was a shambles. Two of the tall windows looking out over the desert landscape were cracked, and the middle one had a huge hole at the bottom, as though a large rock had rolled through it. Food was smeared on the hardwood floor, dumped on the native rugs. Juice and milk and cola and wine dripped from the walls and ceiling, their discarded containers littered about the rooms. Everywhere were Indian artifacts: sitting in corners, perched upon couches and overturned tables, waiting in doorways. They were unmoving, but Glen had the feeling that that had not been the case earlier.

"Alyssa!" McCormack cried out. He ran frantically from room to room, searching desperately for his wife.

They found her in the closet of the guest room, huddled in a corner, whimpering with fear, her eyes wide with terror. She screamed when she saw them, and tried to bat her husband away as he bent down to embrace her. But then he took her in his arms and she began sobbing. She had scratches on her face and arms, dark purple bruises on her legs. Her top was torn, her skirt hiked up, and they both contained splotches of blood.

"Oh, my God," McCormack kept saying. "Oh, my God."

His wife said nothing, just cried uncontrollably.

Glen took Melanie's hand, stayed back.

"What happened?" McCormack demanded. "What the hell happened here?"

It was not a question any of them could answer. They knew that it was connected to everything else that was going on, and obviously Alyssa could fill them in on how she had been attacked, whether by some sort of creature—

the monster with the afro

—or by McCormack's artifacts, which had suddenly sprung to life, but as to why it had happened, they were clueless.

"Let's get you something to drink," McCormack told his wife. He led her through the debris of the discarded containers on the floor, the juice and milk and wine splattered over the walls and ceiling, to the kitchen, where he found an unbroken plastic cup on the counter and filled it with water from the tap.

"It knows we're on to it," Melanie said to Glen quietly. "It's coming after us."

Glen shivered. He'd had the same thought exactly. Whatever power was behind all this, it had sensed them. It knew they were rooting around, and it was sending out feelers, trying to stop them.

Alyssa had ceased sobbing, was thirstily drinking the water, and now it was McCormack who seemed lost and rattled. Melanie approached to see if she could be of help.

Glen reached down, picked up a broken piece of pottery off the floor.

On it was a picture of Alyssa McCormack with her legs spread wide, a carved wooden spear—like one that was lying at his feet—shoved deep inside her.

Embarrassed and chilled at the same time, he covered the picture with his hand, not wanting anyone else to see. But the lines seemed to shift as his fingers closed over the shard, some lengthening, some straightening, and he peeked surreptitiously at the face of the pottery to see that it was now Melanie with her legs spread, being violated by a small doll with a very long penis.

He started to shove the shard into his pocket, then changed his mind and angrily threw it as hard as he could through the hole in the middle window out into the desert, feeling a sense of grim satisfaction as it skipped off a boulder and shattered into pieces.

2

It was happening again. History was repeating itself. That's what history did, though. Right?

No. Not now. Not these days. Not with all they knew. Hell, what was the point of studying the past if you couldn't avoid its pitfalls?

Pace was getting frustrated, not only by his inability to find the skull, but by the fact that every other occurrence he'd heard about and tried to track down turned out to be over and for the most part unverifiable. He'd searched for the missing skull throughout Chaco Canyon, concentrating on a remote, inaccessible area of the park where he had been conducting his own semiauthorized excavation—"The Forbidden Zone," he liked to call it, in homage to the original *Planet of the Apes*—but without luck. After putting that on hold, he'd driven up to Hovenweep and Mesa Verde, down to Navajo and Wupatki, even stopped off at Walnut Canyon, following the trail of unexplained supernatural events that seemed to have broken out not just at Anasazi ruins, but at Sinagua sites as well. Everything was always over by the time he arrived, though. Sentient artifacts were no longer mobile but placed back in their cases. Noises were silent. Figures and apparitions had stopped appearing. There were attempts at documentation—photographs, videotapes—but they were always inconclusive, shot on the run, in the dark, and hard to make out.

There were plenty of eyewitness accounts, however, and the picture they painted was chilling. Everything he and Al had theorized was turning out to be not only true but still valid, applicable to the modern world.

After a thousand years, people were vanishing again.

He wondered how far it would go this time.

He'd been scanning the newspapers at each stop, looking for signs of natural disasters or looming catastrophes. One of the things he'd discovered from his work at Chaco, one of the things he'd wanted to go over with Al but had not, was the fact that previous cultural annihilations, from the Anasazi to the Aztecs, had been accompanied by cataclysms of biblical proportions. The Southwest had suffered not only from the decades-long drought and plagues of locusts, but a period of dramatic geological upheaval, with major earthquakes and uncharacteristically violent volcanic activity. There'd been no such news of late, but he was keeping his eyes open just the same.

Pace drove toward Albuquerque on Interstate 40 through the radioactive town of Grants. He grimaced as he looked out the windshield. Uranium mining, atomic testing, gas and oil drilling. Unbridled geological exploitation. The reward for being a cash-poor state with beautiful and abundant land. An eighteen-wheeler sped past him on the right, gravel bouncing off the highway and hitting his hood. It depressed him to leave Chaco these days, to go out into the real world, and he did it as seldom as possible.

He thought of Al, the skull. Maybe the earth was fighting back. Maybe that's what was going on. Or maybe some of its former stewards were.

He'd heard of crazier theories.

Hell, he'd thought of crazier theories.

The countryside passed by. Red rocks to the north, mesas to the east and south. He was getting tired of driving so much, and his old pickup was pushing the 200,000 mark, but some things could not be done over the phone or via e-mail. Some things had to be done in person.

He drove through the high desert with the pickup's windows open and Copland's *Billy the Kid* cranked up on the under-dash tape player. Aaron Copland was America's greatest composer. People always said it was Charles Ives because they liked his Yankee life story and they didn't want to admit that the essence of the West was captured best by a Jewish homosexual from

Brooklyn. But Ives' music always seemed fussy to him: cloistered, cluttered, claustrophobic, all marching band in the grandstand and piano in the parlor. It didn't capture the majestic grandeur of wide open spaces and big sky the way Copland's ballets did; it didn't speak to the Western spirit.

Pace smiled. What the fuck did he know? He was just an anthropologist.

An anthropologist chasing ghosts.

The office buildings of Albuquerque arose from the rolling plain like missiles pointed skyward, and not until the highway sloped down to the bottom lands of the Rio Grande did the rest of the city come into view. He pulled off at the first exit past the river, stopped at a Fina for gas, and then broke out his street map and found Del Este Way. It was located on the outskirts of town, near the foot of the Sandia Mountains. When he finally drove up the long gravel road that led to the smattering of shacks and cabins and trailer homes, it was late afternoon and the sun was reflecting off the metal mailboxes, making it difficult to see address numbers.

Christiansen Divine was the implausible name of the man for whom he was looking. He'd been tipped off to Divine by Ryan Ladd, a ranger who used to work at Chaco, but was now stationed at Tuzigoot. In a convoluted series of circumstances, Ryan had been visiting his brother-in-law at Walnut Canyon when Pace decided to stop by at the last minute. Pace had laid out what he was doing and what he was looking for, and it turned out that a friend of Ryan's from Albuquerque knew a part-time roofer who'd found an Indian mummy while digging a well on his property. The mummy had supposedly cured the roofer's daughter of spina bifida. Ryan had thought nothing of it, thought his friend was probably exaggerating to make the tale interesting, but after hearing Pace's story, he wasn't so sure. Using his brother-in-law's phone, Ryan called his friend, got the roofer's name, and gave it to Pace. "Might be nothing," he warned. "I'd call first, if I was you."

Pace had called. Or tried to call. But the number was out of service, and while that might mean that the man had simply not paid his bill last month, Pace's mind was conjuring up far more sinister scenarios, and he'd immediately said good-bye and headed out.

He had an address, but he didn't need it. The name DIVINE was written in block letters on the side of a backward-leaning mailbox at the foot of a narrow dirt drive. The drive seemed more suited to a bicycle than a pickup truck, but he turned onto the dusty trail and headed up the slight incline toward an old trailer home whose once-white roof was glinting in the sun.

Pace pulled to a stop next to a black greasy motorcycle at the rounded end of the drive. The trailer home looked abandoned. Situated amidst dried brown weeds as tall as a man, it was dirty and dented, windows blocked from the inside by yellowed newspaper taped to the glass. A lone oak, scraggly and half dead, listed over what looked like an outhouse. On the other side of the outhouse was a primered van on blocks—not one of the new vans, the family kind, but an old one, with a single portal window, the kind used by teenage boys to go to rock concerts and pork babes.

Pace got out of the pickup and walked up a narrow dirt footpath to the trailer. Locusts leaped through the weeds in front of him. A weathered wooden pallet served as a step up to the raised doorway, and Pace stood on the rickety boards and knocked on the metal door. There was no noise from inside—no voices, no radio, no television—and he knocked again. "Anybody home?" he called out.

He didn't expect an answer, was planning to walk around the property looking for someone, but suddenly the door flew open, and a small wizened man in a dirty sleeveless T-shirt peered out at him from a gloomy interior. "Yeah? Whatcha want?"

Pace was nearly bowled over by the smell coming from inside the trailer, a rancid odor of rotted food and bodily waste, but he recovered quickly and even managed what he hoped was a disarmingly friendly smile. "Mr. Divine? My name's Pace Henry. I'm sorry to barge in on you like this. I tried to call but your phone's apparently out—"

"Whadda you want? You sellin' somethin'?"

"No, no. I'm a professor of anthropology working at the Chaco Culture National Historical Park—"

Understanding shone in the man's eyes. "You want to see it."

Pace smiled. "Yes."

The old man nodded, stepped aside. "Come on. I'll let ya look at it. I'm not sellin' it, though. You can't have it."

"I just want to see."

The living room seemed to take up most of the trailer home. In fact, when his eyes adjusted to the gloom, Pace could see lines on floor and wall and ceiling, remnant ridges indicating where kitchen, bedroom, and bathroom partitions had been torn out. There was very little furniture: doorless refrigerator, listing chifforobe, overflowing wastebasket, television with shattered picture tube. An unrolled sleeping bag was stretched out in the middle of the floor amidst empty milk cartons, old whiskey bottles, and greasy fast-food sacks. There was a toilet, shower stall, and small sink against the front wall. Next to a door at the far end that appeared to lead into another room, Pace saw an old-fashioned wooden crib. In it was a dirty naked girl of about nine or ten, curled up and sucking her thumb.

Was that the spina bifida girl?

He didn't want to ask and didn't want to stare, so he simply followed Divine through the living room, stepping over and around the trash, keeping his eyes on the floor as they passed the crib and entered the next room.

Here, it was even darker. If there were any windows, they were completely covered and not just with newspaper. No light appeared to get in, but when Divine said, "Jesse, Absalom," Pace was able to see two shadowy forms detach themselves from the blackness and fall in step with the old man.

The dark dissolved as a back door was opened, and Pace blinked back tears, his eyes assaulted by the brightness. Through a watery haze, he glimpsed both the interior of the room, which was bare save for a pair of rusty grappling hooks on a bloodstained piece of plywood, and his new companions: a male dwarf and a middle-aged woman with only one arm.

There was no stair outside the back door, not even a box. The old man jumped down, landing hard and almost stumbling. He turned around and helped the woman, grabbing her one arm. The dwarf leaped on his own, rolling in the weeds as he hit the ground. Pace stepped out carefully, holding on to the edge of the door frame so he wouldn't fall. He didn't like being alone out here with these people, felt uncomfortable with their silence and, as politically incorrect as it was, with their deformities. He wished he'd told someone where he was going, wished someone else knew where he was and could come after him if he failed to return.

"This way," Divine said.

Pace followed him through the high dry weeds toward a makeshift lean-to, aware at some point that the dwarf was no longer in front of him but behind him, sandwiching him in.

Why? In case he tried to back out? In case he wanted to leave?

He was liking this less and less, but Pace had driven all this way and he was determined to see the mummy.

The four of them reached the lean-to: a rickety plywood roof set atop used four-by-fours propped against a boulder the size of a Volkswagen. There were no walls, unless the boulder counted as one, but the space beneath the roof was dark, and Pace did not see the mummy until he was almost on top of it. They had dressed it in women's clothes. Or, more specifically, women's lingerie. A white-triangled thong covered the ancient pubic area, and a lacy bra was strapped tightly across a flat sunken chest. There was no indication that the figure was female, but neither did it look male. It seemed more monkey than man, all stoop shouldered with black leathery skin, but its face was horrible and unlike either ape or human; there was no nose, deep-set eyes, a toothless mouth frozen in a sneer, and on the top of the rounded head orange stubble. The individual elements were not that frightening, but they came together in a way that inspired dread. He was reminded of the figure painted on the center wall of the storehouse in Chaco Canyon.

Why was the mummy dressed in lingerie, though?

Pace heard a high-pitched cackle from the old man

beside him, and a warning bell went off in his head. He knew he should get the hell out of there, but he continued to act as though nothing was wrong. He was about to ask where the mummy had been found and whether he could examine the surrounding ground, when pain exploded in his legs as a baseball bat slammed into the backs of his calves.

"Worship her!" Divine hissed. "On your knees!"

He fell to the ground, tears flooding his eyes. A sharp cry of pain escaped his lips, and then a filthy hand was clamped over his mouth, shutting him up. He tasted dirt and spoiled milk and fecal matter. He gagged, vomited, and was forced to swallow it back down.

"Don't show her no disrespect, *Professor.* She cured my little girl."

Was it his imagination, or had the mummy shifted position? It was hard to see through his tears, hard to think through the pain. Were his legs broken? He couldn't tell, but every time he tried to flex his foot muscles, tried to test his legs, a newly energized jolt of agony shot up through his body. He had no idea how he was going to get out of this—*if* he was going to get out of this—and he hoped to Christ that Ryan Ladd would put two and two together and steer the cops over to these psychos if . . .

If what?

If he disappeared, if he never came back.

"She keeps growin' hair," Divine said. "I shave her head ever' day, but ever' night it grows back." He bent down, leaned forward, and Pace could smell the old man's rancid breath. "It's the hair that does the curin'."

Pace gagged again, almost puked, but managed to keep his gorge down, afraid that he might choke on his own vomit. Being on his knees was agonizing, and he felt as though he was about to fall forward, when suddenly Divine's hand was taken away from his mouth and strong hands reached under his armpits to lift him in the air. He started crying, and he hated himself for that. He should be screaming for help, trying to get away. Instead, he was sobbing, able only to express the tremendous physical pain in his legs.

Through his tears, he saw that Divine was supporting

his left side, the dwarf his right. He could not see the woman, who must have been behind them.

They were carrying him around the side of the lean-to. The weeds had been cleared from a small section of earth, and in the center of this space was a squarish hole framed by two-by-fours.

The well, he thought. This was where they'd found the mummy.

"I guess this is it," Divine said. "Thanks for stoppin' by, Professor."

He was thrown/pushed forward, and in the brief second before he started falling, he saw a large white object in the black dirt at the bottom of the pit. It was the skull. Maybe not the same skull Al's workers had brought over from Bower, but something damn close to it.

Then he was spinning through space, head and legs smashing into hardpacked dirt and rock on the way down. He landed hard on the bottom, and while it knocked the wind out of him and his already hurt legs shrieked in pain, he was not knocked out.

From above, he heard voices.

"He didn't break," the woman said, and there was both surprise and fear in her voice.

"He's still alive!" The dwarf.

They were silent for a moment. Pace managed to open his eyes and saw next to him at the bottom of the well, in addition to the skull, what looked like broken pieces of porcelain statues.

"We'll leave him there," Divine said. "See what happens."

Pace closed his eyes, surrendering to the pain.

The old man's voice faded, became fainter and more muffled as they moved away from the top of the well. The last thing Pace heard before the voices disappeared completely was the woman saying, "Maybe it wants him alive."

3

Why in Christ's name had he ever run for mayor?

It wasn't the first time Mike Manders had had that thought, but it was the first time he really meant it.

He directed Ted Peters to park the U-Haul in the Burger King parking lot and begin unloading rocks. The sun was starting to sink—his shadow was already lengthening and stretching east—and they needed to finish this barricade before sundown.

That's when the monsters would come.

They'd lost sixteen people in the last raid: four men, ten women, and two children—a boy and a girl. The adults had been gutted and left for dead. The boy and girl had been carried off. That was not going to happen again. Not on his watch.

The barricade was looking strong. This was the last street to be secured, and they'd been working on it all day. Once the rocks were put into place, the militia would take up position. No monster was going to be able to get through.

Mike climbed into his Corvette. "Keep it up, boys!" he yelled. "I'll be back in ten!"

He swung around, out of the parking lot and back down Main to city hall. He'd been hoping they'd finished, but the lobby was still filled with writhing naked bodies. The entire room smelled of musk and sweat and sperm. Janet, his secretary, was squatting over the personnel director's face. Around her shoulders she wore the skin of a dog she'd caught and killed this morning. Down below, blood trailed down her leg. She was having her period.

Mike reached out, grabbed her hair, and dragged her off the personnel director. She screamed in uncomprehending animal frustration, and he slapped her hard across the face. "You're still on the city's clock," he informed her. "Now take a message."

They walked back to his office, and he tired to ignore her swinging pendulous breasts, the trickle of blood on her white thigh. He shoved her into her swivel chair, causing it to spin partway around before he stopped it. "Call up that e-mail we sent to Springerville," he said, pointing at her computer. "I want to rewrite it and send it off to John Eggars, the town manager over at Bower. We might need reinforcements if we survive the next attack."

She looked up at him, eyes wide. "If?"

"They're monsters," he said simply.

Janet was all business now. She printed out a copy of the old e-mail and Mike made the necessary changes in pen, then handed the paper back. "Redo it and send it. Then get on the phone to the police chief and remind him that we need all men—*all* men—out in front of the high school in half an hour. Call Remy at Fire, too. Don't talk to Northrop."

"Okay."

Mike grabbed both his cell phone and walkie-talkie off the desk.

"Where are you going?" she asked as he started out the door.

"Inspection," he said. "I need to make sure the fronts are all secure."

"What if they're not?"

He looked out his office window at the sinking sun. "I don't know. It's too late to fix 'em now."

Mike sat inside Burger King with the police chief and the city's tacticians, looking out at their people. The employees from city hall had shown, although most of them had not bothered to put on clothes. The high school football team stood next to the Elks and Masons, all of them dressed in animals skins and wearing homemade masks. The police and the militia were properly attired for battle, and if some of them sported attachments to their headgear, horns and whatnot, well, they were entitled.

God, he wished this responsibility wasn't his.

Mike stood up from the table, adjusted his flak jacket. "Well, gentlemen, I think it's time." There were glum nods all around, and he walked out the door, the others following.

A hook-and-ladder truck was parked sideways next to the barricade, and Mike strode up to it. The police chief handed him a battery-operated megaphone, and Mike got in the bucket. At his signal, the fire engine operator raised him high, over the blockade, over the buildings, over the trees.

He'd been hoping not to see anything but open desert, hoping the cops and computer geeks were wrong and the monsters wouldn't be returning tonight, but there they were, in massed formation. He could see them already, even without the binoculars, several miles away. Their vehicles were raising a dust cloud that stretched like a wall of sand over the dry lake bed.

Vehicles?

Since when did monsters drive vehicles?

He had no time to ponder that question, no time to do anything but gird for attack. The monsters were moving fast, and though they were still a ways away, they'd be here soon. Judging by the speed at which they traveled, about ten minutes.

He had never been so scared in his life, but Mike swiveled to face his people. He turned on the megaphone, held it to his lips. Below him, before him, the warriors of his town waited expectantly.

"They're coming," he announced. "Get ready."

They weren't monsters after all. The rumors and reports had been wrong. They were people, debauched and crazy, smeared with mud and blood and shit and paint, wearing rags and skins and cardboard and rope. They drove up in their dirt-streaked cars and dented trucks before jumping out and trying to scale the barricade. They were carrying weapons, but it was hard for them to use the weapons and climb at the same time, and Mike was proud of his sharpshooters, who picked off row after row of attackers.

The intruders still kept coming. There were hundreds of them, an entire town's worth, it seemed, and they quickly began to overwhelm the barricade with their sheer numbers. Plus, they had their own sharpshooters, who had gotten into place and started firing, providing cover, and Mike ordered all but the most essential policemen to step down.

Down Main Street, behind Burger King, more people were showing up, ordinary citizens dressed in costumes of their own making, wielding household tools converted into weapons. Mike was heartened to see such civic support. And in such strong numbers. There might be a townful of attackers out there, but they had an even bigger townful of defenders in here, and in the bloody battle to come, there was no doubt as to who would be the victor.

The last three sharpshooters backed off, Cliff Davis leaping from the top of the barricade, Gene Lazaro and Lee Simpson climbing down. Seconds later, the first of the intruders came over the top.

And the war was on.

In the thick of things: Elks swinging hatchets at elk-horned men naked and painted white; Janet and her friend Niki, laughing, with borrowed shotguns blowing the heads off teenagers; hand-to-hand combat between the football team and what looked like a bunch of Hell's Angels, with the football team getting the worst of it until a band of teachers charged from behind with studded baseball bats; a line of housewives with shaved heads and war-painted faces manning antique machine guns and mowing down wave after wave of stupidly advancing old men dressed in costumes of dried human skin.

When the frenzy died down and most of the screaming had stopped, Mike found himself knee deep in corpses, yanking up handfuls of hair and using a machete to whack off the tops of heads. Several were hanging from his belt already.

What was he doing collecting scalps? What the hell had gotten into him? He was a real estate agent, for Christ's sake. He didn't even like to hunt. How did he end up here? Try as he might, he could not retrace the thought processes that had led him to this point, could not think of how he had gone from a mild-mannered businessman and part-time mayor to a machete-wielding scalper.

The monsters did it, he thought.

But there were no monsters, only other people.

He looked around him at the bodies on the ground. They were savages, barbarians, but they were not the fiends he and the other townspeople had originally believed them to be. One man was still dressed in street clothes, jeans and a T-shirt and tennis shoes, and Mike found it hard to look at that one. The dead man was a reminder of the humanity they'd lost, and he felt sad and sick.

But then . . .

But then he realized that this man was part of the attacking force that had driven across the desert with the specific goal of invading their town, killing their people, and taking over.

He wondered if the man still carried a wallet with identification. Mike rolled him over, pulling an overstuffed billfold from the back pocket of the dead man's jeans. He sorted through the contents. There it was, a driver's license.

He looked up. He hadn't noticed before, but he was surrounded by people. *His* people: policemen, firemen, sales clerks, tree trimmers, construction workers, high school teachers, secretaries, housewives. All were looking at him expectantly.

"Jasper!" he announced. "They're from Jasper!"

A cheer went up. Somehow, knowing where they came from, knowing who these people were, made everything seem more manageable, less scary.

Mike reached down into the blood with his finger, painted a stripe across his forehead, bars across his cheeks.

From South Street, where the weakest of the barricades had reportedly collapsed, a police car drove up. The chief got out, walked over. Around them, everyone had gone back to the business of stripping the dead and taking souvenirs.

"Sorry," the chief said.

"For what?"

"Some of them escaped. We didn't get 'em."

Mike held up the driver's license. "That's okay." He smiled broadly. "We know where they live."

Twelve

1

On the road again.

Glen was not only getting used to driving across the long stretches of empty highway, he was getting to like it. He *was* like Bronson, and if the route he'd taken to get to this point was circuitous and more than a little hairy, it didn't detract from the sense of freedom and bedrock contentment he felt while traveling.

Well, it didn't *entirely* detract from it.

Melanie had called one of the friends who'd gone with her to the roadside attraction that featured the mummy, and the woman had confirmed that it was up north, between Flagstaff and the New Mexico border. They'd left this morning, after breakfast, McCormack remaining behind to take care of his wife, Vince staying with his nephew at a nearby motel.

His nephew.

The boy.

He'd told Melanie about his reaction to Cameron, and she had immediately recognized his resemblance to the figure in the triptychs. That didn't make him feel any better. He'd been hoping she'd tell him he was crazy, tell him he was overreacting. Nothing against Cameron, he seemed like a nice kid, but the idea that the two of them were part of some ancient prophecy scared the crap out of him.

The landscape outside the car was shifting from low desert to high chaparral. Saguaros and chollas were giving way to piñon pines and juniper. Rocky sandstone mountains were flattening out into rolling weed-covered hills.

They had an early lunch in Flagstaff at a Del Taco, the first he'd seen since leaving California, and then continued on their way, heading east on Interstate 40, looking for tourist traps.

The first one, some twenty miles out of town on a lonely stretch of high desert, promised on an oversize rooftop sign: FREE PETRIFIED WOOD! DINOSAUR BONES! Melanie didn't think it was the one, but she and her friends had stopped at quite a few and she couldn't rule it out entirely, so they parked in the dirt lot—the only car there—and went in.

He'd never stopped at one of these and didn't know what to expect, but it certainly wasn't this pathetic little gift shop housed inside a dilapidated and only partially completed building. He thought there'd be . . . more. He'd seen these kinds of roadside attractions while traveling with his parents as a child, but his dad had always planned vacations with strict itineraries, even working out where they would eat lunch and for how long they'd stop, and they had not even slowed to read the signs. Truth be told, he had never felt the slightest bit curious about these places. Sure, they were kitschy and had been considered cool in an ironic retro way, even when he was a boy, but they'd always seemed crappy and kind of sad to him. That impression was only reinforced by the crass downscale commercialism of the store.

While Melanie talked with the man behind the counter, a leather-faced senior citizen with a white handlebar mustache, Glen walked up and down the shop's two aisles. One whole shelf was filled with copies of a self-published book titled *How to Find Dinosaur Bones in the Southwest*. On the cover was a poorly drawn picture of a Tyrannosaurus stomping on a saguaro cactus. On the back was a photograph of the shop's proprietor.

"Not it," Melanie said, tapping his shoulder. He put the book down. "Let's go."

Outside, she handed him a piece of white card-stock paper on which was glued a small reddish rock.

"Our free petrified wood," she said. "Keep it for a souvenir."

Ten minutes down the highway, they came across the next one, a stucco building made to resemble a pyramid. It housed a museum as well as a gift shop, although the museum contained mostly taxidermied animals and bad clay sculptures of celebrities. The star attraction was a spooky-looking plaster face that was purported to be the death mask of John F. Kennedy.

"Taken by the coroner who did the autopsy," the gleeful old man behind the register said. "This is one of only three masks in the world made from that original cast."

They were beyond Meteor Crater, past the Petrified Forest, and well on their way to New Mexico, with six roadside attractions behind them, when they finally found what they were looking for. "That's it!" Melanie said, pointing ahead at a rainbow-colored building by the side of the highway. "I recognize the place."

Indeed, as they drew closer, a large sign on the other side of the tilting fence that abutted the interstate announced: SEE THE AZTEC MUMMY!

Glen felt weird, like someone experiencing in real life something that he'd previously encountered in a dream.

There were actually other cars at this place: two minivans, a Ford Explorer, and a small red sports car. Inside, three obviously related boys were drinking root beer floats at three adjoining tables near a small grill and a soda fountain. Their parents and several other families were scattered throughout the store's long aisles, looking at the well-stocked merchandise. While this wasn't his type of place, Glen had to admit that it was definitely a step up from the other tourist traps at which they'd stopped.

Even the entrance to the obligatory museum was impressive—a faux rock door that looked like something out of *The Flintstones* set in the center of a colorful mural depicting an Aztec city. But once they paid their dollar apiece for admission and stepped through the doorway, all that changed. The goal was obviously to get people to part with their money, to entice them into going inside. A place way out here certainly didn't rely on repeat business, so as little effort as possible had been put into the creation of the museum itself. Where the store was new, modern and air-conditioned, they now found themselves in a homemade barnlike structure with plywood walls and glassless windows. There were no electric bulbs; only occasional skylights (or, more accurately, holes in the roof) augmented the natural illumination provided by the windows. It was hot as hell, and humid, and by the time they reached the first exhibit, they were both sweating.

Glen stopped, looked at a bunch of cracked flowerpots containing dead dried plants placed on top of a folding card table. GARDEN OF CARNIVOROUS PLANTS, the sign above the exhibit read. "These rare South American flowers, inspiration for the hit film *Little Shop of Horrors,* eat insects and small animals. WARNING! Don't get too close!"

"That's pathetic," Glen said.

"You think that's bad? Look over here."

Melanie pointed at a rake, shovel, and hoe hanging on a piece of pegboard. ANTIQUE FARMING IMPLEMENTS, the sign said.

"Let's find that mummy," Glen told her.

They walked past a rusted Volkswagen, a department-store mannequin, and a refrigerator painted in psychedelic colors, not bothering to read the accompanying descriptions. At the far end of the building, just before a red door marked EXIT, a square, oversize, black coffin with a Plexiglass lid lay atop a specially constructed cement stand.

"That's it."

Against his will, Glen felt a little spooked. And Melanie was right. This part of the room had a strange smell, a sour, sickly sweet scent that reminded him of rotting flowers.

Melanie's grip tightened on his own as they leaned over to look in the glass-covered sarcophagus.

It looked nothing like the afro-haired figure.

Glen didn't need to see the Polaroid to know this wasn't it, but he took the picture out anyway. Not even remotely similar. This one was thin and bony, with a bald blackened head that looked like a stereotypical Halloween skull.

"That's not it," Melanie said firmly. "That's a different mummy."

"Maybe you just remember it differently."

"You don't forget that hair."

They returned to the store. The boys at the soda fountain were gone, as were some of the adults. At the counter where they'd bought their tickets, a pert blond girl and her equally perky mother were paying for museum admission. After they stepped aside, heading enthusiastically toward the rock door, he and Melanie moved forward. "Excuse me," Melanie said.

The weary-looking, middle-aged woman closing the register did not even glance up at them. "No refunds," she said. "It's there on your ticket."

"We—" *don't want a refund,* Glen started to say.

But Melanie was already slicing through the formalities. "Where's the mummy you used to have?" she asked. "That's a new one in there now."

"That's the Aztec mummy."

"It's different than the one that used to be there. Where's the old one?"

"We have one mummy, the Aztec mummy, discovered in a pyramid in—"

She was starting to go into a rehearsed spiel, and Melanie cut her off. "Look, I'm not in the mood to play games. We came here to see that mummy, and it's very important that you tell us where it is."

"Look, I just work here," the tired woman said.

"You don't know?"

"No."

"Well, who owns this place?"

"Nate Stewky."

"Is there a way to get ahold of him? We need to talk to him."

"Nate's retired."

"I told you, this is important. We're archeologists—" Both of them saw the expression of mistrust and suspicion that passed over her face at the mention of that word. "And that old mummy may help us with a critical problem," Melanie added quickly. She pulled a ten-dollar bill out of her purse, handed it over the counter.

"A phone number for Nate Stewky," she said. "That's all we ask."

The woman looked at her, looked at the money, then took the bill. She reached under the counter, withdrew an old-style rotary phone, and placed it on the counter. She pointed to a phone number taped to the side of the cash register. "Call."

Melanie glanced at him, but Glen motioned toward the phone. She was better at this stuff than he was.

Sure enough, despite an initial denial, she had him admitting within two minutes that the Aztec mummy currently on display was not the original, and within three minutes inviting them to his house in the nearby town of Beltane. Melanie wrote down directions on a scrap of paper she pilfered from behind the counter, thanked him, and hung up. "Let's go," she told Glen.

Nate Stewky's house was a 1950s tract home decorated in a pseudo-Japanese style. Bushes cut into bonsai shapes that made them look like pampered poodles were lined up in front of a square trellis that resembled a folding screen and blocked off a small patio. The roofs of both the house and garage were neither shingle nor shake but loose white rock, and in the center of the black garage door was a vaguely Oriental design made from raised red wood.

Nate himself was out of the house and on the stoop before they'd walked halfway up the driveway. He was an old man, short and bald and skinny, wearing plaid Bermuda shorts, a light pink polo shirt, and a huge smile that lit up his entire face and made him look like a satisfied gnome. "Thank you for coming!" he said, holding open the door as they approached. "Come in, come in!"

Glen shook the other man's hand. "Thanks for inviting us, Mr. Stewky."

"Nate. Call me Nate."

The Asian motif continued inside the house. Japanese watercolors lined the walls, and the living room was decorated primarily with Chinese antique furniture of dark red wood. "I was stationed in Japan during the Occupation," Nate said by way of explanation. "Got a lot of this stuff cheap. Here, sit down, sit down." He motioned toward a loveseat upholstered with red silk fabric. "Can I interest you in a cold beer? Or water? Or . . . a cold beer?"

Glen laughed, shook his head. "No, I'm fine."

"No, thanks," Melanie said.

Nate sat down opposite them in an incongruous reclining chair of worn and heavily faded vinyl. "So you want to know about the Aztec mummy." It was a statement, not a question, and Glen could tell that the old man was tickled to death that someone—self-identified *archeologists,* no less!—was curious about the star attraction in his homegrown museum.

Melanie nodded, leaned forward. "I was there several years ago, when you had the *other* mummy. Like I told you over the phone, we're part of an excavation team working over in Bower under the auspices of ASU. I know this seems a little weird, but we uncovered a very . . . unique skull at the Bower site, and we have reason to believe that there is a connection with your old mummy."

They had discussed ahead of time how much they should reveal, and they'd decided to hide nothing. What was to be gained by such a strategy? People inevitably gave more information to questioners they thought were being straight with them.

On the other hand, neither of them were about to jump right in with the supernatural stuff. That could get them tagged as a couple of loonies and shut off all communication.

So they were going to play it by ear, reveal as much as necessary to find out what they needed, answer all questions honestly.

"You know where I got that mummy?"

"No. Where?"

Nate scooted forward in his seat. "It's an interesting story. A friend of mine name of Jack Carpenter found it in an old ghost town down around Rio Verde. He and a buddy were hunting javelina out there, and they came acrost this little town, just a couple of houses and a bar and a store. Place was intact, all the furniture still in place, nothing looted, no graffiti. Inside one of the homes, in what he said was like a shrine built into the wall, Jack found the mummy. Jack was . . . well, Jack was kind of a looter himself, I guess. He'd already found a bunch of old Indian ruins on his travels, and he'd taken the best stuff he'd come across, metates and such, and given them away to his friends or sold them to gas stations or what have you. So he didn't think nothing of taking that mummy. This must have been around, oh, 1960 or so. I was just putting my museum together back then—we were on Route 66 in those days—and he knew that I was looking for something big, something unique, that would make my place different from all the other ones popping up along the highway.

"So Jack and his buddy—Kent Iverson, I think it was. No, Tommy Heywood, Tommy Heywood—made sort of a makeshift stretcher out of some boards they found in one of the buildings and some twine they brought along. They strapped in the mummy, carried it through the desert all the way out to their truck, then brought it up here to me. It was just the kind of thing I was looking for, and I offered to buy it from 'em, but Jack said, nah, it was a gift, and just gave it to me. Jack was a good guy that way. Always treated his friends right.

"I don't remember how I got the idea of saying it was an Aztec mummy." Nate squinted hard, thought for a moment. "You know what? I *didn't* call it an Aztec mummy at first. I just said it was an Indian mummy. Which it was. Or at least I think it was. Hard to tell for sure with that hair. Jack and Tommy thought so, too, although we never could figure out why some old cowboys or miners or whoever lived in that little ghost town would put up a shrine in their house for an Indian mummy. That's a better story than the one I came up with, and I don't know why I didn't just use it. Habit, I guess.

"Anyway, I called it an Indian mummy at first. But this whole area's reservation central. There's a lot of Indians around here, and some of 'em didn't take kindly to my star exhibit. Not that they came to the museum or paid to see it. There was one young hothead who started telling everyone in town that I had no right to own that thing, let alone display it, that I was being disrespectful and sacrilegious and all that. He *did* pay to see it, but he didn't stay long. Seemed scared of it, if you want to know the truth—"

Glen broke in. "We wanted to ask you about that, too. Did you ever feel that way? Or do you know of any stories of customers or coworkers or anybody being scared or frightened of the mummy?"

"Do you have any ghost stories to tell?" Melanie prodded.

Nate looked at them with narrowed eyes. "What's this about?"

"What do you mean?" Glen asked.

"You're not archeologists. Or not like any archeologists I ever heard of."

Glen sighed. "All right. We're not archeologists. Not technically. But we have been working on an archeological excavation outside the town of Bower." He explained about the skull and the rash of strange occurrences that had been centered around Anasazi archeological sites and artifacts. "The Anasazi disappeared nearly a thousand years ago and no one knows why, but one theory is that a . . . creature, a supernatural being of some sort, was responsible for their disappearance. This is what we believe. And we know a boy who we think got a picture of it." He took out the Polaroid, showed it to the old man.

Nate looked at it, nodded, and handed the photo back. "Hmm."

Glen looked at Melanie. He wasn't sure whether Nate believed him or thought he was crazy, and he could tell from the expression on her face that she couldn't tell either.

"When I saw that, I remembered your mummy," Melanie said. "That's why we're here."

Nate thought for a moment. "I never had any trouble with that mummy, never heard tell of any stories from my clerks over the years either, although a lot of 'em made fun of it because of the hair. But maybe mine had been deactivated at that point or had used up all his juice or whatever. The shrine in that house in the ghost town makes it seem to me like someone sure thought that thing had power, but maybe it had just faded away by the time Jack found it."

"Can you tell us anything else about that shrine?" Melanie asked. "Or put us in touch with your friend Jack?"

"Oh, Jack's been dead some twenty years now. Tommy, too. And I don't know much more about the shrine than I already told you. Fact is, I didn't care that much about it at the time. It was the mummy itself I was interested in, not details about where they found it." He closed his eyes, frowning, as though trying to remember long-forgotten information. "You know, seems like Jack did tell me something else about it, but I can't quite . . . That's right, that's it. The shrine was adobe. He thought that was weird because the rest of the house, and all the other buildings in town, were wood. He said the shrine looked like some kind of Mexican thing, a Catholic thing. I don't know exactly where it was in the room, but like I said, all the furniture and everything was intact, and whether Jack told it to me or I just came up with it on my own, I have the impression that there was empty space in front of it so that the people could . . . I don't know, worship it or pray to it or something."

"But you never—" Glen began.

Nate shook his head. "It might as well have been a fake, a dummy, for all the problems it gave me. But what I'm thinking, after what you told me, is that maybe *it* was the reason that town went ghost. You know what I'm saying? There are ghost towns scattered all over the desert. Most of them don't have names and no one knows what happened to them because no one knew they were there in the first place. The history of the West isn't as well documented as the history of the East. So who's to say what happened there? Maybe that mummy . . . did it."

"Where is it now?" Melanie asked.

"I sold it to an antique dealer from Wickenburg about four or five years ago. He stopped by the museum, hung around in there way longer than any normal person does—" The old man smiled. "You've been through it. There isn't a whole lot to see—and then he left and came back the next day and offered me five hundred bucks. I turned him down flat, gave him the whole spiel, how this was a real Aztec mummy, carried out of the Mexican jungle by a real-life Indiana Jones, but he wasn't buying it and he said he wanted it for what it was, not what I was making it out to be. I'm not sure exactly why I *did* sell it to him. I think maybe I was thinking of selling out entirely instead of just retiring from the day-to-day operations. Business hadn't been the same since they got rid of the fifty-five-mile-per-hour speed limit, and I was getting burnt out. But after I sold my mummy, I was kind of reinvigorated. I found another mummy down near Tucson, a place called The Place. Guy was upgrading, getting rid of the carny stuff, making The Place into a *real* museum. That's the mummy you see out there now. A little more decrepit than my old one, a little more traditional, but I got it for a price and haven't had any complaints—"

"Do you have any photos of the old one?" Glen asked. "So we could maybe compare them?" He held up the Polaroid.

"Oh, I surely do. Step right this way." He led them down the hall to a room he called his "work space," talking all the way about how he built a special case for the mummy and how he'd decided to make it the last exhibit and place it near the exit so that everything else led up to it. The room was decorated with black-and-white photos of the roadside attraction in various decades: sixties, seventies, eighties, nineties. There were also blown-up pictures of the mummy both in and out of its case, and Glen was shocked at how much it looked like the creature in Cameron's Polaroid. He had known that already, but somehow seeing it for himself was different, more jarring. They were putting together a jigsaw puzzle here, but with each new piece in place, the overall picture changed, surprising him every time.

Nate also had several shoe boxes filled with photos, and while most of them were unrelated, snapshots from his army days or pictures of places he'd gone on trips, there was a series of photos in color and in black-and-white from the early days of the museum, when the mummy had just been received and installed. There was even one of Nate, Jack, and Tommy holding up the mummy like a drunken buddy, its huge, dirty orange afro resting partially on their shoulders, a sight that made Glen's blood run cold.

"I think I will take you up on that beer," he told Nate.

The old man grinned. "No problem." He quickly sorted through the remaining photographs and handed one to Melanie, a shot of the mummy alone against a white wall. "That's it for the pictures, but you can have this one if it'll help you."

"Yes," she said. "Thanks."

"Let's go back out to the front and I'll get us some drinks."

They returned to the living room. "Just water for me," Melanie said, sitting down next to Glen on the Chinese loveseat. Nate went into the kitchen and emerged with two cans of Coors and a tumbler of ice water.

"So do you know the name of the antique dealer you sold the old mummy to?" Melanie asked.

"Not off the top of my head. But I still have his card around somewhere. I could give him a call for you."

"That would be great."

Nate put his beer down on an end table next to the recliner, and walked back down the hall to his "work space." He returned soon after, triumphantly waving a small white business card. "Here it is. Preston Alphonse. There's an antique dealer name for you. Couldn't make up one like that. Let me give him a call. Don't hold your breath, though. He didn't have a museum or sideshow attraction. He owned an antique store. Which means that he probably found some buyer for it and sold it. Told me he wouldn't, told me he wanted it for himself, and I believed him at the time, but the more I think about it, the more I think that was probably just a line he fed me. More likely than not he already had some collector in mind and passed it on at a tidy profit."

Nate sat down in his chair, picked up the cordless phone from the end table next to him, and dialed. He listened for a moment, then frowned. "Huh. Phone's out of service." He clicked off. "Like I said, it's been a few years. I guess we could try calling information, see if we can get a number for him. Hold on." He dialed again, asking the operator on the other end of the line if there was a listing for Preston Alphonse in Wickenburg. There was a pause. "Uh-huh," he said. "Okay. Thank you." Nate looked up. "She said that number was unlisted. Which means there still is a number, which means he's still in Wickenburg. He's kind of young to be retired, I think, but maybe he's older than he looked. Or maybe it's just that I'm a workaholic. I didn't retire until I was seventy-five, and I'm still only partially retired. I mean, I don't work the register anymore, but I'm out at the museum at least two, three times a week—"

"You've been a big help," Melanie said, breaking in before he went too far off on a tangent. "We really appreciate it. Do you have a piece of paper and a pen I could use to copy down the name on that business card?"

"Why, sure." Nate kept talking as she wrote down the information, and Glen found himself feeling sorry for the man. He seemed to be so grateful for their company. He clearly lived alone, and the lack of photographs around the living room indicated that he'd never been married. It was no wonder that he couldn't just retire, that he still hung out at his museum several times a week. They'd probably made his day with their visit, and he'd probably be retelling their story for weeks and months to come.

That was one way to get the word out.

The afternoon was getting late, and Nate invited them to hang around, stay for dinner, but in as polite a way as possible Melanie informed him that they had to leave. "Okay, wait a minute!" he said. He ran back down the hall, and they heard the sound of drawers being opened and then slammed shut. He was talking to himself, saying something unintelligible in a clearly exasperated voice. Then he hurried back, two white tickets the size of playing cards in his hand. "Here," he said, handing one to each of them. "Permanent passes. They'll let you into the museum free any time you want. Good forever. So next time you're up this way, stop in."

Glen thought of the museum and felt guilty about the way he and Melanie had made fun of the exhibits. They might be crude and amateurish, but this man took them seriously. He'd devoted his working life to them, and

Glen found that he had a new appreciation for the roadside attraction. This wasn't kitsch, it was Americana, and never again would he smugly dismiss it.

"We will," he told Nate gratefully. "Thank you."

"Yes," Melanie said. "Thank you very much. You've been a big help."

"Let me know how this all turns out, won't you?"

"We will," Glen promised.

Nate followed them outside and stood by his Japanese garage door, waving as they pulled out of the driveway. "Good-bye!" he called.

They both waved as they drove back toward the highway.

"I guess we're going to Wickenburg," Melanie said.

"I guess we are."

They spent the night in Holbrook, within throwing distance of an enormous, ugly power plant spewing continuous clouds of smoke into the sky. For some ungodly reason, nearly all of the hotels in Holbrook were booked, and the only one they found with a vacancy was a ratty little motor inn called the Shangri-La Resort. Their motel room smelled of pine-scented disinfectant, and there were stiff bodies of dead flies in the thick dust of the windowsill. In the bathroom, the toilet ran constantly, a sluicing spray sound loud enough to overpower the sound of the muted television.

"Charming," Melanie said.

"We've still got each other."

She laughed, put a hand on his arm. "Yes, we've still got each other."

Glen opened up the tank and fixed the toilet. Melanie dusted and cleaned with successive wads of wet Kleenex, and they managed to make the room seem tolerable if not entirely pleasant.

He dreamed that night of his mother, and in his dream she was young, younger than he was, the same age she'd been when he was a little boy and she had her paper route. She was sitting cross-legged on the hard floor of a Spanish church in New Mexico, doing needlepoint. The square of yellow cloth in her hands depicted an Anasazi pueblo being overrun by hordes of creatures with bushy heads of bright orange hair. They were of all different sizes, from dwarves to giants, and though they'd been sewn onto the cloth, they seemed to shift positions every time he glanced away. He was standing in the center aisle of the church, facing his mother, and behind her the chancel was lit with dozens of votive candles. It was a warm comforting sight, but he was acutely aware of the fact that behind him was darkness, blackness that he was afraid to turn around and see.

"It's all over," his mother said. Her voice was sorrowful, her eyes sad, but she was smiling crazily, the corners of her mouth pulled up in a Joker-like rictus. "You're too late. You failed."

In full view, one of the afro-headed creatures climbed off the yellow needlepoint cloth, shimmied up his mother's dress, and slid between her lips and down her throat. There was an audible clack, a strangely mechanical sound, and tears began streaming from his mother's desperately unhappy eyes. Her voice, issuing from that insanely grinning mouth, suddenly took on the properties of a skipping record, complete with scratches and clicks: "You failed/You failed/You failed/You failed . . ."

They got a late start the next morning. There was no alarm clock in the shabbily furnished room, so they'd asked the desk clerk for a six o'clock wake-up call. But either he didn't tell his counterpart on the following shift, or the new clerk forgot about it, because they didn't receive their call and it was nearly eight by the time they awoke.

Melanie dressed and packed while Glen took a quick shower, and they hurriedly loaded the car, deciding to skip breakfast and just hit the highway. Melanie took the roll of toilet paper and an unused plastic cup from the motel room before they left. "I'm going to get *something* out of this," she said.

There was supposed to be a shortcut, a back road between Prescott and Wickenburg, but Glen wasn't sure how much shorter it was. The route seemed endless, and the narrow two-lane traveled through country so remote that they saw not a single other vehicle. Melanie tried McCormack on the cell phone, just to make sure it worked out here. As he'd suspected and she had feared, they were out of range.

"We'll be fine," Glen said reassuringly.

"Yeah. Our trips together are always so smooth and problem free."

They did make it to Wickenburg without breaking down or experiencing even the slightest hint of car trouble, but that was where their luck seemed to end. Preston Alphonse was not just hard to find; he seemed to have disappeared. Wickenburg was a small town, but his name was not in the phone book, and none of the proprietors of the other antique stores at which they stopped knew him or were willing to admit they did. Glen suspected the latter. One old man was genuinely hostile when they asked him about Alphonse, and though both of them denied it, it was pretty clear that the old man thought they were cops. The others probably did, too, although why antique dealers would be afraid of the police was a mystery.

They were about to start canvassing door-to-door when Glen saw a white posterboard sign nailed to a telephone pole. ANNUAL LDS RUMMAGE SALE, the sign announced, SAT. 8-3.

"What day is it?" he asked Melanie.

She frowned. "What do you mean, 'What day is it?' "

"I lose track. What day is it?"

"Saturday."

He pointed to the sign. "*Annual* rummage sale," he said. "I'm not an expert, but don't antique dealers get most of their stuff from garage sales and rummage sales and then jack up the price? My hunch is that he's been there before, probably every year, and if we're lucky, someone knows him."

"Good thought," she said.

The LDS church was a big building of tan brick that seemed far too large for a town this size. Tables full of piled clothes ringed the parking lot, along with boxes of records, books, and children's toys. Quite a few cars were parked on the street in front of the church, and several families were sorting through the items for sale. Glen found a spot between a new Cadillac and an old

Jeep, and he and Melanie walked across the marked asphalt to a stand-alone table where two elderly women sat behind a metal cashbox and a pile of used grocery bags.

"Hello," one of the women, a short old lady with tall beehive hair, greeted them. "Looking for anything in particular?"

"Actually, we are," Glen said. "We're looking for a man named Preston Alphonse. He used to have an antique store here in Wickenburg. Do you happen to know him?"

"Preston? Sure I know him."

"Great. Can you tell us where he lives?"

The woman's eyes narrowed. "Why?"

What was with all this secrecy surrounding an antique dealer? The Californian in him was tempted to say, *Because we're IRS agents,* but instead he simply said, "A friend of ours sold Mr. Alphonse something a couple of years ago, and we'd like to buy it from him if he still has it."

"What is it?" the woman asked suspiciously.

Glen saw no reason to lie. "A mummy," he said. "An Indian mummy."

"A mummy?"

He nodded. "It used to be displayed up at a place outside of Beltane, off I-40. But it was originally from a ghost town near Rio Verde. A guy named Jack Carpenter discovered it on a hunting trip."

She looked at him suspiciously, and then the suspicion cleared. Apparently, his story rang true and she was no longer worried that he was a private detective or a federal agent or a mobster or whatever she'd feared.

"Preston's just down the block," she said, pointing. "I don't know the exact address, but you can't miss it. The big Victorian-looking house on the left. White roses in front, a trellis over the walkway. There's an antique plow and old wagon wheel in the flower garden, a white wicker settee on the porch. Like I said, you can't miss it."

"Thank you," Glen said gratefully. "We really appreciate this."

The old woman gestured around the parking lot. "See anything you like? We're kind of winding down here. Everything's half-price between now and three."

"If we don't spend all our money at Mr. Alphonse's, we'll be back."

She laughed. "Fair enough."

They drove down the street in the direction the woman had indicated. For the first block, the houses were all similar-looking homes of fairly recent vintage. Houses on the next block over were older, more individualistic, and halfway down, sandwiched between a remodeled farm cottage and a two-story log cabin, was a large, light-blue faux-Victorian house with white trim and a blooming garden out front.

"This is it." He pulled to a stop, but a sign next to the curb said NO PARKING ANY TIME, and instead he drove into the house's driveway, parking behind an old black T-Bird. As they got out, Glen expected to see Alphonse on the porch, heading toward them, either curious as to why they had pulled into his driveway or furious that he was being disturbed. But the house appeared to be deserted. Alphonse wasn't going to make this easy for them, Glen thought.

He was wrong.

They walked onto the porch, rang the front doorbell, and a slight, pleasant-looking man with a small gray mustache opened the door, peering at them through the screen. "Yes?"

Melanie stepped forward. "Hello. We're looking for Mr. Preston Alphonse."

The man looked puzzled. "I am he."

"My name's Melanie Black and this is Glen Ridgeway. We're here about a mummy that you bought from a tourist trap up near Beltane about four or five years ago—"

"Ah, that," Alphonse said, and Glen thought he heard a tremor in the older man's voice.

"Yes. We just came from Nate Stewky's, and he told us he sold the mummy to you. We"—she gestured toward Glen—"have been working at a newly discovered archeological site near Bower under the direction of Dr. Al Wittinghill from ASU. You may find this hard to believe, and you may think we're overstating the case, but that mummy may be the key to unlocking a centuries-old mystery."

She was so much more articulate than he was, and once again, Glen was impressed. She was a teacher, he thought; she made her living speaking to classes all day long. But that was only part of it. She was quicker on her feet than he was, and he decided in the future he would let her do the talking for the two of them.

"May we come in?" Melanie asked.

Alphonse thought for a moment, then opened the screen door. "I'll come out."

Melanie moved back to let him through, and she and Glen followed him over to the wicker settee on the opposite end of the porch. "Have a seat," he offered. They'd been in the car for half the day, were tired of sitting and told him so. He seemed to have no intention of sitting down either, so all three of them ended up standing and leaning against the porch rail while they talked.

"First things first," Melanie said. "Do you still have the mummy?"

"No. I sold it. A month or so after I got it. You want to know the truth? That thing scared the hell out of me." He paused. "And it killed my dog."

"It killed your dog?"

Alphonse looked uncomfortable. "I believe so, yes. Although that's not something I would ever be able to prove."

"How did it happen?"

"I don't know. Not exactly. But Zelda was afraid of the mummy from the beginning, and she refused to stay in the same room with it, even if I was there with her. This went on for about a week or so. And then suddenly she disappeared. I was frantic! Zelda had never run out on me before, and I was sure it was because of that mummy. I had it moved out of my workroom here at the house and over to the shop. I put up lost doggie posters all over the neighborhood, and for two days I searched and searched, driving up and down the same streets, making twice-daily trips to the pound. Then on the third day, Zelda showed up. At the shop. I found her dead on the mummy's chest when I opened that morning. There wasn't a mark on her, and the vet said she died of natural causes. But how did she get from the house to the shop? How did she get in? And why did she crawl onto the chest of the mummy when that freakish thing terrified her?"

Alphonse shook his head. "I had no answers for any of those questions. My own personal belief is that she died of fright—which to the vet would have looked like natural causes—although that still doesn't explain how she came to be there on that monster's chest in the back room of a locked antique store."

This was the kind of stuff they were looking for, and Glen was filled with an unexpected sense of exhilaration. All previous confirmation of unusual occurrences had filled him with dread, left him feeling overwhelmed and impotent. But somehow this gave him hope. He didn't know why. It was a feeling, a vague intuition that they *were* going to find that mummy.

"That's when you decided to sell it?" Melanie asked.

Alphonse nodded. "Originally, I was going to keep it for myself. I was not only an antique dealer, I was—and *am*—a collector of antiquities. I have always been fascinated by ancient artifacts, and I have to admit, when I saw that beautifully bizarre mummy in that little two-bit carnival display, I simply had to have it. I'd let a genuine shrunken head slip through my fingers just the month before, and I was determined not to make that mistake again. But after I badgered Mr. . . ." He frowned.

"Stewky," Melanie prompted.

"Yes, Stewky. Well, all these peculiar things started happening. So after I buried Zelda, I put the word out and I would say rather aggressively tried to find a buyer. Which I did, about a week later."

"You wouldn't happen to remember who you sold it to, would you?"

"Sure," he said. "It was bought by a historical museum."

"Where is it?"

"McGuane."

2

"Women love the taste of minority genitalia," Ellis McCormack said to the white supremacists' answering machine. "They just . . . taste better than caucasian cocks. . . ." He hung up, not sure where to go with this, aware that his harassment of the bigots wasn't giving him the same lift it usually did.

Because he was secretly a bigot, too?

He wasn't, he knew, but his failure to consult with or even discuss what was going on with a single Native American haunted him, gnawed at him. He'd always considered himself a champion of much-maligned multi-culturalism. Hell, during the anti-Iranian demonstrations of the 1979–1980 school year, he'd been one of the only professors to stand up and defend the school's Arab students, arguing that they were not responsible for the policies of their governments. But he'd been born and raised in Arizona, and as much as he hated to admit it, he was unconsciously more dismissive of Native Americans.

And Native American culture was his fucking field of expertise.

He looked up at the shelf above his desk, at a Hopi Kachina doll bought at Second Mesa for an unconsciona-bly low price. Swiveling around in his chair, he got up and poked his head out the door into the hall. At the opposite end of the corridor, John Campbell's door was open. The Navajo professor had finally arrived.

Campbell was the department's newest addition, and while McCormack, as chair, had hired him, he had made almost no effort to get to know the instructor, other than in the most perfunctory way. He told himself it wasn't because the man was Native American—hell, he hadn't made an effort to get close to *any* of the hirees from the past three years, had he?—but a small nagging doubt couldn't help but point out that Campbell was the only instructor for whom he had not hosted a department meet-and-greet.

McCormack had been thinking all morning about what he would say, trying to come up with a way to broach the subject. Part of the problem was that his mind was on his wife. The doctor said that she'd suffered no permanent physical damage, and Alyssa had assured him that she was all right, that she wanted to go back to work, *needed* to go back to work, but he could not forget the way she'd looked in that closet. The two of them should be taking time off—a few days, a week even—in order to talk this through.

Instead, they'd gone back to their daily routine, and he'd spent half the morning worrying about her instead of thinking about what he should say to Campbell.

Gathering his courage, McCormack started down the corridor. He wouldn't pussyfoot around, he decided. He'd speak plainly. Campbell would probably respect that more than some oblique attempt to ease his way into the subject.

He reached the Navajo instructor's office, knocked on the metal door frame. "Hello, John?"

Campbell swiveled around in his chair, surprised to be approached by the department head during his office hours. "Dr. McCormack."

"I told you: Ellis."

But *had* he told him? McCormack couldn't remember. "Ellis."

There was a pause that started naturally, but quickly grew to uncomfortable length.

McCormack cleared his throat. "I assume you've heard about this rash of unexplained phenomena that has reportedly occurred around Native American excavation sites and museums the past few weeks?"

Reportedly? Why was he still hiding behind qualifiers, couching his words in vague generalities? What the hell was wrong with him? Already he was veering from the conversational course he had set for himself, retreating behind old instinct and bad habits.

"Of course, I've heard about it."

Was that condescension he heard in the other man's voice? Or scorn?

McCormack pressed on quickly. "As you may or may not have heard, I and a few of our colleagues from related disciplines have been acting as consultants to local law enforcement in regard to the events at Scottsdale's Pima House Ruins. Although it now seems to have withdrawn or disappeared, we mapped out the parameters of a phenomenon we've been referring to as 'the vortex,' for want of a better word. Undetectable to the naked eye and virtually unmeasurable with conventional instrumentation, it was the area in which people, animals, and objects disappeared." He paused. "It occurred to me that as an anthropology instructor yourself and as a . . . Native American, you might be able to provide us with some additional insight. As you know, the study of indigenous peoples is my own area of expertise, but I thought you might be aware of pertinent myths, histories, or folktales that might be unfamiliar to me but could shed some light on what has been occurring."

Campbell smiled thinly. "I don't have any secret mystical knowledge. I don't know what's going on. I don't think anyone does." He paused. "Except maybe Al."

"Al's disappeared."

"I heard that."

"In an incident at his dig in Bower."

"That's what I understand."

Another awkward silence.

Would Al have consulted with native scholars, with shamen and medicine men and tribal leaders? Truth be told, McCormack had never really respected Al Wittinghill's academic methods. He'd considered the man's ideas ridiculous, not even serious enough to be contemptible or heretical, and his pop-culture analytical approach was a joke, his conclusions uniformly suspect.

But McCormack was big enough to admit when he was wrong, and he was trying to make up for past sins now.

Only he wasn't quite sure how to do it.

He cleared his throat again. He didn't need to, but the silence seemed to call for some type of prefatory noise. "Al, as I'm sure you know, was working on some sort of unified theory to explain the Anasazi . . . disappearances, as he called them. Although as far as I know, he had not revealed the details of that theory to anyone other than his partner Dr. Henry. I think it was clear from his writings and his speeches, however, that his explanation involved a supernatural component and was not really in line with scholarly thinking on the matter."

"I thought you didn't agree with him on that subject," Campbell said. "At least, that's what Al told me."

McCormack faked a smile, trying to stifle his natural instincts and not become defensive. "I didn't, I didn't. But recent events have forced me to reevaluate my opinions."

"I'm sorry. I'm afraid Al didn't share his theory with me, either. I think he was waiting for publication."

"I understand that. I was simply wondering if he had solicited any input from you, if he had asked you about any, ah, *personal* data you might have."

"No."

"I see."

McCormack thought about Alyssa, the state of the house when they found her. This was happening all over, to Native Americans as well—whatever was behind it did not discriminate as to race—and it was impossible to believe that one or more of the tribes were not attacking this from their own end, putting their own teams on it and utilizing the knowledge of their shamen or scholars or folklorists. Would Campbell know if that were the case? Would Campbell tell him if it was?

"We'll be out there at Pima House again this morning, mopping up as it were. Afterward, we'll be investigating the adjoining neighborhood where an estimated fifty-four people are missing."

Estimated.

"Would you like to . . . come with us?" he concluded lamely.

Campbell met his gaze. "No, I'm busy." He swiveled his chair around, and McCormack could no longer see his face. "But thanks for asking."

3

Cameron stared out the motel room window at the fenced-off pool, where the children of tourists jumped off the diving board and played "Marco Polo." Behind him, his Uncle Vince was on the phone to someone, talking in low hushed tones because he didn't want Cameron to hear.

He wondered what had happened to his parents. And Jay and his family. And Stu and Melinda and their mom.

And Mr. Green and Mrs. Dilbay and Mr. Finch and everyone else. He knew they were probably dead, knew it intellectually, but it didn't really feel that way to him; emotionally it still wasn't registering.

That was good, he decided. Otherwise, he'd be spending all his time crying and feeling sorry for himself. This way, his thoughts were on finding them, getting them back, figuring out what was going on.

He'd learned a lot listening to Uncle Vince and his friends. This wasn't just some isolated occurrence, and it wasn't something that had followed him down from the scout ranch. The monster he'd seen was part of a much larger pattern happening all over the state, maybe all over the country. He was relieved to discover that everything was not revolving around him, that he was not some sort of catalyst. At the same time, that meant that the simple, easy explanation to which he'd been clinging, the hope that killing or vanquishing the Mogollon Monster would put an end to it all, was incorrect. That was as scary as anything that had happened so far.

His uncle got off the phone.

"Who was that?"

"Dr. McCormack."

"What were you guys talking about?"

"You know."

"Oh."

"There's nothing new, though." Vince unwrapped the last plastic cup and got a drink of water from the sink. "We should probably go out for a while, do something, give the maid a chance to clean up in here."

"Is Dr. McCormack at my house?"

Vince shook his head. "He's going over later, after work. They're still looking around, the police and everyone, but he's at ASU."

"You were talking pretty quietly there."

"Yeah."

"There's no reason to keep anything from me, you know. I'm in this as deep as you are. I took a picture of that monster. I was chased by dust devils that looked like Mom and Dad. I can handle it."

"You're right."

"So what were you really talking about?"

"Nothing new. He talked to a Navajo professor and called the Hopi and Navajo governments, but they're as baffled as we are. Or at least that's what they told him. He thinks they might be trying to fight this on their own, in their own way, and just don't want to tell him." Vince poured the last of his water into the sink. "I hope so. I really do."

Cameron was silent for a moment. "What do you think is causing all this, making everyone disappear, making that pottery and stuff attack people?"

"I don't know. None of us do."

"Do you think it's that monster I took a picture of?"

"Maybe. That seems to be the best lead we have so far."

Cameron licked his lips. "I heard you guys talking, you know. Earlier. Mr. Ridgeway said there were old Indian pictures and carvings and things of that monster."

"Yeah."

Cameron paused. An idea had just occurred to him. "Did the Indians have some kind of story about the Mogollon Monster? The scout masters said they did, but that might've just been, you know, for us."

Vince sat down on the bed next to him. "I don't know, champ. Why?"

"At first, when all that stuff started happening to me, after Scoutmaster Anderson died, I thought it was the Mogollon Monster. I thought he'd followed me back down to Scottsdale. But then I thought that was just a story and this was something else, some . . . I don't know.

"But maybe it *was* the Mogollon Monster." Cameron saw that he had piqued his uncle's interest and kept going. "Maybe this thing inspired all those stories. I mean, it's hairy. What I saw in Jay's house wasn't big, but Mr. Ridgeway said that skull he found was big. Maybe it's like a race of these things, and I saw a baby or a kid or dwarf or something. Those old Indians and loggers and trappers and whatever, if they saw it in the forest and it killed some of 'em, they probably spread the word and it turned into the Mogollon Monster and Bigfoot—"

"Sasquatch," Vince said.

"Whatever. But if Indians made all those pictures and carvings, they were obviously afraid of this thing, too."

His uncle nodded thoughtfully.

"I told you, when it passed by my cabin and when I saw it in the backyard, I was frozen, I couldn't move."

"It radiates some type of power," Vince mused. "That's what froze you up, that's what corrupts the animals, the pets, that's what . . . draws people."

Cameron nodded excitedly. "I could feel it when me and Jay went over to the ruins. The same thing. And the closer you got, the stronger it got, and when you moved back to a certain point, it stopped, like you were out of range or something."

"What about when you took the picture of it? You weren't frozen then."

"Not exactly. I felt it, that same thing, but it wasn't strong enough to stop me. Maybe he'd used up all his power getting rid of everyone."

Vince punched his shoulder lightly, approvingly. "Good thinking, Cam. You might be on to something here. I'll call Mr. Ridgeway and Dr. McCormack and talk to them about it. I'm not sure they're thinking along those lines. Dr. McCormack, at least, seems to believe it's some type of wormhole phenomenon. A wormhole is—"

Cameron snorted. "I know what a wormhole is."

Vince raised his eyebrows.

"Star Trek."

"Right. Well, he's thinking some wormhole-type thing opens up, lets these things in, draws our people through, and happens every hundred years or so. But that's . . . too big. Too general. It doesn't explain all these small things that are happening, all these personal things. It doesn't explain what I saw in Springerville, with those guys on the ridge all dressed up in primitive costumes and those people from town going up to collect those artifacts the next day. But if that skull still had some of the power that you're talking about . . ." Vince smiled thinly. "I think we're on to something here."

Cameron's excitement was beginning to fade. He thought of that bushy-haired creature. It had stood on the bed without making any indentation, and it had disappeared without leaving the house. It had also made everyone in his whole neighborhood disappear and had used his parents to . . . play with him.

He remembered his parents sitting on the couch, staring at the dead TV screen, his mom nodding, his dad laughing.

How could they hope to stop something like that? How could they kill it? It had been around for centuries, maybe even longer, and had wiped out entire races of people. What could they possibly do to stop it?

"Are we going to die?" Cameron asked.

His uncle looked surprised. "No, of course not."

"Everyone else is gone, everyone on my street, all my friends. Mom and Dad. It's not that far-fetched."

"But *you're* here, right?" Vince stopped suddenly, his eyes widening. "You're here," he repeated. He looked at Cameron. "What if you're immune?" he said. "You made it through your scout camp. You made it through what happened in your neighborhood. What if it hasn't killed you because it can't? What if you're somehow resistant to this power, this creature, whatever it is?"

Cameron felt a faint stirring of hope. "What if you are, too? Nothing happened to you in Springerville."

Vince nodded wonderingly. "Nothing happened to *any* of us. Not to Glen, not to Melanie, not to us. Not only that, but we're all trying to figure out what's going on and how to stop it, and we've all ended up together. What if that's because we were *meant* to? Or what if some . . . higher power has brought us together?"

Cameron's mouth felt dry. "Higher power? You mean like God?"

"I'm just thinking out loud. Don't take any of this as gospel."

But Cameron could tell that his uncle was not merely thinking out loud. He had only just thought of it, but he believed it, and the expression on his face was almost one of relief. Cameron himself was filled with a renewed optimism. Maybe they could fight back. Maybe they did have a chance.

The two of them sat there for a moment, not speaking.

"What's going to happen to me when this is all over?" Cameron said quietly. "Are you going to . . . adopt me?"

His uncle clearly hadn't thought that far ahead. But he recovered nicely. "Of course," he said.

"Does that mean you'll be my dad, then?"

"No. I'll still be your uncle. But I'll take care of you. I'll do . . . all those things your dad would've done if he was . . . here."

Cameron nodded. He thought of his mom's tooth inside the porcelain carrot that looked like the dust devil. His uncle and the police had broken open the other carrot. While Cameron had said he didn't want to know what they'd found, he'd been able to think of almost nothing else for two days, and now he finally asked, "What was in there? The carrot?"

Vince looked at him for a moment as if weighing options, making a decision. "Your dad's ring finger," he said finally. "With his wedding ring."

They didn't say any more. The image was fixed forever in Cameron's brain without his having to see it or hear any more details.

His parents really were gone.

He stared out the motel window at a father in the shallow end of the pool hoisting a young boy onto his shoulders and flipping him into the water. The boy, laughing, splashed upward. "Again!" he said, holding out his hand to his father. "Again!"

And Cameron started to cry.

4

When George Black returned from the grocery store, his house was not his house.

Oh, it was his house on the outside. When he got out of the car, bearing the grocery sack of syrup and lettuce and spaghetti sauce and orange juice that his wife had sent him to buy, he was in his own driveway in his own front yard. And when he stepped up the stoop and opened the screen door, nothing was amiss. But the second he stepped inside and saw a long dark hallway with corroded metal walls that reminded him of the bowels of the ship that had taken him to Korea, he knew he was far, far from home.

"Margaret?" he called, but only out of obligation. She wasn't here. No one was here. No one he knew.

From someplace far ahead came a deep bass thumping, as though a slave were pounding on a giant kettle drum. George dropped his groceries and turned around, hoping he might be able to get out the way he'd come in, but the doorway was gone. Behind him was only rusted metal.

He walked slowly forward, past puddles on the floor, oily pools of stagnant water that reflected back blackness and turned the dim yellow light from the dirty caged bulb in the ceiling into dull rainbow colors.

Why was this happening to him? He'd been on board from the beginning. Bower had changed and he had changed with it, and when the city council began recruiting volunteers for the wars, he had signed up immediately—despite Margaret's protestations. He had even helped make weapons for the warriors, he and Brian Babbitt both, the two of them basing their designs on pictures from recently uncovered pottery.

So why was this happening?

Why did anything happen? Just because. This was a random world. Bad things happened to good people and vice versa. The churchy crowd might think that God had a plan for everyone and that everything that happened was God's will, but the truth was more haphazard. They'd found that out lately, hadn't they? Would all of this be happening if those county workers hadn't dug up that Indian ruin, if that ASU professor hadn't come out to investigate? He didn't think so. But accidents occurred and accidents had ripples and sometimes the shit hit the fan.

The pounding was softer now, moving farther away. George stepped over the puddles, around the puddles, in them when he had to. He nearly slipped, pressed a hand against the wall to steady himself, and was surprised to discover that the wall was not metal. It felt like the latex-painted stucco of his own hallway, and for a brief hopeful second he thought that this was all a mirage. That hope died fast. His hand came away grimy and greasy, palms and fingers smeared with a dark foul-smelling substance. He could see a streak on the wall where he'd touched it, and it had a tactile dimension that he knew no hallucination could possibly imitate.

This was real. This was happening.

He stopped where he was, heard the pounding retreat even farther. It sounded as though it was going underground. He wanted to get out of this hellish place more than anything he'd ever wanted in his life, but he was afraid to continue on, afraid of where this hallway might lead, afraid it led not out but deeper in. He turned around, intending to go back, but it was darker than it had been. He saw shadows where there should not be shadows and they had shapes he did not like. Nothing about the hallway behind him seemed right, and he started forward again, moving more quickly this time.

The corridor curved, and soon he could see where it ended: a dimly lighted room with a faded yellow floor and filthy once-white walls. The doorway entered the room from the side, at the back, so he could see only a flat expanse of floor, the rear wall, and a portion of the opposite side wall.

He hurried through the oily puddles and the ever-darkening hall, stepping through the doorway onto dry yellow linoleum.

Laughter echoed off the dirty walls, not wild and manic or hearty and friendly, but low and impossibly constant. In the center of the room was a fat man in a stained apron. He was the one laughing, although there was no smile on his thin-lipped mouth.

It was his grandfather.

He knew it but didn't know how he knew it. George had been born three years after his grandfather's death, and if there had ever been any photographs of the man, they had been hidden or destroyed long before he was old enough to see or understand. If he had wanted to do so, he could have gone to the library when he was older, looked up old newspapers—but he hadn't.

This was him, though, this was his grandfather.

The mass murderer.

The fat man was standing before a battered butcher block covered with dried brown blotches, keeping up that low constant laughter. A nicked, rusted cleaver was clutched in his upraised right hand. To the side of the butcher block was a large tub of wet concrete.

George was more afraid of this room than he had been of anything thus far, but the doorway through which he had entered was gone. There were no doors, no windows, only dirty unbroken wall.

The fat man continued laughing quietly, unendingly, cleaver hand upraised.

There was someone else in the room, or some*thing* else, though he had been avoiding it and did not want to acknowledge its presence. It was standing in the far corner, covered by brown butcher paper, and it was short, the size of a child. Beneath the thick wrapping, it was shivering, shaking like a Parkinson's patient, and the paper rattled with the agitated oscillation of its movements.

He knew what was under there, and on some level, he thought, he had known from the beginning, had known from the second he stepped inside his house and saw that hallway that it would lead here, to this.

The crinkling of the paper grew louder, overpowering the laughter of his grandfather.

He thought of the one piece of pottery he had not saved, a piece he had not shown Margaret, had not even spoken about to Brian Babbitt. He'd found it not in the backyard but in the shower. A thin ceramic point had been protruding from between the metal slats of the drain, and he had pulled it up, a long thin bullet-shaped shard that was brown on one side and black on the other. On the black side, etched not painted, was a face, a puckered, buck-toothed, flinty-eyed visage that startled him so much he had dropped it—before picking it back up again, putting it in the soap dish, face-side down, and quickly finishing his shower. The face had been so horrible that he had not simply thrown the pottery shard away afterward, he had destroyed it, smashing it with a hammer in the garage, grinding the individual pieces into powder and flushing the powder down the toilet when Margaret was getting her hair done later in the day.

Maybe that's why this was happening. Maybe he was being punished for destroying what was meant to be the crowning glory of his collection. Maybe whatever power had made all of these artifacts appear and had compelled him to collect them was displeased and angry.

What should he do? Apologize out loud? Pray? Stay where he was and hope the fat man didn't turn around and see him? Walk slowly around the room, carefully checking the walls for hidden exits?

The upraised cleaver slammed into the butcher block with a terrifyingly loud thwack, the powerful blow embedding the blade in the dark stained wood. His grandfather turned around, laughter continuing to issue from that unsmiling thin-lipped mouth.

In the corner, the shaking figure under the butcher paper scooted forward.

"No," George tried to say, but the word emerged as a husky croak.

The fat man was almost upon him, beefy hands outstretched, thick fingers curled into claws, but it was the smaller form that frightened him more. George could see, between his grandfather's left arm and body, the shaking figure skittering toward him. Movement and vibration caused the butcher paper to slip, slide, fall off.

Underneath was the face he'd known he would see.

And he started screaming.

Thirteen

1

The ice cave at Sunset Crater had been closed since the late 1980s, since a roof collapse had destroyed the always fragile entryway and brought the park service's nascent safety concerns into sharp focus. Even before that final collapse, visitors had had to wear hard hats with lights, and crawl over rubble and under wedged boulders, in order to get to the long cylindrical lava tube that made up the main body of the cave. Now the entrance was blocked off, the trail routed around it, but it was still navigable for someone with minimal spelunking skills who knew the terrain.

Like Ryan Ladd.

Ryan flipped on his flashlight. He didn't know why he was jeopardizing his own job by coming down here without authorization, but after hearing Pace Henry's wild theory and seeing how excited Pace was about his Albuquerque story, he'd had his brother-in-law introduce him to a colleague at Wupatki, where he'd done his own informal unscientific research into the rash of unexplained phenomena. Damn if Pace wasn't right. There *was* something weird going on. These weren't just strange little isolated incidents; they were interconnected symptoms of a much larger development that really did seem to have an Anasazi association.

Afterward, since he was in the park already, he'd driven the loop back to Sunset Crater. Time was when he and Hugh had had races up to the top of the cinder cone, and during the hot summer months they'd usually ended up in the ice cave, where the temperature was a constant fifty-six degrees, to cool off. He had the urge to check out the cave again, and that's why he was wriggling on his belly under a cracked boulder that threatened to crush him.

In the old days, a constant stream of people would be trekking in and out of the cave, bottlenecking in the narrow passages. The more experienced hikers would go all the way back to the end, while families and casual tourists remained within sight of the entrance and the lighted world outside. Now, though, he was the only person here, and the cavern was totally still. The only noises were his own breathing and the scraping sounds of his passing.

He emerged from beneath the boulder into a narrow closet-size space that he would have assumed was the end of the cave had he not been here before. Shining his light up, he saw the small opening was still near the roof of the tiny chamber, and he scaled the pile of rubble before him, an almost vertical climb, crawling over the top of the dislodged rocks and dropping into a passage that appeared remarkably untouched by the cave-in.

It was cool down here but humid, and he stopped to rest against a boulder and wipe the sweat from his forehead before it started dripping into his eyes. On an impulse, he shut off his flashlight. Suddenly he was surrounded by blackness so deep he could see nothing whatsoever. He brought his hand to his face, but could not see his fingers, even when they were touching his forehead and nose. It was disorienting to exist in such a total absence of light, but it was not unpleasant, and he decided to remain in darkness a little while longer.

He listened to the sound of his breath, listened to the sound of his heart. Opened and closed his eyes, saw only black. He remembered the way the ice cave used to be and tried to figure out exactly where in it he was.

And whether he was really alone down here.

Of course, his thoughts were turning toward the macabre. How could they not, after what he'd heard? Dave Lentz at Wupatki had told him of a museum curator in Flagstaff who'd been bludgeoned to death after hours by an invisible assailant. A female intern over at Montezuma Castle who had stripped off her clothes in the visitor's center rest room and sexually assaulted herself with an Anasazi ulna. Lentz had also related a story about the Wupatki blowhole just down the road. The blowhole, a deep shaft in the earth from which cool air issued, even during the hot Arizona summer, was at one time a type of natural air conditioner for the pueblo and was now the most popular tourist destination at the park. Two days ago, voices began sounding from within the blowhole, a cacophony of speech uttered in a guttural language that even their experts did not recognize. They'd shone lights into the opening, had even sent down a cable-cam, but the source of the voices was deeper than they could reach—although the cable-cam seemed to capture a swirling movement of darkness, a twisting confluence of shadows toward the bottom of the narrow shaft.

Was that why he had come? Some thrill-seeking desire to discover monsters in the earth? He didn't think so, but Ryan couldn't rule it out. He was a bit of a daredevil, and Sunset Crater was part of the same park as Wupatki and the blowhole, and maybe somewhere in the back of his mind he'd thought he might come across something interesting. He turned on the flashlight, grateful to be able to see again, and pointed the beam around the chamber. As he'd hoped, there was only rock.

He pushed himself away from the boulder and continued on, ducking under the increasingly low ceiling as he neared the end of the cave.

And suddenly it wasn't so cool.

Ryan stopped, frowned. It seemed warmer than it had only seconds before, the air thicker. A faint smell of sulfur emanated from the shadowed area before him, and when he touched a hand to the wall on his right, the rock was hot. For a brief irrational second, he thought maybe he'd died and was approaching hell. But reason instantly reasserted itself as the ground beneath his feet started rumbling. This wasn't supernatural, this was a geological occurrence.

The volcano was becoming active.

But how could that be? Events like this didn't just happen. There were signs, indications, gradual escalations in earth movements and measurable increases in ground temperature. Even if he had not heard about such episodes—which was highly unlikely—Hugh would have, and his brother-in-law would have told him. No, this was not expected; this was completely out of the blue.

The rumbling continued, the shaking not merely below his feet now but all around, and from the dark far end of the cave came a sharp blast of steam that seared his face and hands and made the clothes pressing against his skin feel like they had been soaked in boiling oil. Screaming, Ryan turned around and tried to run, but the quarters were too close and every time he bumped into the wall, agony shot through his body, nearly incapacitating him. Even his throat felt burned, and he tried to close his mouth, tried to swallow and keep his throat lubricated with saliva, but he could not keep himself from crying out as he attempted to make his way back.

He lurched against a fallen boulder, dropping his flashlight.

Up above, their instruments were probably going crazy. Geologists and vulcanologists from all over were being called up and patched in. Within the next day, a team of scientists would doubtlessly be dispatched down into the cave to set up new monitoring equipment and investigate, but for now he was on his own, all alone, and no one knew he was here.

Around him, the rumbling grew stronger. The floor shook, jerked, and though he couldn't see the movement, he could feel it. It was as if the entire cave had abruptly slipped to one side. Rocks rained on him from above, hitting his shoulders and arms, one glancing off the side of his head. Warm blood gushed out. From ahead, somewhere between him and the entrance, came a deafening roar followed by a dusty wave as a piece of the cave collapsed.

He was going to die in here, he realized. For some reason the knowledge did not panic him but made him calm. He sat down where he was, and it didn't hurt. His buttocks had not been seared by the steam blast, and it felt good not to be bumping against rock, not to have his burned skin assaulted.

He closed his mouth, swallowed saliva, and waited for death.

2

This wasn't possible.

Alex Rodriguez checked his gauges. Double-checked them. The reservoir had not only dropped since last month's inspection, it had dropped precipitously, though there was no logical reason for that to have occurred.

It had, though, and he didn't really need instruments to tell him so. A visual appraisal was enough to show him that the basin was down. He could even see the line of last month's watermark.

Five feet.

It was down five feet.

Two years' worth of melted snow and rainfall.

This wasn't the Rockies. In this little corner of Colorado, there was no year-round snowpack. Water was scarce, and it was the job of the SWCWD not only to ensure that water was free of contaminants and toxins, but to make sure that there was *enough* water for all of their customers: agricultural, residential, and business.

This was a problem.

No, not just a problem. A disaster. Within the past two weeks, wells had been drying up throughout the district, not merely dowsed sites but solid stable wells mapped out and drilled by the USGS, and there was talk back at the office of aquifer depletion. They couldn't afford to lose any water at the reservoir. Not this year.

Alex stared across the basin at the bare berm opposite the pump house. He thought he saw pictographic shapes in the hardpacked dirt, large organic circular forms that could have been natural, could have been intentionally made. He was wearing his sunglasses, but he was still squinting against the sun, and from this angle it was impossible to tell exactly what he was seeing.

He walked several paces to the left, until the sun was partially blocked by a bushy juniper. The shapes in the dirt *did* look man-made, and while they made no sense to him, their intentional placement on the berm indicated that they did to someone. He could see the last of the shapes, the end of the line, halfway down the opposite side of the reservoir, some sixty yards north, but the

first ones were hidden from view, the beginning somewhere around the curved side of the berm at an inlet.
He wasn't sure why he was so interested in the pictographs, if, indeed, that's what they were. They couldn't
possibly be connected to the reservoir's sudden unexplainable loss of water. But his gut told him that they
were connected.

His gaze focused on a strange-looking spiral directly
across from the spot where he stood, a spiral that was
reflected in the still water. The two of them formed a
shape that he almost recognized and definitely didn't
like. He looked quickly away, fumbled for his keys, and
hurriedly locked up the pump house.

He tossed his clipboard in the pickup, got in, and
started the engine. Throwing the truck into gear, he took
off down the dirt road on which he had come. He'd tell
one of the supervisors about the defaced berm. And the
shocking loss of water.

Let them deal with it.

3

The two towns met on the field of battle, their war
judged and overseen by an idol of bone.

How in God's name had this happened? Will Green-
burg wondered.

Oh, he knew the facts behind the fight, could recite
the rising progression of insults and assaults and strikes
and retaliations that had brought them to this point. Intellectually, he understood it all. But it was as if, emotionally, he had amnesia. Steps and escalations that had
seemed sensible reactions now seemed unfathomable
and completely illogical. It was as if he'd just awakened
to find himself standing above a murdered body, holding
a bloody knife.

And, really, that was exactly what had happened.

Will looked up at the idol. Taller than the tallest tree
on the field, it had appeared this morning as if by magic,
an elaborate construction of bones and skulls that resembled an ancient Mexican god, a wide squarish figure

filled with static malevolence. The face was fierce: grimacing mouth, beetled brow, angry eyes.

Only there weren't any eyes. Not really. There were
only angled openings above the nose that somehow kept
out the morning light and captured the shadows of night.

On the opposite side of the plain, past the downed
bodies and the current wave of combatants, the other
town's reinforcements prepared for battle. Hundreds of
people—sales clerks, nurses, roofers, teachers—were
checking their weapons, getting into their customized attack vehicles. Those who weren't naked wore animals
pelts. Many of their faces were painted with blood.

A burly man wielding an ax broke through the line of
defense, yelling wildly, and Will shot him in the head.
The man went down in a spray of blood.

Will mentally notched his gun: fifteen.

Behind him came the roar of engines as the motor
crew arrived. He turned to see SUVs with armed gun
turrets, re-equipped fire engines with Caterpillar tires.
Police vehicles and captured National Guard jeeps, he
knew, were circling around through the trees in order to
box in the enemy. Hostilities were about to escalate.

Good. This skirmish had been dragging on all morning, and he wanted to end it. They'd already defeated
two other towns this week—Sundance and Curiale—and
once they finished off West Fork, they'd be able to rest
awhile before stepping up the campaign and bringing
death and destruction to Beltane, Holbrook, Winslow,
Flagstaff.

Or *would* they be able to rest?

He looked up at the idol. The bone figure didn't
speak, but its wishes were clear.

Where did it come from? he wondered again. Who
had made it and why? And how had it just . . . appeared? He had no illusions that it was a real creature.
Despite its horrible appearance, it was an inanimate object, intentionally constructed. And yet . . .

And yet it was more than that. Dark eyes not only
looked down upon him, they *watched* him. And surely
he was not the only one to believe that the figure was
judging them, evaluating them.

All of a sudden, he didn't like the idol. It had emerged

into the open only this morning, but perhaps it had been behind the battles from the very beginning. If it had not existed, there would have been no attacks. They would have all just gone on with their normal lives and right at this moment he would be on his coffee break at the DMV.

Now that world was gone forever.

He looked at the idol with hatred and found himself wondering what would happen if he fired a couple of rounds into the interlocked bones that formed the mouth, the nose, the eye sockets. He smiled as he imagined the face being blown apart, collapsing in on itself as struts and supports gave way and fragments of bone went flying into the air. That wouldn't stop the battle—things had gone too far for that to ever happen—but it might make everyone pause, might make them think, and maybe this would turn out to be the *last* battle. Maybe they would all come to their senses and go back to the way things were—

An arrow penetrated his chest, pierced his heart, moving too fast to see, making a noise like a hummingbird's wings. The pain was explosive, immediate, spreading outward from the point of impact like a shock wave. He saw the shooter as he fell, a young man not unlike himself, who was already stringing another arrow and aiming for Cindy Albano. Will wanted to call out to Cindy, warn her even as he fell, but he had no voice, and he realized that he was not just dying but was nearly dead.

All of this happened instantly, in a second that seemed to take an hour. *The elongated time of the dying,* someone had called it, and wasn't that the truth. He hit the ground hard, and his head bounced sharply and came to rest with the dead weight of his body.

In his last second of life, Will stared up from where he lay, and, with dying eyes, saw the idol smile.

Fourteen

1

Pace woke up, cradling the skull.

He'd been dreaming of Penelope Daneam, a girl he'd dated briefly in college, and in the dream they'd been making love outside, next to a mountain stream, on grass that was softer than any bed. But when he woke up, he was lying on the hard earth of the dry well, his arms around the skull, clutching it to his chest.

He let go, pushed it away, crawled over the pieces of porcelain to the other side of the shaft. From above, he heard cackling, the crazed laughter of Christiansen Divine, and then he was drenched with warm slop, a revolting concoction of thick brown liquid and what looked like pieces of rotten vegetables that splatted on his head and shoulders and soaked through his shirt and pants to the skin. He felt like vomiting, but he refused to give Divine the satisfaction. He did not even bother to wipe off the disgusting goop dripping off his hair onto his face and down to the ground. He remained in place, waiting for the old man to leave.

"Suppertime!" Divine cackled, and behind him Pace heard the laughter of the others.

He looked up, and saw not only Divine peering over the rim of the well but the one-armed woman and the dwarf. Absalom and Jesse. The woman must be Jesse, he thought. That was one of those names that could go either way. Absalom was definitely a male name.

Another head poked over the edge. The little girl, still sucking her thumb.

He should be quiet, he knew. Conserve his strength and not antagonize them. But he jumped up anyway and did a little jig. "A little girl! With spina bifida!" he sang to the tune of "Saginaw, Michigan." "Spina bifida!"

They stopped laughing, and though he couldn't see expressions on the sky-silhouetted faces, their necks and heads stiffened in anger.

Good.

He wiped the slop from his forehead and cheeks, wiped his hands on a small clean part of his pants. "Fuck you, you midget dwarf freak!" He addressed himself to the faces above. "That mummy hair's not making you any taller, is it? And I don't see you growing a new arm, missy!"

He felt guilty for saying such things—it was not how he thought about the less fortunate, it was not the way he'd been raised—but he was filled with a desperate rage, and a base, vindictive part of him felt good as he hurled the insults.

He looked over at the skull. Was he being influenced, corrupted, made to think and behave in ways he ordinarily wouldn't? It was not only possible, it was likely. Like plutonium that remained radioactive for thousands of years, these things—the mummy, the skull—remained strong. Neither he nor Al had had any idea how their unnamed creature had caused an entire people to vanish, but power that potent did not disappear, not even with death.

Maybe that's why his legs didn't hurt. He didn't even feel any residual pain from the baseball bat blow.

A rock flew down, thrown not dropped, missing him by inches, smashing one of the larger pieces of porcelain.

They *were* angry.

"Spina bifida!" he sang.

Another rock sailed down, this one hitting him on the shoulder, drawing blood, though he pretended it didn't hurt.

On an impulse, he dropped to his knees, clasped his hands together. "Oh, God," he intoned. "Hear these words of thy humble servant. I beseech thee, smite Christensen Divine and his entire family, these heathens that have made a mockery of your gift. Make the youngest child a whore. Instead of sucking her thumb, let her suck cocks, a hundred of them, before you tear her limb from limb in the most painful manner imaginable—"

"Shut up!" Divine screamed from above. "Don't say that! Don't you dare say that, you son of a bitch!"

"The other one, I pray, have her brother the dwarf rip off her other arm and use it to fuck her ass in front of her daddy—"

"Stop that!" Divine shrieked.

But Pace did not stop. That psychotic prick was going to imprison him down here, torture him, try to kill him? Well, then Pace was going to do whatever he could to get back at the old bastard. He felt a deep satisfaction as Divine hurriedly moved his family away from the well.

When he was sure that they were gone, Pace moved off his knees and slumped against the cold stone wall. His shoulder hurt like hell, and he was sticky with slop. He could not tell what time it was—the small opening above did not show him a sufficient slice of sky for him to determine the location of the sun—but it felt like mid-morning. Judging by the heat and humidity down here already, this was going to be one hellacious day.

He stared at the skull. He'd been chasing all over creation looking for the damn thing, intending to study it, but now that he had both the time and opportunity to examine the skull, he didn't want anything to do with it.

He was afraid of it.

Not a very professional attitude, he had to admit. But being alone with it in the well for—what, twelve hours now?—he had gained a different perspective. He would still be taking it with him, though. Away from this craziness, back in a lab where he could shield himself from any possible emanations, he and a handpicked team of other scientists and technicians would scrutinize the specimen down to the molecular level.

The skull grinned at him. Its deep-shadowed eyes looked strangely alive, small curved sections of each socket capturing the light from above, and he had the unsettling impression that it was watching him. He remembered that from his brief exposure at Chaco, when

Glen and Melanie had first brought the skull to him—
the air of sentient malevolence it possessed.

Possessed.

Like Al, he'd originally thought that the skull would
provide them with answers. Close inspection would reveal objective, quantifiable information. Now he was not
so sure. There'd always been a supernatural aspect to
their theory, but he had not realized just how far beyond
pure science the reality was.

He also realized that Al had been wrong about one
thing. He had always believed that a single being was
responsible for the disappearance of the ancient tribes,
that it had traversed the desert from pueblo to pueblo
like some itinerant angel of death. But there was a skull
here in the well with him and a mummy up top, and it
seemed clear now that there had been more than one of
these beings. Plus, it appeared that at least one, the one
whose skull had been found in Bower, had been successfully killed by its intended victims.

That gave him hope.

Of course, he had to get out of here first before he
could do anything.

Not for the first time, he felt around the edges of the
well, searching for a handhold, a toehold, some way he
could climb up the walls. But as before, he found nothing, only straight hard stone that rose up and up and up.
He thought of his outburst, his spina bifida song, his
cruel words to Divine's deformed children. He was now
convinced that his behavior had been . . . influenced.
What would happen after he spent another six hours
down here? Another twelve? What would he be like
then?

With nothing to do, he used his feet to clear a larger
area, to push the broken pieces of statuary into a single
pile. There were quite a few fragments, large and small,
many of them covered with the slop that Divine had
poured out here, and he herded them over to the skull,
using the side of his shoe to shove the heap of rotted
vegetables and porcelain against the bone face, covering
the mouth, nearly hiding the eye sockets. That gave him
room to stretch out, and he sat down, leaning against

the stone, looking up at the sky. His mouth was parched, his stomach cramping with hunger, and he wondered if the next time the old man dropped decaying moldy food on him he would be desperate enough to eat it.

If there *was* a next time.

The pain in his shoulder was barely noticeable, and already the bleeding had stopped. Like his legs, his shoulder appeared to be healing fast. He kicked at the floor of the well with the heel of his shoe. Not only was he angry and bored, he was frustrated, knowing that he should be taking the skull back with him to Chaco. He wondered what else was going on out there, what other escalation of this horror was taking place while he rotted down here underground.

The morning passed slowly. He alternated between sitting, standing, and leaning on the wall, but he had nothing to do. At one point, he grew so desperate that he took out his wallet and sorted through the contents, counting his money, reading the backs of his credit cards, examining the business cards people had given him that he had never looked at once. Waves of emotion passed through him periodically, and he could never be sure if they were legitimate feelings or the influence of the skull.

Sometime after what felt like noon, when the temperature was hotter, the sunlight brighter, the heavy air more tangible, he started to become drowsy. He had always disapproved of naps and siestas, had considered all sleep a waste of time. Everyone would be dead soon enough as it was, so why spend a significant portion of the allotted time alive unconscious? But these were extraordinary circumstances, and since he had nothing to do, it was probably in his best interest to rest up and conserve his strength.

Besides, he was having a very difficult time keeping his eyes open.

But what if Divine and his family threw more slop on him while he slept? What if they decided to empty bedpans on his head?

He'd ignore them, pretend to still be sleeping.

That would work.

Closing his eyes, giving in, he drifted off.

He awoke some time later—

—and they were in the well with him.

They seemed just as shocked as he was. And just as frightened. They were flattened against the rounded wall, staying as far away from the skull as possible. Across the well, the skull's face was no longer covered by the porcelain fragments, but was sitting atop the pile, facing them.

Pace stood quickly.

Divine and his children looked at him, saying nothing.

"What are you doing here?" Pace asked.

"It's your fault," the old man said. His voice was cowed, little more than a whisper. "You prayed for it."

"I prayed for you to die. You're still alive."

"Fuck you!" the dwarf said.

Pace turned on him. "Shut the hell up. You're not up there. You're not calling the shots anymore. You're down here with me." He looked from the dwarf to Divine. "If we're ever going to get out of here, we're going to have to cooperate."

The old man scratched his head as though he had lice.

"You hear me?"

Divine nodded reluctantly.

"So now that we're all together, maybe you can answer a few questions for me."

"Like what?"

"What are those?" Pace pointed at the pile of porcelain pieces.

No one answered.

"I'm talking to you."

"The others," Divine said.

"Others?"

"We threw them down here, and they all . . . broke," said the one-armed woman. *Jesse?* "But you didn't break. And now we're down here, too. And now I don't know what's going on." She started to cry. He almost felt sorry for her, *would* have felt sorry for her had he not remembered her cruel laughter after they'd doused him with rotted vegetable soup.

"What's going on," he said, "is that you're being punished. And you deserve it. And maybe you *will* die."

From somewhere above came a high-pitched keening,

an eerie inhuman noise. It was dim inside the well, but the sky above showed blue afternoon daylight, and somehow that seemed worse. Wasn't scary stuff supposed to happen at night, in the dark? The idea that the mummy, after transporting the Divine family into the well, was standing in its lingerie in the hot sun and making weird sounds filled him with a creeping dread.

The keening sound came and went, came and went, came and went, like a siren.

And then it stopped.

That should have been an improvement, but somehow the silence seemed just as ominous. Pace imagined the mummy gliding out of the lean-to, across the weedy ground, over to the edge of the well. Involuntarily, he looked up, but the opening was clear, there was nothing there.

"So now we're all gonna cooperate, huh?" Divine grimaced. "What're we supposed to do to get out of here, *Professor*?"

"Knock off that attitude for one thing, asshole." He glared at the old man, who held the stare for a moment before looking away.

"Fuck you!" the dwarf said again.

"No. Fuck you, you little freak." He glared at all of them, one at a time. "If you want to get out of here, if you don't want to starve to death or turn into porcelain dolls, you're going to listen to me and do as I say, got it?"

No response.

Pace pretended to withdraw, moving away from them, closer to the skull. But not too close. "Eat your soup, then. Lick it up off the dirt."

Jesse looked at her family, then stepped forward, holding out her one hand for Pace to shake. "I'm in," she said softly. "I'll do whatever you say."

"We're all in," Divine said gruffly, trying to make it seem as though he hadn't caved, as though there'd only been a misunderstanding on Pace's part. "Whadda we do?"

"We're going to boost someone up until they can get out. They'll find a rope—there's one in my truck if there's none in your trailer—bring it back, tie one end to a tree or a boulder or something, and then drop the other end down so the rest of us can climb up."

It was a simple plan, easily understood, and even though he had to run through it a couple of times, they seemed to grasp the concept.

There were five of them, more than enough to reach the top if they stood on one another's shoulders. He didn't trust Christiansen Divine further than he could throw him, so the old bastard would be at the anchor spot, on the bottom. But he himself was too heavy to be top man, so he would have to take a chance that one of the others wouldn't double-cross him. Absalom, the dwarf, was out. He'd return with a weapon, try to kill him and then rescue the others. The thumb-sucking girl did not seem able to do what needed to be done.

That left Jesse. She was not a bad choice. Pace trusted her more than the others; she was the only one who seemed genuinely cooperative, and looking at the situation from a purely mercenary standpoint, she would have her hand full carrying the rope. She wouldn't be able to bring along a weapon or do anything else.

But could she tie a knot with just the one hand?

He was about to ask when the little girl suddenly stopped sucking her thumb and, for the first time in Pace's presence, spoke. "I'll do it," she said. Her voice was clearer than he'd expected, more mature. "I'm lighter than everyone else. It'll be easier to hold me up."

Pace stared at her, stunned by the realization that she could speak.

"There's a rope in the storage shed. I know where it is. I can tie it to this tree where we used to have a swing. It'll hold."

He recovered quickly. "That'll be perfect," he said. "Let's do it."

Logically, Pace should have been at the bottom; he was the biggest. But he still thought it best to keep the old man's movements as restricted as possible, so he told Divine to stand next to the wall, then climbed up on the bony shoulders, steadying himself with both hands against the rounded stone. The pressure from the others climbing up and over him caused his shoulder wound to reopen, but he grimaced and held his place as Jesse, then

Absalom took up their positions. They were wobbly, and
Divine was cursing and whining at the bottom, but the
little girl—he didn't know her name, Pace realized—
scurried up quickly. She couldn't quite reach the lip of
the well, but before he could tell her what to do, she
jumped from her brother's shoulders and grabbed the
top edge. She could have fallen, could have knocked
over their entire ladder, but she was more agile than
she looked, and Pace admired not only her abilities, but
her ingenuity.

Had she really been cured of spina bifida?

By mummy hair?

The girl hung there for a moment, her fingers scrab-
bling, repositioning herself, then pulled herself up. She
went over the top. "I'll be back in a minute!" she cried.
And then the rest of them broke apart, Absalom jumping off his sister's shoulders, Divine yelling, "Get off!
You're too heavy!" Pace helped Jesse down, then was
thrown off the old man. He landed on his feet near the
skull, and he quickly turned to look at the others. It
dawned on him that they might try to rush him, take
him down, before the girl returned. His eye lit upon one
of the rocks that Divine had thrown at him.

"How long do you think it's going to take her?"
Jesse asked.

As if in answer, they heard the voice of the girl,
faintly, from up above. "I'm at the shed!" she called. A
moment later: "I got the rope!"

"What's her name?" Pace asked.

"None a yer bizness," Divine snarled.

"Loretta," Jesse said. "Our mother named her." The
implication was that Divine had named the other two,
and this time Pace really did feel sorry for her.

"I'm tying it around the tree!" Loretta called.

Pace moved into position, looking up. He was ready.
He grabbed the rope the second it was thrown down,
and before anyone could take it from him or push him
off, he was clambering up the steep side of the well. He
half-expected Divine to call out to Loretta, ordering her
to unhook the rope and let him fall, but apparently the
old man really was willing to let him escape if it meant
that he could get out, too.

"I'll help pull you up once I get to the top," Pace said. He was thinking of Jesse. "If anybody can't pull themselves, just tie the rope around their midsection and I'll haul them up."

The old man did not respond, not even to say something nasty, and Pace was immediately suspicious. Were they going to attack him? Pausing in his climb, he turned his head and looked down. The three Divines were frozen, unmoving. He thought for a split second that they were merely remaining still as they watched him climb out of the well, but then he realized that they *couldn't* move. Like the "others" who had been thrown into the well, they had been turned into porcelain—he could see light glinting off surfaces that shouldn't have been reflective. As he watched, Absalom toppled over, striking the other two. All three shattered on the floor of the well, breaking like safety glass into thousands of tiny almost uniformly shaped pieces.

Only the skull remained intact, grinning.

Pace had intended to take the skull with him, to have Divine hand it up, but he immediately changed his mind. The skull was dangerous; he did not want anything more to do with it.

And there was no way he was going back down.

He scurried up the wall. From outside came the keening sound again, but at this moment the mummy in the lean-to did not seem half as scary to him as the skull in the well. If he was going to die, he'd rather it be in the open.

The first thing he did as he pulled himself out of the well was look for the mummy. It was standing by itself in a flat open area away from the lean-to, like a scarecrow from hell. The sun was shining full on its face, but that still did not illuminate the deep-set eyes and only served to emphasize the cruelty in that sneering toothless mouth. With no one to shave it, the orange hair had bushed out wildly, and the incongruity of a living mane on that dried dead form was somehow loathsome and abhorrent.

His eyes scanned the area around the trailer, around the outhouse. The girl was nowhere in sight. He hoped she'd gotten away, but he had the feeling she hadn't. If he started searching through those high weeds, he suspected, he'd find little pieces of porcelain, some that matched the color of her skin, some that matched the color of her hair, some that matched the color of her clothes. . . .

Moving slowly, he made his way through the weeds toward the trailer, keeping an eye on that dark wrinkled figure to make sure it didn't try to come after him. It was still wearing bra and panties, and Pace could not help thinking that it was that humiliation which had caused it to turn on Divine and his family.

But why had it spared him? And why, if it really had helped destroy the Anasazi and was part of an effort to purge the contemporary Southwest, was it staying here on the outskirts of Albuquerque and harassing one white-trash family?

The mummy remained where it was as Pace stepped carefully between the trailer and the outhouse. A lizard scuttled in the dirt before him, scurrying into the weeds. To his left, a crow squawked noisily, flying up from a twisted branch on the dead oak tree.

His truck was right where he'd left it, but the tires were flat, the windows shattered, and someone had taken a sledgehammer to the body. Divine, he assumed. The motorcycle next to his pickup had also been incapacitated, knocked over, its frame apparently beaten with the same sledgehammer. He glanced around. There were no other vehicles he could take. It was a long walk back to the highway, a long walk back to the next house, but he saw no other choice.

God, he wished he'd borrowed a cell phone from someone and brought it along.

By the time Pace reached the head of the drive, he could no longer see the mummy. It was hidden behind the trailer, and for all he knew, it was moving back there. If he poked his head around the trailer's edge, he might see it standing next to the back door, waiting for him.

He shivered, though the afternoon sun was hot, and he saw himself walking to the next shack down the road to find the place abandoned and another mummy standing in the field next to the house. And one standing behind the next log cabin after that. And on and on.

Judging by the sun, it was late afternoon. In a few hours it would be evening. The last thing he wanted was to be caught out here when night fell. He went over to the pickup. The doorframe had been smashed in and would not open, but he managed to wiggle halfway through the shattered side window and grab what he needed. He took out a flashlight, a buck knife, and his notebook and pen.

He started walking.

Halfway down the drive, he turned to look back, but everything was obscured by the high dry weeds. He thought of Divine and his family lying next to the skull in broken pieces at the bottom of the well, thought of that blackened mummy with its orange afro hair, dressed absurdly in lingerie and standing alone in the middle of the field.

And he started to run.

2

Cameron had never been to a university before, and it was not the same as he'd thought it would be. There were so many people for one thing, and they were all different ages, most in their late teens or early twenties, but some a little older and some genuine geezers. As far as he could tell, classes were starting and ending at all sorts of times, not merely at standard intervals. There were even fast-food restaurants on campus. The college seemed chaotic and crowded, but exciting and alive, unlike any school he'd ever been to.

He liked it.

But what he didn't like was standing in the hallway, staring at the same closed elevator doors, while he and his uncle waited for Dr. McCormack to finish talking to that fat smelly student. They'd been waiting for ten minutes already, and this guy was going on and on about some class assignment that he didn't understand. They could hear his whining voice even through the closed door, and Cameron wondered why Dr. McCormack didn't just send him on his way.

Another girl had been waiting out here with them, "a hunk of babe" as Jay would've said, but she'd gotten tired of waiting after only a few minutes, and she'd scrawled a message on yellow notebook paper and put the note in a manila envelope hanging from a clip attached to the office door. She hadn't said word one to either of them the entire time, not even a hi, and Cameron thought that that was one thing that was the same about college and middle school: stuck-up snots were still stuck-up snots.

The office door opened, the fat smelly guy walked over to the elevator and pushed the down button, and Cameron and his uncle stepped inside to see Dr. McCormack.

"Hey," the professor said, surprised. "Have you been waiting long?"

"About ten minutes," Vince told him.

Behind them, a bell dinged. The elevator door opened.

"You should've knocked and let me know you were here," the professor said. "I could've used you as an excuse and gotten that student out of here earlier."

"I thought you saw us," Vince said. "We came about the same time he did."

"Sorry. No. But I wish I had." He stood up and started sorting through a pile of books on his desk. "What brings you here?"

"The Mogollon Monster."

Dr. McCormack frowned. "What?"

Vince took a deep breath. "Remember Cameron's story about—?"

"Yes. A campfire tale. Some type of scouting tradition."

"Except that this time a scoutmaster was murdered exactly the same way as in that campfire tale. His face was torn off and left hanging on a branch. And Cameron felt the monster pass by his cabin. There's no Anasazi connection," he said quickly, before Dr. McCormack could object. "I'll grant you that. But bear with me." He looked at Cameron, smiled. "Us."

Cameron smiled back.

"What we're thinking is that this creature that Cameron saw and photographed at his friend's house, the one everyone's looking for, was the inspiration for all of these stories. Cam said the feeling he got when he saw that thing on the bed, a strange heaviness in the air, a sense that he was incapacitated, was the same thing he felt at the scout ranch, the same thing he felt when his friend's dog went crazy and killed a neighbor, the same thing he felt at the Pima House Ruins. They're all connected. I concede that Cameron's our only real link between the Anasazi creature and the Mogollon Monster, but I did an Internet search, and the legend of the monster goes way back. At least to the mid-1800s. And while I couldn't find information about any specific Native American monster myths, the settlers, at least according to what I read, were under the belief that the quote, unquote red men considered the portion of the Mogollon Rim, where the monster supposedly roamed, to be cursed. They avoided it, built no pueblos there, though the escarpment would have provided a natural defense against invaders and, according to written records, including the testimony of an Indian agent, they thought some sort of demon lived there.

"And the fact remains that Anasazi artwork throughout the Southwest depicts the same afro-haired creature that Cameron saw and photographed, and that elicited the same physical reactions as whatever passed by his cabin at the scout ranch and murdered that scoutmaster."

McCormack nodded. "Yes, but isn't it more likely that our genocidal creature killed that scoutmaster rather than the monster from their campfire tale? I'm not doubting you that the murder is connected, and I'm very excited about that development—it's a leap I don't think anyone else could have made—but I don't see the value of crediting this scout story."

"Like I said, it's not just a scout story. It's old. And there are obvious parallels between these two creatures. Not only that, but the tales of the Mogollon Monster have been continuous. There've been gaps in the appearance of this thing, but fifty, sixty years is all. Not centuries. It seems to me that this creature or this race of creatures has been hiding out since destroying the Anasazi civilization and has been living up by the Mogollon Rim, resting, recuperating, building up strength, and coming out occasionally to . . . kill people."

"Interesting," Dr. McCormack said. "So perhaps it hasn't been dormant all these centuries, but has been operating right under our noses, undetected."

"Now here's the weird part. I think Cameron's immune to it. I might be, too. And Glen and Melanie. Possibly you."

"Wait a minute—"

"He's the only person in his neighborhood who survived. I was completely unaffected by the skeleton in the kiva or whatever it was that caused those artifacts to move and compelled those citizens to dress up in their finery and start digging in the dirt. Glen and Melanie survived Bower and that abandoned town and two days with that skull in their trunk. Your wife was attacked but not you."

"And you think this means . . ."

"We're immune, we're resistant. Whatever force or power or energy emanates from that creature or from the bones of its ancestors doesn't affect us. And maybe . . ." He paused. "Maybe there's a reason for that. I'm not religious, and I'm not superstitious. At least I didn't used to be. But maybe we've been chosen."

"Chosen?"

"Not necessarily by God or some higher power— although I'm not ruling that out. It could be a natural occurrence; we could be like the antibodies attacking a disease. I don't know. I just think that . . . well, I think we're the ones who can fight it."

The professor nodded, looking thoughtful.

"I know you weren't a big fan of Al Wittinghill's work. I'm not sure I completely bought into it, either. But that was before. Now think about what's happened and think about the Mogollon Monster. Tell me you think we're crazy. Tell me there's no way it could possibly be the case."

Dr. McCormack sighed. "You know I can't do that. It *is* possible. Anything's possible."

"So what do you think we should do?"

"I have no more classes today, only a few scheduled conferences. I'll reschedule them and we'll go up to this scout ranch and see what we can find."

"I was hoping you'd say that." Vince grinned at Cameron, who found himself feeling suddenly optimistic, excited by the possibility that they might be getting close to solving this thing, to stopping it.

"We'll call Glen and Melanie," Vince said, taking out his cell phone. "Let them know where we're going."

"Where are they now? Wickenburg?"

"Last time they checked in."

"All right. You call them, I'll call Alyssa. After that, I'll tell the department secretaries I'll be gone for the day and have them reschedule my conferences. Do you want to drive or shall I?"

"I'm sure your vehicle's better than mine."

"All right, then. I'll meet you downstairs in front of the building in ten minutes. If you have to go to the bathroom, you'd better do it now because we're driving straight through. I want to be back before dark. If you're hungry, pick something up at the snack bar across the way. Bring something to drink, too."

"All right," Vince said, tapping Cameron's shoulder. "Let's go."

The Rim was only a two-hour trip from Scottsdale, so they were there by one. Following Cameron's directions, they left the highway, drove down the dirt control road, then pulled into the small dusty parking lot outside the closed ranch gates and got out. The cabin looked just as Cameron remembered it, dark even in the daytime. Automatically, his eyes were drawn to the tree, but the branch which had held Scoutmaster Anderson's face had been sawed off, and when he glanced at the ground underneath the spot, he saw only dry dirt and brown pine needles, no blood.

He swallowed heavily. "That's it," he said, pointing. "That's where it happened."

All three of them walked over to the tree, looked around for a few minutes, found nothing, then stepped onto the cabin's porch. The weathered unpainted boards

creaked beneath their shoes, and Cameron was afraid
the whole structure might collapse. He imagined himself
falling through the porch into a deep hidden pit filled
with black water and floating there until something unspeakable with long slimy fingers pulled him down to
his death.

Dr. McCormack pushed aside some of the vines and
branches, and looked into the right front window.

"See anything?" Vince asked.

"No, it's too dark." The professor moved over to the
door and tried to pull off some of the overgrown foliage,
but vines remained caught in the frame and tangled in
the hinges. It seemed to Cameron that plants and bushes
were what held this shack together. Both his uncle and
Dr. McCormack tried to turn the knob and pull open
the door, but they had no luck.

Cameron was not brave enough to look inside. He did
not even like staying out here on the porch. Something
about the cabin frightened him, and he wanted nothing
more than to get away from it as quickly as possible.

The tangle of trees and bushes made it impossible to
walk around the back of the shack without the aid of a
machete, so after peering through the window again and
seeing nothing out of the ordinary inside, the professor
led them off the porch and across the parking lot to the
scout ranch's entrance. Behind the gate, back by the
mess hall, a man in a greenish uniform was walking
away, carrying a rake and a shovel and a broom. He
looked like either a caretaker or a ranger, and Dr.
McCormack called out to him, but he didn't seem to
hear and kept walking. All three of them started shouting, and when that didn't work either, Cameron sucked
in his breath and screamed at the top of his lungs. The
high-pitched cry echoed off the nearby cliffs and sent
the uniformed man running toward them.

The ranch was closed until next spring, the rest of
this year's scouting season had been cancelled after the
murder, and the caretaker—for indeed that's what he
was—was not supposed to let anyone in. But after some
intimidating talk from Dr. McCormack and a twenty-
dollar bill from Uncle Vince, he opened the gates and
allowed them inside. "I'm only here until three," he said.

"So you got an hour and a half. Then I'm kicking you out."

Dr. McCormack nodded. "Understood, sir. And thank you."

The man went off to do his work, and the three of them surveyed the camp. The professor asked Cameron where everything was, trying to get the lay of the land, and he explained what was what. They walked between the bunkhouses toward the foot of the Rim.

"What are we looking for?" Cameron asked.

"We don't know," his uncle said. "Probably won't know until we see it."

"We're looking for some type of Anasazi ruin or some indication that at one time there was a settlement in this region," Dr. McCormack told him.

"Why?"

"Why?"

"I mean, shouldn't we be looking for the monster's cave or something like that? Those Indian villages are what the monster destroyed, right? He went to those places and made all those people disappear. He didn't live there. It's like my neighborhood. He came there and now everyone's gone, but he didn't live there. And once he did it, he left. He probably went back home. Somewhere around here." Cameron looked up at the sheer face of the Rim, the line of pine trees at the top. This was a large area, heavily wooded. Even if they had a team of searchers, even if they spent a week out here, they still wouldn't be able to cover enough ground to look everywhere. It would take a miracle for them to find the monster's lair.

He looked over at his uncle and was surprised to see both Vince and Dr. McCormack staring at him.

"The boy's right," the professor said, and the tone of his voice made Cameron feel good. He heard respect in that voice, respect for a good idea without prejudice as to its origin.

The caretaker was once again carrying his rake and broom and shovel, heading toward the stables.

"Listen," Dr. McCormack said, flagging him down, "are you aware of any caves or Indian ruins or anything of that nature around here?"

The man shook his head. "Nope."

"You've heard these stories about the Mogollon Monster, right?"

"Yeah."

"Well, this is going to sound stupid, but . . . we're looking for it. The monster. We think it lives nearby."

"That doesn't sound stupid at all. It does live nearby, although I couldn't tell you where." He nodded to himself as though confirming something. "I figured that's why you guys were up here." His gaze landed on Cameron. *But why's the kid with you?* Cameron expected the man to ask, but the caretaker said nothing.

"What about mines?" Vince asked. "Are there any mines in this area that you know of?"

"They found footprints by that cabin out front. Big footprints. Right after that scoutmaster got killed. They found his face hanging from the tree."

Cameron jumped in. "I know. I was there."

The caretaker ignored him. "That's the only reason I let you in. Because I don't like being alone here by myself. Not after that happened."

"Have you seen anything since?" Dr. McCormack asked.

"No, not really. But I don't like it here one bit. I can tell you that. And as soon as I find another job, I'm gone."

"What about the mines?"

"Don't know of any mines." He paused, thinking. "But there's the train tunnel."

"Train tunnel?"

He nodded. "Around World War II, there was talk of bringing the railroad up here so they could ship ore from the Verde Valley down to Phoenix. They never did though. They started to build a tunnel through the Rim for the railroad to go through because it was impossible to take a train *up* the Rim. But the rock was too hard and the Rim was too thick, and they abandoned it after going in a hundred yards or so. I think the entrance is all blocked off, but I've never seen it myself. I've heard some hikers have gone in, though, so it's probably not what you're looking for. I don't think the monster lives in there."

"Where do you think it does live?" Vince asked.

The caretaker gave a wry smile. "Anywhere it damn well pleases."

"And how do we get to this train tunnel?" Dr. McCormack inquired.

"Like I said, I've never been there myself." He pointed through the pine trees. "I'd suggest you take one of those trails that lead to the base of the Rim, and then follow along the edge until you come to it."

"Are we going to be able to get off your grounds that way? Isn't this area all fenced?"

He shook his head. "Only the front and the west side, to discourage trespassers. The rear and the east's all open. But you never heard if from me."

"Thanks."

The caretaker headed off toward the stables, and the professor shrugged. "It's as good a place to start as any." He looked at his watch. "We'd better get moving. I don't want Alyssa in that house alone after nightfall."

They followed one of the paths the caretaker had indicated, taking a narrow winding trail that led through the trees, up a small hill, around the edge of a ravine and then along the course of a dry streambed. Despite his years of scouting, Cameron was still not much of a hiker, and he was acutely aware of the fact that he was slowing the party down. His uncle and Dr. McCormack were too polite to say anything though, and that made him even more determined to push himself.

The day was burning hot, and they were all sweating and out of breath by the time they reached the foot of the Rim. The stand of trees through which they'd been hiking opened up, and they emerged in a clear rocky area that reminded him of the desert outside Carefree. Before them, the Mogollon Rim stretched upward into the sky, a rugged cliff of tan and orange where lone pine trees grew on impossibly small outcroppings. Near the top, the ridge was covered with a thick forest of ponderosas.

None of them had brought water, and Cameron thought that they were like those people he heard about on the news who got dehydrated and suffered from sunstroke and had to be rescued. How could they be so dumb?

So much for his scout training.

Vince had gum, and he passed out a piece to each of them. "Chew it," he said. "It creates saliva and will keep your throat from drying out."

"We shouldn't go much farther," the professor said, unwrapping the foil and placing the gum in his mouth. Cameron was glad to see him put the wrapper in his pocket instead of toss it on the ground. "We'll give it another half hour and then head back if we don't find anything."

"There's water at the scout ranch," Cameron said. "We could go and get some and then come back again."

"We'll see," Dr. McCormack said, and Cameron understood that that meant no.

He faced the Rim wall, looked left, then right. The railroad tunnel was nowhere to be seen. How would they know when they found it? he wondered. What if it was hidden by bushes or covered by an avalanche? Hadn't the caretaker said it had been blocked off?

He needn't have worried. They found it ten minutes later, around the edge of a rounded outcropping. The entrance was as tall as a two-story building, and the opening was blocked off only by a two-by-four fence that was halfheartedly erected and half falling over. He didn't know how far a hundred yards was, but the tunnel looked deep and he could not see the end of it. Dr. McCormack and his uncle were already stepping through the rickety fence and walking inside. He did not want to go in there, but he didn't want to be left out here on his own, either, so reluctantly he followed them.

The floor of the tunnel was strewn with rubble, piles of blasted rock mostly, and despite what the caretaker had said, it looked as though no one had been here in years. There was none of the usual graffiti on the walls, no broken liquor bottles or empty beer cans, no candy wrappers or cigarette butts. The tunnel started to get dark a lot quicker than Cameron would have believed with such a massive opening, the sunlight restricted to a dome-shaped area immediately within the entrance. Of course, they didn't have a flashlight. The three of them were without a doubt the worst-prepared searchers ever. They hadn't brought *anything* with them. Not even a camera, he realized, although this was probably not the best time to mention that.

Dr. McCormack saw the objects first.

They were clustered around a tall, freestanding, vaguely oval-shaped rock in the middle of the tunnel. Cameron would have thought it was another boulder and passed right by, but the items encircling the rock indicated that this was something more. In fact, now that he looked at it, the rock, which was approximately his own height, seemed to be a statue or a carving that had been weathered and worn smooth over the years.

The professor crouched down and picked up what looked like a small Chinese vase, holding it up and trying to catch nonexistent light beams in order to see it better. He used a finger to trace something on the porcelain, then carefully put down the vase and picked up a gold bracelet that even in this half-light was bright and shiny and clearly encrusted with jewels. Literally dozens of objects were placed in a wide circle around the rock: bowls and glasses and jewelry and toys and figurines from all the over the world.

Offerings, was Cameron's first thought. People had brought the monster offerings in order to make sure that it didn't attack them or their families. But no one around here had stuff like this, and his second thought was: *souvenirs*. These were things the monster had collected over the years, over the centuries.

Dr. McCormack picked up an intricately carved pipe.

"What's it all mean?" Cameron asked.

"I don't know," the professor said, and he sounded worried. No, not worried. *Scared.* "I honestly don't know."

They talked about the train tunnel all the way back to Scottsdale. They had continued on to the end, which turned out to be not much farther, but they hadn't found anything else unusual—although they could not be absolutely positive since it was too dark at the rear of the tunnel to see much of anything. Both his uncle and Dr. McCormack agreed that the freestanding rock and surrounding collection of artifacts from different countries were fairly recent additions. That meant that the mon-

ster had been living somewhere else until now. Maybe
it still was. They hadn't seen any sign that it actually
lived in the train tunnel, and Cameron was glad of that.
He imagined slimy severed faces draped over boulders,
bloody bodies and bones in the cracks between them.
Things he didn't want to see.

"I'm afraid we're going to have to return and search,"
Dr. McCormack said. "Glen and Melanie should be back
tomorrow. Maybe I'll talk to Captain Ortiz and see if
he can spare some men to help us." He looked sheepish.
"We'll bring flashlights and water this time. And we'll
scour the area to see if we can find where this creature
is and where it came from."

"I don't want to go back there," Cameron said.

"You don't have to," his uncle told him. "But we do."

Cameron thought about it and realized that although
he was afraid to return to the train tunnel, he would
rather go than stay behind. He would not be able to
stand waiting in the motel room, wondering when, or if,
his uncle was going to return.

"What if we do find it?" he asked. "What do we do
then?"

For that, neither of them had an answer.

3

By the time Melanie and Glen reached Tucson, it was
night. They'd driven straight through from Wickenburg,
hoping to make it to McGuane before sunset, but when
they saw they wouldn't arrive until after midnight, they
pulled into a Day's Inn next to the freeway.

"This is getting to be a habit," Glen said.

"So much for saving money," Melanie told him.

"We'll bill it to the university."

They got out of the car, stretched, then walked across
the small parking lot to the lobby. Melanie had a cramp
in her calf from sitting for so long in the same position—
they'd made only one stop between Wickenburg and
Tucson, at a dirty rest area north of Picacho Peak—and
she limped across the asphalt. "Look," Glen said, "a

shooting star." He pointed up to the southern sky, but she was too late and missed it.

"Did you make a wish?" she asked him.

"Are you supposed to? I thought that was the first star you see tonight."

"There are a lot of different ways to make wishes."

"I guess people need something to hope for," he said.

The man in the lobby was dark skinned, wore a blue turban, and spoke in a sing-songy accent that sounded at once utterly alien and completely understandable and that Melanie found fascinating. He rented them a room, but looked upon them with suspicion, and she had the feeling that he wanted to ask them for proof of marriage before allowing them to stay at his establishment.

The room was in a corner on the second floor and, though much cleaner than the one in Holbrook, was equally charmless. There was cable TV, though, so Glen was happy, and he kicked off his shoes and flopped down tiredly on the king-size bed, using the remote control to flip through channels until he found a rerun of *The Simpsons*. She herself had never been a big fan of television. She watched the nightly news and an occasional movie, but for the most part it was an unused piece of furniture in her house. She much preferred reading and listening to music. She liked that Glen liked TV, though. She found that refreshing and she enjoyed snuggling next to him on the bed, watching mindless entertainment.

She had the feeling that they were on the last leg of their little journey, that whatever happened tomorrow they would be heading back to McCormack's house afterward, and she was more than a little sorry to see it end. Despite the circumstances, maybe even because of them, she had enjoyed being on the road. They'd been in their own little world, moving from car to motel to car to motel. More than that, they were good together, comfortable. More than that, they genuinely enjoyed each other's company. It was going to be difficult to return to reality and allow other people into their universe.

She looked over at him. "Do you think we're actually going to find it this time?"

"I think so, but I would have wished on the falling star to make sure if I'd known enough to do it."

She decided to be honest with him and just lay it all out there. "I'm going to miss this," she said. "Being alone with you. Traveling."

He grinned. "In my profligate way."

"I could get used to it."

"I knew you'd come around. What's time and money for if not to spend on the people you love?"

Pleased, she leaned over, kissed him. "I love you, too," she said.

After *The Simpsons,* Glen turned toward her. "So what's the plan for dinner?"

"I don't know. What sounds good to you?"

"Why don't we just order pizza and have them deliver it? Eat in."

Melanie smiled. "I've never had a pizza delivered before."

He sat up. "Never?"

"Never have."

"You haven't lived!" He reached over her to the nightstand, grabbed the yellow pages, and started flipping through the P's. "You're in for one of the great joys of modern life, let me tell you. What do you like?"

"Bell pepper."

"No pepperoni?"

"Bell pepper."

"Half bell pepper, half pepperoni." He found what he was looking for, slammed the book down on the pillow, and reached for the phone. "Your first delivered pizza. Melanie Black," he promised. "This is going to be a night to remember."

McGuane was a sleepy little desert town stretched over two forking canyons at the edge of a massive open-pit mine. There were two museums: a small, one-room mining museum that, according to the carved stone above the doorway, had once been the assayer's office; and the larger Heritage House, which was run by the county historical society and was located in what appeared to have once been a hotel. Preston Alphonse said he had sold the mummy to a "historical museum," and while technically that described both, they figured the Heritage House was the more likely place to start.

It was nine-thirty when they arrived in town and the museum did not open until ten, so they walked down the block to a little café where they bought coffee and sat at small metal tables listening to the conversations of the local people around them. There was talk of sick dogs and honor roll kids and new cars, and it all seemed so innocent and oblivious that Melanie wanted to cry. There was beauty in the ordinariness of everyday existence, a splendor that she had not noticed until now but that touched her heart. She wondered if Glen felt the same, but she couldn't ask him here, so she just looked at him and tried to read his face.

How fragile was the world, she thought, how delicate their lives. She had always done her best to live life to the fullest, but more often than not that had meant grand gestures: white water rafting with her friends in college, backpacking alone through the Maze in Canyonlands, spending her summers working at historical locations throughout the state. Now, she thought, she would take the time to appreciate the smaller things and enjoy the commonplace wonders immediately around her.

Like being here with Glen, drinking coffee.

This *was* nice, and she wished it could go on forever, but the real reason they were here was always at the forefront of her thoughts, and as customers came and customers left, she realized that the time was drawing close.

"It's ten," Glen said finally, looking up at the clock on the wall. "Let's go check it out."

A short bald man with a hangdog face was just unlocking the Heritage House door when they walked up. He opened the door, flipped on the lights, and introduced himself as Rod Huffman, president of the historical society.

"Just the man we're looking for," Melanie said.

"Well, I guess it's your lucky day. I was going to spend the morning birdwatching in Ramsey Canyon, but our curator cancelled out on us and I'm up. We take turns helping out at the museum. Everything's strictly volunteer here." He spoke fast and without pause, his voice betraying more than a hint of Southern twang.

They walked past a tall wooden box inside the entryway on which was stenciled: DONATION REQUIRED $2 ADULTS, $1 CHILDREN 12 AND OVER. Glen stopped, took out his wallet and started digging through it looking for ones, while Melanie followed the bald man into the next room, where he stepped behind an old oak desk and turned on a Macintosh computer. "We need to ask you about one of your exhibits," she said. "It's a mummy you bought from an antique dealer named Preston Alphonse in Wickenburg—"

"The mummy?" Huffman turned pale. "Why are you interested in that? I haven't . . . I don't . . ." He took a deep breath. "It's no longer an exhibit here."

Melanie suddenly felt tired. Not again.

"Where is it?" Glen asked, joining them.

"Why do you want to know?"

She took the reins, explaining that they had found a skull at an archeological site in Bower that they believed was connected to the mummy, telling him that they had tracked the mummy from a tourist trap on Highway 40 to an antique store in Wickenburg to here.

"What do you want to do to it? Just look at it? Take pictures?"

"We'd like to buy it," Glen said.

"You want it? I'll sell it to you cheap. I'm keeping it in a storage locker right now. Haven't opened the door of that place for two years. Don't intend to."

Glen glanced at Melanie. "Why?" he asked.

"I don't like that thing. You want to know the truth? It scares me. I'm only telling you this because if you buy it there's no money-back guarantee. If you take it, it's yours, and I don't ever want to see it or hear about it again."

"What happened?" Melanie asked.

"Nothing." Pause. "Or at least nothing specific."

"But . . . ?" she prompted.

He chewed on his upper lip for a moment, unsure of whether to answer. "Things were moved," he said carefully. "We put the mummy in our 'The Best Before the

West' room, next to some pottery and other artifacts we'd found, bought or were donated. I can show you the room if you want; it's quite an impressive exhibit." He looked at them quizzically, and Glen nodded.

Talking all the way, he led them down the hallway to a surprisingly large space with professional-looking museum cases arranged around a central tableau that included a mock-up of a hogan and a fire pit. "The mummy was going to be our star exhibit, our signature piece. No other historical society in this part of the state has one, and it was in such good shape that our board thought it well worth the expenditure. We'd been saving that money for a new air conditioner, but this seemed so much more worthwhile and—" He stopped just inside the doorway of room. "But you don't want to hear this." He pointed at the tableau. "We were going to redo that installation and build it around the mummy. We even had it temporarily set up."

Huffman took a deep breath. "Then things started to move. Small items at first, things you wouldn't notice unless you were extremely familiar with the Heritage House. We'd just taken on a new part-time janitor, he was still on his probation period, and although he denied rearranging anything, it kept happening, and we let him go because we all thought he was responsible.

"But it didn't stop. In fact, larger items began to be moved. One of us would arrive to open up in the morning and discover that, say, that case"—he pointed— "had been relocated to the Copper Days room or the Pioneer Era room. It was not only frustrating, it was starting to get spooky. Then one night the mummy moved.

"I was the one working that day. I'd worked the night before, too, back in the office, on plans for our monthly meeting, which was going to be a big one. Wyatt Earp's nephew's grandson was going to be our guest of honor. When I left that night, everything was where it was supposed to be. But when I opened the door the next morning . . ." He paused, remembering. "It was standing right there." Huffman held up his hand, flat palm an inch from his nose. "Right in front of my face. It scared me to death, and it looked . . . it looked like it had a different expression, like it was smiling. Maybe it had always looked that way and I just hadn't noticed. I don't know. But I'd been working with that thing for several weeks, seeing it every day, and that day it looked different. It never changed again, mind you—I kept tabs on it, kept watching—but I think on that morning it did. And it seemed to me that it had been trying to escape.

"Now I know how crazy that sounds, and it sounded crazy to me, too. But when I called in the other board members and the curator and the rest of the volunteers and told them what had happened—this was after I'd put it back in the installation—none of them seemed that surprised. It came out that quite a few of them were spooked by the mummy. We didn't know what to do, so we decided to do nothing. We couldn't very well remove what was our greatest asset based on one odd occurrence and some nebulous feelings.

"But it started happening every night. Each morning, one of us would arrive to find the mummy moved out of its display and standing next to another door or window. It got to be so volunteers were afraid to open. We couldn't afford to install security cameras, and no one wanted to stay in the house overnight, myself included, so we hired someone for twenty bucks to stake the place out one night and see what happened, an unemployed construction worker who wasn't afraid of anything."

"What happened?" Melanie asked. "What did he see?"

"We don't know. He died that night of a heart attack, and when we found him in the morning—or when *I* found him, since I was the one to open that day—he was kneeling down before the mummy as though he was praying to it."

Melanie thought of where the mummy had been discovered, in a shrine built into a cowboy's house in a long-abandoned ghost town, and when she glanced over at Glen, she could tell that he was thinking of the same thing.

"It was the eeriest sight I've ever seen in my life, and I got out of there as quickly as I could and went to the police, and after they were through in here, me and Ham Hamson and Eric Amos went and put it in a storage locker, and you know what? We haven't had a problem here since. So we pay the rent on that place by the year, and it stays in there and no one's seen it since."

Glen cleared his throat. "I thought you said there was nothing specific that happened."

"I lied," Huffman snapped. "All right? I lied. Now, do you want to see the mummy or not?"

"Of course," Melanie said. "That's why we're here."

"It's on the other side of town. We'll take my car. Just let me lock up."

Melanie had assumed the historical society rented one of those storage lockers with wide metal roll-down doors that were housed in parallel rows of long buildings behind metal security gates. But the mummy was tucked away in a dilapidated wooden shed in back of a shabby warehouse known as the McGuane Ice Works. There were four such sheds abutting the bare canyon wall, and Huffman gave Glen a tarnished key, said, "The one on the left," and walked back to his car to wait.

"It is a little creepy," Melanie admitted.

Glen smiled. "Big buildup."

They walked up to the shed. From inside she could smell the faint scent of something dead, a familiar sickening odor that brought back memories of that un-air-conditioned room with the so-called "Aztec mummy." She was not sure she wanted to see what was inside. In her mind, she saw the mummy standing right against the door, waiting for them to open it, grinning.

The hanging clasp lock was encased in cobwebs that stretched to the door handle and held trapped the dead brown leaves of more than one autumn. Glen brushed the webbing aside, put the key in the lock, turned it, and opened the door, a tangled train of additional spiderlines pulling with it. To her relief, the mummy was lying flat on a board between two sawhorses at the rear of the shed. Huffman had told them the mummy was wrapped in plastic, but she was not surprised to see that the plastic was gone. A pile of black tarps lay tangled beneath the sawhorses.

What did surprise her were the rats and snakes. She had no idea how they'd gotten into the closed shed, but dozens of them, all dead, many in stages of advanced

decomposition, stretched out between the door and the
blackened preserved form. They were all facing the
mummy, as though they'd died bowing down to it, praying to it.

A god or a demon, Pace had said. Was he right? Was
this a dead god's body? Or a demon's?

Next to her, Glen recoiled, gasping audibly and taking
an involuntary step back.

"What is it?" Melanie asked. "What's wrong?"

He shook his head as if to indicate it was nothing, but
the frightened expression on his face and the sudden
stiffness of his spine said otherwise. He didn't even trust
himself to speak, so shaken was he, and she peered into
the small dark room to see if there was anything she'd
missed. The mummy was scary looking, yes, especially
with that huge orange afro, and the scores of dead ver-
min were disconcerting as well, but she saw nothing that
would engender that sort of reaction in him, not after
all they'd seen, not with all they knew.

"What is it?" she asked. "The rats? The snakes?"

"Nothing," he said, but his "nothing" was about as
believable as Huffman's had been, and though she didn't
press him on it, she couldn't help feeling hurt that he
wouldn't come clean.

They walked in, using their shoes to push aside the
stiff and rotting bodies of rats and snakes so they could
pass. Melanie tried to breathe through her mouth as they
approached the mummy, but even holding her nose was
not enough to keep out that godawful stench. They
walked up to the dried blackened form and looked down
on it. She expected to feel . . . *something*. An indication
of residual power or untapped energy. Gloom, doom,
and dread. The heavy air that Cameron had talked
about. But there was nothing.

They stood there for a few moments, not speaking.

"Let's do it," Glen said.

They turned and left. He closed and locked the door,
and they walked back to the car, where Huffman sat in
the driver's seat, staring resolutely ahead at the road.
Glen tapped on the window, and the historical society
president reluctantly rolled it down.

"How much do you want for it?" Glen asked.

"How much are you willing to pay?"

"A hundred bucks."

"It's yours."

"Thank you."

"I'm not exaggerating when I say that nothing will make me happier than to get that thing out of town once and for all." He looked up at them. "And no money back. You buy it, it's yours. Like I said, there are no guarantees."

"Understood."

Huffman seemed to relax. "Do you want to drive your car up here and pick it up? We can conduct the transaction back at the Heritage House. We're a nonprofit organization, so there are a bunch of forms I need to fill out."

"That'll be fine. But can you wait a minute? There's something I need to do first."

Huffman nodded. "Sure."

Glen took the cell phone from Melanie and called Vince. "We found it," he said. "We bought it. We're coming home."

4

Ron was tired of sitting in this damn teepee motel in this damn town waiting for his damn trial. The cops and the DA had that bitch's signed release. Why weren't they dropping the charges? They had no case here. Jesus Christ on the cross.

Served him right, though, for getting involved with these local yokels in the first place. He should've just put his website on hold for the summer, worked at the excavation and taken photos for the school, collected his money and his extra credit, and then resumed normal life once the fall semester started.

Ron got off the bed, pulled aside the curtains, and looked out. The highway was virtually deserted. It had been strangely quiet the past three days. He hadn't been out much, had only gone to Een's office, Jack in the Box, and Taco Bell, but he didn't like what he'd seen. People were mean, animals unfriendly, and even the buildings themselves seemed darker and more rundown than they had a few days ago.

He was not a superstitious guy and, despite his web addiction, wasn't prone to believing conspiracy theories. He also wasn't a sensitive guy; he usually didn't notice things unless they came up and bit him on the ass. Nevertheless, even he could tell that something strange was going on in this town. The fact that Al and Judi and Randy and Buck had vanished into thin air was only the beginning. All of Bower semed to be undergoing a weird type of transformation. Even Een had seemed odd the last time he'd gone to his office. Or odder than usual. He had dressed not in his customary black pants and white shirt, but in dirty faded jeans that seemed too baggy to be his and a gaudy animal-print shirt that looked like a woman's. He'd seemed distracted the entire hour, and Ron had the distinct impression that the lawyer did not expect this case to reach completion.

Why?

His thought at the time was that Een had been thinking of skipping town. Or even killing himself. But now Ron thought it more likely that the lawyer did not expect *him* to survive to the end of the process.

A single pickup drove by. Slowly. He could not see the driver, but sitting in the bed were four men wearing what looked like fur coats and a naked woman with her face painted in camouflage colors.

He didn't like this. He didn't like it at all.

Ron let the curtain fall and went back to the bed. *I Love Lucy* was over, and now the execrable *Facts of Life* was starting. Shit, small towns didn't even have decent cable. He couldn't wait to get back to the real world and put this whole horrible summer behind him. He picked up the remote, started flipping through channels. Cartoons, auto racing, soap opera, talk show . . .

Suddenly the screen turned to static and snow. He thought he'd come to the end of the channels, and he pressed the down arrow to back up. When it became clear that the television was out, he got out of bed and went to check the cable connection.

He felt a gentle swaying motion beneath his feet, a rattle of windows, and from somewhere far away a rumbling sound like thunder. He had never been through an earthquake before, but he knew that most loss of life in such a disaster was a result of collapsing buildings rather than huge cracks opening up in the ground and swallowing people whole. So he obeyed his instinct and dashed out the door as fast as his feet would carry him.

Into a raging nightmare.

Crows were falling from out of the sky, landing on top of the teepee cabins and sliding down the sloping sides, leaving ragged red trails of blood. A gas main appeared to have ruptured; flames were shooting out of rubble-strewn sections of ground in the middle of the motor court, across the street, and at several spots on the highway. In front of the tallest tower of flame, silhouetted perfectly in a shot so beautifully composed that he wished he had one of his cameras, two men dressed in animal skins with crowns of horns were using long sharpened sticks to spear a crawling woman. A small scrubby tree in front of the motel winked out of existence as though it was a light that had been shut off.

This is what happened to Al and the others, he thought.

A gang of children rode by on their bikes, brandishing bones, their faces distorted with rage. They hit an unseen shimmering wall . . . and disappeared. And then the wall moved forward, down the street, erasing the town as it passed. Gas station? Gone. Bus bench? Gone. Sidewalk? Gone.

A dead crow slid down the side of his cabin, bumped off the window and hit him in the back of the head. He felt rough feathers and small sharp bones and warm slimy innards smack against his shaved pate. Blood trickled down his neck below the collar of his shirt. Repulsed, he swatted at the back of his head, knocking the dead bird away.

In the town, in the homes, in the streets, people were starting to scream. Not cries of pain or cries for help or any yell, shout, screech, or shriek he had ever heard before. These were raw, throat-damaging, piss-in-your-pants screams of sheer terror, sounds worse than any in his most vivid nightmares.

Between two of the teepees he saw the tall pole and sign for Jack in the Box sink quickly out of sight, as though being sucked into a vacuum. Above that section of town, the blue sky was losing color and turning a burnt-charcoal gray.

It's the end of the world, he thought.

And as he watched a cackling old woman skinning a Dalmatian puppy in the back of a pickup truck speeding by on the nonexistent road, he thought maybe that was for the best.

Fifteen

1

They should've brought Vince's pickup truck. How could they be so stupid? They knew before starting this trip that they were supposed to bring back the mummy, so why hadn't they planned things out ahead of time and driven a vehicle that could actually carry it?

Glen looked from the open door of the shed to the open car trunk, then back to the shed and to the open back door of the car. There was no way it would fit in the trunk. They were going to have to wedge it into the backseat. It was stiff and straight, and they couldn't bend it, obviously. That meant its afro-haired head would either be leaning against the backseat window behind Melanie or himself.

He didn't want that mummy in the car with them. Especially not for the three-hour trip back to Scottsdale. The smell alone was enough to make him puke.

Taking out the tape measure Huffman had loaned them, he measured the trunk front-to-back and catty-corner. No way. The mummy was a foot too long, even with the hair flattened down. He measured the backseat. Still not enough room, unless they were able to manuever the mummy so that it was positioned on its side, with its feet on the floor in the corner next to the door and its head bumping the ceiling above the opposite door—an arrangement he did not think would work.

The roof. Tying it to the roof was the best option, and though the car had no rack, they could wrap the mummy back up in the plastic, put it up top, and then tie it through the window, running the rope through the inside of the car. He could only do that in the backseat, though. If he did it in the front, the doors would be roped shut and they wouldn't be able to get in. He'd have to angle all the ropes so that they funnelled through the rear windows. It could work, though. And at least they wouldn't be stuck in the car with that thing.

"So what's the plan?" Melanie said. "Or do we have one?"

"We'll tie it to the roof."

She let out an audible exhalation. "Thank God. I thought I was going to have to sit next to it. I figured you'd lean the passenger seat all the way back, lay it in there and have me sit in the backseat next to it. I was going to suggest we switch. I'd drive and you sit in the back."

He hadn't even thought of that.

"Let's go in there," Melanie said. "Let's get it."

They were afraid to touch the mummy. Huffman had given them disposable gloves, but a thin layer of latex between their hands and the monster did not seem sufficient protection. Huffman himself refused to offer any assistance. He might be able to find someone later in the day, he said, but they didn't want to wait that long. They needed to get out of here and back so that the mummy could be studied.

So, as much as they hated the idea, they decided to do it themselves. Gloves on, wearing handkerchiefs tied around their noses and mouths like bandits, they proceeded to rewrap the preserved corpse. Glen first held up the head and shoulders while Melanie slid the recovered tarp underneath. Then he lifted up the feet and buttocks while she slid it under the rest of the body. They sealed up the plastic, fastened it with duct tape, and then tied the whole kit and kaboodle atop the car.

He still had not told Melanie what he'd seen when they first opened the door of the shed. He wasn't sure why. Too personal, he supposed.

What he'd seen was his mother. Not the young mother of his dream, but his mother the way she'd looked on her deathbed, pain-stricken face, wrinkled skin drained of all color. He'd pulled open the shed door, and she'd been lying on the board between the sawhorses, head turned toward him, mouth open in agony. He stepped back, blinked, and she was gone. But it had not been a hallucination or a case of mistaken identity. She had been there, in the shed, and for a brief second the shed had even smelled like her room, that pungent scent of medicine and disinfectant that he would never forget.

What had caused it? Whatever power was at work here, it seemed to be targeting him personally. Melanie had seen nothing but the mummy. He had seen a horrible vision of his mother. Not just seen it, but smelled it, *felt* it.

But why?

He didn't understand.

And he didn't want to talk to Melanie about it. Not yet.

They drove back to Scottsdale, Glen setting the cruise control two miles below the speed limit. He did not want to get stopped by a cop. They would have one tough time explaining the presence of a mummy to some motorcycle patrolman.

Early afternoon, they pulled into McCormack's driveway and parked behind the professor's BMW. Leaving the mummy on the roof, they walked up and rang the bell. A moment later, McCormack opened the door. Behind him, Glen saw Alyssa and Vince and Cameron, watching what appeared to be a news program on TV.

"Well, we're back. We've got our buddy tied up on the roof. It was either that or put him in the backseat, and we didn't want him in the car with us." The solemn look on McCormack's face made him stop. "What is it?" he asked. "What happened?"

"You didn't hear?"

Glen looked at Melanie, shook his head. "No. What?"

"Bower," the professor told them. "It's gone. It's been wiped off the face of the earth."

Her parents. And her house. And her friends and her coworkers and the school where she worked and the stores where she shopped and . . . everything. All gone. It was impossible for Melanie to get her mind around. She felt numb, hollow. The entire world, Glen included, seemed distant, removed, as though she were viewing it through thick glass. Even the sounds she heard seemed muffled, and it occurred to her that she was in shock.

Glen was holding her hand, but she barely felt it. "When did this happen?" he asked.

"No one knows. Today. Maybe yesterday. They just discovered it this morning."

"This is on the news, right? The national news? NBC, CBS, ABC, CNN? I don't care how small Bower is or how much prejudice there is against the West. There's no way this can be swept under the rug."

"Oh, it hasn't been. CNN's had on nothing but all day." McCormack picked up the remote control from the table, turned up the volume. "They're doing our work for us. The story's finally getting out."

A news flash crawled along the bottom of the screen. "The stock market fell a hundred points?" Glen said. "Is that related?"

"Oh, yes. This is big news. No one's talking about anything else."

"And they're finally putting the pieces together," Vince said. "The local news footage from Pima House is running nationally, all the networks have correspondents in Cameron's neighborhood, and *Dateline, 20/20,* and Larry King have all booked some of Dr. McCormack's most esteemed colleagues."

"Arthur Wessington is bringing along footage shot at the Russell Museum. Stephen Barre will be discussing strange pottery finds with Stone Phillips. They asked me to conduct a Pima House tour for Diane Sawyer," McCormack said modestly, "but I declined."

Melanie could not believe all that was happening. The mummy was still in plastic on the roof of the car, but what just this morning had seemed like an important piece of the puzzle now seemed superfluous.

Bower was gone.

"So our part's over?" Glen asked. "The big guns are on it, the president's assigned the best and the brightest?"

McCormack looked over at Vince. "We don't think so."

"Why? What do you mean?"

"Hang on to your hats," Vince said. And he explained

how they'd found a bounty of ancient multicultural artifacts in a train tunnel near the scout ranch. Now they thought that the Mogollon Monster and the creature that had killed off the Anasazi were one and the same. He said he believed that she, Cameron, Glen, McCormack, and himself were all resistant to whatever psychic power was wreaking this havoc. "I think we've been chosen," he said. "Chosen to fight."

"Jesus Christ!" Glen said. "Why didn't you tell us this over the phone?"

"We told you we were going up to the scout ranch—"

"Yeah, and you told us you came back and we told you we found the mummy and you didn't mention word one. Shit!"

"Not to hurt your feelings," McCormack said, "but you're not the professional here. You stumbled into this, but it's our work. And for you to suggest that—"

"Shut up," Cameron said.

They all turned toward him in surprise.

The boy sat up straighter on the couch. "Why are you arguing over stupid stuff? We're all in this together. And maybe it wants us to argue with each other. Did you ever think of that? If we're the only ones who can fight it, maybe it wants us to separate."

"He's right," Glen said instantly. He nodded at Vince. "I'm sorry."

"It's been a long day for all of us."

"A long week," Glen said.

"A long month."

Melanie was staring at the television, saw a generic map showing where Bower was located in relation to Phoenix and Albuquerque. "I want to see it," she said. "I want to go back there."

McCormack nodded. "I knew you would. And I do, too. I talked to my friend, Captain Ortiz, from the Scottsdale PD. He's willing to fly us up in a police helicopter."

Glen frowned. "Those little two-man things?"

"No. They have access to a big one that can fit up to six people. It's part of a sharing deal between Valley police departments, the DEA, and the INS." He shook his head, waved his hand. "But that doesn't matter. The point is, there's a helicopter we can use. It's late today, but we can go tomorrow morning early."

"I want to go now!" Melanie demanded.

"It'll be dark by—"

"It gets dark at seven-thirty. Right now it's two. A half hour to whatever airport or launch pad this helicopter's on, an hour to Bower, an hour back. That's plenty of time. I want to see it."

McCormack nodded. "All right. Let me call and see if we can go." He retreated to his study, and the rest of them turned their attention back to the television, which was now showing grainy security-camera footage of a totemic figure rocking back and forth in a museum case.

"Have they actually shown Bower yet?" Glen asked. "What it looks like now?"

"They don't have any shots of the town," Vince said. "It's restricted airspace."

Melanie still felt numb, but things seemed to be coming back into focus.

Mom, she thought. *Daddy.*

Glen was holding her hand tightly, and it was starting to hurt. "Remember what Pace told us when we were looking at that mural back in Chaco Canyon?" he said. "That before everyone disappeared it was like Sodom and Gomorrah? Maybe that's what's happening. Maybe it's like a natural phenomenon, and every time a society gets too debauched, a correction takes place and all that's destroyed."

"Do you really believe that?" she asked.

"No."

"I think it's more likely that you unearthed that skull, and that started the ball rolling. If it had remained in the ground, perhaps none of this would be happening."

"You really believe that?"

"Maybe."

"Me, too."

"I don't," Vince said.

They both turned to look at him.

"That skull was buried for centuries. The Mogollon Monster seems to have gone through dormant periods of inactivity, but he was around during that time, killing, living up by the Rim. Maybe he's the last of his kind and has been in hiding, but he's back at full strength and he's not hiding anymore."

"Maybe digging up those skulls and things *brought* him back to full strength," Cameron suggested. "Maybe they're like dilithium crystals, power sources."

"Dilithium crystals?" Glen asked.

"Star Trek," Vince explained.

The professor emerged from the hallway, looking pleased. "The captain said we should meet him at the police department in twenty minutes. That should give us plenty of time. They have a heliport on the roof of the building, and we'll take off from there."

They could only bring four people, so Cameron remained at the house with Alyssa. Glen backed up his car to let McCormack pull out, then drove into the garage to hide the still-bound mummy so it wouldn't be stolen or vandalized. None of them liked leaving Alyssa and Cameron there with the monster—Melanie had visions of finding the mummy unwrapped and upright, the boy and the woman bowing down before its feet—but it couldn't be helped. They would only be gone for a couple of hours.

They piled into the BMW, McCormack speeding, weaving in and out of traffic, driving the way she thought guys who owned BMW's usually drove. Captain Ortiz and one of his lieutenants were waiting for them, and on the rooftop heliport the pilot already had the chopper running. They got in, buckled up, and were off, sailing over the eastern subdivisions, over the reservation, over the desert.

No one spoke. Not that they could have been heard anyway. The noise of the rotors was deafening.

Melanie tried to concentrate on the view out the window. She did not want to dwell on what had happened to Bower, but there was nothing to do on the ride but think, and she found herself remembering not just the people but the objects that were now lost forever. The photographs. The jewelry. The quilts and china and family heirlooms. She had known her parents would die one day, but she had always expected to have pictures of them, presents from them, the physical items that would enable their memories to live on. Now those were gone, too.

Close to an hour later, they reached Bower. Or rather the spot where Bower should have been. For when they looked down, it was just . . . not there. They could see Highway 192, but at the point where it entered the town, where the abandoned building that used to be Tom's Diner sat, the asphalt ended. It resumed three miles away, where the town was supposed to end. In between was . . . nothing, blank prairie land. Only by natural landmarks could Melanie tell where things used to be.

The helicopter flew over the lake, circled back over the town site.

Around Tom's were trucks and tanks and cars of all sizes, a fleet of federal vehicles all dispatched to find out what had happened to Bower. She could see men in suits and men in fatigues down there, all pointing up at them.

The pilot was talking into his headset, using his two-way radio to communicate with someone on the ground as he steadied and started lowering the helicopter.

Melanie looked north, at the small flat-topped rise that she was pretty sure had been her school's football/baseball/soccer field. She was suddenly afraid for them to land. What if there was another vortex here, something spawned by their excavation or that bone land under Ricky's house and they were sucked into it the second they touched down?

Ricky, she thought. *Jerod.*

They were gone, dead, disappeared.

The copter continued to descend. She wanted to tell the pilot not to touch down, but before she could shout out her thoughts, a representative from one of the federal agencies below told him the same thing, ordering the helicopter not to land in an amplified voice that easily overcame the din of the copter blades. The same thing must have come through the radio—and with similar force—because the pilot cried out and swept the wire mike and earphones off his head. She saw him mouth the word "fuck," although she could not actually hear it.

They started up again.

Thank God, she thought. Looking down, she saw no

agents or soldiers or researchers in the area where the town used to be. They were all huddled around the last section of asphalt near the diner.

Maybe they'd already lost people.

The pilot was flying them away, returning along the flight path they'd taken to get here. She saw him shout something to Captain Ortiz, who then leaned over and shouted in McCormack's ear. McCormack bent forward. "We're going back!" he yelled into her face, and she could barely hear him over the blades. She nodded, and he passed the news on to Glen.

Melanie looked out the side window, craning her neck for a last look at the spot where Bower previously stood. Just west of where she thought their excavation had been was a huge bulge in the earth, a swelling protrusion that sloped sharply up at the center. If she had not been so focused on her missing town, she would have noticed it immediately. It was big from the air, but from the ground it must have looked massive, and she saw full-size junipers and piñon pines on the newly created hillside that had been sloughed off and had fallen over.

Melanie tapped Glen and Vince on the shoulder. "What is that?" she shouted. Both men shook their heads and shrugged uncertainly. She motioned for McCormack to look out his window. "What do you think it is?" she yelled.

The professor stared out the window, then leaned forward. He didn't yell, but she could somehow hear him clearly. "I'm no expert," McCormack said, "but I think it's the beginning of a cinder cone. I think it's a volcano."

2

Pace thought he'd be able to hitch a ride with someone heading into Albuquerque, but the one car he saw on the road nearly knocked him into the ditch and sped by without stopping. He walked up to the doors of three houses that looked like they had someone home, but no one was there. At the last one, a faded A-frame, what appeared to be a permanent garage sale sat out front in the gravel driveway: junky tools on a leaning TV tray, a couple of grimy car parts on the ground.

A bicycle.

He walked over to the bike, looked at it. An old three-speed, it seemed to be in usable shape, and the cardboard sign draped over the handlebars said $10. He had plenty of money in his wallet, and without any hesitation, he whipped out a ten-dollar bill, dropped it through the home's mail slot, and got on the bike.

He rode it all the way into Albuquerque.

In the city, the end had already begun. There were cars abandoned on the streets, and an alarming lack of people on the sidewalks, in the businesses. Many of the stores were closed, and closer to downtown a Burger King was burning—with no firefighters anywhere to be seen. He'd been planning to rent a car and drive back to Chaco, but the Avis franchise he passed had been looted and a trio of peculiar-looking German shepherds guarded the parking lot. He kept riding.

Looking south of the city, toward Socorro in the flat basin adjoining the Rio Grande, he saw a tornado. Not just a big dust devil, but an honest-to-God tornado, the sort of huge destructive cyclone he'd seen before only in news footage. It looked to be over a mile wide, and as he watched, it hit the river and temporarily turned into a water spout.

Everything he'd feared was coming to pass, the wholesale disappearances, the natural disasters. Pace had known this would happen, but he hadn't known exactly how. He still didn't know. To his mind, this all seemed random, haphazard, not the sort of orderly destruction he'd envisioned.

He had Glen and Melanie's cell phone number—he'd seen it in his wallet when he was inventorying the wallet's contents in the well—and he found a pay phone, took out his Sprint card, and tried to make the call, but couldn't even get a dial tone. He tried three other phones. Same thing. The lines were down, he thought. He considered finding a store and buying a cell phone, but no stores seemed to be open, and he was not quite up for stealing.

Not yet.

It was getting late. Soon it would be dusk, then soon it would be dark, and he didn't want to be out in the city when the sun went down. He found an Enterprise car rental office nearby. No one was there, but the door was open, and though he felt guilty as hell, he grabbed a set of keys from behind the counter. He considered leaving his Visa number, but someone other than the rental car company might get it, so he just wrote down the make, model, and license number of the car he was taking, wrote down his phone number and address at Chaco, left it on tōp of the desk behind the counter and took off.

It was like traveling through a nightmare version of New Mexico. The sky was a charcoal ceiling. Snow fell concurrently with rain, and the highway was littered with abandoned vehicles. By the side of the road, he saw coyotes and mule deer with twisted necks and loping gaits and terrible smiles, and, farther back in the desert, bands of raggedly attired people with the same afflictions.

A trip that should have taken him two hours took four, and when he finally got to Chaco, there was chaos. The visitor's center was closed, but most of the rangers were still onsite, and the ones who weren't holed up in their cabins were together in the workroom where a sculpture of bones reached all the way to the ceiling.

"Thank God you're back," Steve said when he walked in. "I don't know what the hell's going on here, but it's right up your alley."

Behind him, Jill Kittrick started crying. "I looked for you in your Forbidden Zone," she told Pace. "And I was attacked! Every time I tried to walk into that damn storehouse, something threw sand in my eyes! Then when I finally got in, it . . . it . . ." She gestured toward her crotch, started crying harder.

"We were just going to start tearing that thing apart," Steve said, gesturing toward the bone sculpture.

Pace saw that Miltos and Scott both had pickaxes in hand. "That might not be such a good idea," he said.

"What do you suggest, then?"

Pace shrugged.

Steven threw up his hands. "What is happening here?"

"It's not just here."

Pace gathered everyone together in the visitor's center auditorium, even the rangers from the cabins, and tried to calm them down. He started from the beginning and left nothing out, from Al's earliest original theory to his own hellish experience at Christensen Divine's and in Albuquerque. These were smart people from a variety of disciplines and backgrounds, and he hoped that they'd be able to come at this from a new angle, to see things he had overlooked.

They were quiet when he finished, and then the room erupted. There were a few holdouts, literal-minded rangers unable to make the leap, but enough had happened at the park in the past twenty-four hours that the majority understood instantly that he was telling the truth.

They needed to do whatever they could to protect themselves here, but first he had to call Glen and Melanie. He ducked out quickly while debates were still raging. The telephone lines, thankfully, were still up, and he dialed from his office. Melanie answered her cell phone on the first ring, and he told her that he had found the skull, then went on to describe his adventures since they'd parted.

"It seems clear now that we're not just dealing with *a* creature," he said. "There's more than one."

"We think so, too."

"There was probably a tribe. I don't know how many are left, but they've been resurrected and they're not just putting their toes in the water anymore. Albuquerque is like a war zone. I didn't see any of the creatures themselves, but I saw their handiwork."

"We've seen it on the news," she told him. "Denver, too."

"Denver?"

"Yes."

"Jesus. What about Phoenix?"

"Nothing here. Yet. But Bower, my home, where Al had his dig? It's gone. The entire town has disappeared.

We flew over it in a helicopter, and the land's just been wiped clean."

"There's nothing left at all?"

"Well, it stops at the town limits. There's a diner right past the edge of town that hasn't vanished. The feds are using it as a staging area."

Pace was at a loss for what to say. God, he wished Al was here. From the auditorium, he heard loud, angry, scared voices. "I have some fears to calm," he said. "A bone sculpture suddenly appeared in our workroom this morning, and a lot of other things have been going on that I haven't had time to sort out yet. I don't know if we're under attack or just receiving fallout, but I need to be here right now."

"I understand," Melanie told him. "Stay by the phone, though."

"Why?"

"Because," she said, "I have the feeling we're going to need you."

3

It was impossible to sleep.

Glen lay next to Melanie on the high soft bed in the McCormacks' guest room, listening to the sounds of the desert night through the open window. He would have preferred a television, but the guest room didn't have one, and instead of celebrity chatter and laugh tracks, he heard insect clicking and bird cawing and the far-off howl of coyotes.

Melanie stirred.

"Are you awake?" he asked.

"Yes."

He rolled onto his side, facing her. After returning from Bower, they had untied and unwrapped the mummy, and McCormack and Vince had driven it to ASU, where an entire team was studying it. In the split second they had removed the duct tape and pulled open the tarp to reveal the creature's face, he had again seen his mother, and this time he had told Melanie, though he had not shared that information with anyone else.

"There seems to be a pattern," Glen said. "First the animals, then the disappearances. But with me it's . . . personal." He looked at her. "You know what I mean? All this destruction is happening, and yet I'm seeing my dead mother. It's like the monster is picking on me specifically for some reason, trying to . . . torture me, I guess, although I can't figure out why."

"It doesn't go away," Melanie said softly. "It never goes away."

He wasn't sure if she was talking about his hurt or her own. Maybe it was the past in general to which she was referring.

"It's personal with me, too," she said. "Don't forget, it was my face on that jar and my parents' house on that pottery shard."

"Why, though?"

"Maybe Cameron's right, maybe something is trying to split us up. Maybe we have been chosen and we're stronger together than we are apart, and it's doing this to ensure its survival."

"There's one thing that bothers me, that's been bothering me for a long time—"

Melanie smiled. "Only one thing?"

"Well, one thing in particular. In that church in New Mexico, where we saw the paintings—"

"I know what you're going to say."

"Only me and the boy were fighting that creature at the end. You weren't there. No one else was there."

"I know. And I've been thinking about that."

"What have you been thinking?"

"Those paintings were not part of a prophesy. They weren't telling us what would happen, or even what might happen, but what *should* happen. That last panel was a prescription, direction for what we needed to do if the events in the preceding panels came to pass— which they have. I don't know who might have painted those pictures, but I'm pretty sure I know why, and I think we need to pay attention. Which means that whatever happens, when the endgame arrives, it's you and Cameron. The rest of us need to step aside."

"So where does that leave us?" Glen asked. "How do we get from here to there?"

Melanie sat up. "We have to find out where 'there' is. We've been *re*acting instead of acting, running around after each incident, trying to figure out what happened after the fact. We need to take it to them. We need to find out where these things live and go there."

He nodded. "The problem is, the last time this happened was so long ago. It's almost impossible to piece anything together from the existing fragments."

"We're getting closer, though. Enough has happened recently that we're starting to zero in. That train tunnel they explored, with the artifacts? That's good. That's close."

"And when I go there, I'll no doubt see my dead mother."

"You can't escape the past," Melanie said. "It's always with us. It's what the present is built upon. In personal lives and in the histories of entire peoples. No matter how many generations of schoolkids are taught that brave settlers from thirteen small colonies on the East Coast tamed this wild land, that governor's mansion in Santa Fe says otherwise. It's there as a living monument to a defeated culture, and it's not going anywhere."

She paused, looked over at him. "It's not going anywhere," she repeated.

"What are you getting at?"

"It's still here," she said wonderingly. "Under the layers, like the original surface of a house beneath coat after coat of paint. In Bower, we built the town on top of an old pueblo, right? Well, maybe they built their pueblo on top of an even older civilization, one that wasn't human."

"I understand that much. But what are—?"

"I don't know, not exactly, but maybe there's a . . . a governor's mansion, something right under our noses that we're seeing but not seeing."

He nodded. "A living monument, like you said."

"Yes! Emphasis on the *living*. You know, that's what we've failed to take into account. We've been looking at Anasazi sites and artifacts, assuming anything older than that is gone, that there's nothing remaining of anything prior. But if we're right, these beings were here before the Anasazi and they're still here now. They've always been here. And there's probably evidence of it right before us. Like William Faulkner said about the South: 'the past isn't dead, it isn't even past.' "

Melanie was right, they were getting closer. But what were they to do once they got "there"? If that final panel really was a prescription for action, it certainly didn't tell them much. God damn, he wished they'd picked up their developed photos. There were probably subtleties and intricacies in the paintings that he hadn't seen or had forgotten and that were probably the key to everything.

As far as he recalled, the last scene had taken place in a cave or a dark room with a weird wheel on the wall, a wheel covered with all sorts of symbols that for some reason made him think of the sun. He and Cameron were both there, and they were winning, the afrohaired figure was screaming. But what were the burning ropes, the cables they were carrying that had lightning coming out of the ends?

The . . . *cables*.

Electrical cables.

Yes! It was the only explanation that made sense. The creatures were afraid of electricity.

He told this to Melanie, and she, too, was excited. "Yes!" she said. Everything was coming together. Before the disappearance of the Anasazi, there'd been a prolonged drought. No rain. No lightning. *No electricity*. That was why those creatures had been able to do so much damage. Electricity was everywhere now, but the modern world, with its self-generated power tamed and contained, was a much more hospitable and predictable place than the wild world of old. They were still afraid of it, though, which was why they appeared in ancient ruins and in the wilds. It explained why there'd been no incidents with the mummy at Nate Stewky's roadside museum. That had been too close to the Holbrook power plant.

Glen wanted to wake up McCormack and Vince right now and tell them, call Pace on the phone and let him know, but she convinced him to wait until morning.

McCormack, Vince, and Pace needed their sleep. *They* needed their sleep.

But they were both too wound up to sleep.

Glen thought about the mummy they'd found and Cameron's Polaroid and the dream he'd had of his mother. He imagined Anasazi warriors manning the battlements of a well-fortified pueblo while a horde of orange-haired monsters descended upon them.

God or devil.

How had the creatures been vanquished the first time? A prolonged lightning storm of biblical proportions? That didn't make any sense. Electricity could not have killed them all.

They hadn't been vanquished.

They'd used up their food supply.

Glen suddenly felt sick. That was it. The Anasazi, and perhaps the Incas and Mayans and all of the others, were cattle to be herded and slaughtered, allowed to be fruitful and multiply and then cut down when their numbers reached the target goal. He thought of the disparate artifacts Melanie and the rest of them had found in Bower before his arrival, the objects from around the world McCormack and Vince had discovered in the train tunnel. These beings had followed the food supply, leaving vanished civilizations behind. But unlike those other cultures, the Anasazi had fought back. They'd captured some of the monsters and beheaded them, come up with a ritual to either banish or destroy them, and it had been enough to damage the creatures for hundreds of years. They'd come out to forage only infrequently in the subsequent centuries and became the stuff of legend.

He told this to Melanie, and she nodded soberly. "Food. It makes sense. But . . ."

"But what?"

"But there's not really any evidence of people being eaten. Then or now. Like Al said, there's evidence of cannibalism between tribes, but no indication that these creatures ate or eat people. I'm thinking that they don't use people for food, they use us for . . . fuel."

"Same difference."

"Maybe. But these are beings that can create vortexes and animate stone tools, make line drawings move on pieces of pottery, wipe entire towns off the map. I don't think they eat the way we do, and I don't think their basic needs are the same. I think you're right in that they need to kill humans or draw them into their vortexes, and I'd be willing to bet that they *made* those tribes turn cannibal, but it seems more likely to me that it's for some reason we don't understand."

"Maybe the Anasazi figured it out, though. Whatever rituals they performed, separating the heads and the bodies and all that, they worked."

"I don't think it was rituals."

"What then?"

"Since we're taking big leaps: dirt."

Glen raised his eyebrows. "Dirt?"

"Cameron's dilithium crystals made me think of it. It's true that excavating the skull and these other objects seemed to trigger everything afterward. But why? What was the difference between those things being buried and being unearthed?"

"Dirt."

"Dirt," Melanie said. The way I look at it, it's kept the power of those skulls and bones contained for hundreds of years. That tomb under Ricky's house? The trouble didn't start until it was exposed to open air. Same thing with the skull you found. That's why the buildings at Chaco Canyon were all sealed up. You're right, they did know. At least the people left at the end knew, and whether they sealed in one of the creatures or sealed themselves in from it, it worked."

"It can't be that simple. I mean, these things made Bower disappear. Entirely. The people, the buildings, the trees, everything. And now Albuquerque and Denver are falling apart. Phoenix and Tucson will be next. Who knows what, after that. Do you really think if we just throw a little dirt on these guys, it will all stop?"

"Why not? You can stop a serial killer with a bullet. My great-grandfather murdered who knows how many people all total. And all of that evil was stopped by a single slug of metal no bigger than my thumb. Who's to say this doesn't work the same way? Why does it have to be some elaborate ceremony or arcane ritual that stops these things? Why can't it be something simple?"

"I guess it can. It's just—"

A piercing scream erupted from down the hall, a woman's scream, followed immediately by a man's rough cry.

Alyssa. And McCormack.

Glen threw off the covers, sped out of the guest room and down the wide hallway, Melanie immediately behind him. The professor and his wife, both in underwear, were already in the hall. Alyssa was running toward the living room. McCormack was flattened against the opposite wall, moving carefully sideways in order to see into a corner of the bedroom. Vince and Cameron, who'd been sleeping in one of the other guest rooms, rushed out, pulling on shirts, the boy's face frozen in an expression of panic.

"What is it?" Glen demanded. "What happened?"

Seeing that everyone was all right, Melanie had run back into their room and emerged wearing a nightshirt. In her hand was a flimsy blue robe which she brought out to Alyssa in the living room.

McCormack did not yet trust himself to speak, simply pointing into the master bedroom. Warily, Glen and Vince peeked around the edge of the door frame.

The mummy.

It was back.

The blackened figure stood next to the nightstand on the right side of the bed, its fierce rudimentary facial features mercifully shrouded by the darkness of the room, its wild orange hair illuminated by the soft light from the hallway and looking like the penumbra around an eclipsed sun.

Instinctively, Glen looked toward the window, then glanced down the hallway toward the living room, where he could see that the front door of the house was closed. He needed to check, though he'd known already that the mummy hadn't climbed through the window or walked through the door. If it had been able to get out of the locked lab at ASU and travel ten miles to the professor's home, it did not need to use conventional entrances.

"My wife must have woken up and seen it standing next to her," McCormack said. "All of a sudden, she was screaming and climbing over me, and then I woke up and saw it, and we both ran out." He ran a hand through his wild sleep-tousled hair. "Jesus. What does it want?"

"They know we're after them," Glen said. "Now they're after us."

"They can't hurt us," Vince said. "We're immune."

McCormack shook his head, eyes still wide with fear. "It doesn't look like we are."

"I guess it's time to find out." Vince looked at Glen. "Put some pants and shoes on. I'll get my Nikes. We'll carry it outside."

"And bury it," Melanie said. She'd walked up with Alyssa and the two of them stood a few steps down the hall. "That'll inactivate its power."

Glen explained what they'd been discussing. "I'm thinking we should try to electrocute it," he said. "Do a test run. It's what we'll have to do anyway, at least according to those church paintings." He looked around. "Anyone have any ideas?"

"You could put it in a bathtub filled with water and then throw a radio or something in," Cameron suggested. "I saw that in a movie."

"I have a better idea," McCormack proposed. "There's a portable generator in the garage. I used to use it to run equipment at remote digs. We could try to shock it with that."

"That might work."

"Do it outside," Alyssa said, and her voice was quiet, shaky, on the verge of tears. "Don't do it in the house."

Glen nodded.

"We'll do it out back," McCormack promised.

They got the generator out of the garage, tested it to make sure it ran, and found a place in the desert behind the house, a flat area with sand and no vegetation in case there was some sort of fire. They worked in shifts, one of the men keeping an eye on the mummy at all times, but it remained standing impassively by the side of the bed.

McCormack had gloves, and Glen and Vince put them on before taking the ancient body outside. It was long after midnight, and carrying the preserved corpse of a supernaturally powerful creature into the moonlit desert made Glen feel as though he were part of a weird religious cult.

They placed the mummy on the sand, on its back. McCormack already had the generator running. The professor had cranked up the maximum output and attached two accessory cords with clamps that looked like a car's jumper cables. "Stand back," he said. Holding the two cables, McCormack crouched at the foot of the mummy and touched one to each shriveled foot.

The mummy disappeared.

There was no burning, no sizzling, no frying of orange hair, not even a satisfying electrical pop or a fading cry of fettered rage. The figure simply vanished, leaving nothing behind, not even an imprint in the sand. McCormack put down the cables, turned off the generator, and picked up his flashlight. All three of them searched the immediate area for signs of any residue. Nothing. It was as if the mummy had never existed.

"It works," Vince said wonderingly.

Glen felt as surprised as Vince sounded. He'd thought electricity was the key, but he hadn't believed this experiment would actually accomplish anything. There was no way he believed that their first attempt would make the monster disappear.

But it did.

Inside the house, Melanie was still consoling Alyssa, and Cameron was watching television. The men came back in to explain what had happened. Alyssa seemed not to want to hear, but Cameron immediately turned off the TV, and both he and Melanie listened intently.

Melanie, in particular, was very excited by the news. "We can stop them," she said. "All we need to do now is find out where they are and attack them."

"I think we need to go back to the area around the scout ranch," Vince said. "I think that's the key."

Glen shook his head. "I don't think so."

Vince looked at him askance. "One of them went right by Cam's cabin and killed his scoutmaster. When we went there, we found signs of them in that old train tunnel. That's where they live."

"Maybe. But Melanie suggested that we should be

looking at something more obvious, that we've over-looked, and I think she's right."

"Let's look at Al's map," McCormack said. "We'll figure this out."

They followed the professor into his study. Moonlight shone on the oversize desk in the center of the room, streaming in through the skylight. McCormack flipped a switch, and the office was illuminated in soft white. One of Al's maps had been tacked onto a large corkboard since the last time Glen had been in here, and there were lines and markings all over it, pictures posted all around it.

Glen walked up to the map, which covered the Four Corners states. The marks and lines indicated where incidents had occurred.

"There are probably other events we don't know about or that haven't been reported," McCormack said, "but these are the important ones."

"You haven't added Albuquerque," Glen noted. "Or Denver."

"No." McCormack withdrew a black marking pen from the desk and made two big black dots over those two cities.

"It makes a triangle," Cameron said.

"You're right." Melanie traced the pattern of accumulated dots and circles and marks with her finger. "It's lopsided, but it's there."

"Like the Devil's triangle," Glen said drily. "That's appropriate."

She touched his shoulder. "Do you notice something?"

"What?"

"Look at the center of the triangle, the spot that's equidistant from all sides and angles."

"I don't see what you're . . ." He frowned, looked closer. "Oh, my God."

It was the empty New Mexican village with the abandoned church. Although it was not listed on the map, the center of the triangle was located at the spot where the small town should have been.

Not listed on the map?

There was no such thing anymore as an unmapped town.

He was filled with both dread and excitement. This was the place. He remembered the feeling he'd had in the church, that it was a Christian site but had been built upon something older, something primitive, something frightening and unknowable.

"It *was* under our noses," he told Melanie.

"Yes." She nodded. "If only we'd discovered it sooner."

"Let's go," Vince said. "What are we waiting for?"

"What? Now?" McCormack looked over at the closed blinds, obviously thinking about the hour.

"It's a long trip—"

"Nine hours," Glen said. "Eight if we speed."

"—and who knows what could happen in that time? Look what's happened in the last twenty-four. Bower's gone, the mummy's returned . . . I don't think we have time to waste."

"I don't either," Melanie said.

Glen and Cameron nodded.

"We're going to have to take two vehicles." McCormack pointed at Vince. "We'll put the generator in your truck, so you'll have to drive."

"Not a problem."

"Everyone else can come with me."

"I'm going with my uncle," Cameron announced.

Vince smiled at his nephew, punched his shoulder lightly.

"Let's get ready to go, then. We'll pick up some extra gas on the way. Who knows how long we'll have to run that generator?"

Glen grabbed his wallet and keys from the guest room, ran a quick comb through his hair, then called Pace, who was asleep, but became instantly wide awake when Glen explained what had happened and what they were going to do. "We need your help," he said.

"You've got it."

"Then meet us in Gallup," he told Pace. "We'll pick you up on the way."

4

They saw the sun rise over Winslow.

It was a beautiful sight, Glen thought, made even more so by the possibility that it might be his last. The remnants of a late night summer storm stretched over the eastern sky, and the clouds that had already turned from black to gray were shifting from orange to pink on their way to white. The rundown buildings in the by-passed town looked cinematically picturesque, bathed in the rosy glow of the dawning day.

He had become increasingly less certain of the outcome of this encounter as they sped through the desert darkness toward New Mexico. The more he thought about it, the more he realized that the final painting in the church tryptich did not depict the defeat of the orange-haired figure. The figure was screaming, yes, and he'd assumed it was with agony, but maybe it was rage. Maybe the electricity was only angering the monster. He could not say for certain because he had only memory to rely upon.

Why the hell hadn't they picked up their developed photos?

Why hadn't they used a Polaroid like Cameron?

Electricity had worked on the mummy, he told himself. The painting had steered them right on that. It would work again with the living creatures.

But he could not make himself believe it, and he reached for Melanie's hand and held it tightly.

They'd taken two vehicles, Vince and Cameron driving in Vince's pickup with the generator, he and Melanie riding in McCormack's BMW with the professor and his wife. Alyssa was subdued. In fact, she had not seemed herself since the attack. He hadn't gotten to know her well, but the confident loquacious woman they had met the first day was long gone, and in her place was a cowed jittery ghost who barely spoke. He recalled the piece of broken pottery he'd picked up that had depicted Alyssa's attack and then showed an assault on Melanie. Had that been a threat or a prediction or merely an effort to frighten him off? He didn't know but, since then, the image had never been far from his mind.

They passed Winslow, heading into the sun.

Shortly after they'd hit the road, McCormack had used his cell phone to call Captain Ortiz. The captain's jurisdiction was Scottsdale and they were way past Scottsdale, but the professor told him exactly where they were going and what they were doing and asked him to pass the news along to the FBI or whatever federal agency was investigating the disappearance of Bower. Glen hoped when they arrived at the town they would find a phalanx of tanks and cop cars and official government vehicles, with crack teams of scientists and sharpshooters all ready to give the monsters what for. But he knew that was unlikely. Even if the representatives of law enforcement got to the town before they did, there was nothing those people would be able to do.

They weren't immune.

They weren't depicted in the painting.

They passed the free petrified wood and the dinosaur bones, the stucco pyramid and Nate Stewky's SEE THE AZTEC MUMMY! sign. He felt a nostalgic twinge as he thought of their trip through Stewky's homegrown museum. It had only been a few days ago, but it felt like a lifetime.

Pace said he'd be waiting at "The Best Damn Donut Shop in Gallup," and there was indeed a donut shop with that name just off the highway on the west end of town. Pace was in his pickup in the parking lot, eating a jelly donut and drinking coffee, and at Glen's direction, McCormack pulled up next to him. After a quick bathroom break for everyone and a short stop at a gas station, they were on their way again, Pace's truck the third and final vehicle in the caravan.

Three, he thought. Three paintings in each tryptich. A triangle has three sides. Six of them had immunity: two times three. Father, Son and Holy Ghost. Three. Christ denied thrice. Three . . . three . . .

The lack of sleep caught up with him and he dozed, lulled by the gentle motion of the car and the repetitive thoughts in his mind. When Melanie gently shook him awake two hours later, they were passing through Albuquerque. Or what was left of it. Several large fires burned in different parts of the city, and the freeway was strewn with abandoned cars and dozens of dead animals. In the sky, odd-looking crows spiraled up above a tall rectangular building that appeared to be slowly melting. Pace was right. This was a nightmare. He didn't know what else he'd missed along the way—he'd slept through it—but from the tense atmosphere in the car, he was pretty sure it had been bad.

They were getting close.

"Which way from here?" McCormack asked tersely. Next to him, Alyssa sat silently in the passenger seat, almost curled into a ball.

Glen didn't remember exactly, but he examined the map the professor handed back and directed him to the correct northbound road.

Once again, they traveled through the increasingly rural countryside, past the small primitive villages where he and Melanie had seen dark-skinned people riding horses instead of cars, past dirt roads and adobe buildings and open fields and wooden farmhouses. They saw no people this time, no animals either, and the world seemed still, as though frozen in a moment of time.

Then they were over a ridge, down a rise, winding through trees and into the river-carved valley where they'd stopped in that unnamed village for gas and found the abandoned church.

Only the church was no longer there.

The village was no longer there.

Where the gas station and the restaurant and the houses and the church should have been stood a hideous hellish structure that appeared to be made of dirty rusted metal, a sprawling monstrosity that looked like a demon's house designed by a lunatic. To either side of it, alternating scenes kept winking in and out of existence: bucolic countryside, poor but picturesque village, craggy canyon wall, fire-ravaged forest. In front were three large holes in the ground, ringed with human skulls.

Three.

This was clearly a place of power. Glen could sense it. Cameron was right, the air did feel liquid. But he was not paralyzed. His senses seemed heightened, sight, smell, and hearing all operating far beyond their ordinary capabilities and sending his brain information that was almost too detailed to process.

All three vehicles stopped in the center of the road in front of this fantastic sight, and everyone save Alyssa got out. She remained curled up in the passenger seat of McCormack's car, eyes closed, asleep or desperately trying to sleep.

Glen looked more carefully at the quickly flickering scenes on either side of the horrible building. In one, he thought he saw a downed helicopter in the background. In another, business-suited agents and camouflaged soldiers wandered between trees and through bushes, looking frightened.

The feds *had* gotten here before they did.

The six of them were still standing, facing the structure. So far nothing had happened, but even if the rest of them could resist this power, Alyssa could not, and Glen turned toward McCormack. "Get her out of here!" he ordered. "Get in the car and drive back to the last town. We'll meet you there later. After."

He'd expected an argument, but the professor understood instantly. Wishing them luck, he ran around the front of the car. "I'll call on the cell phone," he announced. "Keep the line open so I can hear what happens."

Glen nodded his assent, and a minute after the BMW had turned around and headed back up the road, Melanie's phone rang. She answered, then clipped it on her belt. "Lot of money for a walkie-talkie," she said.

Glen smiled, put his arm around her, held her close. He had never loved her more than at this moment, had never loved anyone as much, and there was a sudden ache in his heart that made him feel like crying. He forced those feeling away and turned toward Pace. "Have any other ideas?" he asked.

The other man scratched his beard and shook his head. "I wish I did," he said. "But we're in uncharted territory here. Aside from bringing in earth movers and bulldozers and burying that whole damn thing under a mountain of dirt, I guess your plan's about the best we have. But . . ."

"What?"

"I wish we'd brought more generators. Maybe a stun gun or two. More electricity. I think it would be better if we *all* went in, armed to the teeth and ready to do battle."

"You guys weren't in the painting."

"I understand that. But that painting also only showed one creature. Maybe while you were taking care of that one, the rest of us were out of the frame, doing the same thing to the rest."

Glen hadn't thought of that.

"You need someone to watch your back in there."

In there.

It hit him all of a sudden that he would be inside that infernal edifice. He looked up at the grimy rusted walls and tried to imagine what lay within them, but could not. He had no idea what he would find in that place, but he knew it was horrifying.

Vince was already unloading the generator from the back of his pickup, and Glen helped him lift it down off the gate. Pace started digging through the back of his own truck, pulling out a coiled length of well-used rope and a pair of heavy-duty flashlights. Cameron stood nearby, looking away from the dark building at the trees on the opposite side of the road. He seemed much more subdued than usual and had not said a single word since they'd arrived.

In the thick air, currents swirled around them and pressed against them, speeding up and slowing down, depending on where they moved, where they stood. There was no real wind, only this strange liquid movement, like eddies in water. From within the structure came noises, gutteral grunts and odd gurgling sounds that could have been organic, could have been mechanical.

They all might be immune, like Vince said, but Glen was the one who was depicted in the paintings. He was the one who would have to enter that fortress.

He and the boy.

It was the one detail they had not shared with the others, the fact that Cameron needed to go in, too. Now, though, Glen said, "I think we'd better go in."

"Just let me check my flashlight—" Pace began.

"No. Just me and Cameron."

"What?"

"I want Cameron to come with me."

"No," the boy said.

"You're in the painting. You need to go in, too."

"I'm not going."

He grabbed Cameron's arm.

"Let me go!"

"Glen," Melanie said, touching his shoulder.

He shrugged her hand off. "You're coming with me!"

"Uncle Vince!"

"Cameron doesn't want to go—"

"I don't give a shit what he wants!"

"—and if he says he's not going, he doesn't have to."

"Oh, yes, he does."

Pace stepped in. "*I'm* going with you. Cameron can stay."

The boy broke free from Glen's grip and ran around to the front of his uncle's pickup, eyes teary, practically crying. "Why don't you go in there by yourself, you big chicken?"

Glen took a deep breath to calm himself. He hadn't liked the idea that the future was predetermined, had been fighting the idea every step of the way, but the idea of facing this evil on his own, without the painting as a guide terrified him.

Maybe he wasn't as immune as he'd thought. Not here. Not at the source.

"I'm coming with you," Pace said.

Glen shook his head. "No. No, you're not."

"I'm coming, too," Melanie told him.

"No," he said. He glanced over at Cameron, who was still sniffling and glaring in his direction. "I'll go in by myself."

A low-level squawking burbled from the cell phone on Melanie's hip—McCormack wanting to put in his two cents' worth—but they all ignored it.

"What about the generator? How are you going to bring it with you?"

"It has a handle. It has wheels. I'll pull it."

"Come on, now."

"Listen to me. All we know about how to stop these things is what we learned from the painting. What I'm trying to say is, either this is going to work or it isn't. If I go in and I fail, at least you'll still be alive and maybe you'll be able to think of something else." He paused. "Besides, I'd like to stick as close to the painting as possible."

"I agree," Melanie said.

Pace sighed, shrugged. "All right. What's the plan?"

Vince connected the cables, placed them on the proper side hooks, then made sure the generator's gas tank was full and started the engine. Pace tied his rope to the machine's handle, doubling it for strength. It was awkward and inefficient, but as effective as they could make it. They decided the generator would remain on at all times. All Glen had to do was pull the generator behind him and, when necessary, whip out the cables and shove them at any approaching monster. He took both of Pace's flashlights, holding one in his hand, sticking the other one uncomfortably into the waistband of his jeans.

"Here," Melanie said. "I think we should keep in contact." She pulled the cell phone off her belt, clicked it off.

"McCormack's going to be pissed."

"He'll live." She asked Vince for his number, and he called it out as he ran to the pickup to get his phone. She punched in the number, his phone rang, and he answered. Melanie hooked her phone on Glen's belt. "We'll keep this line open. Try to tell us what you're seeing and what you're doing."

"You think this'll work in there?"

"It's worth a shot."

They said good-bye, and he hugged Melanie, kissing her, telling her that he loved her, trying not to believe that this was the last time they'd see each other. To the others, he nodded.

But how would he get inside? There didn't appear to be an entrance, at least not on this face of the malignant building.

The holes.

Yes. That was the way in.

Muscles tense, ready for anything, pulling the noisy generator behind him, he walked up to the line of skulls encircling the center hole in the ground. To his surprise, it was not a bottomless pit or deep well-like chamber. It was only a shallow cavity in which lay a porcelain doll that looked like a miniature version of himself. The other two holes were equally shallow. One was completely empty. The other had a gray stone floor on which was drawn in white chalk a strange spiral symbol that he found unaccountably disturbing.

"Pace!" he called. "Vince!"

The two men came hurrying over.

"Do either of you have a shovel in the back of your truck?"

"Sure," Pace said.

Glen pointed at the chalk drawing. "Cover that up," he said. "With dirt."

"I recognize that symbol." Pace sounded apprehensive.

"You don't want to save it, do you?"

"No. No, I don't. We'll cover it up."

"Melanie says she can't hear you," Vince said. "The generator's too loud."

Glen put the cell phone in his shirt pocket. "Better?" he asked in a conversational voice. He looked back at her, and she nodded, held up her hand in an okay sign.

"Fine!" she yelled.

Glen turned toward the dark monstrosity before him. If the holes weren't the way to get in, how was he going to . . . ?

He saw an entrance. It was tall and narrow, like a gap between sections of wall. Had it been there before? He wasn't sure, but he certainly hadn't seen it until now. He had the uneasy feeling that it had just opened up, that whatever was inside that place knew he was here and it was waiting for him.

Describing what he saw as he pressed forward made him feel better. The heightened senses that he'd first experienced upon arrival had faded, and though he still did not feel the paralysis that Cameron had described, the air felt denser and even more oppressive. The sound of the generator seemed muffled, as though it were com-

ing from behind a thick barrier, and he smelled a heavy
dead odor of rot. The temperature as he approached the
opening dropped precipitously.

And then he was walking inside.

It was like nothing he had ever seen, no place he had
ever imagined. It had walls, a floor, and a ceiling, but
there the resemblance to any other building ended. He
saw no doors, no windows, no furniture, no recognizable
architectural features. The materials used to construct
this place were clearly from this world, but they were
put together in ways that no human would have believed
possible. Angles were neither straight nor rounded, the
undulating ceiling slopped and dipped and rose in a
manner that was profoundly wrong.

He was in a long chamber that could have been a
corridor, could have been a room, and thick freezing air
wrapped around him like a tight blanket, making it hard
to walk and difficult to breathe. Gritting his teeth, he
pressed forward. Exhaust from the generator motor
masked the rotting odor that permeated the building's
interior, and for that he was grateful.

"I'm in," he said, and proceeded to describe the chamber as best he could. He was not even sure if the connection was still open, but he allowed himself to believe
that the two phones were still in contact and Melanie
could hear every word he said.

It wasn't dark, not completely. The far end of the
chamber was shrouded in gloom, but the area immediately around him was merely dim. This phenomenon
continued as he moved forward over a floor that seemed
to be made of ivory or the enamel of teeth. The flashlight in his hand was on, and he swept the beam back
and forth, looking for . . . something. He should be
searching for one of those creatures, but he wasn't ready
for that yet.

He kept talking, hoping Melanie could hear him.

Beyond a section of wall with oddly bulging protru-
sions was an opening, a slanting crack that looked as
though a giant ax had broken through the wall. Beyond
it was a hallway, and some interior compass told him
that this was where he wanted to go. He stepped
through, touching the wall as he did so. It looked like a

rusty piece of filthy sheet metal, but it felt like sponge, and his fingers came away greasy. He wiped them on his pants.

Although from the outside the building appeared to be six or seven stories high, he had not seen any stairs or any indications that there were other floors above this one. Indeed, as he advanced deeper into the structure, the ceiling seemed to get higher and higher. Soon he reached a point where the walls of the hallway continued upward into a blackness that seemed to have no end.

He felt ridiculous lugging the awkward generator behind him. The idea that he would be facing a tribe of these creatures armed with nothing more than McCormack's noisy, crappy little generator and a pair of short jumper cables did not fill him with confidence. Maybe it hadn't been such a good idea to base their entire strategy on the interpretation of an old painting.

But it had done right by them so far.

Besides, why would there be electricity anywhere *near* the creatures' home? It was exactly what the monsters were trying to avoid. It was why they lived way out here in this primitive land. He had no choice but to carry his own power supply. The only electricity likely to be within miles of this spot was what he brought with him.

He spotted light up ahead in the darkness. Electric light. An illuminated white-and-purple rectangle that looked like it was a football field away.

Electric light?

No. It couldn't be. It had to be a trick, an illusion, something made to resemble electric light.

Otherwise, they were doomed.

He kept walking, moved closer, and finally saw what it was: a vending machine. A Delaware Punch vending machine. Was there such a thing? Had there ever been such a thing? He didn't know and it didn't matter, because this could not be real. The hallway ended, opened out into a much larger chamber, and he could see now that the vending machine was in an alcove made to resemble an old general store's porch. On either side of the machine, in rocking chairs, were his mother and father. He shone his light on them. Both looked the way they had at the moment of death, both stared back at him glassy eyed. For a brief wild second, he considered the possibility that this was the afterlife, that this building was where people went when they died, that there was no heaven, no hell, there were only these horrible beings, harvesting souls as they'd done since long before mankind existed. But he pushed that thought away. It was far more likely that these creatures were able to read his mind and extract images from it, or that this building acted as a kind of mirror, reflecting back the thoughts and fears of those who entered.

Either way, this was not real. He would not fall for it.

Pulling the still-running generator behind him, Glen passed the porch, not looking at the figures of his parents. The chamber he entered was darker, and as he shone his flashlight beam around him and above, he realized that it was because the room was gigantic. It was bigger than any stadium or convention center, bigger than even the exterior of the structure would seem to allow. He tried not to think about that, tried to focus his attention on the task at hand. The physics of this place frightened him—the impossible angles, the thick air, the fantastic construction materials—and he kept talking to Melanie, describing what he was seeing, what he was feeling, what he was thinking.

In the beam of his flashlight, shadows moved, shadows shifted, though there were no objects before him that could have thrown any shadows. Beneath his feet, the substance of the floor changed from white tooth enamel to something black, warm, and rough that he could not immediately identify, but that seemed foul.

He kept walking.

To his left were scores of life-size porcelain figures that reminded him of China's terra-cotta army. To his right were man-size boulders that had been polished smooth.

He kept walking.

And then he reached it.

A massive construction of bones and skulls and connective cartilage, a building within the building, several stories high, all graceful arches, elaborate spires, and minarets. A palace in hell.

He stopped, flung the rope aside and moved back by

the generator, withdrawing the cables. If the bone land in the tomb beneath Ricky's house had been imposing, this was overwhelming. Looking at the attention that had been lavished on the creation before him, Glen had no trouble believing that these creatures harvested humans solely for their skeletons. Centuries' worth of skulls had been stacked into an indescribable set of high columns, hundreds of identical leg bones fitted together into a front balustrade.

The horrible thing was that there was a beauty to it all, a strange and terrible splendor that bespoke intelligence, elegance, sophistication.

"Glen!"

It was Melanie's voice, and he frowned as he looked down at his pocket. Had he accidentally hit some sort of volume adjustment on the cell phone?

"Glen!"

It wasn't coming from the phone. It was behind him. He turned around to see Melanie, Pace, Vince, and Cameron emerging from the gloom. They'd found another flashlight somewhere—Vince's pickup, perhaps—and Melanie held it, walking in the lead. He wanted to be mad at them, but the truth was that he was grateful. He hadn't realized until this moment how utterly alone he had felt.

"There's a reason we're *all* immune," Melanie said. "And that reason is not to wait around for you to vanquish to monsters. We're all part of it, and we're with you."

He put back the cables, hugged her, then reached out and touched the others, grabbing shoulders, shaking hands. He had been stupid to come in alone. He hadn't even been following the painting, because he'd decided to go without Cameron.

"You guys're right behind me. How long did it take you to decide to come in? About a minute?"

"Closer to a half hour," Pace said. "After we finished burying that symbol. It was another forty minutes or so after that that we finally came in."

Glen frowned. "Seventy minutes? I've only been in here for fifteen, maybe twenty at the most."

"You've been in here for over an hour," Melanie told him. "Maybe longer."

He looked at his watch. It had stopped. The rules of time obviously did not apply in this place, and Glen found that extremely unnerving. Whatever these beings were, they apparently lived outside the boundaries of conventional physics.

But where were they?

He had been in the building for this long, had come this far, but had yet to see a single creature. Were they hiding? Had they left? Were they traveling about the countryside spreading death and destruction in their wake? What had happened to them?

"We brought some additional firepower," Pace said. He held up a big awkward-looking gun. Vince was carrying the same thing.

"What is it?" Glen asked.

"Taser." Pace grinned.

"How did you . . . where did you get it?"

"A police car. It came speeding out from the side of this place, from that . . . I don't know what you'd call it. Those changing scenes or whatever they are. No one was driving; it just came barreling toward us across the dirt, and we jumped aside. It crashed into a tree, and we went over to make sure there was no one inside and no one was hurt. In the front seat, we found these. No rifles or revolvers. Just these. After that, we came in."

"Do you know how to use them?"

"Not really," Vince admitted. "Point and shoot, we're hoping. But I guess we'll find out for sure when it comes down to the crunch."

"Speaking of which . . ." Pace motioned toward the elaborate palace of bones before them. "Shall we enter?"

"Here." Vince handed Glen his taser, then grabbed one of the handles on the generator and lifted. On the other side of the machine, Pace held the taser with his right hand and picked up the other handle with his left. "This should make it a little easier."

"You're still point man," Pace said to Glen. "Lead on."

Gripping the taser tightly, Glen stepped forward across the warm black floor and stepped onto the raised veranda of bone. He felt a rattling beneath his feet as he passed over the skeletal remains of the dead.

They walked through a vaulted doorway.

Inside, it was more difficult to tell that the construction was of bone and cartilage. Whereas the individual elements that made up the exterior retained their original shape, in here they had been melded together seamlessly. The walls, floor, and ceiling looked solid. They also seemed slightly luminescent, making their flashlights redundant, but neither he nor Melanie shut them off.

"What did you see on your way here?" Glen asked her. He'd been wondering ever since they'd shown up. "Did you see what looked like the front porch of an old general store, with a lighted vending machine on it?"

"Delaware Punch?" Melanie nodded. "We sure did. What was that about?"

He'd been hoping he'd been the only one to see it, that they'd seen something different, that it was some sort of image tailor made to reflect the fears and memories of whoever passed by, but that was clearly not the case. He took a deep breath. "And two dead people in rocking chairs, a man and a woman?"

"Yes."

"Those were my parents."

No one knew what to say, and Melanie reached for his arm, squeezed it. Around them, the room shimmered, shifted. They'd been in some type of rococo foyer, but now they entered what looked like a throne room or a chapel, an elongated space in which all attention was focused on an object at the far end. Before them was a stone circle, like the one in the last panel of the triptych, a round piece of gray rock adorned with incomprehensible symbols. Once again, Glen was reminded of a sun, and he realized that it was because the circle radiated energy. Only it seemed to be a source of darkness rather than light.

The white walls and floor turned black, the ceiling faded to a sickly gray. The thickness of the air dissipated.

Suddenly they were no longer alone. The lone room was filled with the purposeful movement of skeletons and mummies and shrunken heads and skulls, all with bushy orange hair. He didn't know where they'd come from, but they were creeping, crawling, gliding, rolling, moving across the room in eerie silence. He remembered the needlepoint his mother had been sewing in his dream, and her broken-record comment: *"You failed/ you failed/you failed . . ."*

He saw no living beings, though, nothing like in his nightmare, and although all of his instincts told him to run, he held his ground.

"What are we going to do?" Cameron yelled, panicked.

Still unsure of how to use it, Glen pointed his taser at a tall wrinkled figure with dirty bobbing hair that was rolling toward them and would be the first to reach them. It stopped, swerving away.

"They're afraid of the electricity!" Glen announced. He gave Melanie the taser. "Point it at anything that comes close." He turned around, grabbed the cables from the generator. "Put it down," he told Pace and Vince. "I don't want you guys to get shocked. We'll make our stand here."

A huge skull the size of an elephant's, all scowling sockets and fiercely grinning mouth, appeared out of nowhere, rolling into him from the side and knocking him down. The cables flew out of his hands, and the generator fell over, its engine dying. The heavy skull continued to press against him, trying to squish him, but Melanie shoved her taser into its right eye socket. It flew away instantly, shooting backward as though on a bungee cord.

Pace and Vince had righted the generator and were trying to start it up again, but either it was flooded or out of gas, because the engine would not catch. A partial mummy—head and torso—emerged from behind Vince and tried to grab his legs, but Cameron saw it first, screamed, and Pace pointed his taser at the monster, making it hobble away. The silence in the room seemed all the more pronounced without the background clatter of the generator, and while orange afros were moving everywhere, the only sounds were their own breathing and grunts and the mechanical clanking of the motor as Pace and Vince attempted to start it up.

They might be able to resist these creatures' power, but they were not immune from physical contact. It was only a matter of time before the five of them were overwhelmed. Glen looked toward the stone circle at the head of the room. He still thought that was the key. If they had any hope at all, they had to destroy that object.

The generator engine started, coughed, caught, held.

As Glen seized the cables, a ripple in the air passed over them, under them, through them. It was followed by a deafening screech, and everyone's head whipped around toward the head of the room.

This figure was no mummy or corpse. It was the being Cameron had photographed in his friend's house, and it was very much alive. It had also grown. The creature in the Polaroid had been five foot five at the most, but now it was easily twice that height. Standing in front of the carved round stone, it hovered a foot or two off the floor, arms bent at the elbow and stretched forward as though waiting to catch a ball. Its black eyes were deep set and angry, and they scanned the long room, looking for something.

Looking for them.

Where were the living beings? Glen had wondered, and now he knew. There was only one and this was it. The mummies, the skeletons, the corrupted artifacts, and everything else were like a rich man's discarded suits, items that might still have some viability, but that had been worn once and were used no longer. He had no idea what had prompted that comparison, but he had the feeling that was as close as he was going to get to understanding what this creature was and how it operated.

The fierce stony face looked upon them with its hard harsh glare beneath bright orange hair.

And smiled.

It was the most horrible smile he had ever seen, more awful than anything he could imagine, an evil smile that carried with it the knowledge of centuries, of millennia. This creature had been here long before America was born, long before there had been people on this planet, and Glen was filled with a deep sense of despair. How could they ever hope to stop it, a ragtag group of ill-informed do-gooders gamely attempting to battle a power far beyond their ken?

He continued to hold the cables, one in each hand. He glanced to his left at Pace and Vince and Cameron.

Cameron.

The boy was here, he realized. After all that had happened, events had conspired to put the two of them in this place at the same time. It *was* like the painting after all.

Hope flared within him. The entity at the front of the room was vastly powerful, infinitely evil, and if they had the slightest chance, they had to move fast. From deep within its form came a gurgling, a rumbling, like sewage flowing through subterranean passages. Higher up, on a surface level, laughter began, low, steady, even laughter.

The skeletons and mummies were still roving, but they no longer seemed bent on attack. They bopped around the room like free molecules, having handed over the responsibility of killing the infidels to their leader.

"Follow me and run," Glen ordered. He nodded at Vince and Pace. "Carry the generator. Have tazers ready." He looked at Cameron. "I want you by my side. Can you do it?"

The boy swallowed, then nodded.

"Then let's go. Now!"

Cables still in hand, Glen rushed toward the front of the room. Everyone kept up, Cameron on one side of him, Melanie with her taser on the other, Vince and Pace right behind him with the generator. He wished the chamber wasn't so long, wished there wasn't so much ground to cover before they reached the monster. He readied himself for an attack, prepared to be fried by lasers shooting out of those deep dark eyes or thrown backward by an invisible force, but nothing happened. They ran past skulls and mummies, dashed unscathed over shrunken heads.

He reached the giant creature floating off the floor and instantly shoved both cables upward into its midsection. The laughter abruptly stopped. He didn't know why he had been allowed to charge so openly, but he had, and he let go of the cables, yelling, "Taser! Taser!"

Pace shot a wired dart into what should have been

the monstrous being's groin. Melanie's stun gun wouldn't work, but it didn't matter, the damage had been done. The creature spiralled upward, like a deflating balloon whose tie string had been pulled, and suddenly the dark floor, walls, and ceiling were gone. They saw the room for what it was, a space bounded by pelvic bones and shoulder blades and vertebrae. Screeching, the monster shot up into one of the palace's spires, stuck in a prison of rib cages and radii. It struggled, tried to free itself, but its hair became tangled in the bones.

Glen ran up to the round carved stone. It was as tall as he was and balanced on its side. Lunging, he pushed it over, hoping it would shatter into a thousand pieces. It did not, but on impulse he picked up first one cable, then the other. He pushed the cables against the stone, making a specific effort to press one on the disturbing spiral they'd seen in the hole outside. He would not have been surprised if the circular object crumbled or shattered. But instead, it brightened from gray to white and then melted like an ice cube, the symbols disappearing first, then the whole stone dissolving into a clear liquid mess at his feet.

From the hollow spire above, the creature that had been behind all of this, that had destroyed Bower and terrorized the entire Southwest, that had put an end to great civilizations of the past and had been poised to do the same once again, squealed crazily. Glen did not know if this being was the last of its kind or whether it had always been the only one, but as he heard that squeal fade away, as he looked up to see the giant form shrivel and shrink, its hair falling from above like orange feathers off a molting bird, he knew that it would not be threatening anyone else in the future. It was over, it was done, and around the room mummies and skeletons were dropping in place, although they did not disappear.

Sweating profusely, every muscle in his body exhausted, feeling as though he'd just run a marathon, Glen moved next to Melanie, held her, leaned on her. ·

"Is that it?" Cameron asked. "Is it dead?"

"It's dead," his uncle assured him.

"But somebody better come back afterward with bulldozers," Melanie said. "And bury this place."

"Seconded," Glen said.

And they shut off the generator and made sure they had everything they'd brought with them before starting back and heading out.

Epilogue

The morning sun beat down on their heads as Glen and Melanie stood in the desert behind McCormack's house, trying not to listen to the professor and his wife arguing inside. McCormack was returning to New Mexico tomorrow with a team of anthropologists and archeologists from several universities, but Alyssa didn't want him to go. Pace had already returned to Chaco Canyon, and Vince and Cameron were on their way to Springerville—or what was left of it. He and Melanie were the only ones who didn't seem to have something to do or somewhere to be.

Melanie pushed a wisp of hair out of her eyes. "Summer's winding down."

"Yeah."

"I was going to say school will be starting in a few weeks. But there is no school. There is no . . . Bower." She shook her head. "Does that mean I get to file for unemployment? I have no idea how this works. I don't even know who I should talk to about it."

"We'll figure it out."

"My truck's gone, too. I don't even own a vehicle." She suddenly thought of something. "I don't even have any money. My bank's disappeared."

Glen took her hand. "We'll go back to my place," he said. "In California. Even if I decide not to live there, I still have to sort through my mother's belongings. I've put it off long enough."

"Where *do* you want to live?"

"I don't know."

"What do you want to do?"

"I don't know that either." He paused, wondering if he should say what he'd been thinking, took the leap. "But whatever it is, I want to do it with you."

She hugged him, and they said nothing for a few moments. "Were those really your parents in there?" she asked finally.

He nodded, a lump in his throat. "Yeah." He found it hard to speak, and his eyes misted over; he had to blink back tears. He took a deep breath. "I think you would've liked them." The tears spilled onto his cheeks. He held her tightly, pressing his face against her hair, not wanting her to see him.

She squeezed back, and he felt her body shaking beneath his hands. She was crying, too. He thought of her parents, George and Margaret. "I'm sure I would've," she said.

And they stood that way for a long while. Until Professor McCormack, no longer fighting with his wife, called to them from a bedroom window and told them to come inside. It was time for lunch.